With
Neighbors
Like These

With Neighbors Like These

An HOA Mystery

Linda Lovely

LEVEL
BEST BOOKS

First published by Level Best Books 2021

AUTHOR PHOTO CREDIT: Danielle Dahl

First edition

ISBN: 978-1-953789-45-7

Cover art by Julie Kennedy, Digital City Graphics

This book was professionally typeset on Reedsy.
Find out more at reedsy.com

For Kylee and Justin Welch
Love Long, Season with Laughter

Praise for WITH NEIGHBORS LIKE THESE

"Linda Lovely delivers another twisty mystery with the perfect mix of wry humor and quirky characters. Anyone looking for a fun, fast page-turner, here it is!" —*Tami Hoag, #1 New York Times bestselling author*

"HOA communities seem deceptively safe, but the mix of gossip and politics in rule-bound groups can be a fertile breeding ground for murder. For the gutsy Kylee Kane, a fact-finding gig in South Carolina's Lowcountry turns increasingly complex and dangerous. *With Neighbors Like These* offers a distinctive setting, a tenacious female sleuth and captivating suspense." —*Katherine Ramsland, bestselling author of How to Catch a Killer*

"Low Country murder, intrigue, and even a little romance abound in *With Neighbors Like These*. Kylee Kane is a welcome addition to the genre, and author Linda Lovely knows how to stir the pot with crackling dialogue and a tidy little mystery. Highly recommended!"
   —*Richard Helms, Derringer and Thriller Awards winning author of Brittle Karma*

"Multi-layered plots are always central to Linda Lovely's novels. With her fully fleshed out central characters perfectly set up to navigate the twists and turns of the storylines, this entertaining mystery writer always delivers a thoroughly engrossing read. *With Neighbors Like These* is a stellar, page-turning beginning to her brand new HOA Mystery Series."
   —Patti Phillips, Nightstand Book Reviews

Chapter One

Kylee Kane

Friday, September 25, 6:30 p.m.

"Mom, are we eating at the kitchen table?"

Silence.

Not again.

I look outside. Mom's standing by the mailbox, tugging on the blue stocking cap that keeps her nearly-bald head warm.

Crap. I said I'd get the mail. She's a stubborn old cuss. While her skin now looks like wrinkle-mapped parchment, those cagey blue eyes still flash.

Mom stops midway to the house to read something. A postcard? She looks up. Her expression is one I rarely see. Fear? Distress? Definitely bad news.

Ted's Mustang pulls into the drive, and Mom stuffs whatever worried her into a pocket. Ted jumps out, and Mom's thin arms embrace him.

Thirty years ago, Ted was my kid brother's pimpled, bratty best friend, a snot-nosed pest. Last year, when we met up again in the Lowcountry, I couldn't believe it. These days he could model for *GQ*. A lot happens when decades pass between sightings.

I open the front door. Mom's slightly out of breath as Ted helps her up the stairs. While her cancer's in retreat, chemo has taken a toll.

Ted glances my way and grins.

"Hi, Kylee. See you're still having trouble getting your mother to behave. Bet you long for those Coast Guard days when you could give orders and know they'd be obeyed."

"Yep, some days I'm sorry I retired," I answer.

Mom waves her hand like she's shooing flies. "Let's talk about something interesting. Ted, what do you hear from your son?"

"Grant's great, sends lots of love. Says your care package made life worth living last week. Freshman year's tough at the Citadel."

At six feet, Ted towers over my five-foot-two mother. Though he's forty-seven, three years my junior, only a hint of silver threads his thick black hair. His hazel eyes seem to change color with his mood or maybe it's just the light. Tonight, they're green.

Ted looks worried as he studies Mom. He was eight when his own mother died. After that Mom included him in all our family activities. He loves Mom as much as I do.

During our kitchen table dinner, he regales us with tales of HOA intrigue to lift Mom's spirits. Since his management company has more than a dozen homeowner associations as clients, his supply of stories seems endless.

"Once upon a time, there were three neighbors," he begins. "RulesALot is convinced his neighbor, DoggyDo, is harboring three mutts, one more than the two-pet-per-household limit. Since he can't see over his hedge to prove it, RulesALot launches a spy drone. A pilot he's not. His drone crashes in ToplessTina's backyard, who's suing him as a Peeping Tom. Of course, there's only one question on every male owner's mind: Did the drone snap photos of Tina's tatas before it nosedived?"

Ted's eyebrows wiggle up and down, and Mom laughs. "Your HOA stories are certainly entertaining."

"Believe me, the stories are a lot funnier if you're not expected to wade into the middle of the skirmishes. Never dreamed HOAs would be tougher to manage than U.S. embassies on hostile soil."

Mom fiddles with her napkin. "Speaking of neighborhood feuds, I have a confession. I figured you'd be scolding me by now, Ted, since you manage our HOA…"

Ted and I look at each other. *Uh oh.*

"What did you do?" Ted asks.

"I told the moron Hullis Island directors I'll sue if they don't let us vote on what happens to our deer. Emailed copies to all 1,123 owners."

I reach across the table and squeeze Mom's hand. Though I agree with her, she needs to focus on regaining strength, not leading a crusade. "Oh, Mom, kicking over a hornets' nest isn't part of your cancer recovery regimen."

Mom's eyes narrow. "Hey, everyone else bitched and nothing happened. Figured a lawsuit threat might make their little sphincters tighten, and they'd pay attention."

Mom switches to a fake, shaky geezer voice. "I'm a little old lady, their nightmare plaintiff. Who's going to go off on some sick, elderly lady?"

Ted's eyebrows lift. "Exactly what did your email say?"

"Told 'em their plan to shoot our almost-tame deer with no vote on who, what, when, or how was plain wrong. Hullis Island is a nature sanctuary. They can't unilaterally declare an open hunting season without an island vote to change our covenants."

Ted shakes his head. "Myrt, I told the board the same thing, though a bit more diplomatically. The directors sided with Cliff, the board president, and his *expert*, some lawyer drinking buddy, who found a no-vote loophole after they'd tipped a few."

He shrugs. "Welch HOA Management offers advice, but we're hired help. Clients call the shots."

"What loophole?" I butt in. "Don't the covenants require a vote on any change to the island's status as a nature sanctuary?"

Ted nods. "Cliff's citing a provision that allows killing protected animals if they pose a threat to human life."

I roll my eyes. "What? They say zombie deer are preparing to ambush humans? That exception allows trapping rabid raccoons or aggressive alligators, not shooting starving deer."

"I cornered Barb Darrin, a director I thought had sense," Mom says. "Her justification? Deer carry ticks, a health hazard, and they can crash into golf carts."

3

Mom sighs. "Everyone agrees the herd's out of control. Doesn't give these arrogant SOBs the right to sanction a Wild West killing spree. Sure as shoot, some bozo will mistake a human or a big dog for a deer and fire away. You won't be able to throw a rock without hitting some guy in camo with a high-powered rifle."

Ted taps his spoon against his coffee mug. "Myrt, what aren't you telling us?"

"Well…" She shrugs. "Seems one wannabe deer killer has no qualms about threatening old ladies." She pulls the crumpled card from the pocket of her baggy sweater. "Found this love note in my mailbox."

Good grief. That's what she stuffed in her pocket.

Ted snatches what looks like some movie-maker's idea of a ransom note. Black-and-white newsprint cut and pasted on a postcard.

"What a nice closing line." Ted reads, "'It's time us hunters declare open season on diseased deer and busybody bitches like Myrtle Kane.'" He turns the card over to look at the front. "Did this come in an envelope?"

"No, just lying in the box."

"Mom! This is dangerous. Either I'm moving back in with you or you're coming to live with me."

"Nonsense," she scoffs. "It's pure bluster. Took a year to convince you I'm healthy enough to live alone. Anyway, I get seasick just thinking about sleeping on your boat. No-sir-ee, you can't dynamite me out of this house."

Ted raises his palm in a hold-it gesture. "Myrt, do you think Dan Finley pasted this up?"

She shakes her head. "While I'm convinced he's our Grass Slayer, it's not his MO to cut up newsprint and issue threats. More his style to use that big commercial sprayer of his to ruin the Quaids' lawn tonight."

I frown. "The Quaids who live cattycorner? What does Finley have against them?"

"They're one of the couples leading the 'Save Bambi' drive."

"But why would Finley do something tonight?"

"The Quaids are in Savannah for their son's wedding," Mom answers.

Ted sets down his mug. "You may be right about Finley seizing the opportunity."

Mom chimes in. "The deer have cost him big bucks. The poor starving creatures devour plants like I eat chocolates. Plants he's guaranteed. His nursery and landscaping business is hurting. He blames folks like the Quaids, who put out buckets of corn to keep the deer alive."

"Last week, herbicide messages were left on the lawns of two other deer lovers who were out of town," Ted adds. "Dead yellow grass shows up quite nicely against a field of green Bermuda blades."

"What kind of messages?" I ask.

Mom shrugs. "One lawn read, 'Up yours!' He was more artistic on the other lawn, drew a fist with an extended middle finger."

I laugh in spite of my worries that Finley might be Mom's new enemy.

Mom purses her lips. "Sure, it sounds like juvenile hijinks, but the anger's palpable. Folks who golfed or played bridge together no longer speak. That's why I'm adamant we need a vote. Then, win or lose, everyone has a say, and we can move on. It's called democracy."

"Speaking of democracy, I propose a kitchen vote," Ted says. "All in favor of Kylee and me staking out the Quaids' yard tonight raise your hands. That overgrown lot across the street offers a view of their place. Maybe we can catch Dan Finley at work."

While I'm skeptical a one-night stakeout will succeed, that vacant lot also offers a perfect view of Mom's mailbox. And I'm all for hanging around to catch anyone delivering hate mail.

Ted and I raise our hands. Mom harrumphs.

"Just what will you do if Dan Finley does drop by?" she asks.

"Video him doing the evil deed." Ted smiles. "My new phone takes excellent photos in low light."

Mom grumbles, but won't argue with our kitchen table vote, a Kane family tradition.

"Just when do you intend to sneak off in the woods?"

Ted glances at his watch. "Say an hour? I doubt Finley would chance a drive-by while folks are still drifting home from dinner at the club."

"Good. I'll change into some old clothes and sneakers I left here before I was *evicted*."

Ted looks ready for a *Southern Living* picture shoot in his tan chinos, button-down shirt, and polished loafers. "You sacrificing your HOA meeting duds for this outing?"

His hazel eyes twinkle. "Nope," Ted answers. "I was a Boy Scout. Your dad, our scoutmaster, taught us well. I have running clothes in the trunk."

Chapter Two

The Twin

Friday, September 25, 10:30 p.m.

I'm fond of Oscar Wilde's quote "With age comes wisdom, but sometimes age comes alone." It surely applies to the men who killed my brother Jake, my twin. The passage of time hasn't redeemed their characters. All three remain callous, cruel assholes.

It's almost *too* easy to make their impending deaths appear the work of disgusted neighbors. Tons of suspects, and I'm not one.

It's Dan Finley's last night. His blood-lust to slaughter Hullis Island's deer herd has earned him lots of enemies. The nasty HOA feud dictates how I'll pose him.

I switch my car headlights off before turning into Parrot Lane. Only two houses. Finley's and the old biddy's place across the street. Light glows from windows at the back of both houses. Otherwise, it's black as tar. No streetlights.

I coast to a stop about twenty yards shy of Finley's house to drop off a scarecrow and an axe. Props too bulky to carry when I hike back.

I drive to the golf course maintenance building and park behind it. Crack the car windows for Sandy. I pet her shaggy head and assure the drooling lab I'll come right back. Hope it's the truth.

I slip on my backpack and jog across the golf course to Finley's house.

Breathing hard, I stop alongside his front porch to catch my breath. Center myself. I've mentally rehearsed what's ahead a thousand times. Doesn't mean it'll go as planned.

Finley's TV blares. Some action movie with more gunfire than dialogue. Is he hard of hearing? Will he hear my knock?

I pound on the door with my left fist. Need my right free to fire the stun gun.

I pound some more.

"Coming," Finley yells. "Keep your britches on."

He opens the door. Doesn't switch on the porchlight. *Good boy.*

"My car broke down and my cellphone's dead." I smile. "Can I use your phone?"

Finley's head swivels toward the dark lane as he searches for an abandoned auto. His fleshy neck opens to me. I shove the stun gun against his skin. He shrieks as my finger pushes the trigger. I give him a second jolt for good measure.

I stop. Don't want him to have a premature heart attack. Just need him helpless.

He collapses. On the porch, he flails like a hooked fish dumped on a dock. When he settles, I stuff a large handkerchief in his slack mouth and secure his hands and feet with zip ties. *Thank you, Home Depot.* Faster and easier than handcuffs.

Now comes the hard part. I drag Finley down the porch steps and prop him against a large mulch pile. I give him an extra electrical fritz to ensure he remains helpless while I run inside his house. Yesterday, I climbed on his back porch and looked through the window to confirm nothing had changed since my last reconnaissance.

I grab Finley's curved fiberglass bow, a quiver of arrows, and the keys to his truck. I also free a glassy-eyed deer head from its wall mount. When I first saw all those animal heads mounted on his wall, I realized it would be perfect symmetry to swap a trophy head for Finley's. Never seriously considered it though.

It's embarrassing, but I don't do well with the sight of blood. Don't even like excessive gore in movies. One reason I never considered becoming a physician. My orderly plans for revenge reflect my intelligence—okay, and my dark sense of humor. No need to resort to bloody butchery.

As I leave the house, I glance across the street at the old bat's place. She's peeking through her window. Must have heard Finley's single startled cry. Has she called security? I assume that's a yes.

Doubt they'll be in any rush. Too many of the island's old fogies call constantly, mistaking their own dog's farts for gunfire.

Still, I need to hurry.

Finley's conscious. Can see the vein in his temple jumping.

"Remember Jake Turner?" I whisper. Finley's eyes widen. Yes, he remembers. How satisfying.

I ready Finley's powerful hunting bow. "This is for him."

His eyes follow my every move. Frantic, pleading. Must be excruciating to see what's coming and not be able to move. *Good.*

I watched the movie *Deliverance*. Hope the filmmakers had that arrow scene right. Not much blood when the arrow penetrates a chest.

Yep. A nice neat hole.

I snip off the zip ties to free the corpse's hands and feet. Arrange the scarecrow, axe, and deer's head, and take one last look. Smiling, I climb in Finley's truck.

I slowly back out of his drive. The old lady's no longer at her window but I don't want her to hear Finley's truck leaving.

I'm behind schedule. Hate to leave Sandy sitting alone in my car any longer. The lab might start barking and call attention.

Back at the maintenance shed, Sandy is ecstatic to see me. Poor old girl's going to need help to get in Finley's truck. I push on Sandy's haunches to boost her into the cab.

I stroke Sandy's silky head. "Almost done for the night, girl. Only one more chore. Then we'll go home. Give you some treats. Maybe take a nice midnight stroll down the block."

Chapter Three

Kylee

Friday, September 25, 11:15 p.m.

T he incessant buzzing is driving me bonkers. Must be a zillion Lowcountry no-see-ums assaulting my scalp as we crouch behind scrub palms. The forested lot across from Mom belongs to a couple planning to build post-retirement. Meanwhile, nature's claimed it as a bug resort.

I thump Ted's arm, an attention-getter I perfected when we were kids. The stakeout no longer seems a brilliant idea. "Why do I get the feeling you're afraid the author of that hate mail might do more than scribble threats?"

Ted scuffs a foot back and forth in the sandy soil. "I wouldn't put it past some old geezer to play commando and pop off a few drive-by rounds to scare Myrt. When folks get this steamed, reason disappears. Bullets ricochet. People die. If Finley wrote the note, he carries a nine mil, and there's talk he's involved in some right-wing militia."

"If he ventures out tonight, let's hope herbicide is his weapon of choice," I say. "We need to catch the Grass Slayer, whoever he is, and stop the vandalism before it gets uglier."

Ted holds up a hand. "Listen. A vehicle's coming."

An SUV dawdles down the road. At the next cross street, it turns left. False alarm.

10

"If we video Finley poisoning grass, I hope Chief O'Rourke's willing to arrest him. Maybe if one of these idiots stews in jail for a day, they'll realize acting like spoiled ten-year-olds earns a spanking."

Hullis Island is a private, gated island, and its security guards, like mainland cops, carry guns and have arrest powers. If he has cause, O'Rourke can make an arrest.

Headlights appear a half-block away. "Someone's coming."

"Headlights are riding high." Ted lowers his voice to a near whisper. "A truck."

"Let's hope it's Finley's white dually."

"I'm ready to video," he whispers.

I glance at the sky. "Not the best light."

The moon resembles a plump pumpkin, but palm fronds cast deep shadows on the road. I cross my fingers Ted's camera will at least capture the truck's make and color.

The vehicle slows to sea turtle speed. White dually. Ted pushes the record button. The truck's nose comes even with us. A large silver box peeks above the truck bed.

The driver hops from the idling dually and hustles around back. His hunched-over posture and baggy clothes make it impossible to peg height or build. A kerchief covers most of his face. A ball cap hides his hair.

What an idiot. A disguise isn't worth diddly if you drive your own truck.

The man grabs a hose hooked to the silver tank and heads for the Quaids' lawn. Pssst. Pssst. *Pressurized spray?* Can't see a nozzle. Hope Ted's camera can tease out details.

The man throws the hose back in the truck, climbs in the cab, and revs the engine. The truck picks up speed and disappears around a curve.

I'm disappointed. "Dang. Couldn't read the license. Caked with mud."

"Should have tackled him as soon as he left the truck," Ted huffs.

"Yeah? Then Finley could sue. Claim he stopped to check a tire, had no idea why some idiot assaulted him."

Ted laughs. "What a joke! You telling *me* to be cautious."

"My PI courses are loaded with legal warnings," I reply. "One of many reasons I doubt private investigator is a viable second career for me. In the Coast Guard, I believed in the mission—to keep our waterways safe and stop terrorists, drug smugglers, and human traffickers. Not sure I can work up the same enthusiasm to snoop on cheating husbands."

"Hey, it's not always men who mess around. I should know."

Though he chuckles, I'm sorry I opened my big trap. Ted's ex was the marital mess-ee.

"How about we let Finley know we caught him on camera?" Ted suggests. "Maybe I can talk some sense into him and avoid involving Chief O'Rourke. Having Finley arrested might make him a martyr for the shotgun-toting crowd."

"Think he'll listen? You did say Finley might get liquored up for his nighttime raids. Wish you hadn't mentioned his nine mil."

My hand grazes Ted's and comes away slimed with the Skin So Soft Mom slathered on his exposed skin to thwart—or drown—no-see-ums. I refuse to let her plaster that goo on me.

"Let's try to save the lawn. Heavy watering might dilute the poison."

Ted tilts his head like a puzzled cocker spaniel. Though we've spent our adult lives continents apart, his tells haven't changed since we walked the five blocks to Garfield Elementary. His gesture signals internal debate. Probably wondering if dead grass might strengthen the case against Finley.

"Video me taking grass samples," he suggests as he fiddles with his cellphone. "I've got it all set. Just press the white button. Make sure the Quaids' mailbox is in the frame. Once we have video, we'll hose off whatever poison Finley pumped on the lawn."

We abandon our stakeout blind to save the grass. Ted opens the Swiss Army pocketknife my scoutmaster dad gave him on his fifteenth birthday.

As he saws off squares of grass, I video, hoping the blinking recording light means the effort's worthwhile. Too late I hear the chucada-chucada-chucada of a sprinkler system springing to life. I sprint for the safety of the dry road, Ted on my heels.

Not fast enough.

Dang.

The shower turns my long-sleeved t-shirt wet and clammy. Just hope it kills a few gnats.

"Hurry," Ted urges. "We want to catch Finley before he's tucked in bed."

I reluctantly plunk my damp bottom in Ted's car, a refurbished Mustang. He has a passion for restoring rusty relics. He cranks the motor before I can buckle my seatbelt. Ignoring Hullis Island's fifteen-mile-an-hour speed limit for side roads, we rocket toward Parrot Lane at a blistering thirty miles per hour.

Hope we don't collide with any of those kamikaze, zombie deer.

Dan Finley lives across the road from Mom's friend Jenny Elson, a lonely widow. Finley and Jenny are Parrot Lane's only residents. The remaining six lots are undeveloped. No ocean or golf course views to tempt buyers, just palmetto trees and swampy lowland. The graveled lane doesn't rate one of Hullis's tightly-rationed street lights. Money's not an issue. Islanders strive to keep light pollution to a minimum.

When we reach the gloomy side street, I notice Jenny's windows are all lit up. Hunh? Way past her bedtime. I glance at Finley's house. Completely dark. No truck. Unless his habits changed overnight, he's not home. Jenny often natters on about the monster truck in Finley's drive. Says his junk-filled garage has no space for a vehicle.

"Where do you suppose he went?" Ted mumbles.

"Maybe he's spraying another lawn."

Ted's Mustang coasts closer to Finley's house and an odd shape in front of a mulch pile.

"What the heck is that? Too early for Halloween decorations." I gesture toward the mounded mulch.

"Good God!" Ted shifts the Mustang into park and jumps out. I follow.

What does he see?

As I round the car, my brain stutters, trying to make sense of the scene. A scarecrow's straw hand holds an axe poised to behead a seated manikin.

Crap, that's no manikin!

Chapter Four

It's Finley. He's seated, legs splayed in front of him, and he's cradling a deer's head in his lap.

What in blazes?

Ted splashes his cellphone's flashlight over the tableau. An arrow protrudes from the dead man's chest. The corpse's wide-open eyes look surprised.

Though I know he's dead, I squat beside him. My fingers slide over his neck's still warm skin. No sign of a pulse.

Ted's voice finally registers. He's talking to Hullis Island Security, reporting a find better suited to Friday the 13th than Friday the 25th. I rise from my crouch and back away. Have I contaminated the crime scene? I've been present at enough homicides to know the do's and don'ts.

Dead people played occasional cameo roles in my Coast Guard investigations. But finding a corpse on quiet Hullis Island feels different. More shocking than viewing the tragic end for illegals who trusted the wrong smugglers or the victims of a boat collision. I feel ill, chilled.

Ted wraps his jacket around me. "You okay?"

I tug the edges of his jacket, drawing it tighter. "Sure," I lie. "Just my damp clothes giving me goosebumps."

Ted stares at the corpse. "We sure didn't see Finley spraying that lawn. The killer needed more than thirty minutes to set up this scene."

He backs away. "Guess it's symbolism, but putting that moldy hunting trophy in Finley's lap seems over the top. The big antlers prove that deer wasn't bagged on Hullis Island."

I grimace. "The killer stole that scarecrow from the community garden. It's wearing Dad's Iowa State University cap. Mom liked the idea of Dad's spirit watching over her tomatoes. Seeing Dad's ballcap here gives me the willies."

I need to look away. Motion catches my eye as Jenny's front-room curtains twitch. Her backlit silhouette doesn't lack for detail.

"Jenny's peeking outside, probably scared silly. I'll run up and tell her it's just the two of us making noise down here."

"Let's hope you're right. If the killer's smart, he's long gone. Tell Jenny security will arrive in a minute or two."

A horrid thought dawns. "D'you suppose the killer's still tooling around the island in Finley's dually? Is security on the lookout for the truck? For the life of me, I can't figure out why the murderer hijacked his victim's truck and went on a lawn-killing spree after Finley was dead."

"Beats me," he says. "I told security about the truck. Go on, see to Miss Jenny."

I breathe hard as I race up the steep flight of stairs. Like most island homes, this one perches on pilings that lift the main living area well above sea level.

Before I can ring the bell, Jenny throws open her door. "Thank God, I recognized you pounding up the stairs. What's happening, Kylee?"

Her high-pitched voice quavers. Panic dilates her wide, watery blue eyes. "I heard a commotion outside. Phoned security at least ninety minutes ago. No one came. Just now when I heard voices, I called your mother. Didn't realize it was you outside."

Darn it. Mom will be here any minute. The nurse in her will insist, even if it saps every ounce of her strength to scale those stairs. The stubborn woman can't let little things like a double mastectomy, chemo, and radiation slow her seventy-six-year-old body.

I take a deep breath and tell Jenny security's on the way. "Ted's waiting for the officers. Sorry to be the bearer of bad news, but Dan Finley is dead."

Jenny flinches as if I've slapped her. She squeezes Puppy, the rotund dachshund quaking in her arms. He squeals like a frightened piglet and jumps free. I pat the woman's gaunt arm. "Let's sit."

"How did he die?" Jenny asks once she's seated. Puppy—that's his actual name—gives me the stink eye, and his lips curl back to expose yellow, needle-sharp teeth but the ankle snapper keeps his distance. We have a mutual non-admiration pact.

"It appears Mr. Finley was murdered."

Jenny gasps. "My heavens, d'you suppose I actually heard the murder? Maybe that was the commotion I called security about."

I reach across the chintz sofa and take Jenny's hand. Though she's wrapped in a thick housecoat, her bare ankles, hands, and wrists advertise how fragile she's become. I can almost count the protruding bones.

The prim, white-haired widow lost her husband two years ago. After six decades of togetherness, being alone once darkness descends frightens Jenny, who often reports "suspicious goings-on" to island security. Before Mom's cancer treatments, Chief O'Rourke sometimes asked her to sit with Jenny after officers investigated and found nothing amiss. This time a real boogeyman, not loneliness, justifies her panic.

Jenny's blue-veined hands shake as her fingers fiddle with a raised upholstery seam. "I heard a cry and Puppy started barking. That's when I peeked out the window."

She presses a tissue against a tearing right eye.

"I parted the curtains to see what was going on," she continues. "Even with the moon brighter than a new penny, those danged palm trees across the way made it blacker than pitch. All I could see was a shadowy blob moving about. I called security and that new fella, Officer Adam, promised he'd check it out. Never did. Must have figured it was just Old Jenny, scared of her own shadow."

She's undoubtedly pegged it, though I don't say so.

A spray of gravel outside tells me island security's arrived.

"Jenny, I need to go outside for a bit. I promise I'll come back and let you know what's happening."

Chapter Five

As I hurry down the stairs, pulsing lights paint the neighborhood with chilling blue flashes. Chief O'Rourke's SUV and a second Hullis Island security sedan sit right behind Ted's Mustang. And what do I spot not twenty yards behind them? Mom's golf cart. What a shocker.

Chief O'Rourke stands, hands on a utility belt that sags below his round belly. He's loudly chewing out Adam Lowry, a chubby-faced twenty-two-year-old security officer. Finished, he transfers his glare to Ted. It's clear my stakeout buddy already explained how we stumbled across the body.

Chief O'Rourke can't stand Ted. O'Rourke's headed the island's security force for two decades. In theory, he always reported to the Hullis Island Board of Directors. In reality, he reported to no one. The board never interfered or questioned a single request for funds. Then Ted's HOA management firm began to nose around and examine every line item in his budget.

O'Rourke chafes at the unwelcome oversight. Ted knows the chief calls him "the Ayatollah" behind his back, a slur prompted by Ted's last State Department assignment, managing U.S. Embassy facilities in Saudi Arabia.

"What were you thinking?" Chief O'Rourke barks at Ted. "Why didn't you call security soon as you saw someone jump out of Finley's truck to spray the Quaids' lawn?"

In hindsight, O'Rourke's question seems reasonable, though Ted's intent was to try a little diplomacy to stop the feud from spiraling further out of control. Fat chance now.

The chief stops mid-tirade when he spots Mom's golf cart. He waves her over.

"What are you doing here, Myrt? You should be home in bed."

"Jenny's a nervous wreck. She phoned, so I came to keep her company. What's going on?"

When Mom spots Ted and me, her face clouds. "Why are you two here? I saw Ted's car was gone and figured you were cruising the island looking for Finley's truck."

I turn toward the chief. "I'll let Chief O'Rourke fill you in."

The chief has a soft spot for my mother. He and his missus carried casseroles to the house three times after I brought Mom home from the hospital.

The chief waves a hand toward the spotlighted mound of mulch and sums up what he knows about our discovery. "The body's over there," he concludes. "An arrow through the heart. Single shot. The axe is just for giggles."

Knowing Mom, he doesn't try to block her view as she maneuvers for a first-hand look.

She gasps. "Heaven help us."

"What can you tell me about Dan Finley?" O'Rourke asks.

The chief's smart to tap Mom as a prime info source. She has encyclopedic knowledge of island property owners. Give her a name, and she can recite everything from the person's bridge smarts and golf handicaps to the prescription drugs in his or her bathroom cabinet.

She shrugs. "Hate to speak ill of the dead, but Finley was a jerk. He was around Kylee's age. Fifty or close to it. Moved here eight years ago and started Finley Fresh Landscaping. He's divorced. Twice. One kid from a second marriage to some young babe. Neither Dan nor his ex wanted to be parents. They shuffled the boy off to a military school soon as they could. Someone needs to call the ex-wife so she can break the news to the boy."

"Notifying next-of-kin is the coroner's job," O'Rourke says as he focuses on Mom. "You're up to your eyeballs in this deer feud. Any idea which animal lover might have had enough of Finley's gun 'em down crusade to do him in?"

"The Quaids are among the most vocal. Ted and Kylee were hoping to catch Finley spraying the Quaids' lawn tonight while they're off island at their son's candlelight wedding. Can't see them sneaking away mid-reception to off Finley. The other two couples with lawns hit by the Grass Slayer are also at the wedding."

"Did Finley have other enemies?"

Before Mom can answer, the flashing lights of the sheriff's convoy distract the chief. Car doors slam.

"Myrt, go settle Jenny down. We'll talk later," the chief says as he turns to greet the newcomers.

I take Mom's arm. "I'll come with you."

No use trying to dissuade her from playing nurse, and no way I'll let her negotiate those steep stairs solo.

As soon as Jenny opens her door, Mom hugs her, and says, "I'll make tea." As Mom shuffles into her friend's kitchen, I notice she's still wearing her fuzzy pink bedroom slippers.

I seize my time alone with Jenny to ask a few questions.

"Did you notice the time when you first heard the commotion?"

Jenny's eyes squeeze shut. "The TV news had just come on. Must have been a minute or two past eleven."

"Think back to that noise, the sound that prompted Puppy to bark. Earlier you called it a cry. Did you mean a scream…a cry of pain…a shout?"

Her forehead creases in concentration. "Not sure. At first, I thought a screech owl or a small animal being dragged to the lagoon by an alligator. I didn't think about it being human. Then I looked across the street and saw that shadow moving."

"A single shadow?" I prompt.

Jenny's eyes pop open. "Sorry, can't rightly say. It was just a hunched-over dark blob. It straightened, then bent down again."

Mom arrives, struggling to steady a tray loaded with a delicate china teapot and matching cups and saucers. I hurry to take it, and pour three cups of tea. Jenny grips her cup in both hands and takes a dainty sip. Her age-spotted hands can't quite settle the cup in its saucer. Tea dribbles over the cup's rim. "Oh, dear, I seem to have the shakes."

"Perfectly understandable, but the danger's long gone." *Hope that's not just wishful thinking.*

Jenny takes a shuddering breath. A second deep intake and exhale steadies her.

"When you looked outside, did you see any vehicles, any flashlights?" I continue.

"No." She shakes her head. "I figured it was someone walking a dog over to Dan's property to take a dump. Everyone's supposed to pick up after their dogs no matter where they do their business. But a few owners bring their dogs to Dan's yard after dark and encourage them to leave deposits."

"Who would do that?" Mom sounds shocked.

"It's night so I can't rightly say. But I imagine they're folks opposed to slaughtering our deer. Those innocent creatures lived here long before we came on the island."

Jenny's eyes widen. "You think Dan's campaign to shoot our deer got him murdered?"

Mom doesn't answer immediately. "Who knows? He's rumored to belong to some armed militia group," she finally comments. "Could be a falling out among the conspiracy hotheads. Jenny, did you tell Dan about those dog owners leaving deposits?"

Jenny shakes her head. "He mentioned it to me. We were polite. Never had a lot to say to each other. But he asked me to call security if I saw anyone messing with his property. That's why I phoned tonight. Dan's house was dark. First time I looked out I thought his truck was there. Then it was gone. When he's home, that monstrosity's always in the driveway."

Watching Mom comfort Jenny, I fight the pressure building behind my eyes. Mom will scold me if she sees any tears. But sometimes, my throat tightens when I see the toll cancer has taken. Mom will turn seventy-seven next birthday. Before the cancer struck, she could pass for mid-sixties. She was the star of the Hullis Island seventy-and-over tennis team, still practiced her nursing skills for Hospice, and volunteered several days a week at the no-kill animal shelter.

A decade ago, people sometimes asked if Mom was my older sister. A delight for Mom. I inherited her oval-shaped face and dark blue eyes. But Dad gifted me with dimples and a gene for premature white hair.

Before the cancer, no gray had invaded Mom's auburn pageboy, while I became a curly-haired Q-tip by my mid-thirties. Mom claimed my youthful face and white hair looked striking, exotic—"like a seventeenth-century beauty with a powdered wig."

What a load of total bull crap. Still, I refused to sign on for decades of dye jobs and root-reveal anxiety.

Mom stands. "You must be bone-tired, Jenny. Time to get some sleep."

How I wish my mother would listen when I tell her the same thing.

Chapter Six

Mom's foot barely finds Jenny's bottom step when she spies Nick Ibsen and yoo-hoos. Not exactly accepted homicide-scene decorum.

Nick is talking with Ted. *Crapola.* I'd hoped to avoid a potentially messy meet-and-greet with a one-time lover. During a brief period of temporary lunacy, I dated Nick, a sheriff's deputy, and, in his opinion, a detective extraordinaire. Of course, he'd come running any hour of the night to work a newsworthy homicide.

The deputy is ex-military, though he thinks his macho Marine pedigree far superior to my Coast Guard creds. Can't believe it took me two months to discover Nick's handsome exterior hid an ugly misogynist core. He gets real worked up about women with any authority over men.

After I politely informed him I didn't care to see him anymore, he started with the obscene phone calls. I'm thrilled to be rid of a man eager to mess with my head. Too bad a more enlightened male hasn't volunteered to take up messing with other parts of my body.

"Hi, Nick," Mom hollers when the deputy comes within hailing distance. "Nice to see you again. Come say hello."

I squeeze my eyes shut, count to ten. *Good grief, Mom. This isn't a church social.* I was living with my mother when I dated Nick. When Mom was around, he practiced his sweet-as-Southern-iced-tea manners.

I never clued Mom in on my reasons for breaking off the relationship. Never discuss my love life—or lack thereof—with her. She frets about her single daughter's potentially lonely future. *No way I'll let her know I sometimes worry, too.*

Portable lights shine brightly enough to highlight Nick's reddening cheeks. Mom didn't keep her voice down. Sheriff Conroy and Chief O'Rourke swivel to watch our reunion.

Hullis Island abhors a secret. Both Conroy and O'Rourke know Nick and I were briefly an item.

"Hello, Mrs. Kane." Nick smiles. "Good to see you, Kylee."

Does he not remember? Was he completely blotto when he left his last lewd message on my answering machine? Though I can't bring myself to smile, I force myself to stick out a mitt for a no-grudges handshake.

Nick's two-handed grip is crushing, and he won't let go. His calloused thumb lazily circles the sensitive skin above my wrist. My pulse spikes. Irritation, not lust.

He doesn't free my hand so I can't back away as he brings his lips an inch from my ear. "You're still damn hot. You miss me, don't you? Bet you'd like Big One-Eyed Nick to pay another visit."

He cocks an eyebrow, then winks.

You asshole! One-Eyed Nick wasn't impressive or big. How did I ever date a man who has pet names for his weenie?

I smile and lean forward. pretending I want to whisper a reply. Not my plan. My on-deck Coast Guard voice should carry nicely.

"Nick, I'm so sorry *Little* Nicky still can't get up."

My announcement definitely carries. Sheriff Conroy and Chief O'Rourke both guffaw before they attempt to stifle their mirth. Oops, my mother heard, too, and her look isn't amused.

Sorry, Mom, he had it coming.

Nick's nostrils flare. He lasers me with a look of loathing as I rip my hand from his grasp. He stomps off toward the victim's house. Probably to delay returning to the smirking law enforcement cluster. He had to hear the sheriff and chief laughing.

Wonder how he'll try to make me pay for my smart mouth?

The county coroner straightens from his crouch by the corpse and saunters over to join the officials. Mom, Ted, and I sidle closer to hear his verdict.

The coroner snaps off latex gloves. "No doubt about cause of death. Conroy, even you could have called this one without hauling me out in the shank of the evening."

"Hey, I want our taxpayers to get their money's worth," Conroy needles. "Who knows? I mighta figured Finley was a suicide without your 'expert' opinion. Guy coulda collapsed on his own arrow. Too bad you ruled it a homicide. Now I gotta look for a killer."

These good ol' boys have known each other since their mamas bought their first jockstraps. The desultory banter seems to come standard with crime scene tape, sort of like mustard on a hotdog.

"Chief, we talked to Jenny," Mom interrupts. "She heard a noise, a cry, and looked out her window. Says it was around eleven o'clock."

Ted says, "I'd have argued with her timing if we hadn't discovered Finley's body less than a half-hour after someone drove his truck down Egret Lane."

"Ted videoed Finley's dually about eleven-thirty," I add. "We assumed Finley was driving, but that's impossible. Maybe digital wizardry will tell us who was really behind the wheel."

Mom nods. "Jenny's confused about Finley's truck. Thought it was there when she first heard a ruckus. But, a few minutes later, Finley's driveway was empty. There's no room to park his truck in the garage."

"The old lady's got that part of her story right," says Nick, who's returned from his walkabout. "Looked in the garage window. Barely enough room for a bicycle let alone a truck." He pauses and glares at me. "Why were you two videoing Finley's truck?"

Reminded of our snooping, Chief O'Rourke's expression is as unfriendly as Nick's. "Ted and Kylee were making home movies when they should have been calling security."

"Making home movies of what?" Sheriff Conroy asks.

"We thought it was the Grass Slayer," Ted answers. "We were trying to catch Finley poisoning the lawns of his deer opposition."

"Dear opposition? Say what?" The sheriff's jowls sway as he shakes his head.

"Deer spelled D.E.E.R.," Chief O'Rourke explains. "Bunch of island hotheads been feuding over our herd. The animal rights fanatics won't stand for harming a flea on their bony hides. The hunting crowd's itching to shoot 'em all. Folks in the middle like Mrs. Kane here plead for birth control—though I'll be danged if I'm gonna go around neutering horny bucks. The name-calling's vicious; still can't believe someone would murder Finley over it."

"I don't believe it." Mom motions toward the corpse. "Guess that deer head in his lap and the scarecrow executioner are saying, 'execute our deer and your head might get chopped off.' But why would a killer work so hard to make deer lovers prime suspects if he's one of them? The more I think on it, the more convinced I am the murder has nothing to do with deer. I heard Finley played soldier with some right-wing militia group every now and again."

"What group?" the sheriff asks.

"Rebel Renegades," Deputy Ibsen replies. "They're harmless. Good ol' boys who get together to shoot targets, toast the Second Amendment, and get drunk. No way they're involved."

I snake an arm around Mom's waist and tug her toward her golf cart. Time for us to leave.

"Gentlemen, if you don't need anything more from us, we'll head home. Maybe Ted's video of Finley's truck will help. I'll send notes of our talk with Jenny. She's probably asleep by now. Can you wait till morning to get her official statement?"

The chief gives Jenny's house a visual once-over. "Yeah, it can wait. All the lights are out. Hope the killer didn't spot her snooping. Could put her in jeopardy."

Nick squares his shoulders. "I want to question that old lady tonight, while it's fresh in her mind. Probably can't remember where she put her false teeth after she snoozes."

Mom's eyes narrow. The deputy's pushed one of her buttons. "Jenny's exhausted. Keep ragging at her tonight, and you'll confuse her. Her memory's fine when she's not being bullied."

Ted clears his throat. "I'll put together a list of the people Finley sparred with about the deer situation," he offers to change the subject. "The Hullis board has emails from major players on both sides of the controversy."

I frown, realizing both Ted and Mom are going to stay hip-deep in this hot mess.

Chapter Seven

The Twin

Friday, September 25, Midnight

I gently tug the leash, urging the aged dog to quit sniffing bushes and move along. Dogs are truly man's best friends. My throat tightens each morning when I realize Sage, my hyper Weimaraner, isn't waiting at the door for our start-the-day run. It's been six months since Sage died. I'd love a new puppy, but now isn't the time.

I'm housesitting for a fellow animal shelter volunteer, taking care of Sandy, his golden yellow lab. A perfect excuse to be out at night on Hullis Island, sauntering down a street that just happens to run parallel to Parrot Lane. *Hi, officers, Sandy just needed a final pee.*

Weeks ago, after visiting Sandy's human, I scouted this street and found a small break in the trees that offers an excellent view of Finley's house.

Loud, excited voices penetrate the tree line. *Damn.* I reach the break. They've found Finley's body. Knew the old lady clutching her curtains would tattle.

Rotten luck. The death deserves a daylight debut with more islanders out and about to appreciate my efforts. Finley's finale will spark headlines. The tawdry, theatrical details will prove irresistible. I want the men complicit in Jake's death and cover-up to be remembered only for how they died.

Sandy, almost one hundred in dog years, snuffles along. Her piddling gives me ample time to watch the authorities milling about, no doubt lamenting how such a horrible crime could take place on their quiet island.

The Hullis Island security chief, the sheriff, and a deputy are all on the scene. I know each of them, and they know me. The guy kneeling by the body must be the coroner. Haven't met him.

A vintage Mustang is parked near the old lady's mailbox. What's Ted Welch doing here so late? The man lives in Beaufort.

I hear Myrtle Kane's voice. She dotes on Ted. He must have been visiting her. Myrt's okay, even though she's a cat person. Haven't seen her much since her cancer surgery.

What did Myrt just say? Finley belonged to some militia group? How did I miss that?

I smile. Another way to sow confusion. While I still want officials focused on the island's deer fanatics as primary suspects, adding militia hysteria into the mix can't hurt.

May make it even easier to introduce my next victim to his maker before he suspects I'm coming.

Chapter Eight

Kylee

Saturday, September 26, 2 a.m.

After I type up our conversation with Jenny, I Google the Rebel Renegades group, which allegedly counted Finley as a member. According to the Southern Poverty Law Center, the hate group has grown exponentially since talk of taking down Confederate statues began. The gun-happy South Carolina militia is characterized as white-supremacist and neo-Nazi.

Wonder how to find out if Finley really belonged? It's not like they publish a membership directory. Might need to contact some of my Naval Postgraduate School friends. While earning a Master's in Security Studies on the Coast Guard's dime, I had a chance to meet lots of folks who are now high up on anti-terrorism task forces.

I hear a soft knock on Mom's front door, and, almost simultaneously, the creak of the door opening. Ted has a house key, and knows Mom's welcome mat is always out for him.

"Where's Myrt?" He picks up Mississippi, one of the two black cats Mom adopted when no one else would. Superstitions about black cats make their fur color an adoption handicap.

"Mom's back in her jammies and hopefully asleep."

"Good, she needs plenty of shut-eye." Ted returns Mississippi to the floor and drops into a chair beside me. "I grabbed my laptop out of the car to make those lists I promised the deputy."

"Anything happen after Mom and I left?"

"They found Finley's truck behind the golf maintenance building. It's half a mile from Finley's house by road, even less if you hoof it across the golf course. Parrot Lane's been cordoned off to keep voyeurs away until the CSI team finishes."

Ted sneaks a glance my way and smirks. "So does Deputy Ibsen really have erectile dysfunction?"

I roll my eyes. *Dang it. Me and my big mouth. I forgot Ted heard, too.*

"The deputy made a remark that required an emphatic response. That's all I'm going to say, so drop it."

Ted grins and holds up his hands in an I-give gesture. "Good for you. Nick's a jerk. Hated it when you were dating him."

"Enough, okay? I'm not going to discuss Nick with you or Mom." I whisper in case she's still awake. Despite all odds, the woman's bat-like hearing seems to increase with age.

"Okay, I won't mention the deputy again. Let's look at that video I shot. Maybe if we view it on a bigger screen we'll see something we missed."

"I thought the sheriff confiscated your phone."

"He did. Expected it, so I copied the video and emailed it to myself before surrendering my phone. I also griped I needed my cell for work and got it back half an hour ago. I'll load the video on the TV."

"I'll keep researching the Rebel Renegades while you finish."

A few minutes later, Ted announces, "I'm ready."

"Ready for what?" Mom wanders into the room and wags a finger at me. "Don't start. My brain's too hopped up to sleep. Thought I'd have a nightcap. How about you two—the usual?"

"I'll get the drinks." I head to the wet bar, while Ted fiddles with a smart TV four times bigger than the TV that Barry, Ted, and I sat around to watch *Charlie's Angels* kick butt.

I hand out tumblers of Scotch neat. *Yuck.* Then mix myself a tasty Kahlua and cream.

Mom sips the amber liquid as she swivels back and forth in Dad's oversized recliner. While it almost swallows her, it's her preferred seat. Guess Dad's lingering presence is a comfort.

The video begins. "Pretty murky," Mom comments. "But it's definitely Finley's white dually. That big silver tank is a dead giveaway."

I run my fingers through my tangled hair. Though no longer wet, my albino curls, wind-whipped from the ride in Mom's golf cart, are practically tied in knots. "I still wonder why the killer risked an encore performance as the Grass Slayer. He covered his hair and face, but what if someone had stopped him?"

Ted pauses the video on a frame that offers the clearest view of the killer.

"The killer isn't hiding his face like the Rebel Renegades do," I say. "While the group's kin to the KKK, they've abandoned bed sheets for high-tech. Wear the molded masks people who fence put on for protection."

Ted studies the screen while he pries off his wet shoes and socks, and props his bare size-thirteens on an ottoman.

"Wonder if the killer left the island as soon as he ditched Finley's truck," he comments. "Think the guard on the front gate will remember a vehicle leaving Hullis in the last three hours?"

I stare at the paused image. "Doubtful. Security pays attention to arrivals, not departures."

"Bet he's still on the island," Mom adds. "A smart killer would hunker down until the weekend exodus begins and blend in with departing second homeowners, vacationers, and churchgoers."

I notice a dark roundish shape on the frozen image. It appears just above the truck cab's passenger seat. "Ted, go forward frame by frame. Focus on the passenger seat."

The rounded blob changes position ever so slightly as the video advances. Mom frowns. "Too small to be a person's head."

"A dog?" Ted suggests. "But that's crazy. Who'd bring a pet on a murder mission?"

"Maybe the sheriff can access SLED software to sharpen the image."

Mom pulls back a corner of the window curtain beside her chair. "The fog's crept in thicker than pea soup. The two of you need to bed down here tonight. No arguments. Ted, I still have some of my husband's pajamas. You can sleep in the guest bedroom. Kylee, you can share my bed, but you'd better not hog the covers."

"Mom…" I start to argue, then look outside. Crazy to creep through the thick fog to my slip at the Beaufort Marina. It's almost two a.m. Might as well get a couple hours of shut-eye.

I twist my neck back and forth, and raise and lower my shoulders to ease the tightness. I've hunched over the computer too long.

Ted shrugs. "It'll take me a few minutes more to compile those lists. See you ladies in the morning."

"Hope tomorrow's a better day." Mom looks sad. "Never dreamed someone would be murdered on Hullis Island and the prime suspects would be my neighbors."

An uncharitable thought flits through my mind.

Glad I live on a boat. If I quarrel with my neighbors, I can pull up anchor and leave.

Chapter Nine

"A new tropical storm has formed in the Atlantic." The weatherman looks gleeful as he points at an ominous swirl of clouds hundreds of miles away. Sure, it's excitement for him. For us, it's worry.

"September through mid-October is peak season for hurricanes and conditions favor development," he continues. "This storm could reach hurricane strength by Wednesday and make landfall in about a week. The system bears watching. Here are potential storm tracks."

The coastal map looks like the forecaster threw multi-colored spaghetti at it. None of the curvy plots put Beaufort County near a landfall bullseye. Even the European model expects the storm—Maryanne, if it becomes a hurricane—will hit well south of the Lowcountry's slice of the Carolina coast.

The six-thirty a.m. TV report reassures no one at Mom's breakfast table. People who live on the coast know how unreliable early projections can be.

"Just dandy," Ted says. "We need a mandatory evacuation like Finley needed an arrow in his chest."

I yawn. Can't help it. I'm what you'd call an active sleeper. Like an old dog that curls in a circle before he settles, I fidget to find a comfort zone. Sharing Mom's bed, I tried to keep still. Didn't want to disturb her much-needed sleep. The upshot? My brain kept churning over what little we knew about Dan Finley and his death. Could the killer be a rabid deer partisan? Or did Finley violate some militia oath? Was Finley even the original Grass Slayer?

Ted's cellphone trills. "It's Chief O'Rourke," he mumbles as he exits the kitchen. Mom switches off her small kitchen TV and pours more coffee in all our mugs, confident Ted will return before his coffee gets cold. O'Rourke's calls are notoriously brief.

My gaze slides over the kitchen photo collage and pauses on a photo of Barry, Ted, and me. I'm eleven, a head taller than Ted and my brother, both eight. Ted beams as he holds a prize catfish. Barry and I are pouting because our catches are minnows compared to Ted's. Last year, I finally asked Mom why she'd hung a photo that memorialized her offspring looking like surly brats. Her answer? "It was the first time I saw Ted smile after his mom died."

Ted returns. "The ME confirms Finley died between ten and eleven p.m., about when Jenny called security. The doc found what look like stun gun marks on his neck. Appears Finley was immobilized before the arrow did him in.

"The CSI team couldn't find any shoe or tire prints near the abandoned truck," he adds. "Nothing to tell us if the killer walked or drove away after ditching the dually. But when the CSI techs fingerprinted the truck, they bagged what look like dog hairs inside the cab."

I absently chew on my lip. "Maybe your video does show a dog in the truck. Mom, did Finley have a dog?"

"Yes. But it died a while back. Jenny didn't grieve its passing. She was afraid to take Puppy out when Finley's pit bull mix was in the yard."

"So, any dog hair might have come from Finley's mutt," I say. "Don't imagine he was the type to frequently vacuum his truck. Can they do DNA testing on dog hair?"

Ted laughs. "Doubt a canine DNA workup will be a high priority, but maybe the hairs can identify the breed. I'm inclined to agree with Myrt that the killer had only one reason to nuke the Quaids' lawn. He wanted to ensure the deer feud stays front and center in any theory about motive."

"It's plain as the nose on your face," Mom gloats. "If you two hadn't witnessed the spraying, everyone would have assumed Finley did it just before he was killed. Someone is just taking advantage of the deer feud to shift attention from the real motive. Finley had no problem accumulating enemies."

"For instance?" Ted asks. "Can you nominate anyone besides an unbalanced Rebel Renegade?"

Mom glances at me. "When your dad was on the Hullis board, Finley reported Jerry Schevers for chopping down trees without permission. Mind you, Schevers was in the wrong, but it was Finley who told him 'asking HOA forgiveness beats asking permission.' At the time, Finley thought he had a lock on the landscaping work. When Schevers hired someone else, Finley took revenge."

I shake my head. Mom's tales of neighbors weaponizing HOA rules sound like soap opera dramas. I can almost hear the dum-de-dum-dum music swell right before the cliffhanger dialogue—"He did what?"

Ted starts clearing the table. "Sounds as if Finley ticked off plenty of people."

"And whoever killed him definitely dived off the deep end," I add. "That means we should butt out. Right, Mom?"

No answer.

Ted clears his throat. "I need to get home, shower, and change clothes. It'll be a long day. While I give employees the weekends off, I go in on Saturdays to catch up on paperwork and answer calls. We tend to hear from second-homeowners on Saturdays. Today, I'll probably get calls from residents, too, angling for insider dope on Finley's murder."

Mom's fingers trace the top of her coffee mug. "Islanders will be burning up the airwaves, too. Want to wager how many folks nominate neighbors they dislike as murder suspects?"

Happily, my phone's unlikely to ring. Since retiring, I've shared my new cellphone number with five people. With no pesky interruptions, I plan to curl up in my own bed, hog the covers, and nap till at least ten a.m. Need to rest up for an exciting afternoon visit to the library.

* * *

My fingers trail along the walkway's cold stainless-steel handrail as I board the River Rat, my 38-foot Island Packet sailing cruiser. Dad would love it. He spent many happy hours with me, brother Barry, and Ted at the loftily-named Keokuk Yacht Club. Of course, nothing approaching a yacht ever tied up to the club's ramshackle docks on Lake Keokuk, a mile-wide stretch of the Mississippi River just above our dam.

Dad grew up reeling in catfish from granddad's rowboat and loved the water. When one of the firemen under his command ran a sailing dinghy aground, Dad bought and salvaged the wreck. The resurrected boat's name? River Rat, of course.

The dinghy provided tons of family fun—for everyone but Mom, a contender in the frantic dog paddler hall of fame. Even encased in a lifejacket, she got nervous. To her credit, Mom insisted on swim lessons for me and Barry. Wonder if she ever regrets her role in sparking my love of the water, a career in the Coast Guard, and my choice of a home that floats.

I look across the Beaufort River. In minutes, the sun will burst over the majestic live oaks on the opposite shore. I have no plans to watch. I head straight to my stateroom for a deserved nap.

* * *

I rub my eyes and glance at the clock. Nine-thirty. *Darn.* Hoped I'd sleep a bit longer. My stomach's growling. I plod over to my boat's mini-fridge and stare at the uninspiring breakfast options. *Okay, let's call it brunch.* I pop a nukeable, single-portion Mac-and-Cheese in the microwave. The oven's loud and insistent "done" beep almost drowns out Mom's ringtone.

I grab a hot pad and extract my "brunch" before I answer. "Hi. How's it going, Mom? You screening calls?"

"Yes, but I picked up when Jenny phoned. Nick questioned her this morning. You never told me what a horse's patootie he is. Can't believe he's into badgering old ladies."

"Not a shocker," I answer. "What happened?"

"Nick's early morning, third-degree unnerved Jenny," Mom continues. "And that's not the worst of it. The island's avid deer killers are creating some sort of tribute in front of Finley's house. Jenny's scared silly. Says some of the men are carrying rifles. I want you and Ted to go see her. Ted can reassure Jenny her street will get extra security, and you can coax her into sharing insights into her dear-departed neighbor's life. You're good at asking questions."

"Mom, you're the interrogation queen. You visit Jenny."

"Can't. While Chief O'Rourke admits he can't *order* me to do anything, he strongly suggests I quarantine myself for the time being. Guess Ted told him about my mailbox threat. Given my lawsuit notoriety, O'Rourke claims anything I do or say will stir the pot."

I'm thrilled Mom's sitting on the sidelines. Doesn't mean I'm willing to be her butt-in-ski stand-in. "Chief O'Rourke won't be any more thrilled about Ted and me sticking our noses in."

"Don't care. Got another 'love' note today," Mom confesses. "It says I'm responsible for Dan Finley's death. Claims my push for a vote got the Bambi lovers riled up. The note promises I'll pay for my meddling."

A chill careens down my spine. "Mom, please come stay with me."

"You know my answer. No. I already talked to Ted. As the head of the company managing our HOA, he has legitimate concerns. He's on his way to pick you up."

"Ever consider I might have other plans?" I sigh, torn between irritation that Mom assumes I can't refuse her and worry about her new hate mail.

"Well, do you have plans?" she demands. "Reading a new thriller doesn't count."

"It should."

"Conspiracy theories are more plentiful than no-see-ums, and Jenny's spooked. Do your mother a favor. Don't argue. Just help."

We say our goodbyes, and I fork a generous glob of Mac and Cheese before I dump it in the trash. At least Mom warned me Ted's on his way. I'm in seedy nap attire, old sweats, no bra, bare feet. I start to undress.

"You decent?" Ted calls as he clamors below deck.

"No!" I holler, though the fleece layer blanketing my mouth muffles my protest. My sweatshirt is attached at my neck. My arms wave above my head as my bare boobs jiggle front and center. At least the inside-out sweatshirt hides my heated cheeks, undoubtedly bright red.

He laughs. "Maybe I should have asked if you were decent *before* I came below. Let me help."

His warm hands grip my bare midriff, and he spins me one-hundred and eighty degrees before he tugs my sweatshirt over my head. "There. Your back's to me so you can't catch me ogling. It was a nice view while it lasted."

"Gee, thanks." I clutch the sweatshirt to my chest. "Floorshow's over. Give me a minute."

When I return, Ted's thumbing through the Janet Evanovich paperback I planned to exchange at the library. I doubt his mischievous grin has a thing to do with the book's humor.

"Sorry about barging in." His cheery tone isn't the least apologetic. "I have a proposition that would mean we see a lot more of each other—unfortunately with clothes on."

"What are you talking about?"

"Come work for me. Employee or consultant. Your choice."

"What?" I stammer. "Why?"

"You spent years as a Coast Guard investigator, and I need someone to assure our HOA clients we can look into and tackle security concerns."

"Mom suggested this, right?"

"She did, but the more I thought about it, the better the idea seemed."

I shake my head. "Investigating threats to Charleston's harbor or boat accidents isn't the kind of investigating—"

Ted presses two fingers against my lips before I can complete my objection.

"Hear me out. Nervous clients have been calling all morning. Older residents are especially fearful. We need to show we're listening. Yeah, I know the investigations you handled were quite different. Still, you know how to evaluate information, separate fantasy from facts, and see if concerns are legit. Don't answer now. Think about it."

I snap my mouth shut. The offer unexpectedly appeals. I've been taking law enforcement courses online, toying with the idea of getting a PI license. I'm bored. Fifty is too young to be retired. I miss the Coast Guard, the sense of purpose, the camaraderie.

Taking care of Mom lets me shuffle any decisions about the future to a back burner. Now, Mom no longer needs me, and my continued hovering is getting on her nerves.

"I'll think about it." Surprisingly, I mean it. "Would I have to work in an office and wear something fancier than sweats?"

"Sweats are a deal-breaker when you're calling on clients." The corners of Ted's mouth lift. "But I'd be happy for you to work stark naked anywhere else."

I roll my eyes. My cheeks heat. His warm, strong hands felt mighty good on my bare skin. Contact my body clearly misses.

Sometimes I sense Ted's flirting is more than friendly teasing.

Get a grip! He's practically a brother. Almost lived at our house since his dad worked long hours. Mom was a school nurse then, home early to bake cookies and look after strays—especially cats and latch-key kids.

Chapter Ten

The Twin

Saturday, September 26, Morning

I slept soundly. A surprise. Usually have a hard time getting comfortable in a strange bed. Of course, I was exhausted. More from tension than exertion.

I clip a leash on Sandy, and take her for a walk. It's a beautiful morning. Lots of folk out enjoying the gorgeous fall. On our neighborhood stroll, other dog owners recognize Sandy and ask after her owner. I explain I'm housesitting, and my friend will return come morning.

They're all agitated. "Have you heard the news?" … "Someone murdered Dan Finley last night. He only lives a pitching wedge away!" … "Stay inside after dark and lock your door." … "A caller on a morning talk show says Rebel Renegades will storm the island to avenge Finley's death. They're calling him a martyred patriot."

I fake a frown and thank them for their concern. The urge to burst out laughing is strong. Thank you, island jungle drums. Is there any truth to the Rebel Renegades story? Oh, I hope so.

Back at the house, I feed Sandy. After she wolfs down her food, she saunters to her dog bed and collapses. My friend told me not to worry about leaving the old dog alone for a few hours if I need to run errands.

Before my walk, I only had one *errand*. A final reconnaissance of Golden

Treasure. Now I have a second. Need to stop by my house and pick up my night scope. It'll come in handy tonight after all the frightened neighbors lock their doors. I'll wager me and my unregistered Smith & Wesson can trigger a lot more finger-pointing.

But Golden Treasure's my first priority. It's where Chet "Chevy" Cole, my next victim, lives—until tomorrow night.

The Cole family owns the local General Motors dealership, and Chet snagged his Chevy nickname by always driving one. Pretending interest in a new domestic SUV, I visited the dealership last week to eyeball Cole in the flesh.

A chatty salesman told me Chevy'd handed out cigars in honor of his daughter popping out a new grandkid. That's how I learned Mrs. Chevy Cole is out of town, helping the daughter with a new baby. Her absence makes this weekend ideal for my purposes.

I'm delighted Chevy resides in Golden Treasure, an ungated community, with a tax-subsidized beach open to the public. Plenty of options to enter the neighborhood unnoticed. On today's Golden Treasure reconnaissance, I don't expect to see Chevy out with his dogs. Even on Saturdays, he keeps to his routine, taking the dogs out early morning and around dusk.

I drive by his house just as a mail truck pulls into his driveway. The postman rings the bell. I stop my car at the end of the cul-de-sac to watch and listen. His howling mutts sound ready to tear apart the meek public servant who's dared to set foot on the property.

The door opens a crack, and Chevy edges onto the porch, keeping the door angled to prevent any canine escape. Once outside, he shuts the door. Won't risk his ill-mannered dogs chomping on a civil servant's ankles. He signs for the package. God bless, special deliveries!

I smile. Slight change of plan. A perfect way to separate Chevy from his dogs. I'm not keen on hurting them. Not their fault their owner is a dolt. However, I will need to do some quick costume shopping, and I should probably rent a Jeep.

Chapter Eleven

Kylee

Saturday, September 26, Morning

Jenny appears relieved to usher us in. Puppy nuzzles Ted's leg and swishes his stick-like tail with gusto. The mutt ignores me.

Jenny totters toward a chair. "Did you see anyone over at Dan's? I pulled my blinds. Men in military garb and brandishing rifles have been coming and going all morning. Can't security stop them? Isn't there some law about carrying guns around to frighten people?"

"We didn't see anyone outside, though I can't guarantee more won't show up," Ted says. "Unfortunately, the chief can't do a thing about the guns—as long as they don't overtly threaten anyone. While South Carolina doesn't allow open-carry of handguns, long guns are exempt."

"What are they doing?" Jenny asks. "Building a shrine? Finley sure has more friends dead than he did when he was alive."

"It's a memorial, of sorts," I answer. "A big pile of hunter paraphernalia—duck decoys, skinning knives, camo backpacks, and bent-up scopes. Quite a few flags, too. A combination of flags with twined snakes with the 'Don't Tread on Me' message and Re-elect Prudmont banners. Prudmont's practically an NRA patron saint."

I don't mention that the visitors have tossed shell casings around like confetti and posted scary, hand-written signs. The worst? "Kill a Hunter,

Expect a Bullet.".

"We know you've had an upsetting morning. Would you like to stay somewhere else for a few days?" Ted asks.

"No, I don't want to leave my house. Just promise me security will actually come if I call."

"Done," Ted pledges.

"Thank you. Come in, come in. Sit down. You're a nice young man. Not like that snotty deputy. The way he barked at me you'd have thought I killed Dan. How I wish I could remember something to help. No one will feel safe again until that killer's caught."

I pat her hand. "Maybe you could help round out our picture of Mr. Finley. Did you get along?"

Jenny taps a finger against her thin lips. "He was cordial but cool. If we visited our mailboxes at the same time, we'd nod and speak. But I've never been inside his house. Never dreamed of asking Dan to water my plants when I was out of town."

"Did Mr. Finley have many visitors?" I ask.

Jenny shakes her head. "Very few. Leastways not when I was out and about. I don't sit at my window and snoop on my neighbor, you know." Her tone suggests Deputy Nick intimated she did.

"Of course, you don't," I soothe. "But it's hard to ignore a neighbor who hosts parties or engages in shouting matches. Did he do anything to call attention?"

"No. Dan kept to himself. Only heard him shout the one time last week. I was outside with Puppy and heard Mr. Westcott screaming that Dan used some grass killer to write a vulgar message on his lawn. Dan laughed. Said he wished he'd thought of doing just that.

"Mr. Westcott called him a liar. That's when Dan yelled at Westcott to get the hell off his property. Threatened to get his gun if Mr. Westcott didn't get his 'fat ass' back in his golf cart."

Ted nods encouragement. "I'm sure the sheriff plans to speak with Mr. Westcott. Any other conversations or recent visitors come to mind?"

Her brows knit. "Well, yes. I saw Dan greet a chap a couple weeks ago.

It was a Monday, early September. He gave the fellow a bear hug. Never saw Dan show affection to anyone before, not even his son. Wondered if the caller might be some relative, a cousin maybe. They looked about the same age."

"Can you describe the visitor?" Ted asks. "Height, hair color, clothing? His car?"

"Drove up in a fancy sports car. Dan hustled out on the porch soon as the car turned into the drive. The men were about the same height. What was Dan? A little under six feet?

"I was watering plants on my porch. Since it's on stilts, I was looking down. Saw the top of the stranger's head. Bald as a boiled egg, and his bare arms almost as white. Sure was spry though. Ran up the stairs like a teenager."

Ted jots a note and smiles at Jenny. "That's very helpful. Thank you. Here's my card. Call if you think of anything else that seemed a mite out of the ordinary. I promise security will post an officer on this street tonight. Stay inside, and you'll be fine."

"I've been afraid to take Puppy out," Jenny adds. "Could you walk him before you leave?"

Ted carries the roly-poly hotdog downstairs. At the bottom, he clips on a leash. As we stroll down Parrot Lane, I wonder how Ted got the leash, and I got the pooper-scooper.

"Jenny may have given us a lead," he begins. "I'll check early September visitor logs to see who Finley called in."

"Sounds like the man was a good friend," I agree. "Maybe Finley told him about any trouble he was having."

Puppy brakes and barks to let us humans know he's found an ideal spot to relieve himself. "Remember the old joke about aliens deciding canines rule planet earth? Dogs must be royalty if humans follow to pick up their turds."

Ted smiles. "I remember the mutt you and Barry had when we were kids. Brownie's the dumbest dog I ever met. Did you or Barry come up with her *original* name?"

"Barry, of course. I voted for Princess. But since I picked the dog, Barry got to name her."

I'm pleased I can finally share fond childhood memories without raw grief overwhelming me. Hard to believe Barry's been gone ten years. He'd be forty-seven. There was never any question about Barry following in Dad's firefighter footsteps. Unfortunately, he wasn't as lucky as Dad, who made it to retirement with only a few scares.

Whenever I hear a firetruck's siren, I pray an unexpected backdraft or explosion won't harm the brave men and women risking their lives.

I realize Ted's been talking.

"I asked how come there's no Princess—or Prince—in your life? Have you outgrown pets and fairytales?"

I shrug. "Living on a boat, a frog would be a better pet. As to fairytales, haven't met a frog I'm willing to kiss hoping he'll turn into a prince. Besides, Mom made me guardian of Mississippi and Keokuk if anything happens to her. I'm sure she has a clause in her will that forbids my harboring a dog within fifty feet of those spoiled cats."

Puppy tugs at his leash. I almost gag as I bag his odiferous nuggets.

What does Jenny feed him?

After we return the pooch, Ted suggests we hang out a little longer to see if the gun-toting parade has ended. The September sunshine feels warm, and a pleasant ocean breeze keeps the bugs at bay. We stroll to the end of Parrot Lane, a truncated side street in one of the island's older interior sections.

"Who owns all the vacant lots?" I ask.

"Mostly disappointed speculators," Ted answers. "They gambled values would climb once folks snapped up the island's more desirable homesites. Never happened."

I can see why. The empty lots are choked with palms and scrub brush. Poor drainage leaves stagnant pools for mosquitoes to breed.

At the intersection of Parrot and Egret, we turn and look back toward Finley's house. Parrot Lane terminates at a drainage ditch.

Only one way in and out. A true dead-end.

Chapter Twelve

Our return walk brings us to the mulch pile backdrop for Finley's execution. I'm not sure what bothers me more, picturing the posed corpse or seeing the peculiar shrine, which says less about mourning and more about revenge.

"Did the sheriff check on the Quaids and their friends?" I ask. "Were their alibis solid?"

"When a deputy visited the wedding hotel at two a.m., all the Grass Slayer victims were in their nighties, tucked in. In theory, one of them could have shot Finley at eleven and broken all speed limits to make a two-a.m. bed check in Savannah. But the wedding photographer snapped pictures of all three couples dancing just before midnight. Perfect alibis."

"Is the sheriff looking at other 'Save Bambi' candidates?"

"Deputy Ibsen thinks that's the way to go," Ted replies. "But I'm with Myrt. The deer feud motive is too in-your-face. Finley's knack for pissing people off could have extended to the Rebel Renegades."

He glances at Finley's house. "Let's look inside."

"Can we? Is it still a crime scene?"

"No, the CSI techs are finished. Besides Finley was killed outside, not in the house."

I raise an eyebrow. "And you have a key?"

"Sure do. Phoned the ex-wife. Offered to assist with cleaning out the house. She took me up on it. Chief O'Rourke wasn't happy about surrendering the key."

"Where does the ex live?"

"In Greenville." Ted unlocks the door. "Far enough she doesn't want to waste hours driving back and forth. The techs took Finley's computer and business files. But maybe something inside will tell us more about the man's friends and enemies."

The nondescript gray clapboard looks too dull to be a crime location. The dirty white porch railings, window sills, and door trim provide little contrast with the dingy Hardie Plank siding. The scene looks as if it's been painted with dishwater. A leftover snip of yellow crime scene tape adds the only color.

The stuffy interior exudes a halitosis odor. Cigarettes and cooking grease. The guy didn't follow a fat-free diet. I'm tempted to hold my nose. The interior is more depressing than the exterior. The front room holds one stained plaid couch, one lime green chair, and a floor lamp with a sooty white shade. Bare walls, no art. Not exactly an entertainment mecca.

Evidently, Finley didn't like to clean. The grimy mini-blinds admit only knife-edge beams of light. Dust mites boogie in the few rays that slice through the gloom.

Ted turns down a hall. "Looks like he spent most of his time in here."

The den looks—and smells—lived in. It reeks of cigarette smoke. Across the back of the house, large uncovered windows are filmed by years of nicotine deposits.

Still, the den has personality. The wood-paneled wall opposite the windows showcases an eclectic array of hunting and fishing trophies—elk and bear heads, a large marlin, and a stuffed owl with its wings spread. One oval-shaped patch of light wood suggests the recent removal of a trophy. The deer head left in Finley's lap? A gun case holds four rifles.

Framed photos are interspersed with the trophies. A snapshot on the desk pictures a uniformed teen standing in front of a squat building. Finley's son?

I study the photo. "Wonder how the boy's handling the news? Had Finley been in touch with his ex-wife recently?"

"No, but she says Finley phoned his son regularly. The kid's enrolled at Sedgewick Military Academy. Finley's an alum. It's located in the Sandhills area, middle of nowhere."

I shudder. "I've heard of Sedgewick. Hell of a place for a kid. A fellow Coastie spent four painful years there. He claimed it was worse than juvie jail."

On a side wall, a faded color photo shows six young cadets posed in front of the same squat Sedgewick building. Is Finley one of these boys? While lingering baby fat softens their features, their expressions appear too mature. Prison-yard stares.

In another photo, Finley drapes his arms around the shoulders of two soldier pals. "Looks like Finley served in the Army."

Ted glances at the picture. "He joined after college, did two tours. Fought in Iraq. Mustered out as a lieutenant. Didn't stick to make twenty and retire."

"He might have made friends and enemies in the service. Maybe that visitor Jenny mentioned was an old Army buddy."

Ted nods. "We'll check. If the visitor log gives us a name, we have a starting point. Anything else grab your attention?"

"I see a gun cabinet and a case for fishing tackle, but no bow. This seems to be where he kept his gear. Did he actually hunt with a bow?"

"His ex says he hunted with an expensive compound bow. Murderer must have kept it as a souvenir."

"Does a single arrow through the heart mean the killer's a skilled archer?"

"Not necessarily. The stun gun made Finley a stationary target. If the M.E. can estimate how close the killer stood, it might help determine expertise."

I fan out a pile of magazines sitting beside a recliner. Looks like Finley confined his reading to NRA publications and *Field & Stream* type magazines. A flyer for a Rebel Renegades rally is tucked in the middle of the stack.

I show the sheet to Ted.

"Another sign the militia rumors are true," he says. "If Finley wasn't a member, he was at least an admirer."

Ted turns in a circle, giving the room a visual once-over. "Guess we're done."

As we walk out to the porch, I hear the unmistakable click. A gun.

"Hands up!"

When we're not quick enough to obey, the burly man pointing a rifle at us repeats his order. "Hands up, or I shoot."

Ted and I raise our hands. I'm so preoccupied staring at his Winchester that I notice little beyond the guy's stout build and hunter's vest. Definitely not Hullis Island Security.

"What were you doing in Finley's house?" he shouts. "You stealing his stuff now?"

"We're here at Mrs. Finley's request," Ted answers. "Helping with an inventory before an estate sale."

"That's a lie," Rifle Man mutters. "Finley wasn't married."

Ted remains remarkably calm. "He was divorced. Finley's ex-wife is guardian for his young son. I'll call her for you. She can tell you."

Rifle Man lowers his weapon ever so slightly, and I study his face. Don't recognize him. Does he live here or is he one of the Rebel Renegades? Guess he could be both. Finley was.

The fact I don't know this stranger means nothing. I only know a fraction of the island's fifteen hundred permanent residents.

"Do you live here?" I ask. "If so, call island security. They'll verify we have permission to be in the house."

At least I hope they will.

"Don't trust your security," the man answers. "They let some anti-gun, anti-hunter, animal rights fanatic kill a true patriot. That's why we've come. This island's been infected by radical liberals. We're gonna protect the lives and property of Hullis patriots."

"Can we leave?" Ted asks.

"Go," the man answers. "Your hands are empty. Guess you're not stealing nothing, though I can't be sure what you did inside. Don't think about coming back till we check out that story about Finley having an ex-wife. We have our sources."

As he tracks our movements, I match Ted's purposeful stride and fight the urge to run. I also make a conscious effort to memorize everything I can about the man—five-nine or ten, close to two-hundred pounds, longish brown hair, scruffy beard. I search Parrot Lane for his vehicle, too. Must be the rusty white pickup with the gun rack.

Neither Ted nor I say word one until his car exits Parrot Lane.

"I got his license plate," I say.

Ted glances my way. "Me, too. We're going straight to Chief O'Rourke's office to find out if militia man lives here. His tag number should tell us."

* * *

By the time we walk into the chief's office, the cool Ted displayed while a gun was aimed at his chest is gone.

The blood vessel jumping in Ted's temple signals his anger.

"We just left Finley's house where some trigger-happy militia idiot threatened to shoot us," Ted raves at the chief. "What the hell are you doing, letting these idiots have free reign?"

O'Rourke bristles at the criticism. I wait for a brief pause in the ensuing screaming match.

"Chief, we got the license plate of the guy who threatened us, and his pickup didn't have a Hullis decal on the windshield. Must be a visitor. Can you check the vehicle tags issued with recent visitor passes? Could tell us how he got on the island."

O'Rourke grunts and stalks out of his office.

"Thanks, Kylee," Ted says. "Can't believe I lost my temper and lashed out at O'Rourke. I just started thinking about the bloody horrors I've seen in other countries when self-appointed militias start taking over the streets."

When O'Rourke returns, Ted apologizes, and O'Rourke tells us that Aaron Smith, a Hullis homeowner, requested the visitor's pass for a Billy Jenkins. Smith also called in visitor passes for three more visitors this morning.

Since an owner may be hosting a party, guards never question someone requesting multiple visitor passes.

"I know Aaron," the chief says. "I'll talk to him, and call in all our off-duty officers to put more bodies on patrol tonight. And, yes, Jenny's street will get a full-time watchdog."

O'Rourke glares at Ted, indicating the apology is only partially accepted. "You better not give me any grief about overtime and budget, or I swear, I'll make it my mission to get your company fired."

Chapter Thirteen

"That went well." Ted sighs as we drive off the island. "I've never second-guessed security about money spent to deal with an emergency."

"The chief's frustrated," I comment. "He'll cool down. I feel much better about Jenny, given his reassurance her street will be protected all night."

"Wonder if looking into the barrel of a gun triggers a hunger response?" Ted says. "I'm starved. Let's pick up sandwiches at Subway then head to my office. Want you to meet your new co-workers. When the phones started ringing off the hook this morning, I asked Robin and Lyn if they'd come in at noon on their day off for a half-day."

"They're not my office mates yet but I should chat them up," I answer. "Find out how they feel about Ted Welch, the boss. I also need to know more about what you actually *do*. Mom says your HOA clients come in all sizes, from condos with less than twenty units to communities like Hullis with a thousand-plus houses."

Ted keeps his eyes on the island's narrow roads as he answers. "We attend board meetings, look into owner complaints, collect dues, prepare budgets, let contracts, handle architectural reviews, and maintain everything from landscaping and swimming pools to tennis courts and private roads."

He grins. "Cowardice remains a primary reason boards hire us. Some directors serve on HOA boards to push through new rules that address their pet peeves. Things like insisting roof shingles can't be metal or that all mailboxes must be clones of some fancy favorite. Yet directors don't want to be the heavies. That's us—the third-party enforcer everyone can hate."

"When Dad served on the Hullis board, he didn't mind gripes about clear-cut violations, but hated rinky-dink grumbles. You know, 'Joe Schmoe has a patch of mold on his garage door. ... Jill Trill hasn't cut her lawn this week. ... Harry Berry painted his shutters cherry red instead of barn red.'"

Ted laughs.

"Lord, have mercy," I continue. "I might want to murder someone if I had to put up with such nonsense. Glad my home floats beyond the borders of any HOA."

He glances my way. "Good luck avoiding HOA life if you ever put your boat in dry dock. Three-quarters of all new houses are inside HOAs. Don't get me wrong. They can be a godsend. It's just that neighborhoods frequently are allotted either too many idiots or bored, power-hungry retirees. I shouldn't complain. They provide a nice post-retirement source of income."

"Which brings up the subject of pay," I interrupt. "What would you pay me to be a security consultant?

"Well, if you were a licensed PI, it might be different. But since you're a rookie—"

"Rookie!" I explode. My trap snaps shut as soon as I catch Ted's smirk. Knowing me so well, he can push all my buttons.

Ted smiles. "Actually, I'll pay you top of the scale. You're super smart, and have the tenacity of a demented squirrel looking for a buried nut stash."

"Lucky you called me super smart. Not exactly flattering to be compared to a crazed rodent."

Ted puts on his turn signal.

"We're here. Welch HOA Management's humble abode."

Ted bought a run-down Port Royal convenience store for its Beaufort County location. It's near Parris Island and the bridge that links the Beaufort-Port Royal area and its Sea Islands to their Bluffton-Hilton Head cousins.

Ted's roadside signage is tasteful—crisp black letters on a pale-yellow background with line art hinting at homes, trees, and water. The tagline is a bit more braggadocio: "Answers for Every HOA Need."

The squeaky-clean front windows offer a clear view of arrivals. The open interior surprises me. Fabric-covered partitions separate cubicles in the administrative hive.

"I ripped out the grocery shelving and refrigerator cases," he explains. "That left one large undivided room. The screens help sound-proof and give each of us a little privacy."

He gestures toward a front-row cubicle cordoned off by dull-gray cloth screens. "I work here, and my office neighbor and right-hand is Lyn Adair. Lyn, meet Kylee Kane."

The bottle-blonde swivels toward us in her high-backed executive chair. She's what Mom calls well-tended. Expert makeup. Smooth skin. A fitted suit shows off a curvy but fit body.

"Heard so much about you," Lyn purrs. "A pleasure to meet you."

Hmm, who's mentioned me? Probably Mom when she drops by for her weekly lunch with Ted.

Ted jumps in to finish Lyn's introduction. "This lady's a genius at soothing irate clients. Can't believe my luck in snagging her. Lyn had her own successful psychology practice in Columbia before moving to the Lowcountry ten months ago."

None of this is news to me. Ted asked Mom to help him screen job applicants when his company took off. He wanted Mom to have something besides cancer to occupy her mind. As her in-home caregiver, I got an earful about all Ted's hires. When Mom met Lyn, it was instant dislike despite the woman's sterling Ph.D. qualifications. Mom's convinced she took the job to get her hooks into Ted.

"Around Ted, Lyn's sweeter than a sugar cube soaked in honey and dipped in chocolate," Mom groused. "I don't trust her. She could work part-time as a therapist or counselor and make lots more money."

Because Ted's ex-wife royally screwed him, Mom is hyper-critical of any woman who comes within his orbit and has love-interest potential. I try to keep an open mind. Lyn's three-inch heels, mascara-bloated eyelashes, and the glossy smile she beams at Ted aren't helping my neutrality.

The woman's handshake breaks the beauty-queen image. Rough calloused hands, nails clipped close to the quick. A nail biter? A gardener?

"Ted hopes you'll join our *team*," Lyn gushes. "That horrid Hullis Island homicide is making our clients jumpy. Hard to believe an animal control issue could enrage someone enough to murder a fellow human being. Hope you find the murderer quickly."

I frown. Her syrupy "team" reference grates, and she doesn't get what I'd actually do for the *team*. "Finding the killer is the sheriff's job, not mine or Ted's."

Lyn's brows knit. "Oh? Won't you help the sheriff decide which Hullis deer lovers are the best murder suspects?"

Ted breaks in before I can answer. "We're not even sure the murder's linked to the deer controversy." He glances at his watch. "Aren't you meeting with the Golden Treasure Board at one?"

The perfectly groomed Number Two checks the time. "Heavens, I do need to leave. Hope you decide to join us."

Fake sincerity. We're about the same age. Does she think I'll compete for Ted's affections?

We leave Lyn's front-row cube and look in on a chipmunk-cheeked cherub. "Kylee, meet Robin Gates, our IT and social media guru."

Startled, Robin jumps, then giggles. She removes her earphones, and I hear a few beats of heavy metal music before the audio's cut. "Sorry. Didn't hear you."

The young woman's attire leans toward grunge. Faded cut-offs and a long-sleeved t-shirt that sports a few rips. While her frizzy brown hair's pulled into a ponytail, wayward locks form billowing clouds around her ears, each punctured with multiple holes. Her grin reveals a retainer.

I like her. Mom's report? The twenty-one-year-old junior college grad has no current boyfriend and resides with her parents and two younger sisters on Dataw Island.

"Robin designs and manages clients' websites and social media," Ted says. "Ours, too. She's fantastic."

Robin beams. While Ted might be a new entrepreneur, he's an old hand at making staffers feel appreciated.

"We'll let you get back to it." Ted pats Robin's shoulder and waves toward an empty office pod. "This cubicle belongs to Frank Donahue, our maintenance expert and inspector."

Mom hardly approved Frank's hire. He owned a roofing business until a bad fall ended his days of making like Old Saint Nick. Mom says the tumble hasn't affected his ability to climb all over contractors to make sure they deliver.

"There's a phone call for you, Ted," Robin interrupts. "The president of Satin Sands HOA, Roger Roper." Robin's lips pucker like she just ate something sour.

"I should take it," Ted apologizes. "You can claim any of the open cubicles or rearrange the partitions to create a larger workspace. I'll be back in a couple of minutes."

The cloth partitions do a fair job of providing acoustical privacy. Though I'm less than fifteen feet from Ted's desk, I can't hear word one of his conversation. Good time to check out the office potty. I spot a door marked "restroom" in the solid rear wall.

After I use the cubbyhole unisex facility, I peek behind another door that opens to a tidy storage area, and a kitchenette with a small fridge and the all-important coffee maker.

Caffeine and a bathroom. Two positive checkmarks in my pro versus con employment tally. What would a short-term consulting gig do to my sanity? I lack Ted's patience and suck at keeping my lips zipped when people irritate me. Somehow, I sense a number of Ted's HOA clients will prove annoying. Even in the Coast Guard, I had trouble biting my tongue if I disagreed with an officer who outranked me. Could I show more restraint with civilian bozos? Not in my DNA.

Ted's couple-of-minutes call stretches to a quarter-hour. I ask Robin for a password to fire up a computer in a vacant office pod to check the local news. The Hullis Island homicide tops the cyber news list. Headlines hype the deer feud as the murder motive, while photos show emaciated deer at the Quaids' backyard feeder.

I move on to a bait-click banner—"Hullis Resident Threatens Lawsuit."

Crap. Mom's face, with mouth frozen open in a still photo, invites people to tap on the video play arrow.

I tap. A young TV reporter tosses her hair so much I think she'll suffer whiplash. She shoves a microphone in my mother's face.

"We need to take steps to reduce our deer population," Mom says as she looks away from the hair-flinger and focuses on the camera. "As a nature sanctuary, hunting isn't permitted, and our small island deer have few natural predators to keep the population in check. Every year as more homes are built, there's less and less natural habitat."

The doe-eyed reporter interrupts. "Does that mean you support the murder victim's call to kill the deer? I thought you threatened a lawsuit to prevent their slaughter."

"I didn't say I agreed with Mr. Finley's position, young lady," Mom chastises. "Birth control could gradually bring the population back in balance with the food supply."

The questioner tries another tack. "Now that Dan Finley's been killed for his position—"

"Young lady, sorry to correct you again. But you're jumping to conclusions. I seriously doubt our deer debate has anything to do with this senseless homicide."

This portion of the video abruptly ends, and the reporter poses in front of the bizarre Finley shrine. She clears her throat. "While some islanders are in denial that one of their own has killed a neighbor over this wildlife dispute, others are expressing their anger that a hunter who advocated culling the herd has been killed by an opponent who values the lives of deer more than humans."

I switch off the video. So much for my mother staying on the sidelines. *Mom, what possessed you to give an interview?*

I jump when Ted taps my shoulder. "Sorry the call took so long. It's nice out. There's a picnic table around back where we can talk employment. I'll treat. Coffee or a Coke?"

Ted looks upset. "A Coke's good." I decide to listen to whatever he has to say before I tell him about Mom appearing in the latest media circus.

He returns from the kitchenette with two drinks, and my trouble-detector antenna starts twitching. Why does Ted want to sit on a bottom-numbing concrete bench when there are comfy chairs inside?

The picnic table almost looks like it has a polka-dot tablecloth. Bird doodoo.

"D'you see a squadron of Frogmore eagles flying overhead?" Ted quips, but he doesn't even crack a smile as he uses the Lowcountry nickname for its economy-size vultures.

"Okay. What gives? Why'd you hustle me outside?"

He takes a deep breath. "Didn't want to alarm Robin. The president of Satin Sands says his HOA was the scene of a murder attempt this morning."

"What? I just checked the local news. Didn't see a word about any foiled murder attempt."

He sighs. "The victim, Alex Peters, was bitten by a copperhead. A neighbor was passing by in his golf cart when he heard her scream. He clubbed the snake with a fairway wood and drove her to the hospital. The woman's prognosis is good, but she's elderly and has a heart condition, so the doctors are keeping her under observation."

"Neighbors think someone planted the snake? Can't believe a snake tossed in the woman's yard could be counted on to linger until it had a chance to bite her. Never heard of a trained attack snake."

"The copperhead was snagged in netting draping some blueberry bushes. Couldn't get free, and it was desperate. The woman bent to lift the netting and didn't see the snake an inch from her finger."

"Sounds like an accident."

"Doesn't matter," Ted continues. "Ms. Peters' allies are screaming bloody murder about a premeditated attack. She's received anonymous hate mail calling her yard a 'snake pit.' The property is chockful of native plants. Neighbors with neatly-mown lawns think it's an unsightly disgrace. Her friends seized on the hate mail's 'snake pit' wording to conclude the bite wasn't accidental."

"They think someone trapped the snake to teach her a lesson?"

"Exactly," Ted answers. "They're convinced the Hullis murder emboldened

Ms. Peters' enemies. The board president agrees it's attempted murder but blames outsiders. He's hell-bent on immediately installing security measures he's championed for ages."

"Really bad timing," I comment. "Coming on the heels of Finley's murder and the militia turmoil on Hullis."

"You think? Owners in two client properties think hot-head neighbors are assaulting one another over homeowner issues. Not exactly an endorsement of Welch HOA Management's ability to resolve disputes. I need you to visit Satin Sands. See if there's even a remote possibility someone put a snake in the woman's yard. Find out if there are any real security issues. I told the president I'd attend tomorrow's emergency meeting or send a security expert."

I nod. "Not sure how much help I'll be but I'll try. In exchange, please tell Mom not to do any more TV interviews. She might listen to you."

Ted's eyebrows lift. "Interviews? Myrt gave an interview?"

I recap the video currently streaming on the internet.

"Deal." Ted shakes my hand. "I'll read Myrtle Kane the riot act about giving crazies more incentive to focus on her. Not that Myrt will listen. She'll do exactly as she pleases."

Chapter Fourteen

Back inside his office, Ted hands me three sheets of paper—the first labeled Pro-Deer, the second, Anti-Deer, and the third, Other Enemies.

"Since the sheriff's office is laser-focused on the Hullis deer feud, let's see if we can rule out any of these aggrieved Finley customers as possible murder suspects. Having lived on the island, you may know many of these folks."

I glance at the Other Enemies sheet and frown. "No listing of Finley friends?"

"Couldn't find a one—at least on Hullis. He occasionally went hunting with old Army buddies, and every once in a blue moon, he showed up in Beaufort on a date. Otherwise, he was pretty much a hermit. That is if you don't count the Rebel Renegades. Best I can tell, this is the first time they've visited his house."

I shake my head. "Lonely dude. Mom says even the kill-the-deer cheerleaders weren't buddy-buddy with him, though they're acting like it now that he's dead. How did you compile this enemies list?"

"After hearing Myrt's story about Finley ratting out Schevers, I asked Robin to search online for customers who alleged Finley screwed them. She found Better Business Bureau complaints as well as buyer-beware posts on the Hullis Island community board. Schevers never griped publicly, but I added his name to make it an even dozen."

I recognize half the presumed Finley enemies. "The six I know are too old and out-of-shape to play archer or drag Finley's beefy corpse around."

"Okay, let's chat with the rest of the list this afternoon. Driving around Hullis, we'll also see if O'Rourke's making sure Rebel Renegades aren't threatening anyone."

"Good thing I'm a consultant and not an employee. This is Saturday. Weekend and holiday hours mean double time."

"In your dreams."

"That's what I thought," I gripe. "Already we're having labor disputes. But you're in luck. I'm due on Hullis at seven-thirty, so I can join you on a few calls."

"What's at seven-thirty?"

"Bridge. Mom roped me into subbing, so you're off the hook for weekend rates. But I need my car. Drop me at the marina. I'll follow you to the island."

It'll also give me a chance to get my Glock. Just in case some militia idiot isn't keen about islanders gathering to play bridge.

Ted smiles. "Good. We'll drive around and knock out as many interviews as we can, then I'll buy you and Myrt an early dinner at the Hullis Beach Club. Shouldn't be a problem to get a six o'clock reservation."

I laugh. "Don't count on it. The resident population leans geriatric and eats early. Five-thirty is prime feeding time. But, since it's September and plenty of tourists are still on the island, the flock of early birds will be relatively small. Residents tend to spend monthly dining minimums on weekdays to avoid sitting next to rowdy visitors or screaming infants."

* * *

I tune my car radio to a local oldies station as I follow Ted's Mustang over the series of bridges leading to Hullis Island. The drive is a delight unless the final swing bridge traps you on the Beaufort side when you're in a hurry.

This afternoon we're lucky. No flashing lights command us to stop for boat traffic. It's fall shrimping season, and, if trawlers fill their nets early, their horns sound mid-afternoon to signal the bridge tender. Maybe I should consider a career as a bridge tender. A great view and hours of uninterrupted reading time. Then again bathroom breaks would be a problem.

We pass through the Hullis Island security gate with brief waves at the guard. Decals on our windshields identify us as approved regulars. Ted leads the way to the Hullis Beach Club where I park my Honda Fit.

I slide into the Mustang's shotgun seat.

"Who do you want to visit first?" Ted asks.

"Schevers. I know who he is, but I've never met him."

"Let's go." He heads the Mustang toward the south end of the island where Schevers built his mansion on a primo triple lot. My 38-foot Island Packet sailboat could probably fit in one of his palatial bathrooms. *Who needs this much space?*

We park in a circular drive paved in a herringbone design. The lush lawn is emerald green. Numerous large trees provide oases of shade. I'm a tree lover, so I'm glad Schevers was forced to plant mature specimens to replace the ones he axed.

A maid answers the door and shows us into a large sunroom at the back of the house. A couple minutes later, Jerry Schevers hobbles in on crutches. Ted quickly introduces us.

"Have a seat," Schevers says. "I'd offer to shake hands, but it's sort of a tough maneuver while I'm vertical so let's just say we did. Had ankle surgery last week, and I'm not too swift on these crutches."

He eases his doughy, overweight body into a chair and props up his left, boot-encased foot on an ottoman. "What can I do for you?" His dark eyes twinkle, and his lips look like they're having a hard time damming up a laugh.

Like Mom, Schevers is pushing eighty. Other than being pudgy and wielding crutches, he appears healthy. He still cares about his appearance, too, combing his white hair to hide most of his shiny pink scalp. Schevers even ripped the seams on his expensive slacks to accommodate his cumbersome ankle boot. I'd have settled for stretchy sweatpants.

He smiles. "Wondered if I'd be a suspect in Dan Finley's murder. I can give you a doctor's excuse, explaining why I can't be his killer. Then again, maybe you figure I paid someone to do the dirty work. I didn't."

"We're not accusing anyone of anything," Ted calmly replies. "Just talking with folks to get Finley in better focus. Understanding how he operated may help the sheriff's investigation."

Smooth, Ted. Your State Department tact hasn't disappeared.

Schevers chuckles. "That's a good one. Finley was a sleazeball. He got pissed because I checked him out before I signed a contract. His little revenge tantrum cost me a few thou."

He waves his arm to encompass a backyard swimming pool, outdoor kitchen, stone terrace, and picturesque boardwalk across the dunes. "I figure I'd have lost more money if I'd hired Finley. My research told me his mark-up on materials was highway robbery, and his labor charges included plenty of phantom hours."

Schevers pauses to give me a once-over. "Say, you said your last name is Kane. Are you Hayse and Myrtle's daughter?"

I nod.

"Good folk. Was real sorry when Hayse died. Guess it's been five years. I really enjoyed our golf foursome. And your mother was awfully kind to my late wife when she took ill. Give Myrt my best, will you?"

"Of course," I answer.

"Thanks for your time, Mr. Schevers," Ted says as he stands. I follow suit.

We're no closer to a murder motive, though Finley's reputation is steadily going down. His likability quotient is hovering around zero.

We quickly cross off three more peeved Finley customers. Two are fragile, walker-dependent old folks. The third is a single, working mom with kids in grade school. Her "I was asleep" alibi is lame, but she channeled her ire online, and seems satisfied that her blistering, don't-use-this-guy review was ample revenge.

We cross off the remaining two complainers after Hullis Security verifies they were off-island when Finley was murdered. One is on a fiftieth-anniversary cruise, the other visiting relatives in Alaska.

We're lucky someone other than O'Rourke took Ted's call. The officer provides a gratis update on the militia.

"The guy who threatened you is Smith's brother-in-law," he volunteers. "We escorted him off island. He knows we'll arrest him if he tries to return. There was an RV parked in Smith's drive that the brother-in-law's buddies planned to use as their barracks. Covenants don't allow RVs to be parked in plain sight or used as residences. Since Smith doesn't have a garage, the RV had to leave. That set the Rebel Renegades' plans back. Doesn't mean they're gone for good."

Ted consults his watch. "Let's head to the Beach Club. Don't want to be late and get on Myrt's bad side."

"Like you can," I reply. "She loves you and Grant. She loves me, too, but somehow I can still annoy her."

Chapter Fifteen

We walk into the dining room at five minutes to six. Mom's claimed a window-side table and is nursing a Scotch with a splash of water. She always waves away the wine menu, claiming, "I'm no 'whiner.'"

She glances at her watch as Ted pulls out my chair. "Lucky, you just made it. Glad to know you two are working together. One of my better ideas."

"I'm consulting, Mom. Short-term gig. Ted's company won't need me once the sheriff catches Finley's killer and his clients aren't so spooked."

Ted smiles. "It was an inspired suggestion, Myrt. I disagree with Kylee. Bet our arrangement is long-term. We Iowa transplants need to stick together. It'll be fun."

Fun? A waiter's arrival preempts my response. No way does my idea of fun include wading into neighborhood feuds.

We all order Frogmore Stew—a steamed medley of shrimp, sausage, corn on the cob, onions, and spices. Messy and delicious. My drink request—ice water—is my lone deviation from our usual Beach Club dining routine.

"No drink?" Mom asks. "You always have a beer with Frogmore Stew."

"Not before I play bridge. Your buddies are card sharps."

And I don't want to dull my wits in case Rebel Renegades hatch new invasion tactics or the author of Mom's threats knocks on her door.

I flick a look at Ted. "Not used to a boss demanding I work Saturday and Sunday."

Mom asks, "Any progress?"

"Not much," we answer in unison.

"We've eliminated folks who complained online about Finley's business practices from the suspect list," he says. "The Sheriff's Office is busy talking with islanders on both sides of the deer controversy."

Mom shakes her head. "That's a waste. Like I tried to tell that TV reporter, Finley's killer wants us fixated on the deer dispute. Someone has a better motive for offing Finley. 'Course my opinion got edited out. The reporter made it look like I had my head up my butt, denying one of my neighbors was a killer."

Ted nods. "I'm meeting Finley's ex-wife and son Monday for a walk-through of the house. Maybe they can fill in blanks in the man's life, including his participation in the Rebel Renegades and any enemies he made before arriving on Hullis Island."

I lean forward. "Robin is searching for cyber leads on Finley's off-island life. The man didn't seem the sort to post selfies, but maybe he lurked on some social media sites. She's looking to see if the Rebel Renegades have a site on the dark web. Finley also might have joined a Facebook group created by members of his old Army unit."

Ted grins. "I'm surprised you know about Facebook. When I was overseas, I occasionally searched for you on Facebook, LinkedIn, and Twitter. Came up blank. You're not exactly a social media butterfly."

"True. If I was doing something interesting at work, it was classified. And I could never see posting what I did or didn't eat for breakfast."

"Just wish you were still Commander Kane," Ted says. "To the average Joe, Commander sounds much more impressive than Captain, even though I guess it was a promotion."

I sigh. "Yeah, to fellow Coasties, Captain is a serious honor. Who's more important than the captain of the ship? The rank's just below admiral. But ignorant civilians like *Junior* here think of captain as a low rank."

Ted's eyebrows jump. "Junior, a low blow indeed, Kylee. Thanks to Myrtle no one's called me Junior since fourth grade."

I aim a gotcha-smile at Justin Theodore Welch, Jr. In Mom's opinion, calling a boy Junior was akin to saying he's a sequel. "Sequels never live up to the original," she'd say. "Everybody deserves an original name and their own unique future."

Mom asked the kid how he felt about Junior. He said he preferred Ted. Once Mom started calling him Ted, the name stuck.

The waiter arrives with steaming platters of food and puts a bucket in the center of the table for our shrimp shells. Simultaneously, the Beach Club hostess seats couples at the two tables bracketing ours. Their proximity rules out talk of Finley's murder and island security. Instead, Mom asks after Ted's son, Grant.

"How's he getting along at the Citadel? Suggested he read Pat Conroy's *The Lords of Discipline* before attending a military college. 'Course I told Kylee the same thing before she was accepted at the U.S. Coast Guard Academy. She didn't listen either."

"Growing up, Grant and I bounced from country to country. Think he's seeking an anchor." Ted looks wistful. "The Citadel's culture, the close cadet bonds, really appealed to him. The twelve-to-one student-faculty ratio didn't hurt either. Grant's majoring in Intelligence and Security Studies."

"Actually, I'm glad he chose a college in Charleston," Mom says. "It prompted you to spend time in the Lowcountry and gave me a chance to lure you here full-time."

Mom's smile falters. "Just wish Barry could have visited Hayse and me here. He'd have loved all the outdoor fun—fishing, kayaking, golf."

I squeeze Mom's hand.

She straightens and glances heavenward. "Bet your dad and brother are happy as clams that you two are keeping this bony, old bird company."

As we walk to our rides, it's dusk. Ted's Mustang, my Honda, and Mom's golf cart are parked in a row.

"Time to be humiliated by your bridge buddies," I say. "I'll follow you, Mom, and make sure none of those life-threatening deer target you on the way."

Mom starts to chuckle when Ted lets loose with a loud, lengthy string of profanity that would do a sailor proud.

"What's wrong?" I ask.

Mom and I join Ted beside his Mustang. The driver's side is deeply gouged.

Someone keyed his painstaking paint job. This damage is no accident.

Mom shakes her head. "Sorry, Ted. I know how hard you've worked to restore that car."

Ted shrugs. "Don't know what makes me madder. The damage or having to wonder who's responsible. A militia fanatic, a sympathizer, or someone wearing a badge. I've pissed them all off. The militia jerk who hassled us saw what I was driving. I'm going to follow you ladies home. Won't leave till you're safely inside."

Chapter Sixteen

The Twin

Saturday, September 26, Evening

I t's finally dark. Two hours ago, I decided to have dinner at the Beach Club. Then, I saw Ted's car and had to settle for reheated frozen pizza from the marina storefront. Aggravated, I "keyed" Ted a little message he'd pissed me off. He just won't get with the program. Stay off Hullis. Let the authorities focus on community warfare.

It's time to fuel the Hullis fires. If I take potshots at Myrtle Kane's house, maybe it'll convince her and Ted that Hullis islanders are capable of murder and deserve to be prime suspects in Finley's death. Myrt's lawsuit threat makes her more likely to be the target of aggravated neighbors than militia outsiders.

I put a leash on Sandy and shrug into my backpack. My pistol, purchased for cash at a Columbia flea market and unregistered, is inside. So are my night-vision goggles, thought I doubt I'll need them. Won't be near any drainage ditches or lagoons where alligators might be contemplating an evening snack.

A Zillow search found an unoccupied house for sale on the street parallel to Egret Lane. Hullis forbids For Sale signs in yards, the Zillow listing gave the address and noted the heirs were eager to sell. Nobody home. I walk Sandy to the house and look for a comfy spot for her to nap. I tie her leash to a tree. Probably unnecessary. Once she plops down, Sandy doesn't move until I coax her to get up.

A quick slog through the heavily wooded lot behind the For Sale house and I'm on Egret Lane. Across the street from Myrt's house. Two cars sit in her driveway, a little Honda and a big Lincoln. Myrt's entertaining. Even better. Lights glow at the rear of the house.

I slip around the side of the house. In back, large picture windows offer the occupants a view of the golf course. No shades drawn. Not very smart. The windows offer me a view of four women at a card table. They're laughing. Creeping closer, I get a good look at three faces. Myrt and two other wrinkled, old crones. The fourth card player has her back to me, but her white hair says she's another member of the Geritol club.

I take out my Smith & Wesson, a pretty Shield model with permanently installed fiberoptics on the front and rear sights. I decide my angle with care. Want the bullet to shatter the window and end in the ceiling. While the old ladies shriek and dive for the floor, I'll pop a few more shots into unoccupied rooms as I run back around front. Then, it's off to the woods, stuff the gun in my backpack, and retrieve Sandy to finish a leisurely walk.

Chapter Seventeen

Kylee

Saturday, September 26, Evening

I love playing cards, but never got hooked on bridge. In the Coast Guard, we played poker or hearts. When I agreed to sub, I made Mom promise to get out the tablecloth she bought when she was first learning bridge. It shows counts for openings and how to respond to a partner's opening bids.

So far, I'm lucky. My partner's getting all the cards, and I haven't had to play a hand.

Blam!

The window behind me explodes. Tiny glass pieces shower my back.

"Get down, someone's shooting at us!" I yell as I slide to the floor. I look up at the window. A neat hole surrounded by a crinkly fracture web. Thank God, for safety glass. Playing cards fly as Mom and her friends awkwardly launch themselves onto the kitchen floor.

God, I hope no one breaks a hip.

I fumble my flip phone out of my pocket and dial Hullis Island Security. Adrenaline speeds my pulse faster than a hummingbird's.

Blunk. Blunk. Blunk.

Three more shots hit the house as I wait for the emergency operator. No window shots.

Blunk. Blunk.

Two more shots farther away, near the front of the house. Is the shooter running away?

"What's your emergency?" a woman asks.

"This is Kylee Kane. I'm at 42 Egret Lane on Hullis Island. Someone's shooting a gun at the house. Come quick."

I terminate the call before the operator begins her spiel about seeking shelter in a room with a sturdy door and locking ourselves in. I know the drill, but I'm confident Mom and her friends are safer where they are. The gunfire's receding.

Mom and her friends are alarmed, but in one piece. I doubt any of them will try to get up before security arrives. Nonetheless, I add, "Stay down, where you are. I'll be back in a flash."

"Kylee Ann Kane, where do you think you're going? Don't you dare go outside."

"Mom, I won't take any chances."

A small white lie.

Stooping low, I run to the living room, grab my purse, and retrieve my Glock. Then, I carefully slip out the front door and crouch behind a porch column. I scan the area. Can't see shit, but I hear brush rustling in the wooded lot Ted and I used for our stakeout.

I hear a siren. Security. Can't risk being mistaken for the shooter. I slip back inside and put my gun back in my purse. Unfortunately, Mom's crawled to a spot where she can eyeball me.

Caught. Damn.

At least I can tell the officers where to search for the shooter.

* * *

While one officer stays with us, two others race through the woods, looking for the shooter. They find no one. Only catch sight of one dog walker, who swears the dog would have barked if anyone'd sprung out of the woods.

The officers, who come back empty handed, kindly offer to cover the broken window. Good thing Dad cut plywood to size for all the windows, and screwed permanent holders into the frames to put hurricane protection up in a hurry.

Another officer escorts Mom's card buddies home. They'd come together in the Lincoln. The officer promises to walk each frightened lady to her door.

Adam, the youngest member of Hullis Security, is left to sit inside with us. While Mom periodically gives me an evil just-wait-till-we're-not-in-public glare, I won't get a tongue-lashing until Adam leaves.

Looks like another night I won't sleep in my own bed. Tonight I'll opt for the couch. Better chance of hearing any intruder, and I can flail about without worrying about waking Mom.

Chapter Eighteen

Kylee

Sunday, September 27, Morning

I smell coffee. I'm tired and grumpy. Only increases my need for caffeine. Glad I opted for the couch. Noises woke me up a few times since my nerves were on alert. Nonetheless, I got a few hours of sleep.

I glance at my watch. Wow. Nine a.m. Glad there's time for a shower before we have to leave for the island's ten o'clock nondenominational church service. Before we went to bed, Mom told me our nighttime adventures weren't going to change her Sunday worship plans. That announcement came right after her harangue about me running amuck with my gun. She concluded I needed to pray this morning for more brain cells.

Beaufort ministers visit the Hullis chapel on a rotating basis, and the Methodist pastor is up at bat today. I like his homey sermons. No fire and brimstone. His recurring theme? Don't condemn folks who choose to sin differently than you.

Toe-tapping music, too. Beaufort's Hallelujah Singers inspired the new Hullis choir leader to pick joyful hymns. In addition to the spiritual lift, islanders can plan on generous helpings of gossip, coffee, and pastries in fellowship hall after the final Amen.

I walk into the kitchen and pour a cup of coffee. "About time you're up,"

Mom says. "We need to leave by quarter till ten. The parking lot will be packed. Everybody eager to hear the latest gossip about the murder, the militia, and, unfortunately, last night's shooting."

I resist pointing out that Mom thinks gossip rather than religion will be the main draw.

Her parking lot prediction proves accurate. I drop Mom at the door and circle to find an empty space. By the time I enter the sanctuary, the organist is playing the processional hymn. I spot Mom in a back row, her fat red purse saving an aisle seat. The retired nurse always carries outsized handbags to hold a fully-stocked first-aid kit.

Though the minister is one of my favorites, I can't concentrate on his sermon. Instead, I scan the worshippers' faces, mentally cataloguing if they appear on one of Ted's lists.

After the benediction, the pews empty so fast you'd think someone yelled fire. The surge toward the adjacent fellowship hall comes perilously close to a stampede.

"Let's hurry," Mom whispers. "I want a word with Jenny. She'll be like a lame lamb hounded by a pack of hyenas. We'll be celebrities, too, for our shooting encounter."

I dismiss Mom's forecast as hyperbole until we enter the hall. Half the people are massed in a tight knot. Is Jenny at the center?

Mom elbows her way inside the scrum. Following in her wake, I catch sight of Jenny. She looks animated, enjoying the attention. No trace of the fearful woman trembling at the thought a killer might cross Parrot Lane to harm her and her pooch. Having security stationed outside her house seems to have restored her confidence.

Wedged inside the gossip grotto, I listen to Jenny retell how she *heard* the murder. A hand grips my upper arm. I turn, and an agitated Joe Quaid shoves his ugly puss in my face.

"Hear you joined that HOA management company. Also got wind that somebody shot up Myrt's house last night. Got a suspect for the Finley murder?"

I bite back a snarky reply. "I know what you know. If the sheriff has a suspect, he hasn't shared the news."

I figured word of the shooting would get around since one of last night's bridge players is a huge gossip. But I didn't figure she'd also spread word that I'm on the Welch HOA Management payroll.

"I'm not sorry Finley's dead," Quaid continues. "Just hope this doesn't hurt our cause. Those animal killers are already painting that Finley bastard as a martyr, and blaming us for his death. Bet it's a setup."

"Joe, please, we just came from church." Brenda Quaid scowls. "The man is dead. Show some respect."

Quaid glares at his wife. His lips tighten and his nostrils flare. He clearly wants to argue. I wave a verbal red cape to see if the bull keeps charging.

"What's your theory—that deer-hunt proponents murdered Finley because he was too extreme and hurt their cause?"

"That's exactly what I think." With a head jerk, he directs my attention to a clique of worshippers huddled near the refreshment tables. "You ought to question Harry Hofstater. He's always bragging about his archery skills. That macho prick loves to shoot anything that breathes, and he hated Finley."

"Joe!" Brenda's loud rebuke attracts the attention of half the room. Hofstater included. The archer returns Quaid's glare with interest.

Yikes. I half expect the two men to paw the ground and charge. Maybe it's premature to rule out deer militants as murder suspects. These folks—who were praying five minutes ago—have no plans to forgive their trespassers. It almost seems like the fate of the deer no longer matters. Now it's who'll win the fight and get to lord it over the losers.

Once again, I try to talk Mom into moving in with me or Ted for the time being. No luck. Now that Hullis Security is guarding her house as well as Jenny's, she figures she's perfectly safe.

I reach the River Rat with just enough time for a quick bite. Oh, yes, and to pick up those business cards to hand out at Satin Sands.

Boy, does Ted owe me.

I'm wolfing down a pimento and cheese sandwich when my phone beeps. Ted. What now? We already talked early morning so he knows all about last night's shooting spree.

"I phoned Roger Roper, the Satin Sands president, to let him know you'll attend as our security consultant. He'll do a full-court press for his security agenda. See if you can buy time to research his proposals to see if any have merit."

"I'll try. Too bad I haven't the faintest idea how to stop people from believing their neighbors may be homicidal monsters. I'll bet that poor snake willfully slithered into Ms. Peters' garden for a tasty mouse snack and got tangled. No human intervention."

"I agree." Ted nods. "Just make sure all the Satin Sands residents—including conspiracy nutcases—believe you take them seriously."

I sigh. "Wish I were more up to date on civilian high-tech security. Doubt my knowledge of systems created to prevent terrorists from blowing up cruise ships or closing down busy ports will be much help. And I'm totally unqualified to identify or evaluate the mental health of human snakes-in-t he-grass. The fact I dated Nick proves that."

He laughs. "We all make mistakes. Lyn may be able to help you with mental health questions, but her plate's pretty full. She's the initial contact for all HOA complaints. Often, she's able to mediate compromises. But clients don't think of her as an expert on security."

I give up trying to convince Ted I'm a poor choice for this job. I *am* good at investigating.

"Hope you're on your way," Ted adds. "Wouldn't do to be late."

"Mind if I pee first, boss? I know how to tell time, and I've been to Satin Sands before."

Chapter Nineteen

The Twin

Sunday, September 27, Noon

What a delightful day! Sunny skies, mild temperatures, and, best of all, I can close my eyes and picture Dan Finley on a stainless-steel morgue table, sliced stem to stern. My evening outing also gives me reason to smile. Still chuckling over the officers stopping me to ask if I'd seen a shooter. Walking a dog appears to deflect any and all suspicion.

My housesitting gig is over. My Hullis friend returned early this morning, freeing me to spend this Sunday as usual, sitting in my regular church pew and murmuring heartfelt Amens. I'm a Christian with a fondness for the vengeance-prone Old Testament. An eye for an eye.

After church, I joined fellow worshippers for a delicious Sunday brunch of Eggs Benedict with plenty of Hollandaise.

Now I'm settling my lunch with a walk along the Intercoastal at Beaufort's Waterfront Park. I watch teens toss a football on the grassy square, and grade-schoolers squeal as they scamper over a mock fort on the nearby playground.

The bridge to Lady's Island groans open. I sit on a vacant swing as a sailboat glides through the opening. These swings are unbeatable for watching dolphins frolic in this stretch of the Beaufort River.

This break in the action is welcome, especially after sneaking around and taking potshots on Hullis last night. I'm enjoying a little breather to relax and reflect before I visit Chevy Cole this evening.

A brief window between executions means officials have less time to stumble on my victims' common link. Just the same, the timing is somewhat risky. Finley's death and the gunplay and militia drama at Hullis will make everyone in the Lowcountry nervous and more alert to danger.

It's fortunate Dan Finley, Chevy Cole and Ronnie Headley are such despicable schmucks. Each has collected an impressive assembly of foes for the authorities to view as suspects. Each also has achieved asshole status within his HOA. A real feat for Headley, who's lived in his posh community little over a year. The man didn't exactly need more foes. He acquired plenty in the military—and they're trained killers.

However, Ronnie Headley is a problem for another day. First, I need to dispatch Chevy, who is hopefully clueless that Finley's death has anything to do with him.

When Headley learns two of his former buddies have been murdered, it'll put him on high alert. Will he contact the cops and confess why he might be a target? A look into Jake's death could lead to me.

No. Headley won't go to any cops. Until his court-martial, the puffed-up macho shit bragged incessantly about his black ops pedigree and military genius. He's cocky, and undoubtedly armed to the teeth. An experienced killer.

I'm a novice, but learning fast.

I glance toward the cafés and shops lining Waterfront Park. An ice cream sundae at Plum's calls my name. Several outdoor tables are free.

Abandoning my swing, I cut across the green, take a seat, and give a waitress my order. Three ladies claim the table behind me. Their voices high and excited.

"Did you hear a copperhead bit Alex Peters?" a woman asks. "Janice thinks one of Alex's snooty Satin Sands neighbors put the snake in her yard, hoping it would bite her."

Another lady harrumphs. "Oh, come on. That's stupid. What would keep a snake from slithering off? And which one of the snobs who hate Alex has the hutzpah to handle a copperhead?"

A third voice enters the confab. "Maybe that Hullis Island murder planted the seed—why not make troublesome neighbors disappear? I have a few I wish would vanish for good."

Laughter. "Shhh. Not so loud. If that neighbor who cranks up his leaf blower at six a.m. bites the dust, you'll be a prime suspect."

Why didn't I think of this? I feel like smacking my head.

If I concoct a few red herrings, it'll look like the Hullis murder has unleashed a tsunami of pent-up anger, emboldening frustrated neighbors to act out their fantasies. Paranoia and panic will snowball. I won't necessarily need to *kill* strangers. Just arrange mishaps that look like bungled murder attempts or violent attacks. If any of my red herrings happen to die, I'll make sure the fate's deserved.

I smile. Maybe I'll become a comic book hero. The vengeful Robin of the HOA Hood, who punishes the selfish, the bores, the assholes, and gives fantasy fulfillment to the timid common folk.

One more thing to do. Make a list of bullies, hypocrites, and people too stupid to live. Mona Young immediately comes to mind. Not sure she ever takes a day off. First thing each morning, she patrols Marshview, looking for evidence of any possible HOA rules infraction. Mold on a concrete drive? A vegetable garden in plain sight? Shutters painted an unapproved shade? Horrors! Lots of neighbors would applaud Mona experiencing a timely accident.

Then there's the guy my buddy Pat complained about the last time we met. A neighbor who regularly exercises in the nude in front of his picture window. No curtains. A real asshole.

It's a tough choice who deserves my attention first—Mona or the naked dude. I'm thinking the media would find the nude irresistible for top-of-the-hour coverage.

Don't worry, though, Mona, I'll get to you.

Laughter bubbles up. Can't help it. The women behind me lower their voices, probably whispering that I must be eavesdropping.

The best part? Both Marshview and Pat's HOA have contracts with Ted Welch. That will give the authorities and the media another thread to follow. "Death stalks Welch-managed HOAs." Besides, the general may let his guard down if he hears other victims of HOA violence have zero links to his shameful past.

Thanks, ladies. You've made my day—and my night.

Chapter Twenty

Kylee

Sunday, September 27, 2 p.m.

Since I've played tennis at Satin Sands, I know how to find the clubhouse. The ungated three-hundred home community has a tenuous claim to its "Satin Sands" moniker. Though a thin peninsula is sometimes covered with sand, bulldozing winter storms regularly relocate the coveted sand to other coastal outcrops.

I park in the shaded lot that serves the clubhouse, four clay tennis courts, and a pool. Though it's late September, kids gleefully splash in the water. The rhythmic whack of a tennis ball says someone's punishing a backboard.

Inside the clubhouse, a carpeted corridor leads to the Turtle Room where loud voices leak through a closed door. I glance at my watch—1:55. The meeting appears to be underway early.

Ted told me it would be an unadvertised executive session closed to residents. "Almost all of them are, and, any minutes, if they're taken, won't be posted for months."

"Seems undemocratic," I replied. "At least the Hullis board only goes into secret executive session to talk about lawsuits or negotiate contracts. All other board meetings are open. Don't Satin Sands residents care what the board's up to?"

"Out of sight, out of mind. Most don't want to be bothered, and Roper claims open board meetings are inefficient. Many states have sunshine laws that require open HOA board meetings. Not South Carolina," Ted added. "That's perfect for Roper, who prefers to limit who can question or oppose his ideas."

Gee. This could be the high point of my week. Probably prudent to knock.

"Come in," a male voice rumbles.

I poke my head in. "Hi, I'm Kylee Kane, Welch HOA Management's security consultant. I believe you're expecting me."

A tall, acerbic-looking man impatiently motions me inside. Roger Roper. His distinctive hooked nose matches Ted's description.

"Yes, yes. Come in and close the door. We don't want to disturb anyone walking through the clubhouse." Roper, a retired exec, casts a poisonous look at a man two seats away.

Ted had prepped me with a descriptive run-down on the directors. Though he mentioned their given names, all I remember are his short-hand nicknames. I scan the faces and match them with the team roster.

Roper's dependable yes votes are Lap Dog, with his shiny bald dome, and Splenda, who periodically pats her fussy, dyed perm. Roper says he has a mandate to make decisions in the community's best interests. Since he's certain those best interests are identical to his own, he opposes resident surveys.

Sparky and Freckles are the vocal minority directors. I recognize Sparky by the MOM tattoo on his forearm, and Freckles by the dusting across her cheeks. These long-time HOA residents, who own modest homes, can't fathom why the Roper cronies built showy multi-million-dollar mansions here if they thought the community needed a wholesale makeover.

Lap Dog shakes my hand and tells me his real name. Par for the course, I instantly forget it. *This is so not a job for me.* According to my crib sheet, Lap Dog lucked out when a developer needed the land beneath his failing retail store in Nowhere, Ohio. He plowed the windfall into a Satin Sands showcase, and kowtows to Roper, in hopes of being accepted by the high noses.

Splenda wriggles in her seat. "I'm a real estate agent," she boasts in a tone that implies it's the equivalent of a Ph.D. in molecular biology. Ted had warned me. Splenda believes showing homes to people qualifies her as an expert on all property matters.

Ted figures Sparky, a former union electrician, sees Roper as a management bozo. Blunt and to the point, he regularly challenges the president's proclamations.

Freckles looks like a plump Irish Buddha, sitting quietly and taking everything in. That seeming serenity masks a sharp mind and a sharper tongue once she's had her fill. The recent widow owned and managed a fast-food franchise with her husband.

The instant Freckles finishes welcoming me. Roper calls the meeting to order.

"I'm convening this executive session to plan an aggressive response to the attack on Ms. Peters." He nods at Splenda. "Will you take our meeting notes?"

Apparently, Splenda is his go-to secretary. She already has her pad and pencil out.

I catch Sparky rolling his eyes.

Roper deals documents out like poker hands. "I've prepared a list of measures to implement immediately while we determine how to finance longer-term security enhancements. It's imperative that our owners and prospective buyers believe Satin Sands is a safe community. Our enhancements will make a statement—crime makes a U-turn at our entrance. While these improvements aren't cheap, increased property values will more than make up for the cost."

At a glance, I see he's recommending cameras at the clubhouse and both Satin Sands entrances. He also wants unmanned entrance gates. Residents would be issued clickers, like those used for garage doors, to open the gates.

"We can have the cameras in place tomorrow," Roper says.

"Hold on." Sparky waves one of the sheets in the air. "Let's hear if Ms. Kane, a security consultant, thinks we need any of this stuff before we go on a half-cocked buying binge. I don't think we have a security problem."

Roper glares at Sparky, then me. "Do you have something to say before we vote on my list of security essentials?"

The man's arrogant challenge ensures I'll have plenty to say. Though I have more expertise securing coastal waters and ports of entry than HOAs, I know how to assess needs. And that starts with fact-finding.

"First, did the sheriff's investigation turn up any evidence the snakebite was a deliberate attack?"

Peeved doesn't begin to describe Roper's squinty-eyed puss. Clearly, he plans to use the snakebite to justify costly security add-ons. My question is an unwelcome sidetrack.

"The sheriff doesn't believe there's been a crime," Sparky asserts. "Not a shred of evidence it was anything more than an accidental human-snake encounter."

"Ms. Peters agrees." Freckles impatiently taps a finger on the stack of documents in front of her. "Alex says the idea someone planted a snake in her yard is preposterous. Security gizmos won't keep snakes out of Satin Sands. They're part of the environment. Don't need a clicker to open a gate."

Roper's nostrils flare. "Ms. Peters offends many neighbors by insisting her weed-choked property meets our upkeep criteria. And her fanatical environmental crusade has earned her determined enemies outside our HOA."

"How so?" I ask.

"She's one of the founders of FACE, a watch group that goes after developers who fail to meet environmental rules," Sparky replies. "Whenever an environmental issue comes up, local media ask FACE for comment."

Roper jumps in. "I'm certain one of the developers she's harassed is behind the attack. We must monitor and control all those who enter our community."

Roper is full of hooey, but I censor my itch to debate. "FACE is the environmental group's acronym, right? I'll check with members about any developer threats. You mentioned Satin Sands neighbors being upset about Ms. Peters property. Enough to attack her?"

Freckles mutters under her breath. "Roper would top that list." *Did I hear her right?*

"Any off-balance Satin Sands owners who seem quick to anger?" I continue. "It seems prudent to look at potential neighborhood aggression if we're assessing community safety."

"I can name two off-balance people," Splenda pipes up. "Eric Root and Ginger Hamrick yelled and cursed at our last public meeting."

Sparky laughs. "Don't be ridiculous. They yelled because you three dictators tried to push through a thousand-dollar special assessment. As usual, you claimed it would boost property values without a shred of documentation. Hogwash. Eric and Ginger didn't want to shell out money for amenities that only benefit a fraction of the community. If you big shots are all-in for so-called improvements, you pony up the coin. Why should all of us pay?"

Sensing the directors may be ready to spew some obscene language of their own, I interrupt. "What kind of crime has Satin Sands experienced in the past five years?"

"My husband and I were crime victims last year," Splenda huffs. "Criminals stole checks out of our mailbox, whited-out vendor names, and wrote in their own. It was a nightmare."

Freckles snorts. "Yes, quite the crime spree. All three pilfered boxes had flags up all night, inviting petty thieves to score checks. The 'crime wave' ended two days after it began when the sheriff arrested a down-and-out drug addict."

Recognizing I'm getting nowhere, I quit asking questions. "Thanks for the background. If you'll give me a day or two, I'll look into the snakebite incident, take a close look at existing security, and review Mr. Roper's proposals. I can prepare a report by next week."

Roper frowns and clears his throat. "Our members expect prompt action to ensure their safety and protect property values. By sitting around doing nothing, we're failing them. We *will* do a better job at our next meeting. The case studies I provided illustrate that cameras and gates thwart criminals. When we reconvene, we'll establish priorities. We have no more important duty than safety. As a bonus, these improvements will enhance our image as a prestige community."

I smile. *Yep, he'll schedule the next meeting when I'm unavailable.*

My quick glance at Roper's case studies confirms they're manufacturer-s upplied PR fluff.

If a herpetological crime actually occurred—highly doubtful—the culprit is more likely to be a neighbor than some mysterious intruder. In any case, a few cameras and unmanned gates seem dubious solutions.

I stand. "Thank you for letting me sit in. I'll provide feedback on each security option Mr. Roper recommends along with purchase and maintenance cost estimates."

Freckles squeezes my shoulder. "Thanks. I imagine I'll have some feedback of my own."

Chapter Twenty-One

Before leaving Satin Sands, I decide to visit Ms. Peters' property. The snakebite victim's domain is easy to spot. Neighbors have monolithic carpets of turf grass with occasional oases of mulch, in which every resident bush is contorted into a squat round globe.

In contrast, Ms. Peters' yard is a riot of color, shapes, and texture. Must be the "riot" part that irks her neighbors. Grinning, I loop the house on a winding ribbon of pebbled stepping stones. Fat red tomatoes still cling to vines in her raised vegetable garden. Nearby bees and butterflies buzz and float amid wildflowers.

A cedar bench invites me to sit and soak up the sun. A meandering line of robust blueberry and oleander bushes mark the backyard's perimeter, keeping this part of her leafy sanctuary safe from prying eyes.

Wish I could sit here all day, but it's three-thirty—time to get off my butt. I'm eager to meet this fairytale landscape's architect. Hope she isn't in too much pain.

At Beaufort Hospital, I knock softly on the door to Ms. Peters' room.

"Come in." The speaker sounds tired. Hope I didn't wake her.

The pixie-like inhabitant's bed is cranked to let her sit upright. Her grayish blond hair is clipped so short it looks like she's wearing a skull cap. One arm features swollen skin from the tip of Alex's fingers to her elbow. The other arm is hooked up to an IV and a blood pressure monitor.

"And who might you be?" the pixie asks. "Doesn't look like you're part of the jab-a-needle brigade."

"No, ma'am," I answer. "My name is Kylee Kane. I'm a security consultant with Welch HOA Management. I dropped by to ask a few questions about your snakebite."

"Call, me, Alex, and leave off the ma'am stuff." She frowns. "Did that idiot Roper dispatch you to see if I'm gonna sue? Some of my more imaginative friends think a neighbor deposited that copperhead in my yard. What nonsense."

"You believe it was an accident?"

"Of course. My yard's certified as a wildlife habitat. While I prefer inviting butterflies and birds to visit, I have no way to discriminate against snakes, and they have their job, controlling rodent populations.

"It was my fault for netting the blueberries. Should have shared them with the birds, but they were picking the bushes clean this year. My biggest mistake was not looking when I bent to lift the netting. Didn't see the poor snake snagged in the netting. Put my finger right in front of him."

"How are you feeling?" I ask. "That should have been my first question."

Alex sighs. "Swelling's down. My neighbor brought the dead snake to the hospital to prove it was a copperhead. But the docs wouldn't give me the antidote until the swelling reached above my wrist. Actually, they forgot about me sitting in the ER, and the swelling was well past my wrist when they finally remembered me."

"For heaven's sake, why?"

Alex shrugs. "The antidote can cause pretty nasty side effects, and snakes can control how much venom they inject. The docs were hoping my snake was just messing around. Guess he lost control."

"Will you be okay?"

"Sure. He—or she—nailed me through my fingernail. I'll lose the nail, and my finger and hand will stay swollen and damned painful a good while. Worst problem is I can't even get out of bed to go pee or do anything else while I'm all hooked up to these machines." She makes a face at the TV mounted near the ceiling. "The nurse turned on some reality show to keep me company. It's causing my intelligence to plummet. The clicker's out of my reach. Will you turn the damn thing off?"

"Glad to hear you'll be okay. I stopped by your house. Your yard is lovely."

Despite her pain, Alex almost smiles. "I think so, too. Some neighbors disagree. Want me to get with the program, bushwhack my yard, yank out the native plants, put in a lawn, and use fertilizers and herbicides up the wazoo to keep the grass green and the weeds gone. They don't give a shit about what all those chemicals are doing when they drain into our water. Just so their yards look pretty!

"Getting my yard certified by the National Wildlife Federation was one of my brighter moves. While my snobby neighbors don't care for me, they aren't quite so eager to pick a fight with a respected environmental group."

"Is this the same group that checks on local developers skirting regulations?"

"No, a different group entirely. That's FACE, Friends of the Atlantic Coast Environment. I'm vice president."

"Mr. Roper suggested FACE activities may have prompted a developer to arrange a special snake delivery for you."

Alex rolls her eyes. "That's a good one. What's he smoking?"

Her face darkens. "A better question—what's he up to? Is Roper trying to portray my yard as a safety risk? Scare neighbors into voting in new upkeep rules."

I don't doubt that may be the next trick in the man's hip pocket, but I keep my opinion to myself. *Ted would be proud.* Instead, I ask, "Have you always been interested in ecology?"

"Yes. Taught college biology for thirty years, and spent ten of my last summer vacations as a volunteer guide at Yellowstone Park."

"Wow. Bet that was fun. Sounds marvelous." I'm impressed and a little envious.

"Drop by once I'm home and I'm less grumpy. I'll tell you stories about encounters with animals a lot scarier than a little copperhead."

"Will do," I answer and mean it.

On the drive home, I chuckle, thinking my consulting gig may be one of the shortest on record. My Satin Sands report will infuriate Roper. Of course, my boss can always file my report in a circular repository. Didn't notice trash cans in Ted's office, but I'm sure they exist.

90

It's four-thirty when I reach the Beaufort Marina. Can't wait to kick off my shoes and pop open a cold beer. Too bad dinner poses a problem. With all the weekend excitement, I haven't grocery shopped. Potential ingredients for supper consist of one iffy container of leftovers and a half-carton of milk. Shopping is the last thing I want to do. Hmm. Cereal and a banana? Won't be the first time I've eaten breakfast for dinner.

My stomach growls. Maybe I'll order a pizza, a local pie shop delivers to the marina. I pull out my cell and stare at its black screen. *Crap.* I turned it off before the Satin Sands meeting and never switched it back on.

Prior to signing on with Ted's firm, I never felt compelled to leave my phone on. Mom and my friend Kay Barrett are my only frequent callers. I keep my phone number very private.

I check recent calls. None from Mom or Kay, but Ted phoned. Probably wants a report on the Satin Sands meeting.

I listen to Ted's voice mail. Not what I expect.

"A friend made reservations for two tonight at The Jazz Corner. When he had to leave town, I inherited the reservations. It's the last night for a New York jazz combo. My treat. I owe you for spending a sunny Sunday cooped up in a board meeting. The food's excellent. I'll pick you up at five o'clock unless you call to say no thanks."

Five? Twenty minutes away. He issued the invitation at three. Not fair to back out this late. *And there is that mention of excellent food.*

At least I don't need to get spiffed up. I can leap in the shower, and throw on my black pants suit. Ted's seen me often enough with wet hair and no makeup. Won't freak him out. That train of thought heats my cheeks. Yes, he has seen my hooters au naturel, too.

"He won't catch me that way again," I swear as I pull clean undies from a drawer, hang my pants suit on a hook, and lock the door to the compact bath.

I shower and shampoo in record time. Toweling off and dressing in tight quarters isn't easy. I jiggle my damp boobs into a bra and step into my slacks just as I hear footsteps on the deck above. Ted's early, darn his hide.

"I'll be up in a minute," I yell. "No need to come down."

91

Chapter Twenty-Two

I grab a sweater and my purse and rush up the stairs. Kay Barrett peers down at me.

"Did we go for a swim?" she asks. "Or did you just get out of the shower? I hate women who don't own a hairdryer and still look fabulous. Dropped by to see if you'd join me for dinner. But looks like you have other plans. Your clothes say 'date' but the wet ringlets and missing lipstick say no."

"A friend scored two last-minute reservations for a sell-out Jazz Corner dinner show," I explain. "Had all of twenty minutes to shower and dress."

"Is this friend male or female?" Kay lifts an interrogatory eyebrow.

"He's a childhood friend. I'm doing a little consulting with his company, Welch HOA Management."

Kay whistles. "I forgot you know Ted. Met the handsome Mr. Welch at a Chamber of Commerce dinner. Wish he was one of my childhood friends. He's single, isn't he?"

"Yep, been divorced for a dozen years. Want me to put in a good word for you?"

Kay glances toward the parking lot as Ted parks his distinctive Mustang. "Girl, you're nuts if you're not considering getting better acquainted with him as an adult. You're single. He's single. Think hard before you toss him on the discard pile."

Discard pile? I roll my eyes. I've never thought of Ted as a romantic contender.

Kay shakes her head. "What a hunk."

I look at Ted from Kay's perspective. Must admit he's handsome, and a lot nicer human being than Deputy Nick Ibsen, my last, bad gamble on a male companion. My romantic rolls of the dice have mostly come up snake eyes. Maybe it's not my game.

Besides, Mom thinks of him as a surrogate son. Nah. The notion of us becoming more than friends is nuts.

Kay greets Ted as she saunters off the docks a few feet ahead of me. "Have fun tonight," she says. "About time Kylee kicked up her heels."

Ted winks at me. "Couldn't agree more."

Once she passes Ted, Kay swivels and gives me a discreet thumbs-up.

Ted looks dashing. Pale blue shirt open at the collar, tan sport jacket, navy slacks with a sharp crease. Lots of women would think him dressed to perfection if he only wore that grin.

"Ready to go out on the town with your new boss?"

"Yep, you owe me, and I'm starved. Should get hazard pay if the other HOA boards resemble the one at Satin Sands."

"That bad?"

"Yep. I'm kinda hoping you'll give me a pink slip as soon as I write my report."

On the hour drive to Hilton Head, I share my impressions of the Satin Sands directors and my conversation with Alex Peters.

"She's an amazing woman," I say. "The definite bright spot of the day. She fears Roper might use the accidental snake encounter to usher in landscape requirements that would force her to scalp her bushes and uproot plants. I tend to agree."

"Guess you didn't buy into Ms. Peters being the victim of a premeditated snake attack."

"No. But I did due diligence. Checked online to see how one could buy a venomous viper. A purchase like that would be easy to trace. I'm sure the sheriff checked the possibility. Of course, Roper could argue the offending copperhead could have been captured in the woods."

Ted nods. "Roper has an answer for everything. He's pompous and determined. Wears down dissent with long-winded speeches, confident he'll eventually whip everyone into line. Unfortunately, we work at the pleasure of the HOA boards that hire us. We can present facts and advise on legalities, but, if board members disagree, we make like Switzerland."

He shrugs. "If HOA members elect jerks, it's on them to solve the problem, not us."

I nod. "Just not sure I can zip my lips when folks like Roper bend facts to scare owners. You'd better be prepared to soften any sarcasm that sneaks into my report." I shake my head. "I am so not the right person for this job."

Ted glances at me. "Yes, you are. I'm sure."

After a few moments of silence, Ted launches our conversation in a new direction. "I didn't just sit on my butt while you listened to Roper drone on. Well, maybe I did sit on my butt, but my fingers got plenty of exercise. I tracked down and phoned three of Finley's old Army buddies. Last time they talked to him was on a spring hunting trip. Back then, Finley mostly groused about Hullis idiots putting out feed to keep the diseased deer alive."

"Finley didn't mention any threats? Didn't seem nervous or anxious?" I ask.

"Nope. The murder floored his friends. They claim Finley was a skilled soldier with a nose for trouble. Could always sense an imminent ambush. They couldn't imagine anyone taking him by surprise unless he literally was caught with his pants down."

"If that was the case, I'm glad his killer pulled up his trousers before we arrived."

"Amen to that. The murder scene was gross enough."

Ted makes two circuits around the Wexford Village parking lot before he finds a space. "I'm starving," he says. "How about we leave all talk of murder at the curb."

"Deal."

The Jazz Corner is dimly lit, intimate. Tables practically touch. I don't envy the wait staff trying to weave through the maze to deliver drinks and food. Ted and I sit elbow to elbow beside a couple celebrating a golden wedding anniversary. They strike up a conversation with us and make menu recommendations.

"We come here often," the woman says. "You can't go wrong with the She Crab soup and crab cakes."

"Are you kids married?" the man asks.

"Renewing our acquaintance." Ted smiles. "We grew up together in Iowa. Haven't seen each other very often over the years. Now we both live in the Lowcountry."

The question doesn't faze Ted, and since the gent called us "kids," I forgive the discomfort.

The music starts and conversation stops. Table placards ask patrons to keep talk to a minimum while artists play. No problem. I love listening. We order draft beers to accompany our seafood. Two large drafts leave me pleasantly buzzed. I order coffee with dessert—a flourless Chocolate Espresso Cake. After the dishes are cleared, Ted's thumb absently taps my hand in rhythm with the beat. He played saxophone in high school. Wonder if he still plays.

Once the last note sounds and the applause dies, we shuffle to the exit with the rest of the patrons. The founder's widow plays hostess and thanks everyone for coming. Ted walks behind me, his warm hands on my waist.

Chapter Twenty-Three

The Twin

Sunday, September 27, Evening

After watching Chevy Cole interact with the mailman yesterday, I decided to pose as a letter carrier with a Special Delivery. If Cole's heard about Finley's death, he might be super cautious about opening the door to a stranger with an alleged stalled car. But, a letter carrier? Of course, he'll open the door.

I'm wearing a light blue shirt, navy pants, and a ballcap. I Googled postal uniforms. Rural letter carriers aren't required to wear uniforms but must look neat. After scanning several photos of postal workers, I shopped Costco for colors and styles to suggest, at a glance, that I'm legit.

I pull the Jeep, rented at the Savannah airport, into Chevy Cole's driveway. Since lots of rural carriers drive them, its shape will match Cole's expectations. Before I hit the buzzer, I check for any sign of a smart doorbell that sends alarms and video to a cellphone. A rusty faceplate around the bell suggests I needn't worry.

I hold the Express Delivery package I dummied up at an angle to shadow my face. I'm skilled with theatrical makeup, but CSI techs can do amazing stuff with facial recognition software. Why take chances? I could have missed a hidden camera.

Chevy cracks the door open. I try for a bored-with-my-job tone. "You need to sign for the package." I worry my after-dark timing might trigger suspicion. When was the last time a letter carrier arrived with a Special Delivery package at nine p.m. on a Sunday?

The dolt doesn't raise an eyebrow.

As anticipated, I'm not invited inside. The barking dogs sound like the hounds of hell. Chevy steps onto the porch and securely closes the door behind him.

My heartbeat climbs to rat-a-tat mode as Chevy accepts my clipboard. Both his hands are occupied. I jab the needle in his thick neck.

"This is for Jake and my father!"

Chevy's a big brute. He drops the clipboard and wraps his beefy hands around my throat. He's choking me.

Shit, the animal tranquilizer's taking too long to work.

I fight the panic. *He'll pass out before he can choke me to death.*

Still, I pry at the blunt fingers cutting off my oxygen. He presses harder. I see spots. Then, the pressure eases. The fingers spasm as they abandon my neck.

Chevy's body slides down the doorjamb at his back. He slumps almost gracefully to a sitting position. Now his throat will feel the pain. Time for him to panic.

I quickly secure a steel choke chain dog collar around his neck, and cinch it tight. But not tight enough to cut off his air. First, he needs to shake off his tranquilized stupor. I want him to see his death coming. Understand the why of it.

His eyelids flicker, then his eyes widen in fear. I brace my foot against his chest for leverage and pull with all my might. His frantic fingers scrabble at the collar. He's too weak to do more than flail. "Remember, Jake Turner?" I say. "Maybe this will help you imagine how he felt as he died."

I repeat Jake's name again, softly, like a prayer. I watch Chevy's face until his eyes grow dull, blank. All life gone.

Damn. The bastard probably snagged some of my skin cells beneath his nails. Good thing my DNA isn't in any database. Unless the cops ID me as a suspect and get a DNA sample to match, this smidgeon of evidence is useless.

Maybe I should have used a stun gun on Cole like I did Finley. But, if I want authorities to buy that HOA rage is the trigger for these deaths, they need different MOs. It must look like hoity-toity neighbors, who have nothing to do but nurse grievances, have finally lost it. That theory will keep the sheriff from wondering if a serial killer has it in for men in their late forties.

Chevy's eyes look bugged-out and his tongue protrudes. Now, he's just a meaty sack of shit I have to lug to a new resting place. Good thing I'm diligent about weight training.

I huff as I lift his body—got to tilt the scales at 230 maybe 240. I jam him into his golf cart's passenger seat and drive down the dark road's grassy verge.

When I reach the spot I picked yesterday, I position Chevy's supersized golf cart so it shields my exertions from any night-time walkers. A leisure path runs along the opposite side of the road.

I smile thinking about Mr. Shallow, my old high school physics teacher. His experiments weren't lost on this student. Pulleys really do make manual tasks easier. I unwind the braided rope bought months ago at an out-of-state camping store. Cash purchase, of course.

Beads of sweat roll down the small of my back. Thank, God, I'm ninety-nine percent done.

I step back for a last look at the tableaux. Hanging around would be stupid. I have no excuse for roaming Golden Treasure at night.

A murder masterpiece, if I say so myself. Just one finishing touch. I've come prepared. I take a deep breath and pull on the thin plastic gloves I brought for this purpose. One hard yank and the zipper on his pants glides down. I fish around inside. Got it.

Revenge is a dish that's easier to season when it's served cold. I can be as clinical as these men were when they devised their cruel coverup. I'll do whatever it takes to add a dash of humiliation.

Chapter Twenty-Four

Kylee

Sunday, September 27, 11 p.m.

W e're driving down William Hilton Parkway when Ted's cellphone trills. Somehow, he's outfitted his elderly Mustang with Bluetooth for hands-free phone chats. Still, he pulls onto a side street and parks before he answers.

"Sorry. Our answering service takes messages unless it's an emergency. Guess some HOA client thinks he has a crisis."

The emergency message taker needs only a minute to sum up the call. "Jim Monroe, Golden Treasure's board president, says there's been a murder inside the HOA. He wants you to call."

Ted looks at me. "Damn it all to hell. What on earth is going on?"

Jim answers on the first ring. "It's awful, Ted. You have to see it to believe it. How soon can you get here? I don't know what to do."

"I'm on my way," Ted assures him and ends the call.

"Golden Treasure's midway between Hilton Head and Beaufort, right?" I ask.

Ted nods. "Yes, we're pretty close."

"Wonder what happened. Sounds like your client's in shock."

Ted hands me his smartphone before he pulls back onto the road. "I can get to Golden Treasure, but don't know Dolphin Lane, where the murder took place. Need you to give me directions."

When I left the Coast Guard, I exchanged my smartphone for a dumb, flip one. Like everyone who works in secure facilities, I could never bring my cellphone inside. As a result, I never became hooked on apps or addicted to checking for texts. And I was tired of working with high-tech systems that keep morphing. I cursed each new update that forced me to learn new menus and keyboard shortcuts. Decided to give my brain a rest.

Bottom line, I'm not sure how to get directions on Ted's smartphone. "I assume you have a GPS app. How do I get to it?"

Ted chuckles. "Forgot you'd sworn off smartphones."

His concise directions are idiot-proof.

The fifteen-minute drive lets us engage in idle speculation. Ted looks grim. "We now have two homicides, gunplay, and one near-fatal snake bite in less than a week. What are the odds? Even if I write off the copperhead, two murders and a shooting in wealthy Lowcountry HOAs I manage seems an unlikely coincidence.

"If I were suitably paranoid, I'd think someone was murdering people to discredit our company," Ted growls. "With dozens upon dozens of Lowcountry HOAs, this mini-murder spree is confining itself to my clients."

I frown. "You're not really suggesting the killer has a grudge against you? Staging elaborate murders to damage your reputation? There are far more effective ways to sabotage a business, not to mention less risky."

Ted huffs. "Just blowing off steam. No, I don't believe these murders have a thing to do with me. During my State Department career, I pissed off plenty of folks, but most live abroad. Can't think of anyone Stateside sick enough to kill people to tank my business. Much simpler to kill me and get it over with."

"What do we do when we get to Golden Treasure?"

"Not much. Assure Jim Monroe that Welch HOA Management stands ready to help the board through the ordeal of a murder investigation and unavoidable bad press. I'll introduce you. Tell Jim you'll address nervous neighbors' worries about their safety."

"Who's the victim? Did you know him?"

"No. Jim says he goes by his nickname, Chevy, last name Cole. Guy owns a GM dealership and always drives a Chevy."

I focus on Ted's phone. The GPS guides us flawlessly. Technology has its virtues.

We park behind three sheriffs' cruisers and the coroner's van. We're stopped at the crime scene's outer border.

"Let that man in," a tall older gentleman calls to the deputy guarding the perimeter.

Ted leans down to whisper. "That's Jim, the board president."

Sheriff Conroy, who stands next to Jim, signals the okay. The men huddle midway between outer and inner crime scene barriers, while CSI techs process the scene. '

The perimeter guard appears undecided about admitting me since the go-ahead might have applied only to "that man."

"It's okay, Deputy," Ted says. "Kylee Kane is a security consultant."

The deputy shrugs, hands me the sign-in clipboard, and directs us to put on booties and gloves.

Sheriff Conroy yells, "Hurry up, will you? We need to talk."

The closer I get, the more confused I become. Blinding camera flashes don't help. I squint. The victim's lashed to a tall pole to hold him upright. But I can't figure out what's circling the victim's neck? Heavy, shiny loops. A necklace, a silver belt?

My gaze travels from the guy's neck to his broad back and legs. His right leg is tied in an up position at forty-five degrees to his body. He looks like a large dog peeing on a bush.

"Please don't tell me his wanker's hanging out," Ted says.

"I could tell you it's tucked in his pants," Sheriff Conroy answers. 'But I'd be lying."

I choke. "What the hell? Is this guy suspected of flashing or molesting children?"

Conroy looks me up and down and chuckles. "Appears you two were out on the town. Bet it's not the end of the evening you planned. Gonna stay for the duration, Kylee?"

Deputy Nick Ibsen shoulders into the huddle. Only lightning bolts are missing from his thunderclap expression. He glares at Ted and me.

"What business do you have here?" he snaps. "We don't need more civilians tramping about and interfering with potential witnesses."

Seems Nick's holding tight to his grudge that the sheriff delayed his interview with Jenny Elton. My remark about Little Nicky may still sting, too.

"I asked Ted to come," Jim Monroe answers. "He manages our home-owners' association. When word spreads, I'll need help calming frightened owners and keeping nosy reporters at bay."

Nick's eyes narrow as he stares at me, then shifts an unfriendly once-over to Ted.

"When did it become okay to bring dates to a murder scene?" he grouses.

Ted jumps in before the sheriff can reply. "Kylee is our security consultant. It's lucky we were on a *date* in Hilton Head. Didn't have to ask her to drive over and add another vehicle to what looks like a car park."

Ted emphasized the word "date." Does he truly think of it as a date, or is he just pushing Nick's buttons?

Since Deputy Nose-Out-Of-Joint will do whatever he can to keep a *civilian* from having a closer look, I doubt I can be of any help tonight.

Ted clears his throat. "Can one of you answer Kylee's question? What's with the pervert vibe?"

Sheriff Conroy shakes his head. "The fella who found him says the victim wasn't a perv. He thinks the killer posed the corpse to mimic one of his dogs. Apparently, this Cole fella regularly cruises around in a souped-up golf cart with two dogs trailing after him. Refuses to put the mutts on leashes though it's county law. The vic's dogs regularly take dumps in people's yards, chase runners and bikers, dig holes, and tear up gardens. Looks like the killer's making it plain he disapproves of Cole's disdain for leash laws."

"So that's a dog collar around his neck?" Ted asks.

"Yep, a choke chain." The answer comes from the coroner as he walks over to the sheriff. "Looks like he was choked to death with it. The autopsy will tell us for sure. The man's been dead at least an hour."

"It took quite a bit of time to stage this," I note. "Awfully brazen. Isn't that a walking and bike path across the street? You'd think the killer would worry a dog walker would spot him posing the victim."

Nick folds his arms across his chest. His lips compress in a stern frown. He's not about to answer any question posed by unofficial interlopers.

"No streetlights in this patch," Sheriff Conroy answers. "It was black as pitch till we set up lights. Ironically, a dumb dog's the only reason we found the corpse so soon. A fella was walking his collie, and she kept pulling on her leash and whining, wanting to investigate."

Ted looks at the ground near the body. "What kind of vehicle made the tire tracks?"

"Golf cart. We think the killer strangled the victim elsewhere. Drove him here in Cole's own golf cart—a big mother with all-terrain wheels—and used it to screen his activity from the bike path while he posed the body. Then the killer drove the golf cart back and parked it in front of Cole's house two blocks away."

"Was Cole married? Anybody home?" I ask. "Any sign of his dogs?"

"The wife's out of town. We have a search warrant for the house, but, whenever we walk up the porch steps, the dogs go nuts, throwing themselves against the front door. Animal control's coming to sedate the dogs and take 'em to the pound until the Missus gets home."

I tug on Ted's sleeve. "I'm no help tonight though I imagine you want to stay. I can visit with Jim tomorrow. I'll call a cab."

"No. Take my Mustang," Ted offers. "I'll call Uber or Lyft when we're through. I'll pick up my car in the morning."

"You sure?" It seems pointless to loiter at the bizarre murder scene.

"I'm sure," he says. "I'll walk you to the car."

Ted opens the driver's side door for me. We're out of earshot of the folks working the crime scene but not out of sight.

"My Mustang has quite a few years on your Honda. But she just passed a maintenance check with flying colors. Should get you home safely." He grins. "Plenty of gas. I wasn't planning an out-of-gas ruse as an excuse to neck."

I blush. I'm glad it's dark. Is he flirting? Maybe he did think we were on a date.

"Call if you want to talk after you finish," I say. "Doubt I'll be asleep. Not after seeing this. It's amazing the macabre nightmares people dream up."

Chapter Twenty-Five

I roll, and my knee bumps the side of the boat anchoring my bed. Startled, I blink and try to focus on a starboard-side portal. Large angry waves rock the boat. A passing squall?

I check my bedside clock. Eight a.m. I'd slept hours longer than usual. Didn't set an alarm. Figured Ted would wake me with an update on the Golden Treasure murder.

I sit up and retrieve my flip phone. Hunh. No calls. It was midnight when I parked his Mustang in the marina lot. Maybe Ted slept in, too. Not like him, though he probably stood around for at least another hour keeping the board president company.

Caffeine's my top priority. Once the coffee pot's on, I check the weather. Yep, the still distant hurricane is spinning off a series of squalls. A reminder fall weather can be brutal as well as beautiful. Fortunately, the big blow remains hundreds of miles and days away. Looks like this band of storms will pass within the hour. No need to go topside till the winds die down.

Should I call Ted? No, don't want to wake him. Instead, I call Kay, my friend's sure to have the lowdown on that environmental group Alex Peters belongs to.

"Barrett's B&B," Kay answers after a single ring.

"It's Kylee. Not a paying customer. No need to sound cheery."

"Thank goodness," Kay answers. "Had a full house all week, and I'm tired of cleaning toilets and flipping eggs. Why didn't someone warn me B&B owners spend more time with toilet brushes than sipping wine with interesting guests?"

"Does that mean you're ready to reopen your law practice?"

"It's not *that* bad, though I'm hanging on to my license and my old client list. But, do tell, was last evening one you'll always remember? Don't spare any erotic details."

I laugh. "My amusement springs from dark humor. Very dark. The night isn't one I'll forget soon. It promises to give me recurring nightmares."

Kay peppers me with a barrage of questions about the Golden Treasure murder. Once I answer them, I finally squeeze in a question of my own.

"What can you tell me about Friends of the Atlantic Coast Environment? I met Alex Peters yesterday. Think she's the nonprofit's VP."

"Alexandra, one of my favorite people." Kay's tone has a smile in it. "And, yes, I can tell you all about FACE. I'm a member. You should be, too. What's prompting the question?"

I tell her about Alex's snake bite, and Roper's assertion that her volunteer work with FACE has earned her enemies who might relocate a copperhead to her property.

"What horseshit," Kay scoffs. "Yeah, the sleazy developers who want to skirt environmental protections hate FACE, but they wouldn't single out Alexandra for retribution. Several of the group's five-hundred-plus members are more vocal and abrasive than Alex. She doesn't seek the spotlight, rarely speaks to the press. You can dismiss that idea. It's ludicrous."

"Thanks. Always appreciate your local knowledge. But I need to get off the phone. Ted may be trying to call."

"Ah ha! You have him hooked."

"More like he has me hooked—that is to work eighty hours a week for forty hours' pay. The call I'm expecting is business, not pleasure."

"They can mix, you know," Kay reminds.

It's a little after nine a.m. when I hear footsteps overhead followed by Ted's voice. "Permission to board? Don't want to be accused of being a peeping Ted."

"Come on down. How come you didn't call last night or earlier this morning?"

"Couldn't. Handed you my cell so you could direct us to the Golden

Treasure address. You never gave it back."

Ted ducks to clear the narrow opening as he clambers down the stairs.

I slap my forehead. "I'm sorry. Stuck it in my purse and forgot all about it."

"Figured as much. Glad to see you're up and dressed. Finley's ex-wife, Deb, and her son Eric are meeting me on Hullis in forty-five minutes. The man left everything to his son and named Deb executor. She's bringing a copy of the will to share with local authorities. I'd like you to come with me to meet them. If we leave now, we'll arrive before they do. I alerted Hullis Security to issue the ex-wife a visitor's pass."

I retrieve Ted's cell from the side pocket of my purse. Can't believe I stuck it there. "Sure, I'll join you. I'm curious about the ex and the son. Maybe they can give us a better picture of the deceased."

Chapter Twenty-Six

Ted's barely unlocked Dan Finley's front door when a yellow Chevy swings in behind his Mustang. A woman exits the driver's side, and a boy slides out of the passenger seat.

The shapely woman's clinging dress and high heels advertise her main assets. Mom would describe her as "brassy." Bright red lipstick. Teased hair. She'd look prettier if she learned to blend the rouge on her cheeks into her foundation. She looks like an out-of-work clown.

I glance at her feet. How did she manage the five-hour drive from Greenville in stilettos? Seems all too easy to get a spiked heel caught in the gas pedal and wreck the car. One more reason I've never been tempted to wear pointy-toed stilts.

The kid is your run-of-the-mill sullen teenager. Slumped shoulders. Greasy hair. Head down as he simultaneously texts and walks.

Hey, give the kid a break. Just lost his father.

Maybe he's not up to face-to-face social interaction. Don't jump to conclusions about the teen or the ex. Appearances can deceive.

I'm just glad island security has removed the makeshift shrine. Finley's son doesn't need to see that.

"Mrs. Finley, Eric, I'm Ted Welch, and this is my associate, Kylee Kane. We're sorry for your loss. We'll try to make this as easy as possible. Would you prefer we stay outside while you look around, or would you like us inside to help with an inventory?"

"Call me Deb, and come on in. Can't imagine this will take long. Dan and I split ten years ago. I'm not looking for keepsakes. But Eric may want to keep a few things before an estate sale."

"His guns," Eric mumbles. The skinny boy doesn't lift his chin high enough for me to study his features. However, his big feet—way out of proportion to his frame—say the kid has lots of growing to do. What is he? Thirteen?

I open my notebook. Might as well play secretary and list any keeper items while I'm jotting down clues. I don't expect to do much writing on either front.

Dan Finley's heir clearly wants his dad's guns. Will Junior also covet the stuffed remnants of creatures decorating the walls? The glassy-eyed trophies creep me out.

As soon as we enter, Eric marches straight to the back den where his father kept his guns, fishing gear, and the missing compound bow. The ex-wife pauses beside a bureau in the living room and starts opening drawers. Ted inclines his head toward the den, indicating I should keep tabs on the boy while he shadows the ex.

As I walk in, Eric's opening the gun case. "Was the case unlocked?"

He shrugs. "Knew where he hid the key." His tone communicates his opinion of me: adult dullard. I try once more to get the kid talking.

"Did you enjoy visiting your dad on Hullis Island?"

"No," Eric answers. "But anything's better than Sedgewick."

I frown. Sedgewick?

"Oh, right, Sedgewick Military Academy. I take it you're not in love with your school."

"Hate it." Eric finally looks me in the eye. "Might as well be prison. Now that Dan's dead, I hope Deb lets me out. Dan footed the bill. Doubt she'll want to fork over the tuition, even though having me around will cramp her style. She's shacking up with a new 'friend.'"

Some parents encourage kids to use their first names. Doesn't necessarily mean the parental bond is sketchy. In this case, it's a fair conclusion.

Eric's good-looking. If he lost the attitude and snarl, he'd be downright handsome.

I pick up the photo of Dan Finley and friends standing in front of a building on the Sedgewick campus. "Guess your father sent you to

Sedgewick because he enjoyed his time there."

Eric shrugs. "Yeah. I've seen that picture. Don't know why those dudes wanted any reminder of Sedgewick. I sure won't keep a photo of the place. Whenever I bitched about Sedgewick, Dan said I'd make lifelong friends there. Not freakin' likely."

My finger traces over the youthful faces in the fading photo. "Did you ever meet any of your father's Sedgewick classmates?"

"Yeah, some guy who went Special Forces. He took Dan and me to lunch maybe four years back. His stories were supposed to juice me, make me all gung-ho about joining the military. Yeah, right."

"Do you remember the friend's name?"

"Last name was Headley. I remember 'cause I thought he was a head case." "First name?"

"*Sir.* That's what Dan wanted me to call him." The teen straightens and mimics saluting a superior officer.

I try another tack. "You don't like the military, but you like guns?"

"Yeah, hunting's a rush. If Dan's compound bow turns up, I want it."

Wow. The kid wants the bow that killed his father? Not exactly grief-stricken.

Deb sashays into the room. "Didn't find any buried treasure in the living room or kitchen. Eric, do you want anything besides the guns?"

"Like I told the lady, I want that compound bow the dude used to kill Dan if they find it. And I want the gun case, the guns, and the knives."

Ted's mouth hangs open. Taken aback by the kid's nonchalant bid for the murder weapon.

His mouth snaps shut. "Do you want any of these pictures?" he asks.

"You kidding?" The teen glances at the photo of Dan Finley and his friends at Sedgewick. They weren't much older than Eric when the picture was snapped. "I don't need any pictures. I get to live the dream."

Snarky little twerp.

"Deb, I realize you've been divorced for years and may not know any of Dan's current friends, but did you ever meet any of his old school or army buddies?" Ted asks. "Did he stay in touch with them?"

She shakes her head. "We were only married three years. He was deployed overseas most of the time. Barely knew the man." She glances at Eric. "Shotgun wedding. But he did step up and support Eric and me."

House tour complete we exit through the garage. Jenny's right that it's too full of crap to park a truck inside. Pallets of landscaping supplies, open bags of fertilizer, and outsized bottles of chemicals compete for space.

"What a load of shit," Deb comments. "All this stuff can go to the dump."

Personally, I doubt disposal will be that easy. Bet Ted will have a hard time finding a place willing to accept potentially toxic ingredients.

"Where's Dan's truck?" Eric asks.

"Impounded," Ted answers. "It'll be returned once the sheriff's finished processing it."

"I want it," Eric says.

Deb laughs. "It'll be three years before you can get a driver's license."

"I don't care. You told me I could keep whatever I want."

Deb tries to smile as she squeezes Eric's shoulder. "We'll see."

The kid yanks free of his mother's fingers, ones that end with long press-on crimson nails. "Let's get out of here."

Once they drive off, I sigh. Sad, sad, sad. Ted seems as relieved as I am to say adios to the domestic train wreck. "Did Deb give you any leads?" I ask.

"Not a one. How about Eric?"

"Maybe. He met one of Finley's Sedgewick classmates. Last name Headley, no first name. Eric says Headley spent time on a special ops team. Might be enough to track him down. With any luck, Headley stayed in touch with Finley."

"Jenny told us Finley warmly greeted a visitor in early September. I'll ask security to look at logs. Maybe Finley provided a first name for the visitor's pass."

"I'll phone Sedgewick," I volunteer. "School should be able to provide the classmate's full name. Then we can check his service record."

I take a last look at Deb's car as it disappears. "Wish I didn't feel so queasy about that kid inheriting his father's guns. Way too much pent-up anger."

Chapter Twenty-Seven

Ted checks his watch. "Let's have a working lunch at the office. I'll check in with the crew. Bet the Golden Treasure murder is burning up the phone lines."

Before I say boo, Ted phones. Folks who chatter away on their phones while I'm sitting beside them in the flesh annoy me no end. This time, I'm happy to eavesdrop. I recognize Robin's voice when she answers.

"I'm treating for lunch," he says. "Everybody in the office?"

"All present and accounted for."

"Ask everyone what sandwiches and drinks they want."

Robin laughs. "Yeah, right."

What's so funny?

Ted glances at me and grins. "We have a standing takeout order with Bud's Deli. They deliver the same lunches every Monday for our kick-off-the-week staff lunch. Lets us share plans and solve problems. Just need to add your order. What would you like?"

"Uh, chicken salad on rye," I answer, "and a Diet Coke."

"Got that, Robin? Should be there in thirty minutes."

A delivery van from Bud's Deli pulls away from the office as we pull in. My stomach rumbles. At least I'm getting a free lunch—though I'm sadly aware there's no such thing.

At the back of the office, Robin's unpacking our eats. I hadn't noticed the conference table on my Saturday walk-through.

"Hey, Kylee." Robin motions toward a brown sack and to-go drink in front of an empty chair. "That's your sandwich and Coke."

Lyn, already seated, beams a dazzling smile at Ted. The corners of her lips slide back into neutral as her eyes meet mine. *Yep, she's no fonder of me than I am of her.*

An older gent beside Lyn stands and clasps my hand in both his mitts. "I'm Frank Donahue. Glad to meet you, Kylee. Your mom's such a sweetheart."

Frank is close to—no, beyond—retirement age. His leather-look-alike skin says the former roofer never got acquainted with sunscreen. Bright, lively brown eyes peer out from the wrinkled folds.

I smile. "Mom speaks just as highly of you. Says you're one sharp cookie when it comes to making sure any kind of maintenance work is done right the first time."

"You learn all the tricks when you've been around as long as I have."

The chair right of Lyn scrapes against the floor as Ted sits and unwraps his sandwich. "What's the morning been like?"

Lyn glances heavenward. "Phones ringing constantly. Most from Golden Treasure and Satin Sands, surprisingly few from Hullis Island. Guess that would-be deer killer's murder is old news and the militia members packed up and left. The news isn't mentioning how the murders are linked."

Ted pauses mid-chew. "You're saying Dan Finley's and Chevy Cole's murders are related?"

Lyn purses her lips. "Well, not in the sense there's a serial killer out there. No, the Finley murder simply inspired another unbalanced soul to kill a hated neighbor. My gut says a copycat posed Mr. Cole in a bizarre manner as a tribute. Definitely two different killers."

Wow. Lyn's the Ph.D. psychologist, but her hypothesis seems off-kilter. Nonetheless, I keep my mouth closed.

"It does seem folks have gone plum nuts," Frank agrees. "Maybe they all drank the same Kool-Aid and think it's A-Okay to bump off any jerkwad who pisses them off. Makes me wonder, who's next?"

Ted sighs. "Let's hope if there is a 'next,' it happens in a neighborhood with no ties to Welch HOA Management. That reminds me, Robin. Please email all our clients announcing we've hired a highly qualified security consultant. Kylee, share your bio and some heroic Coast Guard stories with

113

Robin. Need you to sound like Sherlock meets Rambo."

I sigh. Don't plan to comply, but it's impolite to contradict a boss in front of his employees.

"Lyn, what do the callers want us to do?" Ted continues.

"Look at security. Jim, at Golden Treasure, specifically asked Kylee to do a security audit today. He wants to tamp down any neighborhood fears about safety."

I speak up. "Ted, I'll head to Golden Treasure after lunch. You don't need me at the Hullis meeting. In fact, Chief O'Rourke will be happier if I'm not there. He's sensitive about being the island's one and only security guru."

Ted nods. "Okay, we'll split up. Lyn and Frank, I'd like each of you to visit HOAs this afternoon. Assure everyone we're all over security concerns."

Lyn and Frank agree to call on several communities before quitting time.

"Robin, you okay with holding down the fort alone? If not, you can work from home."

Robin shrugs. "I'm not worried."

"Okay." Ted smiles. "Listen folks. Have my doubts about Lyn's copy-cat theory, but, even if it's dead-on, there's a limited supply of sickos waiting to murder annoying neighbors. We've been blind-sided. A perfect storm of coincidental violence. Like every storm, this one will blow over."

As he speaks, the wind whistles outside, and fallen palm fronds whip a tat-a-tat rhythm against the office exterior. The distant hurricane isn't finished sending squalls our way. And my gut tells me the Lowcountry hasn't seen the end of this bizarre HOA crime spree.

On both counts, I hope to hell I'm wrong.

Chapter Twenty-Eight

I get Jim Monroe's phone number from Robin and enter it in my flip phone. My cell's job is to make and receive calls. It doesn't tell me stock prices or the weather. I can't use it to buy stuff for next-day home delivery. In theory, its tiny keyboard permits texting. But why spend ten minutes pecking out a message when I can call and get answers instantly?

Jim agrees to meet me at Golden Treasure's entrance in twenty minutes. On the drive, I think about my "security audit." Golden Treasure has no security gate, no private guards. The twenty-five-year-old neighborhood depends on the Beaufort County Sheriff's Department to protect its 121 homesites.

The community has no clubhouse, swimming pool, or tennis courts, not even a common picnic area. A one-mile beach and paved leisure paths for walkers and bikers are its sole amenities. The beach, provided by God, and periodically renewed with government funds, is public property. Street lights are scarce to keep the neighborhood a stargazing mecca.

What can I possibly recommend to make Golden Treasure residents feel safer?

The gates and cameras Roper is pushing have even less value here. Given the tax dollars used to refurbish the beach, the coastline must be accessible to the public. A gate is a no-go. Plus, anyone can beach a boat and walk into the neighborhood via one of five beach accesses.

Cameras? Where? On every residential street corner? If cameras aren't monitored, they do nothing to prevent crime. They only offer potential after-the-fact help with a culprit's identity. No gate or camera would have stopped the psycho who murdered Chevy Cole.

Until last night, security at Golden Treasure has never been a serious issue. In the past decade, it's only seen a few nickel-and-dime offenses—primarily nighttime thefts of tools and building materials at unsecured construction sites. No crimes against persons or break-ins.

At the entrance, Jim motions for me to park behind his golf cart.

"Hi, Kylee. Ride with me. I want people to know you're here. Won't be many people out with these winds, but the word will still spread."

"Are you worried the killer will come back?" I ask.

"Not really." Jim shakes his head. "This murder's personal, not some random attack. None of our directors has ever felt we needed more security. I still don't. Chevy's murder was horrific, but can't see it as the opening salvo in some murderfest. Doesn't mean folks aren't jumpy. I'm hoping some safety tips individuals can practice will tamp down any vague fears."

Golden Treasure pays Ted's company to verify building setbacks and design compliance, prepare budgets, and manage landscape contracts. Security isn't part of the contract, but Ted's offered a security consult "on the house."

"Perhaps you could ask the sheriff to help set up a Neighborhood Watch program," I begin. "A deputy could explain the merits—"

"Good Lord, no. Deputy Ibsen will volunteer. Since Sheriff Conroy announced he's retiring next year, Ibsen's getting on camera every chance he gets. Lord help us if that SOB becomes sheriff."

Jim's spontaneous riff on Nick's career plan startles me. Don't know why. Nick's conceited enough to believe he's the best *man* for anything—women don't count.

"What did the deputy do?"

"We email a chatty, monthly neighborhood newsletter. The *news* items are along the lines of—'Cindy Vidler's in the hospital ... the Gordons are planning a garage sale ... Mary Deacon has a new grandson.' The volunteer who puts the newsletter together said Deputy Ibsen banged on her door and demanded that she immediately email owners, ordering them to report any neighbor who'd expressed anger about Cole's dogs running free. What an idiot! What would a list tell him? Half the neighborhood's griped about his dogs. A list just invites busybodies to tattle on people they dislike. No way does our board want to imply a neighbor killed Chevy Cole."

"I see your point."

While I understand Deputy Ibsen's desire to ID possible suspects, his ham-handed approach sucks. Jim's okay—and not just because we share the same opinion of Ibsen. He's the kind of board president I'd want if I lived in an HOA.

"Do you think there's a chance an irate neighbor did kill Mr. Cole?" I ask.

Jim shakes his head. "No. The killer seized on the Hullis homicide and Cole's reputation as a jerk to distract the cops. And it worked, but only because Deputy Ibsen's easy to sidetrack."

Jim's golf cart tour ends in front of Chevy Cole's home. Three cars fill the victim's driveway. A middle-aged woman, who's marching toward the last vehicle sees us, and heads our way. Uh, oh. A mourner coming to lecture us on respecting people's grief?

Huh? Her arms stretch wide as she walks toward Jim. They embrace, a friendly hug. Jim introduces Lisa Willis. "Lisa heads our volunteer Care Committee."

"Need anything?" Jim asks.

"No, got plenty of neighbors lined up to deliver meals for the family. Chevy's and Abby's three children, their spouses, and kids are here."

"How's Abby holding up?"

"Pretty good, considering. Keeps repeating she can't imagine a killer getting the best of Chevy. Her husband spent time in the Army, even saw combat."

I'm puzzled, too. The man wasn't elderly or infirm, and definitely not scrawny. Six foot, maybe two-twenty, and relatively fit for someone with a sedentary job.

Cole probably didn't sense his attacker's plan until it was too late. Would he have been more likely to let his guard down for a stranger or a neighbor he'd argued with?

Lisa grips Jim's arm. "You two go on in and pay your respects."

Jim frowns. "Think we should? Don't want to intrude."

No way. I'll wait outside. Last thing the Cole family needs is a stranger invading their home. No doubt Deputy Ibsen has already paid an unwelcome visit.

"You should both go," Lisa continues, as if she's read my mind. "Jim, as board president, you should personally offer condolences. Kylee, I think Abby will appreciate Golden Treasure taking a close look at security, given her whole brood's bedding down here."

"Good points." Jim places a hand on my back to usher me down the drive.

Color me skeptical. But my doubts aren't strong enough to try to dissuade Jim.

A woman with puffy eyes answers Jim's knock. She looks to be early thirties. Must be a daughter or daughter-in-law. Jim introduces himself and asks if Abby's up to seeing him. A heavyset woman in her fifties wobbles into the living room and heads straight for Jim. No outstretched arms for a hug, but she manages a tight smile.

"I'm so sorry for your loss," he says. "Is there anything I can do for you and your family?"

"No, thank you." While bloated white skin surrounds Abby's bloodshot eyes, she appears to be cried out.

"Lisa's made sure we have plenty of food for family and anyone who stops by. Would you like a cup of coffee, something cold to drink, something to eat? We have all kinds of casseroles."

Jim has yet to introduce me. Hope he doesn't. Cross my fingers he'll turn down Abby's invitation.

Situations like this make me squirm. Always have. They resurrect the trapped feeling I had when well-wishers swarmed my folks' house after my brother died. I wanted them to shut up and disappear. I didn't need to hear one more person repeat how Barry, the brave firefighter, would be remembered for saving that family. I wanted to scream, "What about our family?"

Jim's voice brings me back to the uncomfortable present. "We can stay for a cup of coffee. Since Kylee has other appointments, we'll need to leave in a few minutes."

Abby ushers us into the living room, and Jim introduces me to the mourners as a security expert. To my surprise, I'm met with "nice-to-meet-you" platitudes. Not a single snide "you're-a-little-late" snip.

Scratching noises and high-pitched whines come from deeper inside the house. Unhappy dogs penned up out of sight. Abby notices I'm looking toward the commotion.

"Our son just retrieved our dogs from the pound, and they're still agitated so we shut them in the master bedroom. Hope they don't wake the baby."

The young lady who answered the door returns from the kitchen with two steaming mugs. The nutty aroma is a welcome distraction. "Take anything in your coffee?"

"No, black's fine," Jim and I answer in unison.

She hands me a mug, and I try to get comfortable on the sofa. The seats are too deep to lean back without spilling the coffee and the seat has too much angle to sit forward. Hope I'm not expected to drain my mug before we can leave.

A picture catches my eye. A gray-haired gentleman has his arm around a uniformed young man. The drab building in the background looks familiar. The penny drops. Sedgewick Military Academy. They're standing in front of the same building I saw in Finley's photo of young cadets.

A jumble of questions runs through my mind. Meanwhile, my brain warns me not to blurt out anything that suggests Chevy Cole's death is linked to Dan Finley's campy exit.

I quit listening to the conversation. My mind's too busy. What are the odds of two murder victims attending the same military academy?

When we finally head for the door, I pause by the photo. "Is the young man Mr. Cole?"

"Yes," Abby answers. "It was taken when he graduated from the military academy. Chevy wanted to throw the picture away, but it's the only one of Chevy with his father. Thought the grandkids would be interested."

I nod. No need to ask which military academy. "I understand Mr. Cole was an Army veteran. How long did he serve?"

"Four years and two tours of duty," the widow answers. "When his father's health began to fail, Chevy didn't re-up. His dad needed help running the local GM dealership."

Abby's answers tell me plenty. Cole and Finley were about the same age. That means they graduated nearly three decades ago. Finley's son said Headley was one of his dad's cadet buddies. Maybe if I can locate Headley, I can find out how Sedgewick figures in the deaths.

Time to visit the military academy.

Chapter Twenty-Nine

The Twin

Monday, September 28, 5 p.m.

The puppy's fur is soft, but her tiny teeth could pass for cactus needles. A nip catches my index finger as I towel her dry. No blood. Like most shelter volunteers, I do what's needed—bathe dogs, walk them, clean pens. If I'm around when veterinarians spay and neuter strays, I'm sometimes called on to help. Unlike many volunteers, I'm strong enough to heft a forty-pound shepherd. While assisting a vet last month, I liberated a spare hypodermic needle and bottles of ketamine. More than enough to put Chevy Cole and Ronnie Headley down.

Listening to the nattering volunteers, I smile. Tuning into their gossip helped me understand the depth of hatred animal lovers had for Dan Finley. Couldn't have dreamed up a better motive for a neighbor to murder the big, bad, evil hunter.

Today, the Hullis Island and Golden Treasure murders have everyone a-twitter. I pick out Myrt Kane's crisp Midwest accent as she says her daughter Kylee's joined Ted Welch's HOA Management firm as a security consultant. She mentions Kylee's trying to track down an old friend of Finley's with Headley as a last name.

"Could she be looking for Ronald B. Headley?" a younger voice asks.

"Who's that?" Myrt replies.

"He's that Army hotshot convicted of sexual assault. Only served a year of his sentence when the president pardoned him. The pardon caused quite a flap."

Damn. Why is the Kane woman looking for Headley? I don't want her talking to him. Would he confess his connection to Finley and Cole? No. He'd just say he knew them long ago. Still…

It takes willpower to shrug off my anger. I don't want some busybody sticking her nose in. Definitely time for another HOA incident. Pat's townhouse complex is managed by Welch. I'll provide the new consultant with a more pressing priority than tracking down Headley. My new quarry will have zero connection to any of my primary victims.

In an hour, I'm due at Pat's townhouse for drinks. I'll study the unit occupied by the dude who gives his pecker total freedom while exercising.

Pat's a liberal-minded guy, but the exhibitionist's attitude pisses him off. Another neighbor, who homeschools her girls, hates to take them outside for fear they'll get an unscheduled anatomy lesson. Pat says the mother asked Mr. Nude to draw his blinds or put on shorts. His "up yours" answer prompted a call to the cops, who said the guy's entitled to walk around in the buff inside his own house. "Don't look if you don't want to see."

Pat says Mr. Nude's an IT-type with a home office. Takes exercise breaks wearing nothing but a medical alert bracelet.

When and how often does Mr. Nude exercise? Does he have a set schedule?

Hmm. What's his medical issue? Heart arrhythmia? Maybe a porch bomb to scare his pumper into overdrive. Time the explosion for ten minutes into his aerobic routine. Make sure he's already sucking oxygen.

Even better, let him be allergic to nuts! What irony. Nuts in the candy do in the nut.

My sudden laughter prompts Mark, another volunteer, to look up.

"What's so funny?" he asks.

"Just thought of a joke."

"Well, share it."

I know all kinds of dog jokes. Which one will Mark appreciate?

"What kind of dog did Dracula have?"

Mark shrugs.

"A bloodhound."

Mark rolls his eyes.

Chapter Thirty

Kylee

Monday, September 28, 5:30 p.m.

A cacophony of barking dogs punctuates my arrival at the no-kill animal shelter. When Mom's SUV started sounding like it had whooping cough, she took it to the GM dealership and sweet-talked a salesman into giving her a lift to the animal shelter. Since the repairs couldn't be completed today, she asked me to pick her up.

Though it's raining, I expect Mom to rush out the minute my car comes in view. She hates inconveniencing anyone doing her a favor.

Seeing no sign of Mom, I park and head inside. I'm not thrilled she's spending time at the shelter again. For physical, not mental health reasons. The air inside sometimes resembles fog, it's so clogged with animal hair and dander. Can't be good for someone with sketchy health following chemo.

"Oh, hi, Kylee." Mom waves me in. "Sorry you had to park. Got engrossed in conversation. Let me introduce you."

I say hi to three of her shelter buddies—Bunny, Mark, and Brent. I figure Bunny for late thirties or early forties, while the two men look to be around fifty. Mark and Brent are something of a surprise. Don't recall Mom ever mentioning male volunteers. The helpers I've met are either retired women or housewives seeking adult conversation while their kids are corralled at school.

I idly wonder if Mark and Brent retired early from civil service or military careers. Most employed folks aren't workday volunteers unless they have flexible hours or are self-employed.

Mark, a six-footer with a runner's wiry body, shakes my hand first. His grin is toothy, and he seems a tad shy. Then it's Brent's meet-and-greet turn. He's a touch shorter than Mark. The hand he sticks out for a shake is attached to a muscled arm that all but shouts he lifts weights. He flicks me a sunny smile.

Bunny, the last to shake hands, has manicured nails and sweaty palms. Based on her grip, she could bench press either man. The woman's maybe five-five, but very, very large—solid large, not blubbery. This robust trio makes my skin-and-bones mother look all the more frail.

I'm primed to say 'nice to meet you, goodbye,' when Mom tells the group we're going to Ted Welch's house for dinner. She turns to me. "Don't worry, Kylee. No need to drive me home tonight. I'm taking up Ted's offer of a guest room. But I will need a ride to the dealership in the morning."

I frown. "Any idea when your SUV will be ready? I was considering an out-of-town trip tomorrow or Wednesday, and I'd want to leave early morning."

"Mid-morning was the serviceman's guess," she answers. "Why on earth are you making an out-of-town trip? Aren't you busy consulting with Ted?"

I look at my watch, pop up an umbrella, and start herding Mom toward the door. "Nice meeting all of you."

I'm not going to discuss anything remotely connected to the HOA murders in front of strangers. Especially if it could start gossip about me digging into a possible decades-old link between the murder victims.

I start the car. "Tell me about your friends. Thought you said men never volunteer."

Mom laughs. "Well, Mark and Brent aren't exactly run-of-the-mill volunteers. They're working off community-service sentences."

I swallow. "What did they do to earn their sentences?"

I try not to show alarm that my outgoing mother appears buddy-buddy with convicted offenders. Fingers crossed their crimes didn't involve snatching purses from old ladies or conning elders out of savings.

Okay, don't go nuts. Mom's too hard-headed to be conned, but I fear she'd put up a fight if anyone tried to steal her giant purse. Of course, the most they'd get is first-aid supplies, but she wouldn't let them go easily.

Mom's amused glance suggests she knows what I'm thinking. "No worries. Their debts to society have nothing to do with old-lady victims."

"So, what did they do?"

"Mark was behind the wheel when he hit and killed a dog. Not a hit-and-run. In fact, he called 911 and tried to help the stray. But, when the cops arrived, they noticed his pupils were dilated. Found his personal stash of drugs in the car. Says he hasn't used since."

"What about Brent?

"Drunk and disorderly. He got into the sauce and raised a ruckus in his neighborhood. Cussed out the cops and scuffled with them a bit when they arrived. Told me he wasn't prone to going on benders, but he'd just found out his girlfriend had died."

"Sad stories," I say. "Hope your new friends didn't leave out any interesting parts—like Brent being a prime suspect in his girlfriend's sudden demise."

Mom chuckles. "Don't be so down on your fellow humans. They made mistakes. Neither one's the sort to make a career of bad decisions. Why didn't you answer my question about needing to go out of town?"

"Some of what I do for Ted shouldn't be discussed in public. If I'd answered your question, I might have started a rumor that Sedgewick Military Academy is linked to the murders. At the moment, that's pure speculation. So, please, watch what you say."

I glance at Mom to make sure she gets the message. She looks sheepish. "So, you're planning to drive to the Sandhills to visit the military school?"

"Maybe. I might phone first. Politely ask for more background on Finley, Cole, and this Headley chap. If I can't get answers on the phone, I'll drive there for a little in-person Q&A."

Mom nods. "Sorry, Kylee, I wasn't thinking. My friends and I were talking about the murders, and I mentioned you wanted to locate an old friend of Finley's, a man with the last name of Headley. Never thought of it as confidential. Beaufort's such a small town. Thought one of my friends might know this Headley and save you some shoe leather."

I fight a sigh. "Okay, Mom. But, please, in the future, no talk about my work for Ted."

"Got it. But the Headley name did elicit a reaction. Bunny reminded me that a Headley—Ronald B. Headley—made lots of headlines last year."

Why do I know that name?

"He's the general the president pardoned, then insisted his military rank be restored. Stirred up quite the controversy. Several high-ranking military officers called it a disgrace."

Finley's son said the man was career military and bragged about his black ops expertise. Headley isn't a common name.

Could Ronald B. Headley be Finley's old classmate?

Chapter Thirty-One

"Come on in." Ted answers the door in a sweatshirt, worn jeans, and bare feet. "It'll be an hour before dinner's ready. Okay, full disclosure, delivery's scheduled in an hour. Ordered from your favorite Mexican restaurant, Myrt."

Since chemo, Mom's become a big fan of spicy. Claims her old Midwest meat-and-potato favorites now taste like cardboard.

"Don't know what you like, Kylee," he adds, "so I ordered multiple dishes."

Myrt kisses his cheek. "What? No gourmet dinner? It was mid-day before I invited myself over. Should have given you plenty of time. Seriously, I hope this isn't an imposition."

"Not at all. Always nice to have dinner companions—especially the Kane ladies. Watch your step," he cautions. "You're entering a construction zone."

The hallway could pass for a World War II movie set—a bombed building standing against all odds. Chunks of plaster hang ominously overhead, and the dust swirls in a dense fog. Missing floorboards add another dimension to the danger.

A heavy drop cloth hangs from the doorway at the end of the hall. Ted holds the cloth aside so we can enter what he calls the morning room. "Ta-da! One of the five rooms I've finished. Only twenty or so to go."

"It's gorgeous," I say and mean it.

"What a beautiful job," Mom crows. "These heart-pine floors look brand new, and the crown molding is spectacular."

"A lot of sweat equity." He hands us a before photo to show the room's total transformation. "Some of the crown molding was too far gone to repair. Found a woodworking shop that can match old samples. They're artists—artists who love cashing ridiculously large checks. Renovation isn't for the faint of heart or poor of wallet. One reason I need Welch HOA Management to remain profitable."

Mom chuckles. "I see you aren't afraid to combine old and new. I'm honored you hung my fish in this lovely room."

I was with Mom when she bought the trio of whimsical, brightly painted steel fish. Two small fish are trailed by one three times their size. Mom thought the mama fish was looking after her young.

"They're colorful," I comment, "though I still say that big fish is thinking lunchtime."

"Oh, posh," Mom replies. "Hank's creations always have the happiest expressions. They may be fish, but they're jolly fish. I love them."

"Visiting Hank's studio on Hemp Isle was fun," Ted says. "The three of us should take the ferry over again soon."

I shake my head. "It won't be soon if we wait for you to finish this renovation. I get you want to preserve historical gems, but why pick a huge mansion for a first project?"

"I did go a little overboard." He smiles. "Couldn't pass up the bargain-basement price, and the architecture's unique in the historic district. Hated the idea it might be torn down."

He motions to a settee and chairs by the bay window. "Have a seat. I'll get our drinks."

Ted returns with Mom's standard scotch and my rum and Coke.

"Was Mom teasing about you whipping up gourmet fare?" I ask. "Do you cook?"

"I have a few crockpot recipes. Pot roast is Grant's favorite. Barbecue pork's a close second. When we lived in Kenya and Saudi Arabia, we had housekeepers and cooks. Could never afford that kind of help in the States. But I learned to whip up a few meals when the cooks didn't show."

Ted's discussions of embassy life never mention his ex-wife. Mom contends the woman was so bored she made sure everyone knew about her torrid affair with a college-age boy. The scandal provided her a twofer—a divorce and an escape from motherhood.

Back in the States, she fabricated reasons why Grant couldn't visit on school breaks. Mom says that bothered Ted big time.

Mom sips her drink. "How do you find time to work on the house with so many HOA clients?"

Ted shrugs. "I only spend Sundays on the house. Not this past Sunday, of course. I take vacation when Grant has school breaks. The demolition part of renovation appeals to him, so we swing sledgehammers together."

"You thought you'd have lots of free time, right?" Mom teases. "Figured HOAs would be a snap to manage after embassies in places like Kenya."

"Guilty." He laughs. "Boy, was I naïve. I have an engineering degree and decades of experience managing huge complexes in third-world countries. Didn't prepare me to deal with cantankerous retirees with too much time on their hands. And now murders are part of the mix."

Mom swirls the liquor in her glass. "Speaking of murders, my daughter scolded me before we arrived." She casts a furtive glance my way. "Okay, I deserved it. My shelter friends were discussing the murders, and I said Kylee wanted to locate an old friend of Finley's, last name of Headley. Didn't see why research would be confidential."

Ted swirls the amber liquid in his glass. "Kylee's right. Our work with HOAs is confidential. Still, I doubt your mention of Finley's old friend will do any harm."

"Actually, Mom's friend Bunny made an interesting suggestion," I admit. "She wondered if the missing friend might be Ronald B. Headley—the Army black sheep the president pardoned. Seems like a long shot, but, when I contact Sedgewick, I'll ask if General Headley attended."

Ted smiles "Why wait till morning? A few internet keystrokes should turn up plenty of articles about Ronald B. One is bound to include where he attended school."

"Good point. Can't believe I didn't think of that."

Mom shifts in her seat. "Could be because you only had a last name until I told you about Bunny's comment."

Credited with providing a clue, Mom's chagrin about blabbing vanishes.

"The food is still a few minutes away," Ted says. "Let's fire up the computer."

In less than five minutes, we find Ronald B. Headley graduated from Sedgewick Military Academy and went on to West Point. Finley and Cole were classmates. A career soldier, Headley became a two-star general before his trial and conviction.

We locate dozens of news articles at the time of his release but nothing since. "Wonder where Headley landed after his pardon?"

"Maybe he lives nearby," Mom suggests. "The Lowcountry's quite popular with retired military. With Parris Island, the Marine Corps Air Base, and the Naval Hospital nearby, retirees from all branches know they're welcome. I imagine that factored into Finley's decision. Chevy Cole grew up here, so it's his hometown. If Cole brought his cadet chums to Beaufort on school breaks, they may have fallen in love with it like I did."

Mom's logic is solid. "Guess it wouldn't be all that strange for two Sedgewick alums to wind up in Beaufort County. But two classmates murdered in rapid succession is hard to swallow as coincidence.

"Tomorrow, I'll phone Sheriff Conroy and let him know Headley was a classmate of both murder victims, and probably Finley's close friend. The general may be able to offer alternative motives for the murders."

Dinner arrives and we dig in. Ted needn't have worried about my entrée preferences. Haven't tasted a Mexican dish I don't like.

As we eat, Mom reminisces about the introduction of Mexican fare in Keokuk, Iowa, when Ted and I were growing up. "Your dad had no interest in trying refried beans." She laughs. "Hayse said, 'if they weren't good the first time, frying 'em again won't be an improvement.'"

Soon after dinner, Mom's head starts to dip. She's worn out.

"Looks like you'll pass out if you stay up much longer, Mom," I observe. "I'm going home. Sure you don't want to sleep on my boat tonight?"

"Hush," she answers. "I can stay awake longer than you, and sleeping on your boat is not an option."

"Myrt, I put you in Grant's room," Ted says. "A nice soft bed with a feather duvet we picked up overseas. I even laid out a pair of Grant's pajamas, a robe, and slippers. You're all set."

Our host raises an eyebrow. "You can sleep over, too, Kylee. I'll give up a pair of my pajamas for you."

Uh, no. A sudden vision of Ted slipping out of his PJs to loan them makes my cheeks burn.

Ted must have had a heavy hand with the rum. Definitely time to leave.

Chapter Thirty-Two

The Twin

Tuesday, September 29, 2 a.m.

Early in the evening at Pat's I steered the conversation toward his nudistically-inclined neighbor. Didn't take long to discover everything I needed to know. One, his medical alert warns he's allergic to stinging insects. Two, a pet door on his screened back porch gives his cat easy access to her litter box. And, three, he begins each day with a get-the-blood-pumping session. Convenient since he has no need to dress. Presumably, he sleeps in the buff, too.

After leaving Pat, I searched YouTube videos. Never imagined I'd need to move bees. But I do. Detailed YouTubes offered step-by-step guidance on relocating a hive. Best done at night after bees return from foraging, which explains why I'm sitting in my car at two a.m., waiting for the driving rain to stop.

I had no problem locating a hive. Saint Helena Island, the Lowcountry's breadbasket, is packed with truck farms and boasts large, fragrant fields of lavender. A honey bee's nirvana and a beekeeper's dream. Multiple hives. Easy access.

About two-thirty, the storm finally passes. Ample time to make my delivery.

Step one, I secure the bee box lid and duct-tape a piece of mesh over the

133

exit hole so fresh air can circulate, and the confined bees don't overheat.

Step two, drive to a public parking lot near the upscale community. The lot's an access point for a rails-to-trails path. It's dark as I arrive. Dense clouds hide any hint of moonlight.

Step three, heft the bee box onto a little pull-along garden cart I wedged in the backseat and begin my trek. YouTube was right. A full hive is heavy. The development's big attraction is a spectacular marsh view. A narrow strip of grass and scrub brush, peppered with a few trees, separates the tony homes from the boggy wetlands. That's where I wheel my cart. I hide with my bees less than five feet from the naked dude's screened porch.

Now comes the boring part. Waiting for the sun's arrival. It seemingly takes forever for streaks of pink to paint the marsh horizon.

Pat says his neighbor exercises early. But how early? Is he at it yet? Can't risk running to the front of the townhouse for a peek in the picture window. Someone might see me.

The time only matters in terms of spectacle. The bees will find Mr. Nude whether he's lolling in bed or doing knee bends. Bees aren't attracted by human scent, but they apparently adore sweet-smelling soaps, lotions, and deodorants.

I'd like him sweating, helping his shampoo or deodorant advertise his whereabouts. If one bee stings, the others will follow. Hope there's a take-charge leader.

A squeak. A tabby cat saunters through the pet door, and jumps on a table in the corner, a fine spot to watch for birds in a nearby tree. Does the kitty's arrival mean Mr. Nude's up and at 'em? My bet is yes.

The screen door's lock is a flimsy hook latch. Simple to insert a pocketknife between door and frame. One flick. Unlatched. The door creaks slightly as it opens, prompting the cat to cease staring at out-of-reach birdies and focus its amber eyes on me. She purrs. Looks curious, not alarmed. I hoist the bee box off the cart and muscle it inside the porch. The buzzing box mesmerizes Ms. Kitty.

I walk over and pick up the tabby. A few soothing strokes of her fur, and a contented purr vibrates her body. I release her outside the screened porch. Don't want Ms. Kitty to suffer any stings. Returning, I use a stick to slightly prop open the pet door. Now it's time to ready the hive. I rip off the duct-taped mesh keeping the bees captive and position a rolled newspaper to create a chute and funnel the bees through the pet door and into the house.

Time to depart. While I'm not allergic, bee stings are no fun.

Abandoning the pull wagon and hive, I sprint to the rails-to-trail path, peeling off my gloves as I jog. I'm just another exercise junky out for an early run.

How I wish I could watch what happens at the townhouse. In my mind, I picture the naked dude swatting at the noisy invaders with one hand as he tries to cover his privates with the other.

Hope there's at least one person outdoors to take in the floor show. If I'm real lucky, somebody will video Mr. Nude's impromptu dance. With appropriate blurring, it might even make News at Eleven.

Chapter Thirty-Three

Kylee

Tuesday, September 29, morning

The storm tossed my boat like a toothpick in a blender until two a.m., waking me once an hour. Glad Mom stayed at Ted's. Trying to sleep in a bed rocked with seismic gusto would have liberated some of my mother's most colorful adjectives.

My immediate need. Strong. Black. Coffee.

I make breakfast—chunky peanut butter on toast—and fire up my computer to research the security items Roper wants Satin Sands to purchase. I need facts. Plan to be well-prepared for a grilling by Roper—if I'm even allowed to speak.

Roper wants security gates that open with garage-style clickers all programmed with the same open-sesame code. He proposes giving each household two clickers, and making residents pay for more. The costly approach seems poorly suited for a three-hundred-door community.

What if a clicker is lost or stolen? Does every homeowner have to reprogram his or her clicker? Then there's the dilemma of commercial vehicle access. Lawn care, termite control, garbage pickup, package delivery, and other services often visit when owners aren't home. Would all these vendors be asked to buy clickers? Not exactly tight security.

If the gates are intended to prevent all trespass, they also get an F.

Unfenced grassy areas border both entrances, making it easy for crooks to stroll around the ironwork. My conclusion? Roper wants the prestige of saying he lives in a gated community; improved security is an afterthought.

I glance at the time on my laptop's background screen. Nine a.m. The sheriff should be at work. Time to call and share my Ronald B. Headley lead.

"This is Kylee Kane. Is Sheriff Conroy in? I have information that may be of interest in the Finley and Cole murder investigations."

"Sorry, the sheriff's unavailable. I'm connecting you to Deputy Ibsen. He's in charge of the homicide investigations."

Crapola.

"Deputy Ibsen." He barks his name. Either he woke up on the wrong side of the bed or he was told I'm on the line.

"Hello, Nick, it's Kylee. Wanted to let the Sheriff's Office know about a possible lead in the HOA murders. Dan Finley, Chevy Cole, and Ronald B. Headley attended Sedgewick Military Academy together. If you can question Headley about his classmates, he may be able to suggest a motive for their murders."

"What would General Headley know about the deer feud on Hullis Island or which crazy-ass neighbor Chevy Cole pissed off letting his dogs run wild?"

Though I can't see Ibsen's smirk, his sarcasm radiates loud and clear.

"Don't you go bothering the general, either," he growls. "Poor guy's been harassed enough by reporters, especially women. He alerted the sheriff when he moved here, in case trespassers gave him trouble. Reporters for fake news media like CNN and MSNBC have practically made him a prisoner on Hemp Isle."

I take a deep breath. Fake news? Don't let Nick push your buttons.

"Always nice chatting with you, Nick. Goodbye."

I disconnect before I utter an obscenity or something that might be regarded as a threat. Imagine most, if not all, calls to the Sheriff's Department are recorded.

Okay, I had no plans to personally call on Headley. Deputy Ibsen changed that. A visit to Hemp Isle is on my agenda.

Water—rivers, streams, estuaries, sounds—covers almost half of Beaufort County's nine-hundred square miles. So, depending on how one defines an island, the county claims more than three hundred. Sure, water only surrounds some islands at high tide. Not Hemp Isle. This private, ten-square-mile hump in the ocean checks all the boxes for a legit island. It can only be reached by boat.

How lucky? I happen to live on one.

For non-boat owners, there's also morning and afternoon ferries.

Last year, Mom talked Ted and me into joining her on a ferry excursion to Hemp. She's one of Hank's biggest fans. He's the artist who creates fantastic fish out of steel. I loved the island, though we didn't set foot in either of its luxury residential resorts. Given his wealth, General Headley undoubtedly resides at Jade Pointe, an exclusive enclave with multi-acre lots and five-million-dollar homes.

We toured the public portion of Hemp with its unspoiled maritime forest, rare Marsh Tacky horses, historical ruins, and deserted beaches. No hospital or grocery store, though there is a rum distillery. Wonder how I can get an invite to Jade Pointe?

My phone trills. Mom. Her SUV's ready and she needs a ride to the GM dealership.

Another intel opportunity? Chevy Cole managed the family business for decades. Employees may feel free to talk about their dear-departed boss.

When I arrive at Ted's home, Mom's huddled in the doorway. It's still cloudy, though not raining, and it's warmer than yesterday. Still, she's shivering.

She climbs in the car. "Before I forget, Ted says the M.E. estimates Chevy Cole died about nine p.m., and he was drugged prior to his death. No signs the killer entered the house. Deputy Ibsen is certain only a neighbor could have lured Chevy outside without his dogs."

"I agree a familiar face—unless it's a known enemy—might seem less threatening. That doesn't mean the familiar face belongs to a neighbor. Chevy could have opened the door for another Sedgewick classmate. That would fit the someone-he-knew profile just as easily."

Mom fiddles with the purse on her lap. "Had a nice conversation with your friend Kay Barrett today. Doubt Kay will blab since she's a stickler for attorney-client confidentiality, but Ted's already heard...."

I glance at Mom. "You didn't." Only one reason Mom would contact Kay.

She smiles. "I did. I'm spending more of your inheritance, dear. The board didn't deign to answer my letter or even acknowledge its receipt. So, I asked Kay to file a lawsuit, requiring the board to hold a vote on the plan to willy-nilly shoot our deer. Though she's winding down her law practice, Kay agreed. She's been our family attorney for almost ten years."

I shake my head. "I don't give a whit how you spend money. Normally, I'd say go for it. But this lawsuit will make you an even bigger villain to whoever is penning your hate mail."

"Life is full of risks, and I've got plenty of heroes cheering me on. Desmond Tutu said, 'If you are neutral in situations of injustice, you have chosen the side of the oppressor.' The lawsuit won't cost Hullis Island a dime, if the board does the right thing and schedules a vote. That happens, the lawsuit goes away."

I take a deep breath. "Okay, Mom. Your moral compass never wavers. One reason I'd love you even if you weren't my mother. But I'm worried. The last few days have convinced me psychos can hide in any community."

Chapter Thirty-Four

En route to the dealership, I ask Mom if she ever met Chevy Cole. "Sure, years back when your dad and I bought our SUV," she answers. "After we signed on the dotted line, the salesman called the big man on campus. Chevy hurried out, all smiles and sunshine. He thanked us for our business. Gave your dad a card, and told us to call him direct should we ever have a concern. Promised we'd get some big bonus—don't remember what—if we referred anyone who wound up buying a car."

"Sounds like he made an impression. Your SUV is seven years' old."

"A nice touch, the owner trying to make the experience personal, but it seemed forced. The man wasn't a natural-born salesman. Our SUV was new, but his demeanor had a 'used-car' vibe."

We park between the dealer's service bay and the main entrance. A man rushes to greet us, probably hoping we're shopping for a new car. Hmm. Maybe I should be.

Mom opens her mouth first, saying she's here to retrieve her SUV from the service department.

I smile at the man, who told us to call him Dick. "I've been thinking about a new car. Mom, no need to wait for me. I'll call you later today."

Mom's mouth is agape, but she shuts it without uttering another word. Bravo.

For the next half hour, I pretend to listen as Dick fills me in on the merits of various models, starting with a top-of-the-line SUV that features a heads-up display and a raft of Bluetooth capabilities. I feign enough interest to keep him talking. Once we're back at his desk and sitting, he transitions to boasting about the dealership's record on fair pricing and service after the sale. Seeing my opportunity, I pounce.

"Wasn't the owner, Chevy Cole, murdered recently? Won't that impact the dealership?"

"No, no, not at all," Dick assures. "It'll stay in good hands. Chevy's nephew, Carl, is assistant general manager. Carl's a good guy, actually had more say in running the place than Chevy in recent years."

"Oh, how so?"

"Chevy wasn't big on details or hands-on management. Left that to Carl. Chevy spent zero time on the lot, but he attended every community function that came up. Liked being seen as one of the Lowcountry's movers and shakers."

Dick bites his lip. "Don't mean to sound disrespectful. Imagine Chevy felt it was the way to bring corporate and group business our way."

"Makes sense. I heard he served in the Army. Did Mr. Cole try to get the local military bases to sign fleet contracts?"

The car salesman shakes his head. "Chevy's father forced him to attend some out-of-town military academy. Didn't want Chevy enrolled in public schools." Dick scans the sea of open-air desks to determine if anyone's in earshot.

He continues, just above a whisper. "Chevy's old man was a bigot. Didn't want his son associating with, shall we say, people of color. Got to give Chevy credit. Said he'd never ship his son off to some military school. Soon as his old man died, Chevy hired blacks, too. Knew it was good business what with the area's sizeable African-American population."

I try for a puzzled look. "Interesting. Sounds like Chevy hated that military school, yet he still joined the Army."

Dick nods. "One of his dad's conditions. Serve your country or you won't inherit the business. His father was a grunt in Vietnam. Chevy was out of the Army in a flash soon as the old man took ill."

Time to try for a subtle conversation shift. "Sounds like you knew Chevy pretty well. Do you really believe a neighbor could have murdered him just because he let his dogs run?"

Dick bites his lip. "Yeah, it's possible. Chevy was moody, and a very stubborn guy. Hated anyone he saw as trying to push him. He told me some ancient biddy in his neighborhood videoed him with his dogs running loose. Posted it on YouTube to publicly shame him. It made Chevy more determined to let his dogs have their daily runs. Said he wouldn't let some decrepit hag tell him what he could or couldn't do. The way he described the old lady—frail and stooped over—I kinda doubt she's his killer. But maybe some other neighbor got just as worked up about Chevy acting like rules apply to everyone but him."

I ask a bit more about service contracts before I sneak in one last question. "Just remembered, I heard General Headley was a long-time friend of Chevy's. Is the general one of your customers? Well, maybe not. Living on Hemp Isle, he wouldn't have much need for a car."

Dick's squint tells me I may have veered off the conversational rails one time too many.

"Don't know where you get your information," Dick says. "The general dropped by once. Didn't hear what was said, but Chevy didn't head up a welcoming committee."

The salesman fixed me with a steady stare. "Now, how close are you to making a decision? Let me see if I can get the floor manager to sweeten the deal a little—"

"Thanks, Dick," I interrupt. "Really appreciate your time, but I need to take a serious look at my budget before I buy a new car. Promise, I'll call you when I'm ready."

I fast-walk to my car. In my rearview mirror, Dick watches as I fire up the engine of my perfectly good, five-year-old Honda Fit. He doesn't look happy. I feel a smidgeon of guilt for taking so much of Dick's time, but our talk didn't cost him any prospects. A very slow morning at the dealership.

Interesting that Dick believes Chevy and General Headley were less than bosom buddies. Maybe another talk with Mrs. Cole is in order. And I do need to chat with the general.

Before I can put the car in reverse to back out of my parking slot, my flip phone rings. Annoying. Ted insists I leave the thing turned on now that I'm consulting.

"Hello—"

Before I can say another word, Ted interrupts.

"You know where Tenyke Townhouses are? Get over here right away. There's been another murder attempt."

Chapter Thirty-Five

I tell Ted I'm on my way. No wonder he's upset. The prestigious Tenyke Townhomes are Welch HOA Management clients. This makes it four for four. Two recent murders and two alleged murder attempts all in Welch-managed neighborhoods.

A long, paved entry road leads to the enclave of traditional, two-story brick townhomes close to downtown Beaufort. I spot Ted's Mustang and park behind it, about a football field away from the crowded circular end of the drive. Townhomes edge the circle.

The vehicle logjam includes Beaufort City Police and Sheriff's Department cars, a TV-broadcast van, and several cars emblazoned with newspaper and radio logos.

Ted spots me and hustles us toward a tight cluster of bodies. On the perimeter, I crane my neck to see the TV reporter who's drawn the audience. She's interviewing a middle-aged woman, who's having a tough time forming coherent sentences between racking sobs.

"I was hurrying...on my way to work." The distraught woman pauses and sucks in air. "I heard ungodly screams and saw a naked man running toward me. I was terrified and started to run when he suddenly collapsed in the middle of the road, spread-eagled, face down on the concrete. Didn't know what to do...what was happening. Dialed 911. Thank heavens the EMTs and the ambulance came right away."

"Did you know the man?" the reporter probes. "Was he a stranger or a neighbor?"

She swallows a sob and stares at the ground. "Neighbor. Phil Gibson. He lives over there." She flaps a hand toward a townhome with an open front door. "Never met him. But I've seen him. Uh, he liked to exercise in front of his picture window. He, uh, didn't wear clothes."

"He exercised nude in front of his window?" The reporter's voice is gleeful. This would definitely make the evening news highlights reel.

"I'm sorry," the woman sobs. "I can't do this." She turns and stumbles away.

I tug on Ted's sleeve and whisper, "Did you know there was a neighborhood exhibitionist?"

He shakes his head. "No," he whispers back. "Our contract is for grounds and building maintenance. No involvement with any other board matters."

As soon as her first victim escapes, the TV reporter latches on to someone eager to parade in front of the television audience. Sheriff's Deputy Nick Ibsen. Looks like Jim was right about Nick trying to get as much media face time as possible before he runs for sheriff.

"Can you tell us what happened? Was Mr. Gibson attacked?" the reporter asks.

Ibsen puffs out his chest. "Someone released a swarm of bees into Mr. Gibson's house as he was exercising. He's allergic to bee stings. Definitely attempted murder."

"What's Mr. Gibson's status? Is he expected to survive?"

"Yes, thanks to the quick EMT response. He's in intensive care, but the prognosis is good."

The deputy focuses on the camera lens instead of the reporter.

Trying for intimacy with the TV audience? He looks as if he's trying to seduce a young lady in a bar. Bet he practices in front of his mirror.

"Do you have a motive for the attack?" The question's transparent. If the deputy's answer is salacious enough, this segment will headline the news hour.

"Not at the moment," he answers. "The Sheriff's Department is collaborating with the Beaufort Police since we're investigating two recent murders and another alleged murder attempt. All occurred within the confines of homeowner associations—HOAs—in Beaufort County."

Ibsen pauses a beat. Waiting for a drum roll?

"The neighborhoods have little in common, with one exception. All four are clients of Welch HOA Management."

The TV reporter's eyebrows zoom up. "Are you saying there may be a connection between this management company and the crimes?"

"Too early to say." One of Ibsen's eyebrows lifts suggestively. "But all the attacks appear connected to unresolved neighborhood disputes."

Ted's fingers dig into my arm as he pulls me backward. "The deputy may just be the next murder victim." His hoarse whisper vibrates with anger. "Let's get out of here before Ibsen claims I create ideal breeding grounds for aspiring killers."

"Can't leave too soon for me," I agree. "Don't trust myself to be civil in any conversation with the deputy. I'll come back and talk to the neighbors once this circus is over."

Chapter Thirty-Six

As agreed, I meet Ted back at the office.

"Wow," Robin hurries our way. "Just live-streamed a video about the townhome murder attempt. What did you do to piss off that deputy? He went out of his way to imply Welch HOA Management is connected to the murders."

"I fumed all the way here," Ted growls. "Came up with very imaginative ways to send Deputy Ibsen to hell."

He stops and scans the room. Making sure no unaccounted for ears are listening?

"I wasn't going to linger and give reporters a chance to shove microphones in my face," he continues. "But maybe I should have stayed, been proactive. Not let Ibsen have the last word. I could have pointed out all four communities also contract with Charter Cable and Palmetto Electric. Nothing sinister about any of these links. No cause and effect."

I shake my head. "No. I think your instinct was right to get out of Dodge. Deputy Ibsen intentionally planted a seed. He suggested neighborhood wars don't happen in well-managed communities, and ipso facto Welch HOA Management must shoulder its fair share of the blame." I sigh. "It's baloney, and you don't deserve the deputy's venom. My fault. I'll quit. You need to hire someone else to consult on security."

Ted's face flushes red. "No way I'll let that piece of shit ruin my company's reputation, and I certainly won't let him dictate how I do business or who I do it with."

Lyn leaves her cubicle to join Robin, Ted, and me. She rests a manicured hand on Ted's arm. "I understand you're angry, but, perhaps, it's best if Kylee steers clear of the deputy and his investigations and focuses exclusively on preventive security measures."

I bite my tongue. Lyn has a point, but I'm leaning toward a different option than the one she's selling. As soon as Ibsen blew off my suggestion that authorities talk to General Headley, I vowed I'd follow that lead. But maybe it would be better for all concerned if I did so as a private citizen. Not on the Welch HOA Management payroll.

"Ted, it's time we end this consulting gig. Once I'm no longer associated with your firm, the deputy will only sling mud at me and leave you out of it.

"No," Ted's tone is vehement. "Kylee, I recognize that stubborn look. You won't let the deputy dictate what you do or don't do. But, don't kid yourself. Your resignation won't get Ibsen to go easy on my company. He's pissed because you dumped him, and he saw us on a date. Jealousy. Pure and simple. Deputy Ibsen has it in for me, too."

I blush. Not sure why. Maybe it's Lyn's and Robin's surprised—and disapproving?—looks. The *date* was just two old friends going to dinner. Not really a date-date. But, if I open my mouth, I'll stick my foot in it. *Don't overreact.*

My brain is churning, considering and rejecting responses when Lyn says, "Oh, heavens, I only meant Kylee should make an effort not to get crossways with the deputy. I know what an asset she is."

She's such sweetness and light. *Gag.* I grit my teeth.

"The deputy had better not get crosswise of me," I spit out. "He's an asshole."

Once more my mouth engages before my brain. Best to chat with Ted in private. Maybe Mom's right about Lyn wanting more than a professional relationship with Ted. His mention of our *date* may make it even harder to be part of what Lyn considers the Welch *team.*

"What's on the agenda today?" Ted asks, abruptly switching topics.

Robin responds to his cue.

"Frank called. Says he'll be at Marshside all morning, assessing water damage from a leak in the clubhouse roof. This afternoon he'll head to Hullis and read the riot act to the company that paved the Beach Club parking lot. The pavement's only a month old and already has major cracks."

A phone rings. "I'm working on October newsletters for three communities," Robin calls over her shoulder as she hurries to the phone. "Also have to update two HOA websites."

As Robin vanishes, Lyn steps to the conversational plate. "Have a lunch date. This afternoon, I'll reply to owner emails. Most have security concerns. Perhaps Kylee can put together a list of common-sense precautions I can cut and paste to customize."

She focuses on me. "I need to know what times you're available so I can schedule your conferences."

I let the silence hang a minute. Shouldn't blurt out another up yours-style reply, but there's no way in hell she's gonna schedule—read *handle*—me.

"I created a safety checklist for Golden Treasure and Satin Sands that you can use. I'll email everyone a copy. I prefer to set up my own meetings, just give me contact numbers for folks requesting help so we can talk and agree on mutually convenient times."

"It's more efficient if I set up the meetings when they call," Lyn pouts.

Ted cuts her off. "I don't want Kylee overloaded with meetings. I need her help torpedoing the deputy's innuendoes."

Ted checks his watch. "I have to review bid proposals for resurfacing tennis courts, and visit three construction sites to verify setbacks before footers are poured. Should be free by two o'clock. Kylee, can you meet me at Tenyke Townhomes then?"

"Sure," I answer.

He frowns and glances toward Lyn. "Aren't you friends with someone who lives in those townhomes? Ever hear any mention of that exhibitionist before today?"

Lyn studies her shoes. Uncharacteristic when she has a chance to bat her eyelashes at Ted.

"There was gossip. My friend said the board saw nothing to be gained in getting involved. Left it up to the neighbors to work things out."

Ted frowns. "Well, I guess attempted murder is one way to work things

149

out."

Ted's fidgety hands indicate he's ready to end the meeting. Did the newest crisis crowd Mom's lawsuit and possible Hullis Island blowback out of his mind?

"Any updates on Hullis Island?" I prod. My question leaves it up to Ted to decide if he should let his employees know Mom's suing the HOA.

Ted sighs. "Yes, I should warn everyone. Sooner or later a Hullis board member will call, wanting to know what we plan to do about the lawsuit Mrs. Kane filed yesterday. It's designed to compel an HOA membership vote. Our answer? The directors need to discuss their response with legal counsel. Should they elect to avoid costly litigation by allowing a community vote, we'll be happy to assist with ballot and meeting preparation."

Lyn's dropped jaw and eye roll relay her thoughts. She finally closes her mouth. "That's great, just great."

While she doesn't elaborate, I'm pretty sure I know what she's thinking—*Are Myrtle and Kylee Kane trying to sabotage Welch HOA Management, or are they just plain stupid?*

Chapter Thirty-Seven

The Twin

Tuesday, September 29, 1 p.m.

I grab a quick bite, and, on a whim, drive to the animal shelter, thinking Myrt Kane might be there. I need to discourage Kylee's interest in General Headley, which could lead her to the link between my victims. While it was bee-u-tiful stirring up—dare I say it—a hornets' nest at Tenyck Townhomes, a threat closer to home's more likely to distract Kylee. Thanks to the shelter's thriving gossip network, I know about Myrt's hate mail and her decision to bulldoze ahead with a lawsuit. Time to piggyback on those anonymous poison pen letters. Make Myrt's welfare a more pressing concern for her daughter.

Myrt's SUV is parked in a shady corner of the animal shelter lot. Perfect. If she stays put for another hour, I can ratchet up her threat-o-meter without a time-consuming trek to Hullis Island. If Myrt's gone when I return, my efforts won't be wasted. I'll be totally prepared when the next opportunity pops up. No expiration date on dead flowers.

The alley behind Lisa's Flower Emporium is empty. As I'd hoped, the dumpster in back of her store has everything I need—wilted flowers, slimy, days' old greenery, twine, and a damaged wicker basket.

I slip on a pair of neoprene gloves, make my selection, and drive to a secluded spot to assemble my artistic floral arrangement. Only wish the gossip had detailed the form of Myrt's hate mail. Typed notes? Printed in block letters? Scribbled with crayon?

No matter. If the style doesn't match previous notes, Myrt—and her loved ones—may worry she's acquired a second, more deadly stalker. Hmmm. A frightening threat from a new source suggests escalation.

I carefully consider the wording before I pull a blank sheet of paper from my briefcase.

Hello, Myrt—Do all witches—or bitches—have black cats? Hope you've arranged for someone to care for those felines once you're gone. Maybe I should save you the trouble and kill the cats before your special send-off. Too bad you can't mind your own business. Your lawsuit will cost your neighbors big-time legal fees. If you disappear, so will the lawsuit. Don't worry. I can find you on or off Hullis Island. Since you won't see the flowers I send to your funeral, I'm offering a preview.

I smile. Not bad for an off-the-cuff ramble. At the animal shelter, I park in a spot where Myrt's SUV hides my car. I pop inside the shelter and ask staffers what the volunteer situation looks like this week, since I may only be able to work a few hours. It doesn't appear as if Myrt or anyone else is getting ready to leave.

Fortunately, no exterior cameras aim at the parking lot, and my actions won't be visible from any window. I grab my special dead-flower bouquet and place it on the SUV's hood. Mission accomplished. Five seconds flat.

Who says attention to detail and personal service are dead?

I slowly drive off. Can't afford to be missing in action too long on my paid job.

Chapter Thirty-Eight

Kylee

Tuesday, September 29, Early Afternoon

Before leaving Ted's office, I phone to ask Abby Cole if I can stop by late afternoon. I half expect a hostile reply, a scolding for my insensitivity in her time of grief. To my surprise, Chevy's widow sounds almost happy at the prospect of a stranger's visit.

Next up is a call to my friend Kay Barrett. I ask her to meet me for a quick lunch at Ord's Sandwich Shop, halfway between Ted's office and her B&B.

We arrive within two minutes of each other, and order shaved roast beef sandwiches, the shop's specialty. Luckily, a shaded picnic table beside the building offers privacy.

One of Kay's eyebrows lift. "You've never suggested meeting for lunch before, and you promised it would be quick. Hope this has nothing to do with your mother. If so, forget it. She's my client."

I smile. "Wouldn't dream of asking you to violate attorney-client privilege. Mom told me you filed the Hullis lawsuit for her. Have no problem with that—other than worrying some lunatic might graduate from threatening Mom to harming her. But that's not why I called."

In an exaggerated gesture, Kay swipes her forehead. "Whew. I can breathe again. So, what do you want to know? Should make you pay for my lunch since you obviously want to mine my wealth of local knowledge."

I smile. "Hey, I'll buy you a fancier dinner later this week. Your knowledge is worth its weight in shrimp and grits. You handled lots of real estate closings before you got bored with lawyering. Did you happen to close the sale of a Hemp Isle property to General Headley?"

Kay takes her time chewing a big bite of beef. An escaped dribble of horseradish sauce gets her napkin's undivided attention.

"Guilty as charged," she finally says. "Only reason I can answer is the sale's public record. He bought the historic Carlyle Estate. It predates Jade Pointe by more than a century. The developer made a deal with the owners to incorporate it within the resort. The Carlyles called when they received Headley's offer. Their property wasn't even on the market. Headley had done his homework. Knew Mr. Carlyle had heart trouble. Age and health made the secluded home, accessible only by boat, risky. No hospital on Hemp Isle. The general made an above-market bid. With no real estate agents involved, the couple made a tidy profit.

"Headley's only stipulation was the Carlyles weren't to disclose details of the sale for a full calendar year. When the Carlyles bid friends goodbye, they said they were off on a world tour. Of course, the sale had to be recorded, but the new owner is an LLC, and not easily traceable to Headley."

"Headley managed all this while he was in the brig?" I ask.

"His attorney made the cash offer when the general still had many years on his sentence. Headley must have known the president's pardon was imminent. He was free for the closing. Let's see, that was fourteen months ago. I remember because I'd just closed on the B&B."

"What did you make of Headley?"

"He looked the part of a two-star general. Stood erect as a flagpole. No flab. Must have seriously worked out behind bars. Though he was bald as a billiard, he looked younger than his age. Headley was all business, no attempt at pleasantries.

"He brought a bodyguard to the closing. Said he'd received threats, which was one reason he wanted to get settled before the press got wind he'd relocated to Beaufort County. He mentioned his four bodyguards would live in the estate's guest cottage. Said two were always on duty."

"Did he say who was threatening him?"

Kay smiles and shakes her head. "How did you miss all the gossip when the president pardoned him? He's a big-time political donor. Headley's not rich, he's *stinking* rich. The Headley empire has large financial stakes in companies that manufacture weapons and supply ex-military soldiers for security at home and abroad. Money and those connections can produce powerful enemies, not to mention his reputation as a sexual predator."

I shrug. "I sort of tuned the world out when Mom was so sick. But it's hard to believe there's been no talk of Lowcountry sightings. Surely Headley must come to Beaufort or Hilton Head for business or just to dine?"

"Can't help you there. You should ask folks at your marina if Headley ever docks there. When he purchased the estate, he bought the couple's yacht. It's a forty-five-foot Hatteras, strictly diesel, no sails."

Kay pauses to wipe her hands on a napkin and take a long drink of iced tea. "Now, it's your turn. I assume the general is somehow linked to the murders on Hullis and Golden Treasure."

Kay has an ear for gossip, but knows how to keep a secret. The lack of chatter about Headley becoming a Lowcountry resident is evidence of her zip-the-lips discretion. So, I confide. Fair is fair.

"General Headley attended Sedgewick Military Academy with the two victims. That's why I hope to chat him up. I bet he has a good idea why someone would want to kill two of his old school chums. The victims appear to have nothing in common beyond their academy school days."

Kay frowns. "What if Headley had a hand in murdering his old classmates? Maybe they knew something that could put him back behind bars."

I slowly shake my head, though I can't entirely dismiss her suggestion. "The general's way down my suspect list. Headley appears to have been one of Dan Finley's only friends, though it does sound like he and Chevy Cole weren't bosom buddies. I'm visiting Chevy's wife this afternoon. Maybe she can shed some light on the relationships."

We leave the picnic table and throw our paper plates and cups in a trash bin. Kay hugs me before I slide behind the wheel.

"Be careful, Kylee. If your hunch is correct and the same person murdered

Finley and Cole, you don't want the killer to find out you're digging into his past. Even if Headley isn't involved, I'd be cautious. This killer's smart, and he impresses me as one cold, ruthless SOB."

* * *

It's five till two when I pull into Tenyke Townhomes. No problem finding a parking place for my Honda Fit. Only three vehicles—a battered Ford pickup, a gleaming BMW, and a carpet cleaning van—are parked curbside in the horseshoe road.

Tucked away from busy roads, the enclave is pleasingly quiet. The twitter of birds provides the primary soundtrack. It's low tide, and the ripe, salty aroma of the marsh is strong. Since Ted hasn't arrived, I take a stroll on the community's raised boardwalk to savor the view. Crabs scurry in the pluff mud below, and blue herons poke their slender beaks in shallow tide pools. Something brushes my leg and I jump.

"Where did you come from?"

I bend down and stroke the plump tabby's fur. The purring response and expensive jeweled collar tell me this is no feral kitty. She sure looks like she's had a rough time, though—a muddy coat and a sore, bleeding paw. I pick her up and read the ID dangling from her collar.

"Hello, Miss Agatha. Good grief, you belong to Phil Gibson. Did you flee the bees when he did?"

"Talking to yourself again?"

Ted's voice startles me, and I almost drop my furry find.

"No. Phil Gibson's pet just found me. Definitely a house cat. Defenseless with no claws. Wonder how she wound up outside."

Ted looks thoughtful. "One more reason to knock on doors. Maybe another cat lover will take care of her until Mr. Gibson comes home from the hospital. He's out of ICU, and the hospital expects to release him tomorrow. In the meantime, let's take the neighborhood temperature."

"Do we start with his next-door neighbor?" I ask.

"I'd like to try the HOA president first. Dr. Robert Sapp lives in A-12.

I've never met the man, and an introduction is past due. The doctor wasn't on the HOA board when they signed our maintenance contract. Frank has spoken with Dr. Sapp a couple of times regarding roof repairs. Though the units are quite new, the builder didn't properly flash around the chimneys, and there were leaks."

We walk to A-12, midway around the horseshoe. His unit's front entrance features a small camera angled toward us. Ted rings the bell, and I stand beside him, cradling Miss Agatha.

A woman's tinny voice issues from a metal speaker beside the bell.

"Who are you, and what do you want?" It's evident the woman can see us.

Ted holds a Welch HOA business card up to the camera and explains we've come to address any safety worries—free, of course—related to the morning incident.

There's a click, and an elegant older lady, dressed in beige linen slacks and a soft pink silk blouse, opens the door. She appears to be about Mom's age, mid- to-late seventies.

Mrs. Sapp's smile is wistful. "Sorry for the curt interrogation. We've been careful about opening the door to strangers today. Amazing how many reporters have rung our bell. Bob only talked to the first one. Said we live in a wonderful neighborhood, and we hope Mr. Gibson recovers quickly. The reporter tried to egg Bob into saying Mr. Gibson was a pervert and we were cowering in fear that some neighbor might be planning another deadly assault."

Mrs. Sapp notices the muddy tabby in my arms. "Oh, my, where did you find Miss Agatha? My husband's a retired veterinarian, so we know all the pets. Bob was worried about Agatha when the officers went inside Mr. Gibson's house and reported no sign of a cat."

She reaches her arms out, and Miss Agatha happily clings to a new rescuer. "We'll take care of her until Mr. Gibson returns. Won't you come in and sit down? I'll fetch Bob and make sure Miss Agatha has some food and water. She'll be comfortable in the laundry room until I can clean her up. Bob went to the den to *read*. That means he's taking his afternoon siesta. Guess he was under deep enough he didn't hear the doorbell."

"Oh, please, don't wake him for us," Ted says.

"Nonsense. He'll never sleep tonight if he naps too long."

When she leaves, I walk to the oversized French doors that open onto a screened porch. I assume the layout matches Gibson's. Outdoor lounge chairs and a wrought-iron dining set suggest the Sapps make the most of the panoramic view.

The townhouse looks quite comfortable. The large rooms are handsomely furnished. I'm glad Dr. Sapp didn't fall for a reporter's attempt to solicit a quote about community terror. I just hope the doctor and his wife aren't keeping their fears secret. This tranquil neighborhood is too lovely to be infected with doubts and unease.

Hearing the Sapps' footsteps on the stairs, I take a seat next to Ted. No sooner had I sat than Ted stood to greet the doctor.

Dr. Sapp tells us to call him Bob. "The doctor title confuses folks. They start asking me about their sciatica and runny noses. One reporter asked why I didn't rush outside to offer medical assistance to Mr. Gibson. For heaven's sake, I wasn't even home."

Mrs. Sapp disappears in the kitchen to fetch ice tea. Meanwhile, Ted explains that I'm available for a free security consultation if the HOA is interested.

Mrs. Sapp returns and hands around frosty glasses of tea complete with sugared mint leaves. Bob smiles at his wife, and says, "Thanks, Deb, dear."

He carefully places his sweating glass on a coaster. "Not sure how other owners feel," he begins. "I should call a board meeting. We don't have them often. Not many worries in a small development, especially when it's new."

He glances at Deb, who takes the chair next to him. "Whoever released those bees into Mr. Gibson's house used the pet door he installed to give Miss Agatha access to her litterbox on his screened porch.

"It's not as if an axe murderer thwarted our security systems to bludgeon one of us to death. Every townhouse has its own security system, including a front-door camera and pressure-sensitive alarms on all windows and doors. Owners can even set the system to detect movement inside their homes if they're away."

I jot a note. The system he describes is fairly standard in upscale homes. The main weakness? It only works if it's activated. Too often, people quit using them after they've accidentally tripped the alarms a few times.

"A good system," I comment. "Yet an intruder accessed Mr. Gibson's screened porch without setting off an alarm. Does that mean porch doors aren't wired, or did Mr. Gibson have his system turned off?"

Bob swivels his ice tea glass as he thinks. "Doors between the house and the porch are wired, but doors on the screen porch have simple latches. Wiring them is impractical given how they rattle with every wind gust. We don't have cameras around back either. They wouldn't have prevented the attack, but they might have proved helpful in identifying who did it and how."

The doctor's a smart cookie.

"Whoever released those bees knew Mr. Gibson had a pet door," I comment. "That suggests the intruder scouted the place or a neighbor provided the information. How do your neighbors feel about Mr. Gibson's penchant for exercising nude in front of his window?"

Mrs. Sapp sighs. "Most neighbors thought the situation funny. There was cocktail talk of setting up chairs in his front yard and holding up cards to rate his efforts. Jan Benson has been the most distressed. She homeschools her little girls and didn't want them to accidentally catch Mr. Gibson's show. But I'm certain she had nothing to do with the assault."

"What about Mr. Benson?" I ask.

"He's in the Army, deployed overseas," Bob answers. "Not a suspect. In hindsight, maybe the board should have gotten involved. Mr. Gibson wasn't, uh, pleasuring himself or making suggestive moves. And he was predictable. Once you knew his schedule, you could avoid passing his window when he was exercising. We feared board involvement would make things worse. Nudity isn't addressed in our bylaws. Adding it would create unwanted publicity and possible legal jeopardy. Not sure it's wise to try and regulate what people do inside their homes. Mrs. Benson talked to the police. They declined to get involved."

We thank the couple for their time. As I walk toward my subcompact, a man unlocks the BMW I noticed when I arrived. He's dressed in a sport coat and carrying a briefcase. He has his back to me. Yet something about him seems familiar. He turns. It's Brent, the animal shelter *volunteer*. Does he live here or is he visiting?

Maybe I'll ask the Sapps if Brent's a resident or frequent visitor.

Yeah, yeah, I know. Just because Brent got in hot water with the law once doesn't mean he's a murdering psychopath. But since Mom's spending time with him, I'd like to make certain his transgression was a one-time thing.

Chapter Thirty-Nine

I t's three p.m. I drop by the office, call the security firm that services Tenyke Townhomes and ask them for a proposal to add video surveillance of the units' rear entrances.

I'm disappointed Lyn isn't in. I'd hoped she could tell me if Brent owns a townhome. I ask Robin when Lyn will be back. She shrugs. "Lyn keeps her own appointments. Just calls in periodically to check for messages and see if an emergency's popped up. She's attending a board meeting at Marshview now. You've got her number, right? Call her."

I don't want to give Lyn or Robin the impression Brent is an urgent concern. I smile. "Not a big deal. Will catch her next time we're both in the office."

Since it's earlier than I told Abby Cole to expect me, I give Jim Monroe a call. Golden Treasure's affable board president answers on the first ring. He invites me to drop by his house and gives my kind of directions. "Turn left at the white stucco with the red tile roof. We're the second house after the turn."

Jim is pulling weeds beside his driveway when I pull in. He stands and brushes the sandy soil off his pants. "Glad to see you. Gives me an excuse to call it a day. My knees and back aren't as young as they used to be."

I follow him to his backyard where branches from a huge live oak overhang a cozy brick-paved patio, and nicely shade an eclectic collection of lounge chairs and rockers.

"Wow, what an incredibly gorgeous tree."

Jim's smile grows wider. "Yep, that beauty's why we bought this lot. Took extra care to make sure construction crews didn't drive over its roots or compact the soil while we were building. That tree is at least two hundred years old. Irreplaceable."

He motions me to an Adirondack chair, softened with plump flower-print cushions, and offers refreshments. I decline, explaining Abby Cole is expecting me in twenty minutes.

Jim frowns. "She's had a rough time. Glad all her children could come so quickly. While Chevy's behavior peeved neighbors, Abby wasn't tarred with her husband's brush. She's soft-spoken, polite. Frankly, people felt sorry for her, having Chevy as a husband. If he lost his temper over some little thing, you could hear him berating Abby half a block away."

"How's the neighborhood coping?" I ask. "Are people frightened? Do they believe a psycho killer might be living next door?"

Jim shakes his head. "Frightened? No, we're in the denial and disbelief stage. Can't accept that anybody who lives here could get worked up enough about those damn dogs to kill Chevy."

"I understand a woman took photos of Chevy's dogs running amuck and posted them on social media to shame him. Did she also complain to the board? Did the directors attempt to get Chevy to cease and desist?"

Jim sighs. "Yes, Claire asked the board to act. In hindsight, we should have tried to do more. But what? There's nothing in our covenants or bylaws about keeping dogs on leashes. That's a county ordinance. We recommended Claire talk with local authorities."

"Did she?"

"Yes, she was told an animal control officer would have to catch the dogs loose outside their yard. Then, they'd be taken to the pound, and the owner would be fined and get a warning. After an owner's third warning, the dogs are taken away. Unfortunately, Beaufort County is huge. An officer would almost need to park his butt in our HOA around the clock to catch the dogs on the loose. Claire called in reports a few times, but Chevy always corralled the mutts before an officer could get here."

"How frustrated was Claire?" I ask. "Should she be considered a suspect?"

Jim laughs. "Ask Lyn about Claire's frustration level. She called your office as well as our directors regularly. Naturally, Lyn wanted to help, but, like the board, she couldn't figure out what your company could do.

"Is Claire a suspect?" He chuckles. "Hardly. She's eighty years old. Needs a walker. That's the main reason those dogs terrified her. They'd come bounding toward her at full tilt when she was scooting down the path with her walker. Claire was sure they'd bowl her over, and she'd break a hip."

"Any thoughts about who might have killed Chevy?"

"Not a one. I remain one of the deniers. I don't believe a neighbor did it. But Deputy Ibsen's convinced otherwise. He's returned several times to question me and dozens of other neighbors. Tried to get me to complain that Welch HOA Management—or, as he would have it, *mismanagement*—created a toxic atmosphere that escalated into violence. Ridiculous. No neighborhood can escape its share of unlikeable fools and idiots. For the most part, we're a friendly, generous community. We don't have a lot of rules. No architectural review committee. No rules about what you can and can't plant in your yard—front or back. It's live and let live."

While I refrain from saying I dismiss most of the deputy's opinions, I can't stay quiet.

"Well, Jim, count me in with the deniers. I doubt any of your neighbors had a hand in Chevy's murder. Whoever killed him knew enough about his unpopularity to stage his death, and make it look like an act of neighborly rage. Haven't a clue what the murderer's real motive might be, but I'd bet big bucks it has nothing to do with Chevy's dogs."

Jim claps his hands. "Bravo! Glad to hear someone outside Golden Treasure say that. My thoughts exactly. Wish I felt more confident the Sheriff's Department will uncover the real motive for Chevy's murder and catch his killer. Can't wait for our community to return to normal. A widower friend put his house on the market last week. He's in poor health and wants to move into one of those CCRCs—Continuing Care Retirement Communities. He fears no one will buy his house until the killer's caught."

We say our goodbyes, and I head to Abby Cole's home. No cars in the driveway, and Abby answers the door. As I step inside, my ears tune for any hint of paws thumping my way for a knockdown. I'm pleased to hear no barking, whining, or scratching at a door.

"Come in," Abby says. "I'm enjoying a little peace and quiet. My children and grands are out running errands. My daughter-in-law, bless her heart, took Chevy's dogs to a kennel. I'm boarding them for the week. My not-so-secret hope is that one of my kids will adopt them. Those big German shepherds were never trained, and they're too much for me to handle."

Not surprisingly, Abby looks better than when we first met. The heavyset woman's eyes are no longer puffy. Her salt-and-pepper hair is curled, and she's even wearing a little lipstick.

"I won't take much of your time, I promise. Just have a few questions about Mr. Cole's days at the military academy. I'd also like to know if he keeps in touch with any old friends from his school days."

Abby's eyebrows knit. "Why on earth would you care about that?"

I suck in a deep breath. How much do I spill about my suspicions? "I imagine you know another man was murdered recently on Hullis Island. His name was Dan Finley, and he attended Sedgewick Military Academy with your husband. The fact that two schoolmates have been killed within days of each other seems a mighty big coincidence. One worth exploring to see if the deaths have any connection."

Abby's mouth hangs open. "Chevy refused to talk about that military school. He loathed Sedgewick, and hated his father for forcing him to leave his Beaufort friends and go there. He said his father was a racist who sent him to a virtual prison just so he wouldn't rub elbows with Beaufort blacks. Never heard Chevy mention any school friends. And I never heard Dan Finley's name before."

"How about General Headley?" I ask. "He was a classmate, too, and I understand he recently moved to the Lowcountry."

She rolls her eyes. "Him I've heard of. Chevy may have hated him more than his dad. Why I don't know. My husband laughed like a hyena when General Headley went to prison. He kept muttering, 'It's past time that bastard got his due. Always the big shot, ordering people around. Too bad more people don't know the big general is a cowardly SOB.'"

"Did your husband comment on the general's pardon? Did he know he moved to Hemp Isle?"

"Yes." She closes her eyes. The eyelids twitch. Is she trying to remember or hoping to forget?

"General Headley showed up at the dealership, and Chevy made quite a scene, yelling at him to get the hell out of his sight. My husband never mentioned the incident. My nephew Carl told me. Said he'd never seen Chevy so worked up. And that's saying something. Chevy had a bad temper."

I really want to ask, "Why in blazes did you stay married to the jerk?" I don't. Love and loyalty are indeed complicated, and it's none of my business.

Abby gives me a hard look. I hope she hasn't read my mind.

"Chevy wasn't a bad man," she adds softly. "He yelled a lot, but he had his moments. I made a big mistake talking Chevy into buying this house. I fell in love with the setting. As we got older, I wasn't keen about living in the boondocks, miles from a hospital. The Golden Treasure HOA didn't have a lot of silly rules that I knew would drive Chevy crazy. I figured it would be okay."

She sighs and her shoulders droop. "I didn't consider the dogs. On our farm, Chevy let them run free. He didn't think he or his dogs should be subjected to restrictions put in place by 'wimps,' who thought the dogs might bite. I pleaded with Chevy to put the dogs on leashes. He refused. His attitude was catch me; I dare you. He chafed against any authority telling him what he could or couldn't do."

Wow. I'm an independent cuss, too, and hate unnecessary rules, but any smidgeon of empathy I might feel for Chevy is erased by sympathy for Claire-of-the-Walker. Leash laws aren't stupid. Claire should have the right to walk in front of her own home without fear of dogs bowling her over or biting her.

I thank Abby and promise to let her know if I learn anything new about Chevy's time at Sedgewick. She admits I've piqued her curiosity about why Chevy hated General Headley. My promise to keep her informed doesn't mean I'll pile needless grief on the woman.

I've yet to figure how to meet the general. My first step is a visit to Sedgewick Military Academy. See if anyone still remembers Dan Finley,

Chevy Cole, and Headley. Given that thirty years have passed, a complete staff turnover's likely. But former instructors may live nearby. It's just one hundred and fifty miles away.

What have I got to lose?

Chapter Forty

Done with consulting for the day, I head home. As I park, I remember Kay suggesting folks in the Harbormaster Store might know if General Headley ever docks in one of the transient slips.

Inside the compact store, Julie perches on a stool behind the counter. The college student works at the marina part-time. Can't quite read the title of her thick book.

"Hi, Julie. Reading anything good?"

The pretty young lady laughs. "Not unless you consider *Case Studies in Aberrant Behavior* a page-turner."

"I may borrow it," I say. "Aberrant behavior seems to be the new norm."

We chat about Julie's psychology course at the University of South Carolina Beaufort campus. Then, we talk weather, an obsession among boat people—especially if there's a hurricane churning in the Atlantic. The newly christened Maryanne is now a Cat 2. Fortunately, it still looks like she'll come nowhere near us. Looking at today's blue sky and puffy clouds, it seems impossible a monster storm lurks anywhere over the horizon.

With our standard chitchat finished, I ask if General Headley ever comes into the shop or reserves a slip.

Julie puts her book down. "Is he the guy who bought the Carlyles' 42-foot Hatteras and their home on Hemp Isle?"

Bingo! "That's him. Have you seen him lately?"

"The Hatteras makes a supply run every couple of weeks." Julie rolls her eyes. "Can't miss the boat. It flies a huge, gaudy 'Re-Elect Prudmont' flag along with one of those 'Don't Tread on Me' snake flags. He's a big fan of the idiot president. Ugh. Don't know how often the general's aboard. He's never come in the store. Usually, a big dude, name of Jacob, stops in. Guy looks like a sumo wrestler, forearms the size of tree trunks. He pays the bills, buys anything needed in the way of marine supplies."

"Is a supply run due soon?" I ask. "If so, I'd like to talk with Jacob, or whoever's aboard the yacht when it docks."

I jot my cell number on the back of one of my new Welch HOA business cards along with a brief note, saying I'd like to speak with the general regarding a security concern. The front of the card IDs me as a security consultant, but only lists the main office phone number.

I hand the card to Julie. "Next time the Hatteras yacht docks, could you ask whoever's working to pass along my card? It's really important for me to speak with the general."

Julie's sunny face clouds. "Imagine someone will cruise over before the weekend. Is this urgent? You look stressed. Why wait for the supply run? Can't you just call the general?"

"Would if I could," I reply. "Unlisted phone number."

"Why not use your boat's VHF radio? It's equipped with DSC, right?" Julie asks. "I have the MMSI number for the Hatteras. Wrote it down. Sometimes they radio ahead to ask about diesel prices, marine supplies, or recommendations for local tradespeople. Here, I'll write it down for you."

"Thanks, Julie. I'll try the radio. But, if I can't raise anyone on the Hatteras before the next supply run, relay my message, okay?"

"Will do."

I leave the store pleased with my progress. To someone who doesn't own a boat, Julie's VHF suggestion would sound like gibberish. Me? I can't believe I didn't think of it. Most recreational boats that cruise large bodies of water come equipped with VHF radios for safety reasons, and the newer VHFs offer Digital Selective Calling. One DSC feature is the ability to broadcast a distress or "mayday" call with the push of a single button.

Every DSC user also has a Maritime Mobile Service Identity number, which is akin to a private phone number. If you know a boat's unique MMSI, you can radio it without broadcasting to every boat in the vicinity.

Of course, people can ignore MMSI calls if they don't recognize the caller's ID. My hope is someone would pick up out of curiosity. Before I radio, I need to think what to say to him—or, more likely, one of his flunkies. As my business card makes plain, I have zero authority to require anyone to listen to me or answer my questions.

Inside my cabin, I change into stay-at-home comfort clothes. That's when I slide my simple, dumb phone out of my jacket pocket and notice it's off. I turn it off while driving since I have no hands-free option, and can't respond to an emergency while I'm on the road. Anything else can wait. Trouble is, I sometimes forget to turn the dang thing back on.

Three new messages. The first, from Mom, is short and sweet. "Call me when you get a chance." Ted's the second caller. "Phone me. Myrt couldn't reach you. Claims she's not scared, but she got another poison pen letter attached to a dead flower bouquet. The note and flowers were left on her SUV while it was parked at the animal shelter. She's back on Hullis Island, and I'm headed to her house."

I bite my lip. Don't even listen to the third message before I call Ted. I'll get more details from him than Mom.

Ted answers immediately. "Hey, Kylee. Guess you got my message. Where are you?"

"Just came onboard the River Rat. Are you at Mom's yet?"

"A couple blocks away. Myrt's doing her stiff-upper-lip number, but I think this threat spooked her. I'll stay with her till you get here. Try to talk her into coming home with me."

"Will be there soon as I can. I'm with you. Mom needs to stay with one of us."

* * *

On the drive to Hullis Island, I try to think rationally about the best way to safeguard Mom. Neither Ted's house nor my boat offers good security. Not a big concern if Ted or I are with her. But we both work. Would my stubborn mother willingly spend her days as one of our sidekicks? Doubt it.

169

Improving security at her house isn't an answer. Not unless she barricades herself inside. Her psycho stalker has demonstrated his ability to reach her wherever she goes.

Suddenly, I have a brainstorm. Aunt Linda can help me hatch a compelling reason Mom needs to visit her in Atlanta. I smile. Linda's a great co-conspirator.

I unlock Mom's door. "It's me."

"We're in the kitchen," Ted answers.

A heavenly aroma says something loaded with chocolate is fresh from the oven. Mom's a baker. She bakes when she's happy, and when she's sad. She's most prolific when she's worried.

At the kitchen table, Mom and Ted are wolfing down brownies topped with a thick layer of icing. "Come join us." I can see chocolate coating all of Ted's teeth as he issues the invitation with a mouth full of goo.

Mom lifts a big brownie onto a plate for me.

"Thanks. Can I have this served with a side of details? What happened, and how are we going to make sure you're safe?"

Mom describes the dead flower delivery as a stupid prank designed to scare an old lady. "I should stay in my own home and ignore the blowhard, whoever he may be."

Working in tandem, Ted and I convince Mom that prank or not, we won't be able to think straight if we're constantly worried. Negotiations begin. Mom agrees to sleep at Ted's house tonight.

"Tomorrow, you can join me on a road trip to the South Carolina Sandhills," I say. "I'm going to visit Sedgewick Military Academy. It's in the country, nearest town is Melsville, really tiny."

"You're going to Melsville?" Mom says. "Sure, I'll go. I can visit an old friend. She taught at Garfield Elementary when I was the school nurse. Always meant to visit her now that she lives so close."

While Mom packs an overnight bag, I make sure Mom's cats won't want for anything for the next thirty-six hours. Mom has an automated food and water dispenser. So much easier to leave cats on their own than dogs. As I put cat food in the dispenser, I share a highlight reel of my afternoon.

"Right after we left the Sapps, I spotted Brent, the mysterious animal shelter volunteer, at Tenyke Townhomes. I want to find out if he lives there. Seeing him at the scene of the latest murder attempt makes my trouble antenna twitch. He knows when Mom visits the animal shelter. He could easily be our dead flower delivery boy."

Ted nods. "I'll check. If he's not a resident, maybe the good doctor or his wife know who he visits. But I think your antenna needs a tune-up. Why would Brent threaten Myrt over the Hullis deer? Pretty sure he doesn't live on the island."

"True. Maybe he delivered the message for a friend. Afraid I'm turning into one of those conspiracy nutsos. Still, it would be nice to know more about the man."

I freshen the kitty litter before moving on to my next update—my Golden Treasure visits with Jim Monroe and Mrs. Cole. I fill him in on Chevy's overt hostility toward the general. Finally, I explain I may be able to contact General Headley without a landing party raid.

When Mom returns with her bag, we discuss travel and dinner logistics. We talk her into leaving her SUV in the driveway so it appears she's home. We program the lights to come on at dusk and off at bedtime, while Mom lets Hullis Island security know she'll be away for one or possibly two nights.

Since Mom dislikes my "cramped" Honda almost as much as the River Rat, she opts to ride with Ted. I volunteer to pick up our take-out pizza order. Naturally, the pan of still-warm brownies goes in Ted's car.

In the pizza parking lot, I phone Aunt Linda and leave a message on her answering machine, urging her to concoct some reason Mom needs to visit immediately.

The delicious aroma of pizza practically makes me dizzy. It's been three days since I've been swimming—my favorite form of exercise. Need to figure out how to work more exercise into my new routine, especially with all the carbs I'm scarfing down.

Chapter Forty-One

After a good night's sleep, I take a brisk early-morning walk in downtown Beaufort to burn off a few of the pizza calories. Then, bakery aromas sabotage my resolve, and I buy breakfast goodies to bring to Ted's.

The three of us munch on them as we swill copious amounts of coffee.

"I need to catch up on paperwork and pay bills this morning," Ted says. "The afternoon's a goner. Meeting with three boards. Happily, none of these HOAs has seen any violence."

"We should be going soon," I add. "I've planned a scenic, back-road route that avoids I-95 and all the semi-truck traffic. But it will take two-and-a-half hours. I just hope there are restrooms along the way, given how much coffee we've downed."

"Can't wait to see my friend, Emily," Mom adds. "She sounded delighted when I asked about paying a surprise visit."

We started our road trip in good spirits. Before we even reached Beaufort's city limits, Mom powered up her smartphone. Unlike me, she's a devotee. Texting keeps her in touch with the young people she loves—Ted's son Grant, and her grand nieces and nephews.

Mom looks up Melsville on Google. "Wow, population is only 871. It's named for Milton Mels, who was a hero in the War of 1812. Old Milton had quite a cotton plantation spread over a thousand acres."

I'm half-listening. Love history, but my brain's preoccupied, trying to decide my initial approach at Sedgewick Military Academy. I'll likely encounter a gatekeeper trained to give minimal info to outsiders. Should I admit I'm worried a killer is targeting alumni? Would the admission make stonewalling more or less likely?

I hope Mom's phone rings soon. When Aunt Linda and I finally spoke, she promised to beg Mom to help her babysit. "Don't have to fake desperation." Linda laughed. "My daughter and her husband are away on business, and I have my three grandkids for a week. Not sure a sixty-five-year-old should be trusted with these wildlings. The nine-year-old twins are a handful. And the fourteen-year-old? What can I say? She's a teenager."

Mom loves Linda as well as her baby sister's children and grandkids. She'll accept Linda's plea.

"Are you listening to a word I say?" Mom asks.

My mind's wandered, and Mom's changed topics.

"Uh, yes. Just have a lot on my mind."

"I'm surprised you don't remember Emily McVea. She was your brother's energetic first-grade teacher. He adored her."

I laugh. "Unfortunately, I didn't have Ms. McVea. My first-grade teacher was old Mrs. Gunter. She was so cranky and mean she gave me nightmares."

Mom chuckles. "Don't know about the *old* part. Back then, Mrs. Gunter was probably ten years younger than you are today. But you weren't the only little kid who didn't warm to her. She scared me, too. Always scowling, and those black Mother Hubbard shoes looked like Army boots laced up to kick butt."

"How did you and Emily become friends?"

"Emily was single, straight out of college, and there were few teachers her age. She was lonely. I made it a point to chat with her whenever it was my day to play nurse at Garfield Elementary. Turned out, we liked the same types of books and movies. She met her husband, Jeff Beck, when they were both pursuing Master's Degrees at the University of Iowa."

"How did the Becks end up in Melsville?"

"It's Jeff's hometown. He always hoped to come back, so they retired here. Emily's Christmas cards describe Melsville as pretty, and the lifestyle as unhurried and cheap."

Mom's phone rings and she greets Aunt Linda. Before we go twenty miles,

Mom agrees to visit Atlanta.

She awards me *the look*. "I know you and your aunt concocted this visit. But I won't fuss. It's been ages since I've seen Linda and her rambunctious grands. If I don't go, you and Ted will pester me to death. But there is a quid pro quo. Since Linda's allergic to cats, either you or Ted need to take care of Mississippi and Keokuk while I'm gone."

"Deal."

I'll lobby hard for Ted to give the kitties a temporary home. His mansion renovation offers dozens of rooms to explore. Mom's cats would be bored on the River Rat. Despite my boat's name, there isn't a single rodent to chase.

Mom directs me to Emily's house, a well-kept Victorian with lots of fancy trim and a lush garden. Emily rushes to hug Mom the minute we arrive. I promise to return about two o'clock. "I'll call if I'm late."

* * *

Sedgewick Military Academy sits seven miles outside Melsville. My first visual does nothing to change my preconceived notion that life inside its walls would be joyless. A cluster of drab gray buildings sits atop a swell in the land. The complex is surrounded by a few scraggly trees and acres of grass shorn to look like a brownish-green military crewcut.

Did some military tactician scour the landscape to ensure anyone who dares to approach could be spotted miles away?

I turn into the long drive. If anyone in that main building looks out a window, my bright red car will not go unnoticed.

The circular drive has no other cars. Staff parking and the service entrance are probably in back. The front door opens before I push the buzzer.

"Can I help you?"

The gatekeeper is the female equivalent of the buildings she guards—gray, drab, unsmiling. While she asks if she can help, her demeanor proclaims she only wants to help me back to my car.

I smile. "Yes, may I come in? I need some help researching Sedgewick alumni who graduated about three decades ago."

The human blockade doesn't budge. "I'm sorry. Not even cadet parents are allowed visitation during the week. If you had bothered to telephone, it would have saved you a trip. You need an appointment to speak with our superintendent or any staff."

"I understand." *Actually, I don't, this isn't the Pentagon.* "But I drove all the way from Beaufort in hopes of finding some answers. Perhaps you'll allow me to look at old yearbooks. You must have an historical collection."

Her eyes narrow. "Who are you, and what are you looking for? Student records are confidential."

"Surely, there's nothing secret in the yearbooks," I counter. "I'm a security consultant, and I fear someone may be targeting Sedgewick alumni, who now live in the Lowcountry. Two Sedgewick classmates were murdered in the past few days. I hope to identify any friends of theirs who graduated around the same time. If they've settled in Beaufort County, I'll warn them they might be in danger."

The matron swings the door open a little wider, and stands aside. I try not to shudder as I enter the dim interior.

"I'm Miss Landis," she says. "Can you show me identification?"

Finally, I'm glad to have business cards. I hand her a business card, my driver's license, and a card identifying me as retired military. That one does the trick.

"I suppose it won't hurt for you to look at yearbooks. You can sit in Assistant Superintendent Hand's office, he's away on business. I'll bring the yearbooks one at a time. What year do you want as a start?"

I request the year Dan Finley graduated. Miss Landis ushers me into an office that has a hint of humanity. Photos of smiling family members sit on the massive oak desk. I take a seat in an oversized chair and twiddle my thumbs.

When Miss Landis returns, I'm glad I'm quietly sitting in non-snoop mode. I'm tempted to giggle. *Maybe Miss Landis and my old first-grade teacher are cousins.*

I open the yearbook and count the number of graduating cadets in Finley's

175

class—thirty. From the info I gleaned online, the academy accepts male students in grades seven through twelve. Assuming an average of thirty cadets per grade and six grades, less than two hundred students would have been on campus each year the murder victims attended.

Small class size means each graduating cadet gets a big mug shot. Seniors' activities are listed under the photos. If the cadet was accepted into one of the service academies, the achievement is bolded and capitalized: **Accepted AIR FORCE ACADEMY!**

Dan Finley's picture has no bolded accolade. His activity list is meager—track and rifle teams. I flip to the photo of Chet Cole, who had not yet claimed his Chevy nickname. Activities? Zero.

I use my cellphone to snap pictures of both pages. While my phone isn't "smart", it includes a camera.

Headley doesn't appear in this yearbook. Must have graduated before Finley and Cole. I ask Miss Landis if I can trade for the prior yearbook. Ronald B. Headley's photo is easy to find with its big **Accepted at WEST POINT!** accolade. His string of activities suggests he was big man on the small campus. I snap another picture.

I jot down the names of cadets who appear in activity photos with Headley, Finley, or Cole. I recognize none of the classmates' names. If they live in the Lowcountry, they fly under the radar.

Looking through the small photos of underclassmen, I notice a picture rimmed in black. Beneath Jake Turner's name, his date of birth and death are printed. No other details. A car accident? While most young people don't die from disease, cancer and other illnesses do strike teens. I write down the boy's date of birth and death. Maybe his death certificate will tell me more.

I also copy the names of staffers who look relatively young. Maybe Emily can tell me if any still live near here. I capture a few more pages with my phone's camera.

Periodically, Miss Landis opens the door to spy on me. While she never offers so much as a glass of water, she does fetch all four of the yearbooks I request. When I relinquish one year, she replaces it with a new one. My bet is she leafs through each return to ensure I didn't rip out a page or add graffiti.

Every now and then, a loud bell breaks the tomblike silence. I assume the bells announce the beginning or end of class periods. Yet I never hear the shuffle of feet or a chorus of boys' multi-octave voices. This building must not include any classrooms.

I close and return the last yearbook.

"By chance are any faculty who worked here thirty years ago still on staff?"

Miss Landis shakes her head. "No, I've been here the longest, twenty-five years."

Of her lengthy tenure, I have no doubt. Who would dare fire her?

I thank Miss Landis and leave. It's not quite one o'clock. Have an hour to kill before I pick Mom up at Emily's house. Arriving early might spoil their chance to catch up. I spot the required rural "meat-and-three" café in downtown Melsville. I predict two of the meat choices will be fried chicken and meatloaf. The three sides will include an array of starches and grease-coated vegetables. Lucky, I went for that morning walk. I do love fried chicken and mac-and-cheese.

I claim a shady parking spot half a block from the café. Though it's a little after one, the restaurant's crowded. Looks like everyone in Melsville ventured out for a leisurely lunch. Since there's no "wait to be seated" sign, I pull out a chair at an empty two-top near the back. A minute later, a friendly waitress takes my order. After she leaves, I call Ted.

"Just checking in. My visit to Sedgewick Military Academy was uneventful. No buckshot in my bottom, but I didn't learn much either. The gatekeeper begrudgingly let me examine old yearbooks. If she was telling the truth, no one on campus was around back then."

"Sorry it proved a dead end," Ted says.

"I did get a list of cadet names to research, including one student who died while our victims were at the academy. The dead boy was younger than our victims and the general. The connection seems tenuous, but it doesn't hurt to check. How's your day going?"

Ted groans. "Lyn was here when I came in, but left half an hour later. Blamed a really bad migraine. Hope she'll be in tomorrow. Didn't accomplish much of what I wanted this morning. Had to handle the calls she usually takes. She's a lot better than me at sounding sympathetic or at least pretending to care."

A prerequisite for a master manipulator.

"Did you ask Lyn about Brent, the animal shelter volunteer I saw at Tenyke Townhomes?"

"Sorry, no. Totally slipped my mind, and I don't want to bother her at home. Says she needs total silence and darkness when a bad migraine hits."

"Mom agreed to go to Atlanta tomorrow and spend a week with Aunt Linda."

"Terrific. One less worry."

I end the call as the smiling waitress delivers a week's worth of cholesterol. Must say the fried chicken looks and smells divine. I sip the iced tea and sputter. Sometimes, I still forget Southern tea comes with a week's ration of sugar unless you request it un-doctored.

Chapter Forty-Two

The Twin

Wednesday, September 30, Morning

Didn't see that one coming—Kylee dragging Myrt along on her snoop outing.

Damn. Wouldn't a loving daughter opt to keep her mother safe at home? Does Kylee think driving beyond Beaufort County's borders eliminates all risks?

Guess it's up to me to prove her wrong.

I start my drive an hour behind the Kane women. Since I know where they're going, it doesn't matter. Myrt didn't make their Melsville destination a secret. Gotta love her compulsion to explain. When she phoned the animal shelter, Myrt could have simply said she wouldn't be in today. Not like the shelter demands a doctor's note if a volunteer's a no-show. But Myrt felt obliged to elaborate, nattering on about why and where. She didn't mention Kylee, but I'm not stupid. Sedgefield Military Academy is a stone's throw from Melsville.

I'm optimistic the trip will prove a time-waster for Kylee. If it weren't for John Hart's deathbed confession, I still wouldn't know how Jake died. The academy's current tight-asses probably still believe in a circle-the-wagons code of silence. Their predecessors excelled at it. Stymied any investigation of Jake's death.

179

I expect this generation to work just as hard to bury any whiff of scandal. Anyway, it's doubtful any current Sedgewick staffers know a thing about Jake's demise. Still, it galls me that Kylee's sniffing around the connection that links my victims.

I can't prevent her visit. But I can send a message she should focus more on protecting her mother and less on sticking her nose where it doesn't belong. What kind of message? *Think.*

She'll spot my car in a New York minute if I loiter near the entrance to Sedgewick and tail her when she leaves. The academy's long approach is too exposed, and traffic is almost nonexistent.

Five miles south of Melsville and two miles north of the military academy's long drive, I spot a deeply shaded country lane. After I make sure my car's hidden from the road, I settle in to watch for Kylee's scarlet Honda to reappear. How quickly she leaves the academy will provide a clue about her research success. If the visit's short, I'll know some Sedgewick admin told her not to let the door hit her ass on the way out.

As long minutes tick by, my frustration builds. My stakeout is ninety minutes old. Somehow Kylee avoided a bum's rush. What has she found?

Finally! The snoop's car zips past my discreet vantage point. Kylee's the sole passenger. That confirms she dropped Myrt off at some friend's house before the Sedgewick visit. Myrt's verbal diarrhea didn't include the name of her long-lost Melsville friend. Otherwise, I'd know the address. However, it shouldn't be hard to find the Kane women. Melsville makes the fictional Mayberry look like the Big Apple.

I tug down the brim of my ballcap and snug my oversized sunglasses to the bridge of my nose. Not that the sunglasses are needed. The sky's dark, and it's drizzling. I listen to a weather forecast while I count backwards from one hundred to make sure Kylee's far enough down the road that she won't notice me in her rearview mirror. The weather forecast makes me smile. Rain will arrive within the hour and increase to a downpour. Visibility will be next to nil on the highway.

As I cruise Melsville's main drag, I spot Kylee locking her car and hurrying through the drizzle to a café. Great! Not knowing how long she'll be, my plan's a bit dicey but worth the risk.

I park beside the Honda and cross the street to an old-timey hardware store, a virtual requirement in every small burg. I pay cash for a package of nails. Since it would take too much time and muscle to force nails into Kylee's tires, I'll count on the Honda to do the hard work. I squat like I'm tying my shoe, and place a nail—business side up—directly behind the back-left tire. I scan the street. No one's paying attention. I repeat my charade three more times, trusting at least one of the four nails to embed itself in a tire when Kylee backs out of the angled parking slot.

I'm counting on a slow leak rather than an instant flat. The best outcome? A tire will lose enough air to be a problem when the Kane women reach the lightly-traveled backroad between Melsville and the interstate. If Kylee's forced to replace the flat with a donut tire, it will slow them even more. Between the rain and the donut, the car will be creeping along. Not stationary, but a hard-to-miss target.

My pistol may be useful again. I smile as I visualize the headline: "Stranded Mother and Daughter Shot in Roadside Drive-By."

But what if Kylee was able to dig out a lead at the academy? Maybe she's already phoned Ted. If so, he won't buy a drive-by shooting as an attack on Myrt or random violence. He'd be more inclined to link their deaths to Sedgewick.

I sigh. Best to settle for scaring the shit out of the pair. I have ample time to get in position and plan a hair-raising, non-lethal attack to fluster Myrt and Kylee. The rain should prevent them from recognizing my car or me.

When I'm twenty-five miles out of town, the rain starts in earnest. I make a U-turn and pull onto the shoulder to wait for a limping Honda to venture into my web. The flat landscape should make it easy to see the Honda's headlights well in advance. The road isn't heavily traveled, and it's doubtful any farmer will be driving around in a small Honda Fit.

Chapter Forty-Three

Kylee

Wednesday, September 30, Afternoon

It's quarter till two, fifteen minutes ahead of schedule to pick up Mom. But I can't dawdle any longer in the café. The once-crowded tables are empty, and I'm the sole patron. Unfair to ask the nice waitress to refill my ice tea a third time. Not to mention I might go into insulin shock.

At Emily's, an older Chevy sedan sits in the drive. Does it belong to the husband? He was out when I dropped Mom off. Hate to park and block the Chevy's exit. Unfortunately, a trailered pontoon boat and a plumbing van are hogging nearby parking.

I'll just pop in. Don't want Mom to get soaked in the rain. Given the weather, I'd like to leave soon. Maybe the women have run out of things to gab about. Yeah, fat chance.

Emily greets me with a big smile. "So glad you're here. We were worried Tim might need to leave before you arrived."

Tim? Is that her husband's name? No. It's Jeff. Jeff Beck.

Emily herds me inside as an older gentleman rises from a club chair to shake hands. "Tim, meet Myrt's daughter, Kylee. Tim's one of my husband's boyhood friends, a lifelong resident of Melsville. When Myrt told me about your Sedgewick research, I invited Tim to join us. He's a virtual encyclopedia when it comes to Melsville history."

"Nice to meet you," Tim and I murmur in unison. I sit on the couch beside Mom and Tim returns to his chair.

"Emily tells me you're interested in anything unusual that happened at the academy around thirty years back," Tim begins. "I only know of one incident, one death. My family owns the town's funeral home, and, back then, I served as deputy coroner. Not uncommon for funeral directors to do double-duty in the Carolina boondocks. You don't need a medical degree to figure out the reason for ninety percent of the deaths. If a corpse is inside a wrecked car or pinned under a tractor, the manner and cause of death are pretty clear."

I nod and smile, though I'm itching to urge Tim ahead to the punch line. *Who died, how, and why do you remember a death that happened so long ago?*

Tim pauses to sip whatever's in his mug and takes a big chunk out of one of the cookies stockpiled on an adjacent napkin. "Anyway, real early one Saturday, the academy commandant called the sheriff to report an accidental death. I was sent to make it official.

"When I got there, a young boy was laid out on a bed with a sheet covering him up to his chin. Looked like he was sleeping. When I pulled the sheet away, the boy was naked as a jaybird, and his neck was badly bruised. I told the commandant it looked more like a suicide or murder than an accident."

Tim's cheeks color. "The commandant didn't try to hide his disgust. He lowered his voice to a whisper to tell me how it was. Up to that moment, I'd never heard of autoerotic asphyxiation. The commandant showed me the closet where a staffer had found the boy hanging from a closet rod and the noose that had been around his neck. He pointed to a passel of dirty magazines they'd picked up around the boy's feet. He was adamant. 'The boy didn't mean to hang himself. We have to tell his folks how he died, but there's nothing to be gained in turning this into a lurid, public scandal. We will keep this quiet and preserve Sedgewick's reputation. You are going to rule this death accidental. Understood?'"

I frown. I already know the dead cadet's name. "The boy was Jake Turner, right?"

Tim's eyes never left his hands while he replayed the scene. Now he focuses on me.

"How did you know?"

"A Sedgewick yearbook had his photo edged in black with the dates of his birth and death printed below." I look back at Tim. "I take it there was no autopsy?"

"No. Not the norm for accidental deaths. The academy's version of how Jake Turner died shook me. Later, I worried the poor boy's death might have been staged to cover up a murder. By not asking questions, I worried I'd let a killer go free."

The temperature in the room seems to plummet. Goosebumps race up my arms, and the tiny hairs on the back of my neck prickle.

I almost blurt out, "Not a killer. We're talking killers, plural."

I bite my tongue. No need to fuel Tim's sense of guilt.

"Hindsight is twenty-twenty," I comment. "It's impossible to know what happened. Murder isn't the only possibility. It could have been suicide, and the academy didn't want that verdict public either."

My white lie is for Tim's conscience. Not for a minute do I believe Jake Turner committed suicide. My gut tells me Dan Finley and Chet 'Chevy' Cole had a hand in his death, and now someone's claimed their lives in revenge. But who? Could it be another cadet who was forced to keep silent but is now determined to right a wrong? Are there more victims to come?

I sense General Ronald B. Headley knows the whole story. Even if he wasn't involved, he was there, and he remained Finley's good buddy.

But will the general break three decades of silence?

Tim checks his watch. "I promised to handle a viewing at the funeral home so my son and daughter-in-law can attend my granddaughter's installation into Rainbow Girls. I have to go."

I stand. "We should leave, too. My Honda has you blocked in."

"Nonsense, let Tim out and come right back," Emily responds. "I have a pot roast in the oven, and I know Jeff will be disappointed if Myrt leaves before he can say hello. We don't get company often. You must stay for dinner. We'll eat early. Always do. I promise you'll be on the road by six."

Mom's eyes tell me she hopes I'll agree. I give a slight nod.

"We'd be delighted," Mom answers with a big smile. "We still have some catching up to do, and I promise our dinner conversation will be cheerful. Not a word about suspicious deaths."

Chapter Forty-Four

The Twin

Wednesday, September 30, Late Afternoon

Revenge is helping me cauterize my painful memories. But seeing Sedgewick Military Academy again has pricked at the scars. An attorney delivered an audiotape of John Hart's death-bed confession after his funeral, and I transcribed every word of it. Didn't want to forget a single sentence, though listening to Hart's voice made it somehow worse.

It's been months since I looked at my transcript, though I always carry it with me. I might have made peace with Jake's senseless death if it weren't for Hart's description of the coverup. Cruel. Cowardly. Calculated.

Jake and I never knew our mother. She died minutes after we were born. Dad was all we had. The sordid coverup those teens dreamed up put a pistol to Dad's head. Grief and shame drove him to suicide and condemned me to my uncle's *loving* care.

Now Jake's dead, and Dad's gone. I'm half a twin. Alone. A single.

I read my transcript of Hart's tape. In my head, I hear his voice.

To the Family of Jake Turner—

While I don't know who will receive this letter, I hope my confession will let you remember Jake the way he deserves.

It was maybe two a.m. We—Danny, Chet, Ronnie, and I—were drinking. I almost left my buddies to race to a john when my stomach rebelled with the last swigs of moonshine. Wish I had. I was fifteen, younger than my friends. Eager to prove I was tough.

The year before, I'd been the 'dog' on a leash obeying any orders my upper-class masters barked—rollover ... drink out of the toilet ... raise your leg and piss. My collar was leather, studded with metal. Jake wasn't so lucky. Ronnie fitted him with a choke chain.

At Sedgewick Military Academy, cadets who refused to take part in the hazing became ghosts. Invisible. Ignored. Lord knew, a cadet needed pals to survive.

Jake was scrawny for a fourteen-year-old. He wheezed as the chain cut into his neck. Out of air, he panted and shook his head trying to gain some breathing slack.

I wanted to help but didn't want to be shunned. It's no excuse.

I remember Ronnie saying, "It's time to go outside, bitch." As Ronnie dragged him toward the stairs, Jake strained to keep up on hands and knees. Any tension in the leash made it harder to suck in air.

Danny and Chet ran downstairs to open the dorm's back door. I was to sound the alarm if any faculty turned up. Hardly mattered. Most instructors believed hazing toughened us.

Ronnie started down the stairs with Jake crawling behind doggie-style. As Jake's palms thumped one tread, his kneecaps smacked the tread above. I can still hear the popping noises.

Ronnie weaved side to side. I smirked, thinking our leader couldn't hold his booze either. Midway down the stairs, Ronnie turned, and his foot slipped. He tumbled backward. Didn't stop until he slammed against the wall at the foot of the stairs. The leash still tight in his grip.

Jake was sprawled on his back halfway down the stairs. Motionless. Eyes wide open. I rushed to ask him if he was okay. No answer. His head was at a weird angle. No pulse. I knew right then. Jake was dead.

I put down the transcript. The rest of the details are burned in my mind. How they undressed Jake. Dragged his naked body into his closet. Tightened a noose around his neck to cover the choke chain's telltale marks and hung him from a clothes rod. The boys scattered skin mags to make it look like

Jake was choking himself to achieve a grander orgasm.

Those boys cast Jake as a pleasure-seeking pervert, who screwed up and hung himself.

Now they're paying. They liked theater. I'm making sure their finales command center stage. Only one more to go. It won't be long, Ronnie.

* * *

I can't let emotion trip me up. That's how you make mistakes. To calm myself, I lean back in my car seat and stare at the soybean field. The rain plays hide-and-seek with a huge object. Not a structure. Something mechanical.

A combine harvester, and it has a cutter apron!

My laugh is as spontaneous as my idea. How convenient. Maybe something good will finally come of the three loathsome years spent on my uncle's farm after Dad blew his brains out. Uncle Wade never bothered to take the keys out of the combine's ignition. "It'd take a real idiot to try and steal something this big and slow," he'd say. "A three-legged turtle could catch a combine crawling down a highway. Impossible to hide a monster this big."

Hope the local hayseed who owns or rents this monster shares Uncle Wade's nonchalance. I don't plan to steal the combine, just borrow it.

In this weather, Kylee's Honda won't be coming fast—flat tire or not. Even if the combine's top speed is fifteen miles an hour, should be fast enough to give Kylee a nasty surprise. *The monster materialized out of left field.*

I laugh at my wit.

The morning weather forecast prompted me to bring along my Frog Togs. I put on the lightweight rain suit, cinch the hood, and slog through the mud toward the combine.

Glad there's time for a little refresher on how to use the cutter apron's hydraulic lift.

Chapter Forty-Five

Kylee

Wednesday, September 30, Late Afternoon

It's six o'clock on the dot when we leave the Becks. Wish I'd worn my Thanksgiving pants with the elastic waistband. Pot roast, gravy, and all the trimmings were a mere prelude for Emily's piece de resistance—homemade ice cream and Dutch apple pie.

"You do see that bright yellow exclamation point on your dash, don't you?" Mom asks when we're five miles out of Melsville.

"Yep, it's the tire pressure warning light. Comes on all the time when temperatures fluctuate. A real nuisance in spring and fall. Usually means zip."

Mom frowns. "Hope you're right. Not like our route's littered with gas stations, and you can't count on cellphones in the boonies. If we get a flat, we might have to send smoke signals to summon AAA."

I laugh. "Mom, I do know how to change a tire. Remember, Dad made me practice changing a perfectly good tire before he'd entrust me with the family station wagon. Didn't want me stuck somewhere, flagging down, as he put it, 'who-knew-what-maniac' for help. 'Course back when I got my license, calling AAA on a cellphone wasn't an option. Kids like Grant can't imagine the *hardship* of growing up in a world without texting and Facetime."

I drive another twenty miles. The car is pulling right, hard. *Crap.* The yellow warning light may not be foolin' this time. My tires are almost new. Don't want to ruin one by driving even a little distance on a flat. I slow the car, edge off the asphalt onto a grassy berm. The sloped shoulder makes the car list even more to the right. Wish I'd seen how close we were to a steep ditch before pulling over. The steady rain makes it a bitch to see anything clearly.

"I need to check the tires," I tell Mom. "Think the right front is going flat." I ignore her smirk. Figure she's aching to add an I-told-you-so. She doesn't need to say it. I'm quite aware of my mistake. Had I paid attention when the light first came on, we'd be sitting at a gas station waiting for the tire to be fixed.

I walk around the hood. *Shit.* Definitely flat. Not quite pancake mode, but already at the bread-won't-rise-because-I-forgot-the-yeast flat. To add insult, the rain's beating me like a drum.

I rap on Mom's window. "Stay in the car. It's miserable out here. I'll change the tire as fast as I can."

I barely hear Mom's muffled reply. "I'll try my phone again."

Before opening the trunk, I notice the car's rear end is also listing farther right than it should, even allowing for the slanted berm. Another flat? What the hell? This is my first flat in years, and I have two? It isn't as if I've been cruising through debris-strewn construction sites.

I squat. Sure enough. Though rain has darkened the early evening sky to twilight, there's enough light to spot a shiny circle on the rear tire. I touch it. A nail's firmly embedded.

A shudder frizzes every nerve end in my body. Did someone want to strand us out here?

That's not rational. Nobody followed us to Melsville. Impossible to miss a tail on these rural roads. Just get to work. The faster the better.

With one spare, the front tire wins the flattest contest. I start to change it. Maybe if we limp another mile or two down the road, Mom's cell will find a signal and she can call AAA—or Ted—for help.

Worries for Mom's safety prompted me to stick my Glock in the glove compartment. When I left the Coast Guard, I bought a Glock, the same model as my service sidearm. Toting a handgun isn't part of my everyday routine, but I'm glad I have it tonight. Have visited a firing range infrequently since leaving the Coast Guard. Doesn't mean I forgot how to hit center mass.

Gun or no gun, I plan to heed Dad's long-ago advice and greet anyone who stops with suspicion. Paranoia doesn't mean the next stranger isn't a maniac.

What's that noise? It takes a minute to recognize the rumble of a massive engine. The noise grows steadily louder. Bright lights—too high for a car or pickup—are creeping down the opposite side of the road. The machine's a monster. A semi-trailer?

No, way too slow. I look again. It's actually off the road, moving through a field. A combine? Growing up in Iowa, I have more than a passing acquaintance with combine harvesters.

Thank you, God! I frantically wave my arms to get the attention of whoever's sitting in the cab's high, glassed-in catbird seat. I squint. The lights are too bright to make out the driver's face. Can he see me?

He's come within fifty feet, just across the road. I shout till my throat turns raw. Wind, rain, and engine noise drown out my pleas. Can't decipher my own words. A flashlight. I'll get his attention with a flashlight. I hurry to the driver's side, open the car door, and lean inside.

"Mom, open the glove box and hand me the flashlight."

Mom screams.

Huh? She's looking past me. Eyes wide, mouth open.

"Get in the car. Now!" she yells. "Close the door."

I twist around to see what scared her. The mammoth harvester has pivoted, and, holy shit, it's taking aim at our car.

"What the hell!"

Like a slow-motion nightmare, the monster creeps across the pavement. My mind replays movie scenes of war tanks, rolling over jeeps, crushing boulders, people. Nothing stops them.

But we're not at war. We're in rural South Carolina. Is this a dream, a nightmare?

The icy water coursing down my cheeks convinces me the nightmare's real. The rain along with the giant combine's lights totally destroy my vision. Mom grabs my sleeve and yanks, tearing me away from the machine's mesmerizing, deadly approach. "Get inside," she screams again.

I tumble into the car. Scrabbling behind me, I search for the door handle. I manage a two-fingered jerk. The car's tilt and gravity slam the door.

Does the poor little Honda Fit's frame offer any protection? Halfway across the road, the damn harvester is in an entirely different weight class. How many tons do combines weigh? Who cares? We're talking *tons* plural. If there's a machine BMI, this monster's morbidly obese.

Metal screeches. Mom screams. I scream. Our car shimmies, and we're shaken like French fries in deep fat. My fingers go on a frantic foray, hunting for a piece of my unbuckled seatbelt. Eureka! I'm terrified I'll crush Mom if the shake-and-bake action tosses me to her side. The cancer's left her so thin, so frail. I squeeze the webbing in a death grip.

The harvester backs off, and my side of the car thuds back to earth. Is the psychotic farmer leaving? Please!

The rain sounds like machine-gun fire on the metal roof. But the roar of the monster machine's revving engine is louder. Its white-hot headlamps blind like camera strobes. I see only spots when I look away.

God in Heaven, he's not leaving. Trying for a better angle?

Wham!

The Honda bounces like a picked-on carnival bumper car. My fist tightens on my seatbelt-life preserver. *Oh, shit!* I feel the car levitate. My side rises off the ground. No! No! He's going to roll us into that deep ditch. We're going to turtle.

Despite my seatbelt grip, my upper body slides relentlessly toward Mom, who's buckled in place. My feet flail above my head. I kick my left leg. Can I hook a foot on the steering wheel? Please don't let me crash on top of Mom.

The car teeters, and rolls. My body crashes against the roof. My head explodes in pain.

* * *

I wake to darkness. Where am I? I blink. Oh, no. I make out a car seat—above my head. My car's upside down. Memory, reality, and dread rush in. I listen. No growl of a monster engine, and Mom isn't screaming anymore.

My heart gallops. I search for Mom in the darkness. Why can't I see her? I'm afraid to call out. Afraid there'll be no answer.

I swallow the lump in my throat.

"Mom, are you okay?"

Chapter Forty-Six

"Glad you're coming round. You hit your head while you were bouncing around like a pinball. Knocked you out cold, but only for a couple minutes. Since I didn't smell any gas and your pulse was steady, I let you be. Not like I could have hauled you out of the car if I wanted to. You're not a svelte feather-weight like yours truly."

Mom's voice is clear but muted. As if we're in a tunnel. Where is she? Not in the car. Guess I'm still dazed.

Knuckles rap on glass. I sort of make out the pale oval of Mom's face, inches from a side window.

"Got my door open, but doubt I could budge the driver's side door," she adds. "When the car flipped, my side landed uphill. Scoot your butt my way. Passenger door's open enough for you to crawl out. Help's on the way. Imagine Ted is, too."

My head feels like someone's swinging a ball-peen hammer inside my skull. Way worse than a hangover. But the fog's lifting. Mom's acting like all danger's past. Is it? I can't see much, but I can listen. With the exception of Mom's voice, all I hear is a croaking chorus of frogs. The deafening drumbeat of rain is gone, replaced with a gentle pitter-patter.

Using my elbows and legs I scuttle toward the passenger door. The cool, rain-scented air prompts a shiver. I slide out feet first and drop down. Mud sucks at my shoes, and I topple doing a less than graceful face plant. Mud now cakes my clothes. I wipe my slimy hands on my untucked shirttail.

Multiple portions of my body lodge angry complaints. But my night vision's improving. Mom waves her hand, and the flashlight she's holding pulses light hither and yon. I blink. The strobe-like effect makes me nauseous.

"Are you okay?" I repeat. "Is that homicidal farmer gone?"

Mom harrumphs. "Don't know who was driving that combine, but it sure wasn't any local farmer. Fortunately, whoever it was, is gone.

"To answer your other question, I'm a lot better off than you. You turned into a Mexican jumping bean when the car rolled. Lucky, you didn't conk me in the head. Seatbelt kept me from joining you. Undoing my belt while hanging upside down like a bat proved a challenge. But not enough to drive me bat shit."

Mom's babbling. A sign she's more worried than she wants me to realize. I rub my throbbing temple. Something sticky coats my fingers. Blood. A trickle, not a gush. Wonder what was sharp enough to cut my scalp.

"You said help's on the way?" I manage.

"Yep," Mom replies. "Used the flashlight to flag down a car just before you came to. Pocketed your gun in case we'd stumbled into some twilight zone. Not a worry. The driver was a nice, white-haired lady, who looked even more ancient than me. She promised to send help the minute she reached town. Gave her Ted's phone number and asked her to call him, too. Figured this car won't be going anyplace soon."

Mom stops talking as a siren's wail shatters the silence. In minutes, the deserted road transforms into an all too familiar traffic accident scene. Lights flash and what seems like an army of earnest men spill from a firetruck, a sheriff's SUV, and an ambulance.

Mom sighs as the ambulance medics head our way. "While you weren't knocked out long, I am worried about a concussion. You're going straight to a hospital, and I won't brook any argument."

As the medics reach us, Mom assumes bossy nurse mode and orders them to examine me first. The first responder who pokes and prods me is a middle-aged woman. She shares Mom's presumption that being knocked out means concussion, and I need an MRI to assess how bad it is.

Nurse Mom informs the EMT checking her vitals that she's no worse than before the accident. She manages to shoo him away.

Over my strenuous objections, two EMTs join forces to trundle me off to the ambulance.

"Don't be a pill," Mom scolds. "I'm sure the nice sheriff will drop me at the hospital to hold your hand as soon as I've answered his questions."

I'm too wet, achy, and exhausted to keep protesting. Though I haven't the faintest idea where the nearest hospital might be, I give. Maybe I'll just take a little nap en route.

Chapter Forty-Seven

An ambulance attendant tells me I'm headed to Sumter, South Carolina, where I'm assured the Prisma-run hospital is first-rate. Having never been transported in an ambulance before, I'm surprised at the bumpy, jarring ride. Most occupants must either be unconscious or in too much pain to bitch about it.

At the hospital, I'm whisked to an examination room, then handed over to an MRI tech. I'm feeling the effects of whatever relaxation elixir they gave me. I feel like giggling at the notion I need my head examined.

The problem with hospitals, particularly if the docs are worried about brain damage, is you're not allowed to sleep. Just when you're feeling drowsy and comfy, a nurse takes your blood pressure or shines a bright light in your eyes. I'm tired and irritable. I want to go home.

It seems forever and a day before I hear familiar voices outside my room. "What did the MRI show?" Mom prods.

Mumble, mumble. I can't make out an answer.

"Tomorrow?" I'm sure it's Ted's voice.

I want to scream, "Hey, I'm awake. Don't talk about me behind my bedpan."

Finally, the door cracks open, and Mom and Ted enter.

"Mild concussion." Mom smiles, answering my unspoken question. "They insist on keeping you overnight, but, if all goes well, they'll release you in the morning."

Ted and Mom choose opposite sides of my bed. Mom squeezes my hand. "You'll be right as rain. Other than the mild concussion, nothing's broken. You sprained an ankle and bruised your ribs. No doubt you'll be sore."

"Myrt and I checked into a hotel about a mile away," Ted adds. "I'll drive you home to Beaufort in the morning. I had Frank postpone any HOA work. He's driving up here to chauffeur Myrt to your Aunt Linda's house."

Mom rolls her eyes. "I still can't believe you talked me into showing up on my sister's doorstep without so much as a toothbrush."

"I'm sure Linda will fix you right up, though you're too skinny to wear her clothes. Imagine two of you could fit in one of her outfits," Ted says.

The mental image makes me chuckle, and instantly reminds me I have bruised ribs. Any temptation to laugh again disappears.

"What time is it?" I ask. The medical pickpockets stripped me of all jewelry right after they filched my clothes. Yeah, I'll get my watch and clothes back, but I feel next to naked in the scratchy hospital gown.

"It's eight o'clock," Ted answers. "Time to deliver Myrt to the hotel. She's had a rough day, too."

"Wait. Not so fast. Do they know who was driving that killer combine?"

"Too long a story to tell you now," Ted answers. "I promise I'll fill you in later."

I'm ready to have a hissy fit when he leans in, gently kisses my cheek, and whispers, "Don't go postal. Soon as I get Myrt settled, I'll come back."

I'm pissed and feeling downright surly. Someone could have killed us. I deserve to know what's going on. I'm tired of people telling me to behave. I'm ready to let Ted have it when I look in his eyes. His subtle nod toward Mom makes me really see her. Exhaustion puckers the skin around her tired, bloodshot eyes. She needs to be in bed.

I slip his watch off his wrist. "I'm timing you," I whisper before I let his arm go.

In under an hour, Ted's back. He pulls a chair up to my bed and takes my hand.

"Visiting hours are over. Not sure I should have sweet-talked that cute nurse into letting me see you. But I figured your blood pressure would climb if I didn't come back with a quick update. And I do mean quick. Hold the questions. We'll have plenty of time to dissect what happened on the drive to Beaufort."

I sigh. "Okay. Let's hear it."

"The sheriff talked to the farmer who rented that combine. When he saw the weather turning ugly, he left it in the field with the keys in the ignition A farrier, who spent the afternoon in his barn, gives him a solid alibi. Another neighbor recalled seeing a black BMW abandoned on the side of the road near the combine late in the afternoon. The neighbor figured the BMW owner had car trouble and hitched a ride. Assumed a tow truck would haul the car off once the weather improved."

"I can't believe someone followed us to Melsville," I begin.

Ted touches his fingers to my lips. "We'll try to make sense of all this come morning. I don't want to leave Myrt alone for long. You'll be safe in the hospital."

"I—" My answer is smothered by Ted's lips. A kiss, and it's not the brotherly-type peck on the cheek.

His eyes twinkle when he comes up for air. I'm too astounded to say boo.

"Always wondered if there was a way to make you stop talking." He smiles. "Glad I discovered the secret."

He leaves before I recover enough to protest.

Hey, what do you know? Ted really is a good kisser.

Chapter Forty-Eight

The Twin

Thursday, October 1, Morning

Thanks to daylight savings time, it's seven-thirty before it's bright enough for Mona Young to start her golf cart inspection rounds. That's good and bad news for me. Good since I'm not an early morning person, and I didn't get to bed until midnight. Bad because a lot of Marshview residents are out and about now, walking their dogs or en route to tee times or breakfast dates. Since I run most days before work, I know the HOA's morning routines. My rental condo is less than a quarter-mile from the golf club.

I often spot Mona on patrol with a jumbo coffee in her golf cart's cup holder and a small notebook and pen handy for note-taking. Her mission? To find at least one HOA covenant infraction to report or, failing that, some individual faux pas worthy of ridicule. As a transient, I don't count, and haven't made it onto one of her lists.

Mona smiles brightly and chirps hello in her high-pitched voice to every person she encounters—especially ones she reviles. Clueless newcomers peg the old bat as a cheerful soul until experience wises them up.

It's a game to her—trying to force folks who detest her into returning pleasantries. If they refuse, their churlish behavior is called to everyone's attention. If they bend to social pressure and greet her, Mona mocks them and celebrates the victory with her cronies.

Getting inside Mona's head might prove interesting from a psychological point of view. People with her pathology often consider themselves model citizens, no mental health issues. It's their victims who are more likely to seek help dealing with stress and anger.

I hear a golf cart stop at the front of the house I selected for my ambush. Marshview has established a list of plants approved for landscaping to make the community look cohesive. The owner of this second home had the audacity to bring cuttings from beloved, but unapproved, plants at her primary residence to see if they'd take root.

Yesterday, I overheard Mona say she bet the owner would remove the offending plants from her front yard and replant them in back where they'd be harder to see.

Will Mona do what I hope? Exit her golf cart and follow the pavers around back?

I hear footsteps, and Mona, the beanpole, comes into view. Hard to guess her age. Maybe seventy-five. While she's sidestepped some of aging's physical curses like flabby upper arms and stooped posture, her weathered leather skin and dye job sell her out. Looking at her matte black hair is akin to staring into one of the universe's black holes. No light can escape.

Mona hasn't put on sunglasses. Good. I'm told she wore bifocals until two years ago when cataract and lens replacement surgery brought her beady eyesight to twenty-twenty. All the better to see HOA violations and people's flaws.

My plan is to reduce her visual acuity for the good of her neighborhood.

I spring from behind a hedge and zap Mona with my stun gun. She folds like a cheap tent. My ski mask should prevent her from recognizing me. Important, since she'll survive.

While she's immobile, I wad one of the HOA's paint color guides and cram it in her mouth. Then, I wrap duct tape around her head to hold it in place and gag her. I use zip ties to secure her hands and feet.

Once she's nicely trussed, I steady my pistol. Smith and Wesson makes this version for paintball aficionados. It's loaded with neon pink and orange balls. Her eyes are wide open when I fire the first ball. I'm almost certain she blinked before it splattered. Amazing how quickly our nerves fire to protect our eyes.

Nonetheless, Mona's not going to be seeing clearly for quite some time.

I'm about ready to leave when I see a pair of hedge clippers left near the path. Why not? I loosen random hanks of her black-hole hairdo and whack them off.

Finally, I walk to the front of the house and glance up and down the street to make sure no one's around. In the clear, I fire the remaining paintballs at her golf cart. The windshield and hood are now nicely streaked with Day-Glo orange and neon pink.

With one of those inverted markers landscapers use to show flower-bed perimeters, I spray a message. "Down with HOA Tyrants!"

I leave all my tools, except the stun gun, and stuff my gloves and ski mask in my fanny pack. Time to run home. Wonder how long it will be before Mona manages to crawl to the street or a passerby sees the golf cart graffiti and looks for her?

Chapter Forty-Nine

Kylee

Thursday, October 1, Morning

I grumble as Ted wheels me to his car. No matter what you're in for, hospitals insist you leave in a wheelchair.

My muddy duds add to my surly disposition. My pants didn't wash themselves overnight, and they smell like mold. What the heck was in that mud? Whatever it is, I'm leaving a trail of it. With every move more flakes off my britches. Still preferable to my other option—exiting in a hospital gown and flashing Ted with my bare butt.

On the bright side, my headache is now a dull throb, despite my lack of sleep. While nurses take the blame for waking me every time I managed to nod off, my brain bears considerable responsibility for my insomnia. I couldn't switch off its jumbled attempts to make sense of the combine attack.

"You comfy?" Ted asks as he buckles his seatbelt and glances my way.

He's grinning. I want to punch him.

"What's so funny?" I snarl.

"You. Haven't seen you in full-out pout since your dad grounded you for riding with Bill Lundquist the night he got a DUI."

He laughs. "Plus, your hair is really cute."

I give Ted my best glare, and self-consciously comb my fingers through my hair. A waste. Hitting a pillow with wet hair is a foolproof recipe for wayward curls and annoying cowlicks. Mix in mud and you have a complete disaster.

"Did Mom try to wiggle out of leaving for Aunt Linda's?" I ask as the car speeds up.

"Surprisingly, no. Maybe it has to do with her chauffeur. When Frank arrived bright and early, she was all smiles. Perhaps a mutual attraction? Frank always goes out of his way to be in the office if he knows Myrt's planning to visit."

Wow. The possibility of a romantic attraction never crossed my mind. Mom's been a widow for five years. Why wouldn't she be attracted to a nice widower like Frank?

"Myrt demanded a quid-pro-quo for being bundled off to Atlanta without a suitcase," Ted says, interrupting my train of thought. "She made me promise to move in with you until our psycho killer is safely behind bars."

What the ...? My whole body tenses as if I've been sucker-punched.

"No way. I'm not a child nor an idiot. You can't make decisions for me. I'm better trained to handle threats than you are."

Ted's laugh is gleeful, reigniting my desire to pummel him.

"Myrt suggests you think of our new living arrangement as protecting me. After all, two heads—and two guns—are better than one. I'm a good shot, you know, and we pledged to keep Myrt's hellcats safe, didn't we?"

I bite my lips to keep quiet until I can make my voice calm. Ted's a logical guy. He should see this is a really bad idea. "The River Rat is comfortable for one person. There's not enough space on my boat for two people, two cats, and a litter box to coexist."

Ted shakes his head. "When Myrt made her roommate ultimatum, I suggested you and the kitties bunk at my house. She pointed out that renovations make my place a security sieve. Too many unsecured points of entry. In contrast, the River Rat's easy to secure because it's so compact. And, don't forget, your dad taught both of us to sail. I can be your first mate if we need to leave Beaufort in a hurry."

Crap. He has a point. But having Ted onboard restricts my options. Say I decide to pay General Headley a visit? I'd prefer to keep him in the dark, provide Ted with plausible deniability should I screw up. Living together makes it impossible to keep secrets.

"We're getting ahead of ourselves," I calmly counter. "We need to figure out the who and why of the combine attack. I assume Mom filled you in on my Sedgewick research and the retired coroner's story about that dead cadet."

Ted glances in my direction. "She did, and I agree it's likely that Dan Finley and Chevy Cole were killed to avenge that boy's death. If so, the killer has good reason to torpedo or, at a minimum, slow your investigation. But, if you were yesterday's target, how did the killer know you'd be visiting Sedgewick? You didn't warn the academy you were coming, and you're convinced you weren't followed."

I close my eyes.

"Only three people knew about our trip—you, me, and Mom. Maybe Mom told folks at the animal shelter why she couldn't volunteer yesterday."

Mom answers on the first ring.

"Hi, Dear. Hope you're not calling to gripe about Ted staying with you. Frank and I just stopped in a nice little restaurant for breakfast, and I don't want an argument to ruin my appetite."

I look heavenward. "Just a quick question. Did you tell anyone about my plan to visit Sedgewick Military Academy?"

"Of course, not," she huffs. "You must think I'm a real ninny."

"Okay. What reason did you give the animal shelter for skipping your shift yesterday?"

"Told 'em I was driving to Melsville to visit an old friend from Iowa. Didn't mention you and didn't say word one about Sedgewick."

"Okay, thanks. Enjoy breakfast. Call tonight after you get settled at Aunt Linda's."

I disconnect and turn to Ted. "Mom told the animal shelter she was visiting Melsville. but didn't mention that I'd be with her. The killer could have put two and two together, given that the military academy is just outside the town. This ups the odds our killer has some connection to the animal shelter."

Ted tightens his grip on the steering wheel. "I agree. The combine attacker must either spend time there or he knows a gossip who does. But this connection doesn't rule out the possibility Myrt was the target, and not you."

I shake my head. "We were in my Honda Fit, not Mom's SUV. If the killer was waiting for Mom and didn't follow us, how did he know to target my Honda? That witness sighting of an empty, black BMW near the combine makes me want to learn more about Brent. I saw him leave Tenyke Townhouses in a black BMW."

"I'll run a background check once I have his last name. Lyn probably knows it since she occasionally volunteers at the shelter. Maybe she can get a list of volunteers to crosscheck against Hullis fanatics."

"What kind of info will Brent's background check include?"

"Nothing in-depth. But it should tell us if Brent attended Sedgewick, and might hint at any family ties to the cadet. It'll also turn up arrests and convictions."

We ride in silence for several minutes as I ponder how to pursue other leads.

"I'll research the dead cadet," I say. "Old news stories and his obituary may gloss over how he died, but they should mention his hometown and surviving relatives."

"Good idea. It's after ten now so Robin and Lyn should be at work. I'll call and get the ball rolling on that background check."

Ted taps his steering wheel and makes the call. Lyn answers.

"Great to hear your voice," Ted says. "How's your migraine? With Frank out-of-town, I'm glad you came in."

I half-listen as he updates her on my wrecked car and Frank's chauffeuring assignment. Ted adds he'll return to the office around lunchtime, and Lyn gushes, "That's wonderful."

You'd think Ted was returning from a war zone.

Lyn's Pollyanna act seriously irritates me. The human chameleon slips in and out of whatever role promises the most atta-girls.

Lyn says my name, and I tune in.

"I told Roger Roper that Kylee could attend a board meeting at two-thirty this afternoon. Is that okay?" Lyn asks.

Oh, joy. Ted looks at me, and I nod.

Finally, Ted quizzes Lyn about Brent. We learn his last name is Jackson. He's fifty years old and moved to Beaufort a year ago. He works for an accounting firm owned by his uncle—none other than Cliff Jackson, president of the Hullis Island Board. Lyn says she'll request a backgrounder on Brent.

"It'll be at least two hours before I get to the office," Ted adds. "Have some errands to run."

It's lunchtime when we reach Beaufort's outer limits.

"Want to pick up takeout before we head to the office?" he asks.

"No. Just drop me at the marina. I can't sit in these filthy clothes another minute, and I desperately need to shower and wash my hair. If you intend to live aboard the River Rat, I want a leisurely turn in my bathroom before I'm forced to share."

Ted smiles. "Deal. Imagine Lyn, Robin, and, most certainly, Roger Roper will appreciate you showering. Can you make the two-thirty appointment Lyn set?"

I frown. "Jeez, I forgot. I don't have a car, and I can't run that fast. I could sail there but it would take two hours."

"Not a problem." Ted smiles. "As I recall, your dad made you learn to drive a straight shift. Take my old Ford pickup. I'll bribe one of the men putting new tile in at my house to drive it to the marina and leave the keys in the office."

The image of me arriving at the Satin Sands clubhouse in Ted's smoke-belching rattletrap makes me grin. Fingers crossed Roger Roper will witness my classy entrance.

Chapter Fifty

I t's 2:25 p.m. when I pull Ted's rusty pickup into Satin Sands. Sadly, Roper isn't around to see my ride. I'm freshly scrubbed and presentable, assuming sticklers give me a pass on damp ringlets. A hairdryer is among the luxuries this boat owner forgoes to conserve space.

I enter the clubhouse meeting room and stop dead in my tracks. What the...? Deputy Nick Ibsen and Roger Roper are side-by-side, yucking it up. A sinking feeling tells me their high-five frivolity has everything to do with taking a common enemy down a notch or two.

"Come in. You're the last to arrive." Roper checks his watch and frowns. *Disappointed he can't chastise me for being a minute late?*

I nod and smile at Freckles and Sparky, the only board members willing to make eye contact. Both friendly directors look dejected.

Roper raps a knuckle on the table. "Let's begin. I invited Deputy Ibsen to join us because he's a *true* authority on local crime and can offer expert advice on how communities can best protect homeowners. He's reviewed my suggestions and enthusiastically endorses them. Deputy, please share your valuable insights."

Ibsen stands and puffs out his chest. "First, Roger, thanks for inviting me. It's a pleasure to serve Beaufort County's citizens and have an opportunity to be proactive and help *prevent* crimes instead of solving them after the fact."

I resist rolling my eyes and gagging. *Since when have you solved any crimes?*

Ibsen lets his gaze linger a moment on every face in the room. When he gets to me, he smirks. "Beaufort is a large, sprawling county, and, try as we might, the Sheriff's Department can't always reach crime scenes as fast as we'd like. While all citizens deserve to feel safe, people living in gated communities with video surveillance have a substantial leg up because criminals prefer soft targets like Satin Sands. Gates make it harder for criminals to enter, and even the dumbest thugs know video surveillance can ID them later if they're not caught in the act."

Yeah, and most thugs know to wear ball caps and keep their heads down as they pass cameras. Cool it. Don't spout off. Be polite and patient. Wait for my turn.

"I've lived here fifteen years," Sparky interjects. "No gates, no guards, no security cameras, and we've experienced virtually no crime. I feel as safe walking down our streets as I do in gated communities like Hullis Island."

Freckles vigorously nods. "Despite its gates and guards, Hullis Island is reeling from a horrendous murder. Satin Sands has never had a homicide, or even a burglary. The sheriff's investigation found no evidence that Alex's snakebite was anything more than an accident. Why spend a fortune on security systems we don't need?"

Deputy Ibsen strokes his chin and glances my way. "It's true the sheriff could not find evidence the snake attack was premeditated. That's not the same as confirming it was accidental. I agree with Roger. The snake victim's environmental activism created enemies. They could easily have entered Satin Sands and cleverly trapped a copperhead in her netting.

"The Hullis murder is a different situation," he continues. "The prime suspects are neighbors, not some criminal who snuck through the island's gates. Note, too, that Welch HOA Management oversees the Hullis Security force, and has recently shown its inability to prevent neighborhood disputes from escalating into lethal warfare."

"That's preposterous." I stand so quickly my rolling chair bangs the wall. "There's strong evidence the Hullis murder had zero to do with a community disagreement."

Ibsen's smug smile makes me want to strangle him. "Sorry, *sweetheart*, but your attempt to scare up an alternate murder motive for some homicidal stranger is wishful thinking. Given the facts, any intelligent law enforcement officer would draw the same conclusion, Welch HOA Management failures are a primary factor in the recent HOA crime wave."

"*Sweetheart?* How dare you—"

"Sit down, Miss Kane." Roper cuts me off. "You do not have the floor. Nor is this board interested in your theories or half-baked opinions. You're present to inform your employer that Satin Sands is today terminating its contract with Welch HOA Management."

Sparky stands. "Wait just a minute, Roper. You're not king. The board has not voted to terminate the contract."

"You are correct. It's time for a vote." Roper smiles. "Ira, would you like to make a motion?"

Lap Dog grips a sheet of paper like it's the Declaration of Independence, and clears his throat. The motion is typed. *Want to bet whose computer spewed it out?*

"I move that the Board terminate its contract with Welch HOA Management immediately," Lap Dog aka Ira reads. "Furthermore, I move that our Board authorizes Roger Roper as Board President to solicit bids from property managers to replace Welch HOA Management and to sign contracts to install entrance gates and video surveillance systems with a cost not to exceed fifty-thousand dollars."

Splenda smiles like a Cheshire cat. "I second the motion. As a real estate professional, I'm confident these actions will enhance resident safety and increase all our property values."

"Hold on—" Freckles bangs the table with her fist.

Roper ignores her. "All in favor of the motion?"

Three hands shoot up and simultaneously voice loud "Ayes."

What a shock. The meeting is a mere formality. Roper had the votes in his pocket. No discussion.

"The motion passes," Roper proclaims.

"You're violating our covenants," Freckles says. "There's a five-thousand-dollar cap on how much the board can spend on improvements without giving homeowners a chance to vote."

"Ah, but our treasurer verified we have sufficient funds in our reserves to cover the cost of these improvements. That's one reason we don't need a vote. It won't cost owners a penny. I also checked with an attorney friend. I'm paraphrasing here, but, under Board duties, our covenants assign directors the responsibility of maintaining the property for the safe enjoyment of all owners. We're just doing our duty."

"This isn't over," Sparky says.

"Want to bet?" Roper gloats. "Do I have a motion to adjourn the meeting?"

"So moved," Splenda says.

"Second," Lap Dog adds.

"All in favor?"

Gee, another shocker. The ayes have it.

I'm fuming, but see no point in getting into a row. Ted's the diplomat. I just need to report what happened. Hopefully, his contract with Satin Sands guards against a dismissal without notice or compensation.

Freckles takes my arm. "Would you like to join me for a drink?"

"You bet," I answer.

As I leave the room with Freckles, Ibsen grabs my arm.

"Don't even think about interfering again in my investigations," he says. "You and your boyfriend need to find another hobby and leave solving crimes to professionals. You have enough problems."

I wrench my arm free and clamp my mouth shut.

While I'm not a gifted or frequent user of cuss words, my Coast Guard years equipped me with a salty vocabulary suitable for any occasion. I mentally scream a stream of expletives.

"You don't have high blood pressure, do you?" Freckles asks. "Your face is redder than a fire engine. Let's get out of here."

Chapter Fifty-One

As Freckles and I walk toward the clubhouse bar, my anger subsides enough to make room for guilt. Would Ted or Lyn, experts in diplomacy and psychology, have outmaneuvered Roper?

I touch Freckle's arm.

"Will you give me a rain check on that drink? I need to fill Ted in before he's ambushed by a reporter. I have a horrid feeling Nick may be giving his pet TV journalist a scoop that Satin Sands fired Welch HOA Management."

Freckles nods. "Wouldn't doubt it. Roper, his director acolytes, and that deputy orchestrated how the meeting would go long before it started."

"Yeah, and if Nick and Roper come to the bar to celebrate, I'll be sorely tempted to sock the deputy in the jaw. That would only make things worse."

"Yes, but it would be oh so satisfying." Freckles smiles. "Promise me you'll call soon for that raincheck. I'd like your opinion of Roger's plans for gates and cameras. I'm going to send a letter to every owner. Since Roger refuses to hold open meetings like we used to do, folks only hear his version. Meeting minutes are a joke. No transparency.

"The minutes will report the deputy's opinions and the board's vote. Period. Scare tactics may well convince owners we'll all be bludgeoned to death or knee-deep in anacondas if we don't fund his favorite security add-ons."

I open my briefcase and hand Freckles three typed pages. "Here's my report on gate and camera considerations, pros and cons. Look it over. Even if Satin Sands opts for gates and video surveillance, there are better options than Roper's expensive boondoggles."

"Thanks." Freckles kisses my cheek. "Don't let the blowhards get you down. I've been around the block. The likes of Deputy Ibsen and Roger Roper are eventually undone by their own selfish arrogance. Just hope I'm still breathing when they go up in flames."

* * *

My stomach knots. My unbending resistance to petty tyrants has cost Ted a client. Maybe several. What if the Satin Sands firing causes a domino effect? Deputy Ibsen will spread the word. Make it sound as if communities are wising up to Welch HOA Management failings.

Not hard to imagine the Hullis Island board viewing the Satin Sands dismissal as permission to do the same. The Hullis directors must resent Ted's reticence to approve their autocratic deer solution. Though he hasn't publicly opposed them, the directors know the woman suing them is someone he considers family.

I straighten my shoulders and walk into the office. Lyn is sitting in Ted's chair. Why?

"Hi, Kylee, Your Satin Sands meeting was short." She attempts a chuckle. "Not sure I recall Roger Roper ever winding up a board meeting this quickly. He enjoys having an audience. How did it go?"

"Not well." I don't elaborate. "Where's Ted?"

"He left for Marshview half an hour ago. Seems a woman was attacked there this morning. No attempt at murder this time, but vicious. Someone fired paintballs at her face at very close range. She's in the hospital. May have some permanent eye damage. He's meeting with the board."

"Should I go out there?"

Lyn's incredulous look tells me she thinks I'll make matters worse. "Ted said he'd handle the situation by himself. He has a good relationship with the Marshview board. Oh, he also said he'll drive on to Hullis and pick up Myrt's cats after the meeting. He'll bring them to your boat around six o'clock."

"Crap, I need to warn him not to take any calls from reporters—especially if they've gotten word of the Marshview attack."

"Why?" Lyn's precisely-tweezed eyebrows shoot up.

"Satin Sands fired Welch HOA Management. Deputy Ibsen, a guest at the meeting, provided ammunition for my summary execution and the company's dismissal. All choreographed in advance. My fault. Didn't see it coming."

Lyn's frown deepens. No disagreement with my assignment of guilt.

"Text Ted," she snaps. "He usually checks texts before returning phone calls. You can share the sordid details when he drops off your mother's cats. I just hope Satin Sands isn't a harbinger of things to come. We never had a problem with Deputy Ibsen before. I've dealt with him on several occasions, and he's been very helpful. You should apologize and mend fences with Nick."

When hell freezes over...

Lyn's unsolicited advice on cozying up with Ibsen boosts my annoyance with the in-house psychologist. Her professional skills aren't all that red hot if she can't interpret my death-ray glare as a sign to shut up. Maybe she's trying reverse psychology and wants to egg me on? If so, she's doing a superb job. I want to *find* new ways to irritate the deputy—and Lyn.

"To mend fences with Ibsen, I'd need to quit seeing Ted," I blurt. "I used to date Nick, and he's jealous. My relationship with Ted isn't negotiable. By the way, Ted's not 'dropping off' Mom's cats tonight, he and the cats are moving in with me."

Lyn's gaping mouth and sky-high brows telegraph her horror. While it's exactly the reaction I wanted, I'm ashamed. I implied Ted and I are an item. We're not. Now, I'm caught. To recant, I'd have to explain why Ted will be living aboard the River Rat. I don't trust Lyn enough to share my suspicions about a Sedgewick link to the murders, and Mom's fear the killer is now after me.

I zip my lips. I'll confess to Ted. Let him correct the impression. It's only a major faux pas if he has romantic feelings for Lyn.

God, I hope he's not attracted to that woman.

I suck at texting on my flip phone's teensy keyboard, but leave a brief text and back it up with a succinct voicemail. I'll grovel in person tonight. I chat with Robin a few minutes, then head to the front door.

"Where are you going?" Lyn's abrupt tone is barely civil.

"Robin knows how to reach me if anything urgent comes up. Otherwise, I'm off the clock. One advantage of being a consultant, no set hours."

I'm halfway out the door. "Fine," Lyn snaps. "Thought you might want to see the background check on Brent Jackson. Ted said you were concerned about his association with your mother."

I step back inside. "Yes, I would like to see it."

Lyn hands over a single sheet of paper. "Not much there. Only so many sources a company can reference without the subject's Social Security number or his permission."

She's right. The info is skimpy. Current and previous addresses are provided for the past several years, all in the Lowcountry. But, Tenyke Townhomes, where I saw him exiting his black Beemer, isn't on the list.

Scanning the printout, I see he was born in Atlanta and has a B.S. in Accounting from the University of South Carolina. A ten-year marriage ended in divorce three years ago, and his only criminal misstep—at least where he was caught—is the Drunk and Disorderly conviction that led to his community service at the animal shelter.

I give the sheet back to Lyn without comment. "Thanks. See you later."

I leave. Two hours until Ted arrives at the marina. Plenty of time for some in-person snooping. First stop, the family accounting firm where Brent Jackson works.

* * *

The small Jackson Accounting office is located near Beaufort's downtown public library. I've walked by dozens of times and never noticed the mundane storefront. A bell tinkles as I enter. Brent, phone to his ear, stands behind a glassed-in partition and motions me inside. He puts his hand over the receiver. "Be right with you. Have a seat."

True to his word, Brent leaves his cubicle to greet me in under two minutes.

"We've met." He shakes my hand. "You're Myrt Kane's daughter, right? She's such a delight."

"Good memory. Yes, I'm Kylee Kane. I'm planning to obtain a private investigator's license and open shop in Beaufort. Thought I'd ask your opinion of what type of corporate organization would be best from a tax and accounting standpoint."

My private investigator mention fails to rattle Brent. He smiles and invites me to sit. His quick, practiced spiel on the tax considerations of Sole Proprietorship, LLCs, and C corporations tells me he's no dummy.

"Do you have plans for dinner?" Brent grins. "I'd love to learn more about what a PI does and how she investigates. You like Italian? There's a new restaurant, Luigi's, on Lady's Island I've been dying to try."

Okay, is he hitting on me or trying charm to discover if I'm investigating him?

"I'd love to, but I already have plans for tonight."

"Tomorrow night then?"

Uh, how do I gracefully wiggle out? Hmm. Maybe I shouldn't. Ted won't care if I leave him on his own for dinner tomorrow. A perfect opportunity to see if Brent has anything to hide.

"I'd like that," I answer. "Could we make it around seven and meet at the restaurant? I'm not sure where or how long I'll be working tomorrow."

"Sure. By the way, how's Myrt? Haven't seen her in a few days. You must know my uncle—he's president of the Hullis Island board—isn't too fond of your mother. But I think she's terrific."

"Me, too. Mom's visiting her sister. She'll be out of town for a week or two."

Oops. I've inherited Mom's tendency to offer information before it's asked. We left her SUV parked at Hullis to make it look like she's home.

Thinking about Mom's car brings me back to Brent's vehicle, a black BMW, which may or may not have been abandoned yesterday near a lethal combine harvester.

"By the way, I think I saw you at Tenyke Townhouses. You drive a black BMW, right?"

"Yep, that was probably me. I keep the books for a client, who runs a marketing company out of her townhome."

Good, I can check out his excuse for being there.

"Do you like your Beemer?" I persist. "I've heard they're great cars. In fact, I'm thinking about getting one." *And I'm getting good at faking car-buying urges.*

"Want mine?" Brent chuckles. "I have an itch to get a sports car, a convertible. Unfortunately, the itch won't get scratched anytime soon. But, if you're interested in a used BMW, I can put you in touch with someone who's thinking of selling hers. Your mom probably knows her, Lyn Adair, she volunteers at the animal shelter, too."

I'm sure my mouth falls open. I snap it shut, and try for a neutral expression. Lyn?

"Uh, I know Lyn. I'll ask how much she wants for her BMW."

Yes, indeedy, I will certainly quiz Lyn about her black BMW. Starting with, why have I never seen it parked at Ted's office? Does the woman keep two cars?

Brent's phone rings, offering me an excellent excuse to mosey on out.

I wave as I get up from my chair. "See you tomorrow night at Luigi's."

Chapter Fifty-Two

The Twin

Thursday, October 1, Afternoon

Damn it all to hell. Bashing Kylee's compact and dumping it roof first into a ravine should have kept the bitch out of commission a few days. Can't count on hospitals anymore. Don't know why they even bother to have beds. Pretty soon they'll offer drive-through appendectomies.

At least, I'm warned. Kylee's blabbermouth mother called the shelter to tell everyone about the wreck. She boasted her daughter wouldn't let a minor concussion keep her from returning to work today. Wonder why Myrt takes such pride in her daughter's hard head?

Fortunately, my research on the general is complete. I can move up my timetable.

I worried I wouldn't be able to use an HOA motive for Headley's murder. Since he's occupied his new home for little more than a year, I figured he hadn't had time to enrage any neighbors or join any spats. I wrongly assumed a man recently pardoned and released from the brig would keep a low profile.

Not Headley. He flies gargantuan Re-Elect Prudmont flags on his boat and his home balcony. Guess he thinks a presidential pardon gives him a get-out-of-jail-card for future as well as past offenses. If anything, Headley seems to flout his deviations from social norms.

His bad-boy behavior offered me choices. He's alienated ecology-conscious neighbors, feminists, and political foes during his brief Jade Pointe tenure. No small accomplishment given his estate's large acreage. Hard to piss off neighbors when your house isn't even visible beyond your property lines. Still Headley's succeeded.

First, he violated salt-marsh protections, filling in wetlands to eliminate what he felt was a haven for mosquitoes that buzzed his firepit and outdoor kitchen. To make matters worse, the wetlands he destroyed weren't his property. They're common green space owned by the Jade Pointe HOA. Incensed neighbors complained, but the board of directors did nothing. While everyone knew Headley was guilty, there were no eyewitnesses, no documentation. Reporting the destruction to authorities would mean the HOA would be responsible for a costly restoration.

Shortly after the marsh incident, the misogynist had one too many drinks at the Jade Pointe Club. On his way to the men's room, he shoved a nubile young waitress against the wall and felt her up. The server sobbed out her story to club management, who, in turn, reported it to the all-male board of directors.

The board dithered and talked the matter to death. I played to their fears that bad publicity might hurt property sales. Money always talks. Jade Pointe badly needs more buyers to maintain costly amenities. In the end, the board followed my advice and sent a polite note to all owners outlining Code of Conduct expectations. No sanctions, no fines, and no mention of Headley. Just as I wanted.

When gossip about the sexual assault made the rounds of the small community, one wealthy owner, a former rape victim, knocked on the general's door. Said if she heard of another incident, she'd personally slice off his pecker.

Staging the general's death as revenge by an angry environmentalist would offer Deputy Ibsen the biggest pool of suspects. But where's the satisfaction? No, I have something else in mind. Like my dear uncle, the general has never paid a price for abusing women.

Closing my eyes, I picture potential death scenes. In all of them, he's nude, but I wonder if I could outfit him with a garter belt, fishnet nylons, and high heels to suggest he's a crossdresser? I think about posing him bent over with something appropriate shoved up his ass. A cattle prod? A very big gun from his collection?

But, no, the scene should echo how he staged Jake's death.

I'm determined that Headley feel helpless as he experiences the pain and indignity. But he's strong and wily. I'll need to subdue him like the Cole bastard. Immobilize him with ketamine. I still have two of the vials I pocketed at the animal shelter. Based on my experience with Cole, I have a good idea how much is needed for quick paralysis.

Tonight, I have a chance to size him up. The general's invited me to dinner at his private estate. He thinks I'm Alexia Bottom, a freelance writer for ultra-right media. Sent my letter last week, asking for an interview. I claimed to be researching an article that will expose the sick psychology of women who wrongly accuse men of sexual misconduct. Said I was eager to report how false accusations damage the virile men these harpies target. Naturally, the general was delighted to be given a soapbox.

I'm to arrive at six p.m. via the luxury water taxi that provides 24/7 service to Jade Pointe owners and guests. It'll still be light. A great opportunity to scope out Jade Pointe security, in general, and any extra layers of protection the general's instituted.

My heart triphammers thinking about coming face to face with the general.

Calm down. Practice deep-breathing. Meditate.

I need to charm the general so he'll welcome me with open arms and thrusting hips when I make a surprise repeat call at his home. My voice, my expressions, my gestures need to convince him I'm one of those female submissives longing to be dominated by a strong man.

Wrong! I'm an executioner with a strong-woman complex. The wait is almost over.

Chapter Fifty-Three

Kylee

Thursday, October 1, Afternoon

I clear space on the River Rat for a litter box and clean out a cubbyhole for Ted to store whatever he brings. I hope his nomadic State Department days school him to pack light.

As the minutes tick by and Ted doesn't phone, my stomach knots. What does the silence mean? Did a reporter blindside him with news of the Satin Sands fiasco before he got my message?

To take my mind off Ted's justifiable ire, I fire up my laptop to research Jake Turner, the Sedgewick cadet who died under suspicious circumstances thirty-odd years back. My gut tells me his death is connected to the Finley and Cole murders. Before contacting General Headley, I want to find out everything I can about Jake Turner. Then I'll know what to ask. That is if I ever manage to speak to the arrogant recluse.

I find Jake's obituary. He grew up in Seneca, SC, and was survived by his father, Victor Turner, his twin, Blake, a grandfather, Wade Turner, Sr., and an uncle, Wade Turner, Jr. Hometown for grandfather and uncle is listed as Orangeburg, SC. The cadet was preceded in death by his mother, Helen Lynd Turner, and three grandparents.

Okay. A start. I Google Victor Turner, Seneca, SC, and find an obit dated just nine months after his son's. The terse announcement provides no new information.

I search for the twin, Blake Turner, Seneca, South Carolina. Zero results. Widening the search to South Carolina finds eight possibles. Given Blake was Jake's twin, he's forty-seven now. None of the eight are the right age. Blake probably moved out of state or died.

Uncle Ward's the only lead left. He was probably mid-thirties to mid-forties when Jake died. By that age, I speculate he'd sunk deep roots. Perhaps he still lives in Orangeburg.

A search for Wade Turner, Orangeburg, provides an immediate hit for a seventy-five-year-old male, Wade Turner, Jr., with a property on Rural Route 4A. There's a phone number, too. Eureka!

I tamp down my excitement as I tap his number into my cell. The phone starts to ring. I panic and disconnect.

"Tell me about your dead nephew" is a tasteless conversation opener. Need a better approach before I redial.

Footsteps overhead. Someone's come aboard. No attempt at stealth. I glance at my watch. Five-thirty. If it's Ted, he's early.

"Ted, is that you?"

"Yep. Me, and Myrt's cats, who aren't thrilled. Wish she'd told me to don Kevlar mitts before trying to coax these hellions into a carrier. I may need stitches."

Ted's feet and the pet carrier come into view. Can't yet see his face, but I don't detect any anger in his tone. Must not have gotten my messages or called the office. Otherwise, Lyn, the suck-up tattler, would have regaled Ted with a litany of my failures. I'm so sorry to add to his woes, especially since he's just been dealing with another attack.

Okay. Woman up. Give Ted the news. Right between his friendly eyes. Maybe he can salvage the Satin Sands account.

Ted's head pops into view. He grins as he sets down the carrier. "You ready for the wildcat release? No telling what these cats will do once the cage opens."

I nod, and the pet jail opens. While the cats didn't want in the carrier, they're in no hurry to escape into unfamiliar terrain. Their heads slowly swivel to assess the landscape before they skulk through the open door. Wary. Aloof.

After a minute, Mississippi leaps atop a cushioned bench seat by a portal, curling her pudgy body in a spot where sunlight, though absent at the moment, promises to warm future snoozes. The alpha cat has claimed her new napping fiefdom. Meanwhile, Keokuk slinks into my boudoir. Fingers crossed she doesn't shred my favorite bedspread.

"Ted, you better sit. I have bad news."

"Oh, no!" He presses his hands to the sides of his face and his mouth gapes wide, mimicking the horrified reaction of the kid in the *Home Alone* classics.

Ted drops his hands and chuckles. "Hey, I got your message. I'm not upset. Even though our contract with Satin Sands requires a thirty-day severance notice, I won't argue. That's a life lesson learned the hard way—never try to coerce an unhappy party into staying in a relationship. Applies to countries, business, marriage.

"Roper is a pain in the butt," he adds. "Never was happy to have competing views to his dictates. He's a genius. Always right. For months, he's wanted an excuse to get rid of our company. Better to exit gracefully than give Roper more fuel to badmouth us. Not worth it."

"Phew." I mimic swiping a hand across my forehead to shake off sweat. "You or Lyn would have handled today's meeting better. Lyn made that point crystal clear. And, speaking of your in-house psychologist, I have another confession."

I look at my feet, embarrassed to meet Ted's eyes. "Lyn suggested I make nice with Nick Ibsen to smooth things over. That riled me. Since the woman appears to have the hots for you, I intentionally told her you were moving in with me. Childish. I know. Did it to get her goat. Implied our living arrangement is something other than what it is. Sorry."

Ted laughs so hard he wheezes when he tries to stop. "Wish I could have seen Lyn's face. I have no plans to wise her up. She's an asset—as an employee. But she's ignored my none-too-subtle hints I'm only interested in an employee-employer relationship. Maybe thinking you're my significant other will convince her."

Ted pauses and waggles his eyebrows. "We could make love and email her a video. That would be even more convincing. What do you say?"

I lightly punch his arm. *He's kidding, right?* Actually, Ted sounds like he's kidding on the square, testing my reaction. And, damnation, part of me wants to take him up on it. My concussion must be worse than I thought. Scrambled what's left of my brains. Don't answer.

"I needed a laugh after my visit to Marshview." With his change of subject, little worry creases pop up between Ted's eyebrows. "The newest victim, Mona Young, has never been my favorite person but, it's a wonder she didn't die from fright or a massive coronary."

"What happened?"

Ted shares all the details of the paintball assault. Mona wasn't found until noon when someone spotted the neon graffiti on her golf cart. She was so dehydrated she couldn't speak. Dried paint on her face made it painful to open her eyes. The doctors indicate her eyesight will be impaired for some time but should improve as the inflammation subsides. She won't be blind.

"I'm surprised you don't seem more upset," I comment. "Won't this add more weight to Nick's theory that Welch HOA Management spawns rage?"

Ted shrugs. "Marshview sits within Town of Port Royal boundaries, so its police are investigating. In fact, the policewoman I spoke with has no plans to even notify the Sheriff's Department. I didn't even nudge her. She volunteered her low opinion of Deputy Nick Ibsen. Her folks also live within Marshview and, apparently, have had nothing but good things to say about me and the company."

I shake my head. "Still, sooner or later, Nick will find out and make hay of it. When I heard about the attack, I even had second thoughts about the Sedgewick connection. Maybe the fact that Finley and Cole were classmates is the real coincidence."

Ted frowns. "What are you saying? HOA rage is driving all these incidents. You think my company is guilty of contributing to the anger?"

"Good God, no! I didn't mean to imply that at all. I just meant societal norms seem to be breaking down everywhere. Disagree with a protest? Then show up to oppose them and be sure to bring guns. Dislike a politician's stance? Then video yourself taking a crap in front of her house. No, Ted, I'm not buying into Nick's malicious theory. If anything, I believe Welch HOA Management helps instill and maintain civility."

"That's my hope." Ted sighs.

"My doubt about the Sedgewick link being important was fleeting, too," I add. "A knee-jerk mental flipflop when I first heard about the paintball assault on a woman, who like the bee sting victim, has no connection to Sedgewick. But the more I think about it, the more certain I am that the murders of the former military cadets are one thing, and the non-lethal attacks are another. While the attacker might be the same, the intent is totally different. The bee stings and paintballs seem more like vicious pranks than attempted murders."

Ted nods. "For the sake of my own sanity, I hope one person is behind the murders and the attacks. Much less frightening to think we're dealing with one psycho instead of multiples."

Chapter Fifty-Four

I notice Ted didn't bring a suitcase on board. Of course, he had his hands full with the pet carrier. "I cleared some space for you to stow things. Hope you packed light."

"Just brought a duffle bag. Don't have any meetings that require me to dress up tomorrow. Brought clean underwear, a spare pair of jeans, and a couple polo shirts. That'll get me through the weekend. If I need anything else, my house is within walking distance.

"The duffle's in my car," he adds. "I'll get it later. I say we treat ourselves. We've both had tough days, and I'm in the mood for Italian. Want to try that new place on Lady's Island?"

"Luigi's?" I laugh. "Why not? I can eat Italian two nights in a row. Want a beer? Take a load off, and I'll catch you up on what happened after I got booted at Satin Sands. Then we can go to dinner."

I pop two brewskis. We sit at my all-purpose table, and I fill Ted in on my visit with Brent Jackson.

"Don't think he's a murderer or even Mom's demented stalker," I conclude. "Actually, Brent was charming. Invited me to dinner tomorrow night at Luigi's. That's why I laughed when you suggested we eat there."

Ted frowns. "You accepted?" He sounds incredulous.

"Yeah, I'm meeting Brent at Luigi's. Public and safe. He's cute. Thick, wavy blond hair. Blue eyes with real long lashes. Nice smile.

"Don't worry, I'll be home by curfew," I kid.

Ted stares at his beer as he twists the bottle back and forth. "Just decided I'll eat at Luigi's tomorrow, too. Brent's cute, huh? Don't forget this *cute* guy owns a black BMW, a car he may have traded for a combine to flip your Honda and put you in the hospital."

"I do plan to keep that in mind. And I'll submit another owner of a black BMW as a murder suspect. My candidate has ready access to detailed information about the squabbles in all the HOAs where murders or attempted murders have taken place. She also frequents the animal shelter, and she has insider information about my whereabouts."

Ted's puzzled look tells me the penny hasn't dropped. "Who?"

"Lyn Adair. I didn't realize she owns a black BMW until Brent mentioned it. How come I've never seen her Beemer at your office?"

Ted chuckles. "She's a suspect because she parks her car around back in the shade. Have to be dozens of black Beemers registered to people in the Lowcountry. A pretty big suspect pool. You sure you aren't making Lyn a suspect because she pissed you off?"

There is that.

"Mom always wondered why Lyn joined your company when she could make lots more money working as a psychologist. She decided Lyn wanted to sink her claws into you. I think her come-ons are part of her act."

I pause and tip my head like I'm judging Ted's appeal. "Sure, you're cute, too. But, in my opinion, not *that* cute. The job gives Lyn access to details about the communities her potential victims call home."

Ted smirks. "Pretty far-fetched. What's Lyn's motive for killing Cole and Finley? Do you credit her with the bee and paintball attacks, too? You think Lyn knows how to drive a combine? And she delivers dead flowers to scare Myrt, right?"

My chin drops. "Laugh all you want. Women can drive combines, and they can and do kill. Neither Finley's nor Cole's murder required excessive brawn, just subterfuge. And who's better equipped than a psychologist to con people? Lyn did call in sick yesterday, which means she could very well be the mystery combine driver. The attack was meant to stall my search into the link between Sedgewick and the murders. Though I have to admit I'm puzzled by the other incidents."

Ted's expression—just short of an eye roll—says he's humoring me. "Okay, it's worth investigating a little to eliminate Lyn as a suspect."

"You did a background check on her, right?"

Ted hesitates. "No. When I looked at her resume, I asked friends in Columbia about her reputation. She'd been in business a long time. No complaints, no scandals. And Dr. Adair is on one of her alma mater's alumni boards. Since she wouldn't have access to any company bank accounts, I didn't think I needed to know about her finances or anything more."

I lift my chin. "You know nothing about her before college, right? I want to find out if she has any connection to Sedgewick Military Academy, Jake Turner, Dan Finley, or Chevy Cole. If there are no links, no motives. I'll say I'm sorry, and we move on.

"One of us needs to question Wade Turner, the dead cadet's uncle," I add. "He's listed in the Orangeburg phone book. I started to phone, but hung up. I hadn't come up with a good strategy to get him talking."

Ted's stomach growls, and he laughs. "I'm starved. My gut tells me our first step should be getting a table at Luigi's. We can figure out the best way to approach Wade Turner over clams linguini."

Chapter Fifty-Five

L uigi's is crowded. We're seated at the last available two-top, jammed between two others. Can't pull my chair all the way out without knocking an elderly lady off her perch. I suck in my gut and squeeze sideways to sit. With the cramped seating, it's all too easy to eavesdrop on neighbors. Looks like discussing murder suspects is out.

Ted's fine with PG-rated chitchat. Without naming names or citing HOAs, he shares an amusing story—to the uninvolved—of condo odor wars. Apparently, the folks in Unit A like to cook Kimchi, a favorite Korean dish of fermented cabbage, and its eye-watering fumes waft through shared ventilation to unit B. To retaliate, Unit B is now cooking collards for breakfast.

"Okay, Solomon, did you propose a solution to make everyone happy?" I wave at a fragrant platter of lasagna on its way to the next table. "Forbid them to cook anything but Italian?"

"Much easier solution," he grins. "Asked Frank to investigate. Construction debris in the air vents was hampering airflow. 'Course I also offered a few secrets from my days in, shall we say, unique foreign housing. Namely, tape scented dryer sheets to air vents and simmer a vinegar-water mixture on the stove."

"You're a wonder, Ted. Who'd suspect your knowledge extends to kitchen hacks?"

Ted waggles his eyebrows. "My know-how extends into other rooms in the house, too, if you'd like a tutorial tonight."

I smile and feel the blood rush to my cheeks. Can't believe I'm blushing.

Ted's good company, and, if I'm honest, he's better looking than Brent. Still, I'm impatient to forget the inuendoes and come up with a way to get Wade Turner talking.

Service is excruciatingly slow. Not surprising for a new restaurant. But, the food, when it comes, is excellent. I practically groan as I taste the gnocchi in a rich cream sauce. I can happily eat here two nights running—hell, every night of the week. But it's bound to be even more crowded tomorrow—a Friday night. Luigi's doesn't take reservations. Can I chitchat with Brent for an hour at the bar if there's a long wait?

The adjacent two-tops empty as I fork the last smidgeon of pasta. Perhaps five minutes before new eavesdroppers arrive or our waiter returns. "Any brainstorms on how to get Wade Turner to share family secrets? Think he'll spill how to reach the dead boy's twin?"

Ted nods. "My idea involves a little fibbing—okay, lying. Found money is always a sure-fire conversation lubricant. Say you're calling on behalf of an estate attorney hoping to locate heirs of the twins' mother. What was her name?"

"Helen Lynd Turner," I answer.

"If the money's coming from Helen's blood relatives, Wade won't figure he has a chance to cash in. He's not a blood relative. Still, he should want to help Blake get the dough. When you ask about heirs, he might even talk about Jake's death."

"That's good." I'm impressed. "We need to find Blake. He's the key. His twin's death must have hit him hard. Since he was only fourteen, his dad may have spared him the lurid details. But twins share. Maybe Jake confided in Blake about being tormented by other cadets."

Ted puts down his napkin and pushes back from the table. "I'm a little puzzled why the father separated the twins. There's no record of Blake attending Sedgewick Military Academy, right?"

"Correct. Otherwise, he'd be pictured in the yearbook alongside Jake. I thought it strange, too, though a split might encourage twins to develop as individuals or keep a troubled kid from influencing a sibling. Maybe Jake was sent to military school to straighten him out."

The waiter clears our empty plates and asks if we'd like to see the dessert menu.

I preempt Ted. "No, we need the check."

He lifts an eyebrow as the waiter leaves. "Hey, I saw a chocolate cheesecake go past that looked mighty tempting."

"Sorry, but I want to call Wade before it's the old guy's bedtime," I answer. "I'll make it up to you. You can raid my candy stash—a drawerful of candy bars, cookies, and dinner mints. Claim all you want."

Ted grins. "Just how many candy bars reside in your stash, and when do you raid it? You don't look like a closet muncher."

I roll my eyes. "I enjoy my chocolate out in the open, thank you. Keep sniping and I won't share."

* * *

When we reach the River Rat, Ted retrieves his duffle bag from the trunk, opens it, and pulls out a pistol.

Wow. Really?

He edges in front of me as we climb aboard. "The rule is ladies first, but, not tonight. I'll yell when I'm sure it's safe."

He hurries below deck. My pissed-off status has me tongue-tied. Never guessed Ted would be packing. My territory.

"Hope you remember how to shoot that thing," I mutter. "Men."

With Mom safe, I didn't think about bringing my Glock to dinner. Maybe I should have.

"All clear, except for two indignant cats," Ted calls up. "Being dumped in a strange place and left alone seems an unforgivable sin."

As I climb below, Mississippi arches her back as Ted bends to pet her.

You're one spoiled tabby. Suck it up. No room for prima donnas in close quarters.

I start coffee perking, and reveal the whereabouts of my candy drawer. Though it's October 1, grocery stores have been hawking big bags of Halloween treats for weeks. I succumbed when a giant bag of bite-size candies went on sale. I could say I bought it for trick-or-treaters, but that would be a lie. Kids look for big houses with porch lights and pumpkins. Not small boats on dark docks.

Ted grabs a handful of the gooey delicacies. In a great show of restraint, I select a single pint-sized Snickers bar.

Once we're seated with steaming mugs, I switch my phone to speaker mode and dial Wade Turner's number.

The third ring brings a brusque "Yeah." The voice is husky, the tone aggrieved.

I will my jaw to unclench and launch into the inheritance spiel I've been rehearsing in my head. I keep expecting Wade to interrupt and ask questions. I hear only heavy breathing, and I'm running out of phony palaver. The silence stretches. Seems like forever.

Is he still there? Did he leave the phone off the hook and walk away?

"Don't know where Blake is," the uncle finally responds. "Don't give a tinker's damn neither. Any money from my sister-in-law ought rightly come to me. When my brother took the easy way and blew his brains out, I took in Blake—an ungrateful brat. Kid made me out a monster for expecting help on the farm for room and board. Haven't heard a word since Blake landed a scholarship to Clemson. La di da. Ain't gonna wish you luck with your search. Blake don't deserve no free money."

Click.

Call over. Wade's voice may be gone, but his malevolence lingers in the silence.

"No family love." Ted sighs. "But we got a lead. I'll check with Clemson's alumni office come morning. See if the university will tell us Blake's major, and, if we're lucky, his current address."

"Why wait? Let's assume Blake took four years to earn his degree. Most colleges put their graduation programs online. Let's look at the program the year Blake should have graduated."

I power up my laptop and download a PDF of the Clemson commencement program. A search for Blake finds nada. Crapola.

"Search for Turner without Blake," Ted suggests.

CHAPTER FIFTY-FIVE

B. Lynd Turner, Bachelor of Arts, Psychology, pops up.

"Gotta be Blake, right? Too big a coincidence for another Clemson grad to have the mother's maiden name and Turner as a last name."

"Agreed." Ted impatiently drums his fingers on the table. Doubt he realizes he's doing it. The man's itching to seize control of my keyboard. "Search for Lynd Turner in South Carolina," he says.

In seconds, the screen fills with options. A quick scroll finds B. Lynd Turner, Ph.D., University of South Carolina. "Got him," I practically shriek.

I tap on the link. It's a research paper by B. Lynd Turner on "The Psychological Needs of Teens in Foster Care."

"Shoot." My excitement fades. "Not the ah-ha moment I hoped for. No help with his whereabouts."

"Given the uncle's attitude, it's easy to see why Blake—or, guess it's Lynd now—chose this research topic," Ted observes.

"Too bad it doesn't tell us Blake Lynd Turner's whereabouts," I complain. "Guess it's time to invest a little coin in one of the online record searches. What name should I check? Blake or Lynd?"

"Hey, go crazy. Try multiple combinations. See what pops up."

Forty-five minutes and two cups of coffee later, the name Lynd Turner appears on a marriage license. The spouse's name? Jeffrey Adair.

Ted practically levitates. "I'll be damned. Lyn, short for Lynd—our Dr. Lyn Adair. We've been hunting for Jake's brother, not his twin sister. Explains why Blake wasn't enrolled at Sedgewick Military Academy. They only take boys."

"I knew there was something off about Lyn," I crow. "Now, do you believe Lyn should be a prime murder suspect?"

"Perhaps—"

"Perhaps my butt! She's—"

"Let me finish," Ted's deep voice drowns out my protest. "If Lyn knows Finley and Cole played some role in Jake's death, there's a murder motive. But, if so, why wait thirty years for revenge? And, if she just discovered these men were culpable, how? Who told her?

"For all we know, the Sedgewick link may be something entirely different.

Maybe the killer is another cadet who was abused by Finley and Cole."

"There's one person who knows the truth," I snap. "General Headley was not only a classmate but Finley's life-long friend. He must know the history—what happened in that military academy to spark this rash of murders. I say we grill him."

"Right," Ted scoffs. "Like we have the authority to grill anyone. The general would just tell us to screw off. I say we call Sheriff Conroy and lay out the facts."

"You think he'll listen? Deputy Ibsen, his own homicide guru, claims people are dying because you've let toxic neighborhood feuds turn lethal. Nick would say Lyn's nomination as a suspect is a desperate scapegoat ploy. Without concrete evidence, it's a hard sell for the sheriff. We need to talk to General Headley. Does your company have any relationship with Jade Pointe? One that would get us through the gates?"

Ted chews his lip. "Jade Pointe is a client. Frank and Lyn work with the resort's on-site property manager, Ralph Myers. Haven't met him. Frank negotiated a lucrative 24/7 service contract for emergencies like broken water pipes. We give tradespeople lots of business so, if we're calling, they'll boat over to Jade Pointe in the middle of the night."

"What's Lyn's role?"

"She's consulted on some HR matters. She told me she developed their procedures for hiring, firing, and handling complaints."

Ted rubs his jaw. His unfocused gaze doesn't fool me. His mind's churning. "I asked Lyn to send offers of free security check-ups to all our clients. I don't know if she did. I could call Jade Pointe and make a persuasive personal offer."

"Good idea. Let's go in early tomorrow. Can you access Lyn's computer files and emails before you make the call? Helpful to see any Jade Pointe chatter about security. Maybe Lyn's computer will offer some cyber breadcrumbs, too. Would love to know if she's shown any interest in stun guns, ketamine, bees, or paintballs."

Ted yawns. "Sorry."

"Me, too. I'm beat. Just not sure I can go to sleep wondering what Lyn's next move might be."

"*If* she's the killer," Ted adds, and gets up from the table. "Don't get fixated on her. We need to keep open minds."

He yawns again. "If I remember from the boat tour you gave me, there's a pull-out bed hiding around here somewhere."

"Right." I show Ted his berth and offer him first dibs on the shared bath.

I turn to leave. Ted's hands grip my shoulders. He pulls me tight to his chest. "I do get a goodnight kiss, don't I?"

He leans in. My pulse speeds up. *Do I kiss him back?*

His lips meet mine. My lips answer "You betcha," before my mind stutters, "He's like a brother…"

But he sure as hell doesn't kiss like one.

Chapter Fifty-Six

The Twin

Thursday, October 1, Evening

I designed my prior murders to encourage the authorities to assume the killer was male. Purposely chose methods not typically associated with female killers. This time is different.

My tart costume works on every man I meet. Screw-me stiletto heels, red-silk suit clinging to all my curves, jacket open to expose a low-cut filmy blouse that shows off ample cleavage. In sum, the whole woman-in-heat package, including an expensive red wig, glossy lipstick, mascara-lengthened eyelashes, and jangly gold earrings. Meet Alexia Bottom.

Forty-seven can be sexy late thirties if you work at it. I do.

Jade Pointe's white-jacketed boat captain personally escorts me to the water taxi's interior lounge. I sink into one of the plush chairs and decline a drink from the complimentary bar. Need to keep my wits.

The boat ride is smooth. I'm the salon's only passenger, thank God. No need for polite, mind-numbing conversation. I silently rehearse my lines. Need the general to buy who and what I'm selling.

* * *

We dock. I'm greeted by a burly man in an ill-fitting black suit. Not the general. Meeting a woman at the docks is beneath his station. Black Suit introduces himself as Jacob. Says he's the general's aide.

Okay, honey, you can call yourself an aide. Whatever. You're a bodyguard, who may not live past tomorrow.

Jacob proves to be a courteous gorilla. Doesn't ogle my boobs as he ushers me to a limousine version of a golf cart. The miniature trolley's three rows of bench seats could comfortably handle nine passengers. It's just me. Once I take a seat, Jacob lowers darkened side screens. To keep my hair from blowing or to limit gossip about the general importing female companions? Either works for me. I'm wearing a wig. Contacts turn my blue eyes brown. Still, the fewer people who see me the better.

The electric trolley rolls along at a zippy fifteen miles an hour, even slower on inclines. It takes twenty minutes to reach Headley's front door. The motorbike I rented and chained to a tree should make my eventual commute from Headley's to a rental cabin a fast, ten-minute ride.

Jacob unzips the side screen, and my pulse quickens. We're here. The bodyguard offers a calloused hand to help me exit the trolley. I study the old-style Lowcountry mansion. Large wraparound front porch. A generous roof overhang for shade. Pots overflowing with colorful flowers hang from the porch roof and sway in the breeze. Artifacts from the previous owners? Posies don't seem the general's style.

Jacob escorts me up an impressive front staircase. We're halfway across the porch when the door opens. General Headley, bald as a billiard ball, steps out. Exceptionally dark eyes, almost black, laser in on me. No attempt to disguise his head-to-toe inventory of my assets. Headley's tan chinos feature a razor-edge crease. Two buttons undone at the collar of his blue cotton shirt allow thick, salt-and-pepper chest hair to peek through. Sleeves rolled up to just below the elbow reveal thick forearms with no hint of flab. No paunch either. Headley's stayed fit.

Definitely need to surprise him.

He reminds me of a human buzzard. Graceful body, ugly head. I smile.

"What a pleasure to meet you, General," I gush.

"My pleasure, Alexia," Headley answers. "A delight to meet a woman who's not been brain-washed by radical, left-wing feminists."

He pauses and lets his gaze linger on my boobs.

"And one who isn't afraid to look and dress like a woman should."

He ushers me inside. Takes the opportunity for his hand to casually brush my ass.

"Thought we'd sit in the sunroom until dinner's served. Magnificent view, and, with the windows open, there's a pleasant breeze."

I follow him. The long hall's lined with Headley photos, picturing him with prominent men. There are two with the president, who pardoned him. In others, senators, pro athletes, and military hotshots shake his hand or clap him on the shoulder. Bet he chose the sitting room so I'd have full exposure to his ego wall.

Jacob appears and asks my drink preference. Bodyguard and butler. How nice. I've researched what the general drinks and request his favorite. Subtle psychology. *I'm your type!*

I anticipate no difficulty selling the general what he wants. I'm Alexia Bottom, a right-wing journalist/blogger, who's come to hear how he's been wrongly maligned.

I wind him up and let him spew. An occasional nod and a sorrowful pout tell him I sympathize. Oh, woe is me.

Just wait till tomorrow. You'll learn the real meaning of suffering.

I make it through dinner without hurling. The food is excellent, but swallowing takes all my willpower. Once the dessert dishes are cleared, Headley assumes there's another treat on the menu. Me.

I pretend my cellphone vibrates, apologize, and walk a short distance away to take the call.

I force a sad face as I tell him my editor insists we go over a last-minute update on a story about to go to press. I bat my eyelashes. Smile seductively. Tell the general how sorry I am to leave.

"Can I possibly come back tomorrow for some follow-up? I so enjoyed your company."

The general practically drools as he agrees.

"Until tomorrow then. Can't wait. I like men who know what they want and take charge." My voice oozes with lusty promise.

My enthusiasm isn't faked. I am passionate about our coming date.

My departure is the arrival dance in reverse with Jacob as my partner. The white-uniformed boat captain welcomes me back, though he looks surprised. Don't imagine too many women who come to see the general escape so quickly.

My scalp's hot and itchy under my wig, and the cosmetic contacts are making my eyes burn. Can't wait to strip. Then it's time to see if Ted really moved in with Kylee. She may have lied to make me jealous. The woman isn't skilled at hiding her true feelings. She doesn't like me.

The feeling's mutual, honey.

Chapter Fifty-Seven

The Twin

Thursday, October 1, Just Before Midnight

A long cold shower and I feel human again. I don't perspire—a biological oddity. Makes me easily overheat. The tense hours spent with Headley didn't produce so much as a sheen of perspiration. But they did trigger my body to exhale an unpleasant odor.

I choose clothes for my next mission—turtleneck, yoga pants, tennis shoes, all black. Once I'm dressed, I pull my hair, still wet from the shower, into a ponytail and don a dark ball cap. A glance in the mirror confirms I'll be next to invisible on the marina docks, a fleeting shadow near Kylee's boat.

I smile. My third costume today. No one can say I don't get into my roles—dedicated professional...hot-to-trot slut...crafty killer.

Multiple personality disorder? I chuckle. Nope. Well, maybe.

I've grown rather fond of all my faces, especially the crafty killer one.

Tonight, I need the cunning. But killing is a no-no. Can't risk raising any alarms before tomorrow's visit to Headley.

The urge to punish Kylee is strong. She's messed up my timing. Plus, the notion Ted might choose her over me is insulting. I let the man know I was interested and available.

Ted's quite attractive for late forties. Having sex with him would have been pleasure not hardship. However, my primary interest in Ted had nothing to do with orgasmic release. Screwing a man makes his little head override any contrary notions bouncing around in his big head. I hoped to hardwire Ted's brain, make it impossible for him to think of me as anything other than a generous, skilled lover and dedicated employee.

Unbelievable that Ted is putting it to Kylee. How does he find that white hair and scrubbed face sexy?

But is he screwing her?

Maybe not.

I drive to Beaufort's Waterfront Park. Pull my BMW in a space near the street, almost a football field from the marina docks. Check my watch. Almost midnight. I hunch down in the shadows of cars and buildings and creep toward the docks.

Dammit. Ted's classic Mustang sits under a street light.

Ted's habit is early to bed, early to rise. A friggin' Boy Scout. He's almost always home by now. Maybe they're just talking, having a nightcap before he leaves.

I need to know. Worth the risk.

I tiptoe down the pier to Kylee's boat, the River Rat. Name is typical of the woman. No class. Adjacent slips sit empty. A big cruiser, cattycorner across the pier, is lit up like a carnival ride. Music blares from stereo speakers. A party boat. Good. Less likely a squeaking plank will prompt Ted or Kylee to look outside. Bad because the blasting stereo will make it next to impossible to hear their conversation.

I flatten myself on the pier. Rough wooden planks scratch my cheek. I squirm until I can look through one of the River Rat's cloudy portals.

Shit!

They're kissing. Not some friendly peck on the cheek.

Don't need to worry about listening in on conversation. No desire to hear "oh, baby" or "yes, yes, yes."

I rise. Saunter down the pier toward the marina lot. Kylee and Ted won't venture topside anytime soon. The party boat ensures no one will think twice about a stranger strolling along the pier at midnight.

Do I need to make any changes to tomorrow's plans?

Once upon a time, I thought about forcing Kylee at gunpoint to sail me to Jade Pointe. After docking, I'd kill her and exit the boat as her double. The River Rat would serve as added authentication. Kylee's death a bonus.

Satisfying as this scenario might be, risks outweigh potential rewards. Ted is a wild card. Knew the two were close—though not lovers. I could have sent Ted off to Hilton Head to defuse some HOA dust-up. But what if he stopped by the marina first and found Kylee's boat missing? Couldn't guarantee he wouldn't turn up at an inopportune time.

The plan minus Kylee and her boat is no less perfect. Jade Pointe expects one Kylee Kane late tomorrow to test their security. It will be one humdinger of a test.

I'm the Kylee who arranged all the details with Jade Pointe. I'm the Welch HOA security specialist they expect. I have the woman's business cards. Even procured a fake driver's license with her name and my photo.

One more acting performance to pull off.

I'll go to the office early. Act cheerful until mid-afternoon when a sudden migraine forces me to bolt. My headache will magically occur before three p.m. I have to make my reservation on the afternoon ferry. I also reserved a rental golf cart on Hemp. Booked both using a company credit card and Kylee's name.

One more day. In twenty-four hours, justice will be done. General Headley will be dead. And I'll be free.

Chapter Fifty-Eight

Kylee

Thursday, October 1, Just Before Midnight

My lips aren't the only body parts betraying me. My tongue willingly darts between Ted's parted lips. My arms spontaneously circle Ted's neck and pull him closer. My body greets the heat of our full-body embrace with a near-combustible reply. My mind takes a vacation as I give in to desire. It's been too long.

Ted pulls back. Space opens between our bodies.

What? He grips my shoulders to separate us even further. "We need to talk."

He wants to talk? Really?

He laughs.

I want to hit him. Did he stoke my furnace as a joke? My cheeks, undoubtedly deep red, are on fire. I'm mortified.

Did Ted forget I can dispense pain in close quarters. Maybe Mom never told him about the martial arts style moves I learned from a fellow Coastie.

Ted's laughter stops, but he continues to smile. "Wanting to kiss you—really kiss you—is the one obsession I could never shake. Had a bad crush on you as a teenager, but knew you considered me akin to pond scum. Your little brother's buddy. A brat."

"Now you can deep-six that obsession." My voice is ice. "Too bad the

243

reality was a huge letdown. Should have just stayed with your imagination."

Ted chuckles as he brushes a curl away from my cheek. "Oh, no. I'm totally satisfied with the reality. But my obsession goes well beyond kissing, and now isn't the time. I want to make love to you. And I need to be sure you want it, too. Can't be a spur-of-the-moment, one-night stand that erodes a life-long friendship. Couldn't handle that. So, I'll be a gentleman and sleep in your guest bed. When and if you're ready, you let me know. Okay?"

He turns away. "Is the guest bed made or do I need some sheets?"

My tongue—the one so eager to perform gymnastics seconds ago—is in park. I'm stunned. Speechless. Ted wants to be my lover? Not for one night? For many nights?

Is that what I want? Ted's my friend. Been like a brother. Mom loves him like a son. Ted is right. Not a decision to be made in the midst of—have to admit—heart-pounding lust.

"The bed's made," I croak, my dry throat makes me sound like a frog. "Do you have an alarm or should I wake you in the morning?"

Blood rushes to my cheeks again as I imagine waking him. Does he sleep in the nude? Does he wake with a stiffy?

Stop it!

"I'll set my watch," Ted answers. His voice normal. Matter of fact.

Okay, I can pretend there's no big, fat elephant occupying the room. "I'll set my alarm for six a.m. If we get to the office early, you'll have more time to snoop through Lyn's emails before she arrives."

"Good idea. See you in the morning. Sweet dreams."

Yeah, right. Not nice to get a girl all worked up right before it's sack time. Might as well have served me a Full Throttle energy drink with a Death Wish coffee chaser.

Like I can sleep anytime soon.

Chapter Fifty-Nine

The Twin

Friday, October 2, Morning

I'm tired. Who wouldn't be with less than two hours' sleep? Spent from one to four-thirty a.m. sanitizing my apartment. My muscles are tighter than guitar strings. I shrug my shoulders to try and relax as I drive into a county recycling center.

The gates open at six-thirty a.m. It's 6:32. As the first customer, I can choose my parking spot. My pick prevents the attendant from watching me as I lift the first of three trash bags from my backseat. I heave the bag in a mammoth trailer, labeled "household." Soon piles of rubbish will cover my deposits, and then they'll be buried in some landfill.

I toss the last oversized garbage bag. It clunks against the trailer's metal bottom. Relief. My trash is full of "leftovers"—everything from my paintball gun to Finley's composite bow.

Amazing how many miscellaneous sundries one needs to create enthralling death scenes and rage attacks. I'm not trying to prevent my identification as Finley's, Cole's, and the general's killer. I just hope to delay anyone confirming my ID as long as possible. That's why I'm dumping any on-scene leftovers that could provide a "gotcha" moment when strangers enter my house. And they will go inside once I'm reported missing. Still, it irks me to be so wasteful. I'm obsessive about recycling.

Now, it's off to the office for my last day. My little secret. My new timetable makes this a busy, busy day. For starters, I'll search for and delete any emails related to my nighttime activities. I never know when Robin, our computer admin, might add an application or do some other computer housekeeping. I'm well aware "deleting" emails and files only means I no longer see a way to view them. Unfortunately, they remain on the main server for whatever length of time Robin has set for backup.

Other than hiding a few red-flag emails, I'll maintain my routine. No unusual activity. That means listening to any HOA clients who call to whine about their petty dramas. Their bellyaching helped me conjure up plausible motives and murder suspects for my victims. But I'm weary of pretending sympathy.

I stuffed the trash bags in the backseat because my trunk is full. It holds all the essentials for my Kylee imposter gig and my evening meet-up with Headley. The trunk also holds my passport to leave Jade Pointe and the Lowcountry free as a bird. A bird who's winging it to England Saturday morning. New name, new identity.

I started building my alternate ID—passport, credit cards, college degrees, work history, driver's license, and birth certificate—shortly after receiving John Hart's confession. While I hoped no one would link the deaths of my twin's killers to Sedgewick, I couldn't count on it. A backup plan seemed prudent. As time moved on, I realized Lyn Adair had to die. The more I thought about it, the happier it made me.

As soon as I murder Headley, Lyn Adair will cease to exist, and Jan Bishop will be born. Perhaps I should buy a cigar for the occasion.

Sooner rather than later, Kylee, or someone else, will uncover Lyn Adair's link to Sedgewick and Jake. It's inevitable. I never made a conscious effort to hide my identity. Pure serendipity that I cut all ties to my scumbag uncle and senile grandfather. Started using Lynd—my mother's maiden name and my middle name—because my given name, Blake, constantly reminded me of my missing twin. Only good thing about my brief marriage to that turd, Jeff Adair, was a new last name.

After I started my psychology practice, several clients admitted they had qualms about making that initial appointment because they thought Lynd was a man's name. Shortening Lynd to Lyn was a business decision. I wanted to attract patients who prefer confiding in a woman psychologist.

My name metamorphosis didn't make me a new person. Hart's confession was the catalyst. Transformative is the term we psychologists use. Before the confession, I used my professional skills to help people through the five stages of grief—denial, anger, bargaining, depression, and acceptance. The born-again me recognized a better, healthier way to deal with grief. Righteous anger could burn away the grief, the sadness, a lifetime of regrets.

As a healer, vengeance is a superpower.

Once I get to my desk and power up the computer, I'll start deleting yesterday's emails to Jade Pointe and work back in time. After I dispose of my Jade Pointe communications, I'll deep-six my digital back-and-forth with Hullis board members about the deer controversy.

I already deleted my Hullis friend's request to housesit and take care of Sandy. Couldn't have it place me on the island when Finley died. If Robin's timeframe for retaining deleted files is short, that sucker is already history.

Hope I have a solid hour for my computer purge before anyone arrives.

Chapter Sixty

Kylee

Friday, October 2, Morning

L ast night feels like a dream, makes me wonder. Did I imagine the kiss? Imagine Ted saying he wants me as his lover? When we pass in the narrow space outside the River Rat's head, Ted practically hugs the cabin wall so our bodies don't touch.

His morning conversation is all business. "I already put food out for Mississippi and Keokuk. Made coffee, too, if you want a cup. I helped myself to your cereal."

I nod. Pour a cup of coffee and slice a banana on my cereal. Finished with breakfast, Ted pecks away on his laptop. He's dressed for the office. Crisp khaki pants and a button-down cotton shirt.

He looks up when I sit across from him. "Robin and I both have admin capabilities. That means I can access any office terminal," he says. "But, if Lyn's on her computer, I think she'll see I'm in her system. I never bothered to learn how to do most of the admin stuff. Didn't need to with Robin around."

"When does Lyn usually come in? Can you copy her emails to your computer before she arrives?"

"Worth a try," Ted agrees. "She usually shows up around nine. Everyone has flexible hours. While Lyn arrives later than me and takes some long lunches with friends, she makes up the time with evening hours. Can't complain. Gets her work done."

"What about Frank and Robin? Will they be in today?"

"Never know with Frank. He may get called out for an emergency. But I think he's supposed to be in this morning. Robin? She won't be there. She's helping one client troubleshoot a computer glitch and teaching another how to update a new HOA website. Said she'd try to be back early afternoon."

Ted glances at my bare feet and bed-rumpled hair. "How soon can you be ready to go?"

"Five minutes?" I speed eat my cereal.

From what Mom told me about Ted's ex-wife, my get-ready speed should impress him. Then again, I've seen how he admires Lyn in full war paint. Maybe I should primp more.

* * *

We walk into the office.

"Hi." Ted greets Lyn. "Surprised to see you in so early. Is there a problem?"

Dang. She's two hours early. Why?

"No problem." She smiles sweetly. "Just catching up on emails. I short-changed you the day I took off with a migraine, and I have to leave before three today for a doctor's appointment. You're a terrific boss. I owe you some hours."

As Lyn simpers through a please-the-best-boss-in-the-world suck-up schtick, I fight a gag response. Want to ask if the doctor she's seeing is her shrink.

Ted returns her smile with interest. Is he acting or still on the fence about Lyn being our primary killer candidate?

"Lyn, could you do me a favor?" he asks. "Forgot all about the Chamber of Commerce luncheon at that new Ribaut Road diner. Starts at noon. Will you go? It pays to show different faces at these events. You said you're catching up on emails. No emergencies, right? Anyway, it's a free lunch."

Bravo, Ted. Either Lyn has to invent an excuse or reveal she's not truly the always-ready-to-please employee. The luncheon should keep her out of the office at least ninety minutes.

Lyn's answer isn't prompt. Can almost hear the wheels grinding behind her tweezed eyebrows and pouty lips.

"Of course," she finally replies. "Though I'm sure the other business owners would much rather talk with you. Do you have something pressing? If so, I can stay and help you. It's not like these Chamber get-togethers are rare."

"Nothing pressing," Ted says. "Just want to review bids for some projects, and thought I'd call some of our newer clients to see how we're doing. Pays to ask for feedback. Shows we care. Haven't ever spoken to anyone at Jade Pointe since you landed that account. Must admit I never considered that an HOA with its own in-house management was a good prospect. You must have poured on the charm. I should at least introduce myself."

Lyn's smile falters. Her face pales. Mentioning Jade Pointe may be pushing the woman too far. I suspect she went after the account because a relationship made it easy to visit the island resort and perhaps meet General Headley.

"Uh, well, maybe you should wait," she pauses. "Uh, not much to talk about until Jade Pointe actually sees us perform. Frank hasn't arranged any service calls yet."

Ted tilts his head. Mock thinking mode. "Sounds right. Your intuition about clients is invaluable. I'll wait on Jade Pointe. Still, I'd like you to attend the luncheon. Okay?"

"Sure." The half-lift of Lyn's lips resembles a grimace more than a smile. "Since the restaurant's so close, I won't need to leave until just before noon."

"Great." Matter settled, Ted heads toward his cubicle.

Lyn refocuses on her computer screen. Doesn't bother to greet me. Okey-doke. I meander toward my own doorless space. Not a big fan of open office design, though a gap in the screens lets me monitor Lyn out of the corner of my eye. The finger on her mouse moves up and down so fast it's practically a blur. Deleting incriminating files?

Lots of luck, honey. I bet Robin can bring them back to life.

I Google Jade Pointe. Read everything I can from promo come-ons to scathing complaints about the tony resort's environmental practices.

Ted startles me when he pulls up a chair.

"Wanted to share a little good news." He keeps his voice low so it doesn't carry. "Chief O'Rourke phoned. They caught the Hullis idiot who's been pasting up threats putting a new one in Myrt's mailbox. Man's eighty-two. Doesn't own a gun. Had a beef with Hayse when he was on the board. Myrt was right, all bluff. Unfortunately, the crank swears he hasn't left the island and knows nothing about Myrt's dead-flower delivery."

"Thanks for letting me know," I say. "One mystery solved, but not the big one."

I go back to my research. Maps and aerial photography prove helpful. Jade Pointe's an easy sail in the River Rat. An aerial shows the general's house has beachfront and a pier, but no private dock. The same is true for his neighbors. Fishing piers but no docks. Too shallow?

I check aerials of the private Jade Pointe marina. The huge political flag makes the general's yacht easy to spot. It's docked in a slip on the second pier.

I've studied everything I can find about Jade Pointe and Lyn's still here. Waiting for her to leave, minutes ooze forward like molasses.

Frank stops by my cubicle as he's leaving for lunch.

"Hey, Kylee. Imagine you came in with Ted this morning. He's such an early bird. You know you don't have to ride with him every morning."

My eyebrows jump. *Does everyone know Ted's moved in with me?*

"Understand you're without a car," he continues. "I'd be glad to play chauffeur. That way you don't have to keep Ted's hours."

"Thanks."

I sigh in relief. Frank's comment doesn't imply I'm shacking up with Ted. He just knows my car got wrecked outside Melsville. After all, he drove up to chauffeur Mom to Atlanta. While I claim I don't give a whit what people think of me, having Ted's and my living arrangement become common knowledge makes me uneasy.

Duh. I was the one who opened my big mouth to taunt Lyn. If she blabs and shares her disapproval with Frank or Robin, it's on me.

I hear Frank's cheery goodbye to Ted. "See you tomorrow. Will be at Hullis Island all afternoon. Call if you need me."

Five minutes later, Lyn's butt finally sashays out the door. Ted stands and stretches. Figure he's watching to make sure her BMW pulls from its back-of-the-building spot and drives away.

He rubs his hands together. "Okay. We should have an hour and a half. Let's see what surprises Lyn's computer holds. Pull up a chair. We have the place to ourselves."

"Did you notice Lyn's panic at the notion you might contact Jade Pointe?" I ask. "Let's search for any Jade Pointe emails first."

There's no record that Lyn's sent or received any Jade Pointe emails over the past three weeks.

Puzzling.

Ted decides to search back to the time when Lyn made her initial pitch and finds several emails. She boasts her psychology credentials make her an ideal consultant for any HR—human resources—conundrums. She also touts Frank's value as a maintenance troubleshooter. Never mentions Ted. You'd think she was the talented brains, and Ted, a figurehead owner.

"Can't believe her gall. She makes it sound like she runs the company," I say.

Ted shrugs. "Hey, hard to complain. She landed the account."

Minutes later, as Ted moves forward in time, he finds a flurry of emails that make him mad. About five weeks ago, Jade Pointe sought advice on handling a sexual assault complaint filed by a waitress. She described how General Headley trapped her against a wall, squeezed her breasts, grabbed her crotch, and clamped a hand over her mouth so she couldn't scream. The young lady quoted Headley as saying, "Want a bigger tip? We can do this without clothes."

Lyn's response? She volunteered to find the young woman a higher-paying job on Hilton Head. She advised against reporting the incident to authorities or sanctioning the general, saying either could mushroom into a publicity nightmare given Headley's notoriety. Instead, Lyn drafted an innocuous Code of Conduct notice to be sent to all owners.

Anger burns my cheeks to fever range. "That poor waitress. The incident swept under the carpet, and she's shunted away like she's to blame."

"I never would have allowed Lyn to send this. Not in a million years." Ted's low voice has dropped into basement territory. "No organization should ever bury a sexual assault complaint. Not only is it morally wrong, it's plain stupid. Invites legal action and a public relations shitstorm when it comes to light. Lyn knows better."

"So why did she do it?"

Ted slowly shakes his head. "Maybe Lyn didn't want to rock the general's boat. That's the only answer that makes sense. Could mean she's the general's ally or the opposite. Perhaps she wants Headley to stay right where he is, fat and happy, until she can pounce."

"I vote for the latter."

Ted glares at the screen. "Why are there no recent emails? I don't even see the one I asked Lyn to personalize and send to every client offering a free security audit."

"This morning Lyn looked like she was giving her delete button a Jane Fonda workout," I point out. "Probably trashing anything she didn't want you to see. Whatever she deleted is still somewhere, right? D'you suppose Robin can help?"

"I know she can. Robin told me not to worry if I accidentally deleted any emails or files. They go into a temporary system folder for a couple of weeks before being purged for good. Robin should be able to resurrect anything Lyn deleted today."

"But that means we need Lyn to be gone and Robin to be here."

"You're right. Robin hoped to be back early afternoon. I just need to invent another reason to send Lyn away."

I snap my fingers. "I know. Kay Barrett's heading a Chamber committee putting together a 'best practices' guide for employers. I'll twist her arm to request Lyn's help this afternoon. Then you can ship your psycho employee off for an in-person meet at the Chamber."

I phone Kay, who fortunately skipped the Chamber luncheon, and explain our dilemma.

"No problem," she replies. "A psychologist's input would be helpful. Who do I call, Ted?"

"Yep. Wait till one-thirty to phone. Lyn should be back from the luncheon by then, so we can send her away again."

Chapter Sixty-One

The Twin

Friday, October 2, Afternoon

I flee the Chamber glad-handing as quickly as I can. It's a little after one when I walk back into the office.

Do Ted and Kylee suspect me?

Ted's last-minute request for me to attend the Chamber luncheon registers high on my bullshit detector. I tried to discern signs of subterfuge in his expressions and body language. Didn't see any, but the guy worked for the State Department, a training ground for professional liars.

Everything seems normal. Ted and Kylee appear engrossed in their own projects. Without even trying, I hear Ted on his phone, questioning some vendor about bids.

Let's amble over and see what Kylee's up to.

"I have a few minutes. Can I help with anything?"

While I pose my question, I study Kylee's screen. She leaves it up, no attempt to blank it.

"Thanks, but no," she answers. "I'm researching suppliers of HOA video camera systems, and comparing costs for cloud and hard-drive storage."

The screen image confirms Kylee's story. Good. The two snoops just need to stay out of my way a few more hours.

"Lyn, can you come see me?" Ted motions. He's on his phone. What does he want now? Hope to God he didn't call Jade Pointe.

"Hey, Lyn, Kay Barrett's on the line." Ted holds his hand over the receiver. "Kay wants some input from a psychologist on an employer guide the Chamber's preparing. Wants to know if I can spare you this afternoon. Can you meet her at the Chamber?"

"Uh, remember, I have a doctor's appointment this afternoon. I'd be able to spend less than an hour. Perhaps we could schedule for another day."

Ted takes his hand off the receiver and shares my response.

"Kay says whatever time you can spare today would be great. She's being pushed to get this guide going so she'd like to meet this afternoon."

I shrug. "Okay, long as she knows I need to leave before three."

Ted confirms with Kay and hangs up.

"Thanks so much, Lyn. Helping the Chamber out is good PR."

I smile. *Like I care.* Though it's going to do away with any extra leeway in getting to the ferry on time.

Fortunately, everything I need in the next twenty-four hours is packed in my trunk. But, knowing Chamber meetings, I won't have time to change clothes at my house. Looks like I'll be performing a striptease in a restroom at some fast-food dive.

Can't wait till it's time to board the ferry. Then no one can stop me.

Chapter Sixty-Two

Kylee

Friday, October 2, Afternoon

I scoot my chair next to Ted's so we can both see his computer screen. "Think you should call Robin and see when she'll be back?"

"No, we have all afternoon. Robin can scare up any missing emails in a matter of minutes. No need to call her away from a client in the middle of a job."

I lean forward. "Since we don't know when Lyn might act—yeah, yeah, *if* she's the killer—Headley needs to be warned. Though he may be a misogynist creep, I don't want a cold-blooded execution on my conscience. Any luck reaching Headley through your friend?"

Ted's fingers drum restlessly on his desk. "Yeah, I got in touch with Dave, a retired general I met in the Middle East. Dave isn't a fan of the disgraced man, but he was able to retrieve Headley's cellphone number and personal email address from a West Point alumni roster.

"I left Headley voice and email messages warning that a woman named Lyn Adair may be planning to kill him. Asked him to call. Not a word. If he picked up the messages, he probably decided I'm a crackpot."

I rack my brain for some other way to reach the general. "Maybe Headley's on his yacht. If he doesn't call before we leave the office, I'll radio him from the River Rat. Even if I don't get the general, maybe I can convince a crew member to talk to him."

"I should call Jade Pointe," Ted adds. "Not sure what the hell to say. 'Lyn Adair, your primary contact with my company, has been giving you horrible advice. Incidentally, even though I own Welch HOA Management, I hadn't a clue what she was up to. Oh, by the way, my employee may be planning to murder one of your homeowners.'"

I give Ted a wan smile. "A message like that will definitely get your client's attention."

Ted calls up a client database. "At least Lyn entered an office phone number for Ralph Myers, the primary contact. Unfortunately, no cellphone's listed."

Ted takes a deep breath and punches in the Jade Pointe office number.

"Great. An answering machine. The automated voice says Friday office hours are eight a.m. to one p.m., yada, yada. I can leave a message, but my guess is it won't be picked up until Monday morning. They do give an emergency number. What do you think?"

"Write it down," I reply. "But, first, let's notify the Sheriff's Office. Maybe Conroy will listen, even if Deputy Ibsen won't. Surely, the sheriff has a way to quickly reach Myers or Jade Pointe's head of security, whoever it is. The sheriff's our best chance for fast action. Hemp has no police force, so the Sheriff's Office is the island's go-to for law enforcement."

"Worth a shot." Ted puts his desk phone on speaker and calls the Sheriff's Office. Amazingly, the operator immediately puts Ted through to the man himself.

While Ted shares what we've learned about the cadet's suspicious death and Lyn's identity, Sheriff Conroy stays silent.

"We believe Lyn may be killing men she holds responsible for her twin's long-ago death," Ted concludes. "We think General Headley could be next. We left a message on Headley's phone and sent him an email. Haven't been able to reach any officials at Jade Pointe. The main office closes on Friday afternoons."

Ted pauses to give Conroy a chance to ask questions. The silence lengthens.

"Sheriff, can you sound the alarm at Jade Pointe? Maybe you should send deputies over to reinforce the resort's private security," Ted suggests.

Conroy clears his throat. "Did you try to 'sound the alarm' with Jade Pointe security?"

"Uh, no. Lyn's been the contact with Jade Pointe. I have the manager's office number, but no direct line to security."

"Goddamn." The sheriff doesn't disguise his disgust. "Your theory's a pile of crap. Not a shred of evidence placing Lyn Adair at the scene of the Finley or Cole murders. So what if her brother died decades ago, and attended the same academy as two murder victims? You're making a gigantic leap accusing this woman, a respected psychologist, of being a murderer. Have you been drinking?"

Conroy pauses a few seconds to suck in more air for his tirade. "And, even though you think your employee may attempt to murder someone soon, your response is to send her to a Chamber confab and leave a few voicemails for the presumed next victim? Unbelievable."

"Sheriff," Ted interrupts. "We're doing the best we can to warn everyone. We want to stop this insanity before someone else dies. Tell me how to reach Jade Pointe security, and I'll make the call."

"Don't bother," Conroy snaps. "Nick will notify the HOA's security force of your *theory*—on the remote chance it has merit. If Jade Pointe requests assistance, we'll send a deputy or two over. I doubt they'll feel any need. As far as you're concerned, I have only one request: butt out!"

Conroy doesn't bother to say goodbye.

"Think we ought to sail over to Jade Pointe?" I ask.

"Sure." Ted smirks. "Imagine Jade Pointe security will welcome us with open arms given whatever heads-up they get from Nick."

I stand. "Might as well go back to my desk. I have a list of Jake Turner's Sedgewick classmates. I'll try to locate and talk to them. See what they remember about Jake's death. I'll also ask what kind of relationship existed between Finley, Cole, and Headley."

* * *

It's a few minutes to three when Kay rings me on my cellphone. "I kept Lyn as long as I could. Minute she arrived, she warned me she had to leave before three no matter what. Couldn't make her stay longer without handcuffs."

"You did great. Thanks. I'll tell you the whole story when I figure it out myself. That's a promise. Talk to you later."

Hands settle on my shoulders, and I almost jump out of my skin.

"Hey, it's just me," Ted says. "I've been checking Lyn's emails periodically. A new one just arrived. While it came to her inbox, the message is addressed to you—Kylee Kane."

"What?"

Ted hands me a printout, which I quickly scan. The email reminds Kylee Kane that she'll forfeit her Hemp Isle ferry reservation if she fails to check in at the Port Royal marina by three-fifteen. The scheduled departure is three-thirty."

I read it a second time. "Why would Lyn make a reservation in my name and guarantee it with a Welch HOA Management credit card. I don't even have one."

Ted's forehead wrinkles. "Come to my office. We'll look online at the company's credit card activity. Should tell us when she made the reservation and which ferry she booked for her return."

Lyn's ferry reservation is a one-way ticket with no return. She also used company plastic to rent a golf cart from "See Hemp." Both ferry and golf cart reservations were made yesterday.

Chapter Sixty-Three

The Twin

Friday, October 2, 3 p.m.

Outside the Burger King, I open the BMW's trunk and grab black tights and a top from my backpack. In a restroom stall, I wriggle out of my stylish suit and into my Goth-like get-up. Just missing the piercings.

While I'm too old to dress like an angst-ridden teen, folks in the Lowcountry are used to seeing artsy-fartsy pretenders and scuzzy tourists dressed—or undressed—in appalling attire. Unbelievable how many dumpy men and obese women don't mind displaying rolls of puckered white blubber in next-to-nothing swimsuits.

I hate to throw my favorite business suit in a trash bin. But I brighten at the notion of buying a whole new wardrobe in London.

I pin my hair under a ballcap and slip on a pair of wrap-around sunglasses. My incognito get-up's complete.

My stomach cramps. Nerves? Understandable with the finish line in sight. Then it dawns on me. I'm sorry to see my revenge mission end. Not only has it given me purpose, it's been exhilarating. Dare I say fun. While seeing Jake's killers suffer and die is satisfying, my success at fooling everyone around me is an unanticipated pleasure.

I phone Alan Watson, Jade Pointe's security muckety-muck. He's the contact for this Kylee's security audit. Alan's met me as an improved Kylee upgrade, and I've thoroughly charmed him.

"Hey, Alan, Kylee here." I'm Miss Cheerful. "Ready for your security test? You didn't warn your people, did you? Remember our deal. You monitor your radio from six o'clock to midnight. If one of your people catches me during our four-hour test, you congratulate your vigilant guard, and tell him to send me on my merry way."

Alan laughs. "I'm expecting quite a few calls. Have total faith in my officers and patrol procedures. Bet you a bottle of ten-year-old bourbon they catch you at least once."

I snort. "You're on. I'm just as confident I can sneak into Jade Pointe and knock on some resident's door without so much as a sighting."

"The deadline's midnight, right?" Alan asks. "That's when you'll call and tell me where to pick you up. You'll be a good enough sport to toast me, right?"

"You got it."

You have more than toasting in mind. That was plain when we met for drinks. Once I'm safely out of Jade Pointe, I may phone to tell you where to find Headley, a secret best kept until my plane takes off.

I drive to the Port Royal marina, the Isle ferry's home base. After strapping on an oversized backpack, I wheel a large suitcase to the pier and check in. About a dozen other passengers are waiting. I slink off to a corner, hold my cell to my ear, and pretend to be engrossed in conversation. Almost as good as a Stay Away sign.

All the late-day ferry passengers will spend the night on Hemp. They either live on the island, own second homes, or have reserved a vacation rental. Day-trippers, who come to tour the island, arrive on the morning ferry and board this one when it makes its end-of-day return to Port Royal. The ferry's the only way most folks have to get on or off the island.

Privately-owned boats and Jade Pointe's luxury water taxi are two exceptions.

Me?

I have options.

At three-fifteen, the captain announces it's time to board. A first-mate takes our tickets and directs us into the enclosed cabin.

Once everyone's seated, the loudspeaker screeches as the captain clears his throat. "Since all passengers are present and accounted for, we'll depart a little early. That should help us reach Hemp Isle on schedule. The weather's a challenge, and it's going to be a bit rough. Winds are freshening, and the sound's choppy. So please stay seated."

Just get us there. I built plenty of extra time in my schedule. And foul weather may actually be a help.

Chapter Sixty-Four

Kylee

Friday, October 2, 3:10 p.m.

Ted puts his phone on speaker and calls "See Hemp."

"I'd like to check on a golf cart reservation made yesterday and guaranteed with a Welch HOA Management credit card," he says. "I'm reconciling company accounts, and I'm not sure which employee made the reservation. There's no problem with the charge, I just need more detail for our client billing."

"Not a problem," the woman answers. "Kylee Kane rented the golf cart for two days, starting this afternoon. It's parked at the Hemp Isle ferry pier, ready to go, as requested. Since Kylee signed the liability waiver and proof of driver's license online, the pier attendant will give her the keys as soon as she arrives."

"Thanks for your help," Ted answers and hangs up.

"What in blazes? Why didn't you cancel the golf cart reservation? Leave Lyn stranded at the pier?"

"A canceled rental would tell Lyn we're on to her. While there's no police force on the island, there's no shortage of rental options. You've been there. Entrepreneurs greet every ferry, offering to rent everything from rattletrap DeSotos to rusty motorbikes. Lyn could easily pay cash to some hard-up islander. Then we'd have no idea what she's driving."

"You're right. At least Lyn didn't use my personal credit card. Will the pier attendant ask to see any ID before handing over the keys?"

Ted shrugs. "Doubtful. Remember, Lyn—or rather Kylee—signed a rental agreement and insurance waiver online. She assured the rental company she's duly licensed and accepts full responsibility for any damages or injuries."

I check my watch. "It's three-fifteen. Maybe there's time to stop her from reaching Hemp Isle. Let's call the Port Royal marina, tell them Kylee's ferry reservation was made with a stolen company credit card and Lyn should be detained."

Ted's call reaches the woman who handles ferry reservations. "I'm calling about the three-thirty ferry to Hemp Isle," he begins.

Before he says another word, the bored woman interrupts. "Sorry, sir, there's no space on the three-thirty ferry. In fact, it's already departed."

"What?" Ted interjects. "It's only twenty after three."

"The ferry was full," the bored voice answers. "It's Friday, the start of the weekend. All our passengers arrived early. Since the winds are coming up, the captain left ahead of schedule. I assure you; no one was left behind."

"Thank you." Ted hangs up with an audible sigh.

I wait till Ted looks me in the eye to make my pitch. "Time for us to sail the River Rat to Hemp Isle. Our only option, though I'm not certain what we do when we get there. The fact Lyn's taking the Hemp Isle ferry instead of the Jade Pointe courtesy shuttle suggests no one at the resort expects her. She must plan on driving the golf cart to a spot where she thinks she can sneak into Jade Pointe undetected."

The office door opens, startling me. It's Robin.

"Glad to see you," Ted says. "How fast can you find any deleted emails between Lyn and Jade Pointe?"

Robin grins. "Under five minutes. Our server's deleted folder is a lifesaver when people accidentally hit a delete button. Did Lyn throw away something important by mistake?"

"Something like that," Ted answers. "I need to eyeball those deleted emails as quickly as possible."

Robin frowns. Ted's long face tempers her glee at being the company's email savior. "Okay. Should I send them to your computer terminal?"

"Perfect," Ted answers.

Robin's true to her word. The string of emails arrives in Ted's inbox in three minutes. I read over his shoulder as he opens them.

What do you know? I'm auditing Jade Pointe security this evening. And, unlike my other audits, I'm not simply inspecting. No, I'm posing as an armed intruder attempting to foil Jade Pointe security and stage a mock attack on a random homeowner.

If an officer happens to catch me, I ask him to call the security director, Alan Watson. In turn, Alan will commend the officer, and tell him to release me. I have an automatic get-out-of-jail card to continue on my commando mission.

"What the hell?" I'm flabbergasted. "It's clever, going in on a supposedly legitimate mock-insertion test. Got to give Lyn her due. She's arranged a risk-free way to penetrate Jade Pointe security. These emails prove Lyn's hiding her identity and is up to no good. This should convince the sheriff. Plus, you can call that Jade Pointe emergency number and leave a message that the audit's a ruse to clear Lyn's path to Headley's estate."

Ted stands and walks to Robin's cubicle. "Great work, Robin. Kylee and I need to leave the office. Why don't you head on home? You've done more than enough work today."

Robin's eyebrows scrunch together. "Uh, thanks. Okay. It'll take me a couple of minutes to shut everything down. Have a good weekend."

* * *

We climb in Ted's Mustang. He's on Bluetooth making warning calls before he even finishes backing out.

For all the good those calls will do.

The Sheriff's Office operator claims—rather testily—that Sheriff Conroy and Deputy Ibsen are unavailable. Ted leaves a voicemail. Then, he relays a succinct message to the woman who answers the Jade Pointe emergency number.

Who knows when either message will reach someone who might do something? Of course, there's also the distinct possibility the messages will be shrugged off as paranoid delusions.

Ted glances at me. "How long will it take us to sail to Hemp Isle?"

"Depends on the winds," I answer, "as well as where we attempt to dock. Lyn will reach Hemp Isle at least an hour before us."

"I doubt that matters," Ted says. "She told Alan Watson her security test would begin sometime after six p.m."

I chew on my lip. "What do you suppose she plans to do between four-thirty and six? We've both visited Hemp. The island's pretty primitive beyond the borders of the posh resorts. But, even traveling on the island's dirt roads, she'd need less than an hour to reach Jade Pointe's perimeter. She must have arranged a hidey-hole, a staging base."

"Makes sense," Ted agrees. "That gives us more time to beat her to Headley's estate. Especially if we bypass the Jade Pointe marina and beach the River Rat in front of the general's house. His mansion's oceanfront, right?"

"Right." I frown. "But the Google aerial doesn't show a dock, and the general's yacht is moored at the Jade Pointe marina. Have to assume the water near his house is too shallow or rocky for an approach."

"Will your marine charts help?" Ted asks.

"Not much in bad weather and low tide. When we get to the River Rat, I'll check the weather forecast. The winds are picking up. If we're going, we need to get underway. We'll have to figure out where we'll put in on the way."

Ted weaves through traffic. Totally unlike him to drive his treasured Mustang like a formula one racecar. We're twenty miles over the speed limit as we shoot across the arched bridge linking Parris Island to Beaufort. *Hope we don't get pulled over.*

"At first, I wondered why Lyn didn't want the Jade Pointe courtesy boat to pick her, er, you, up." Ted honks at a car dawdling in the left lane. "The woman's meticulous. The free courtesy shuttle would have saved time and money. Why dock miles from Jade Pointe and rent a golf cart? The chummy emails with the security director, Alan Watson, explain it. She has permission to sneak in, carrying whatever she needs to off Headley without being searched for little items like choke chains."

A shiver shimmies down my back. Wonder what *props* Lyn is bringing to make the general's death into macabre theater. I have no doubt she plans to stage General Headley's corpse in some hideous manner.

Chapter Sixty-Five

On board the River Rat, I put on kitchen mitts while Ted fetches the pet carrier. I've arranged for Julie to keep Mom's cats at the marina until Kay can pick them up. She'll care for them until Ted and I return. The mitts prove useful. Once the cats are corralled, Ted carts them to the marina while I check the weather.

The forecast is miserable. While no hurricane's bearing down, small craft advisories are up. The sail to Hemp Isle won't be smooth. In fact, we won't raise the sails.

I search for Headley's MSI radio identifier and find it tucked under a paperweight next to my radio. The minute Ted returns I try to contact Headley's yacht. Given the weather, I'm not optimistic anyone will be on board.

"Who is this?" a gruff voice demands. "I don't recognize your MSI. How did you get this number?"

I try for a calm, even tone. "Julie at the Beaufort Marina gave it to me. My name is Kylee Kane, and I need to speak with General Headley. Is he on board?"

"I'm General Headley. What do you want? Are you a goddamn reporter? Julie shouldn't give this number to anyone. For Christ's sake, I can't even get away from you scumbags on my private yacht. We just docked. Should have followed my instincts and ignored the call."

I sense I have seconds before he hangs up. What can I say to keep him on the line? "I believe a woman plans to kill you tonight" would probably earn a laugh and a disconnect.

"I'm retired military, not a reporter." I don't say Coast Guard since I know, courtesy of Nick, that some macho Army and Marine officers regard Coast Guard vets as wusses.

Before he can react, I hurry on. "I have good reason to believe two of your former Sedgewick classmates—Dan Finley and Chet 'Chevy' Cole—were killed by Jake Turner's twin. I think the twin's planning to murder you, too, perhaps, tonight."

Heavy breathing. Got Headley's attention. He's still on the line.

"Why would this twin want to kill me?" Headley attempts a dismissive laugh. I don't answer. Let the silence egg him into filling the void.

"Uh, I believe I recall a Jake Turner," he continues. "But he wasn't in my class, a couple years younger. Didn't really know him. Why would his twin have a beef with me?"

Headley's fishing to see if I know what role he played in Jake's death. I don't.

"I have no idea," I answer truthfully. "But the twin, a woman named Lyn Adair, is on the late afternoon ferry to Hemp Isle. She's posing as a consultant—actually she's pretending to be me—and she's arranged to test Jade Pointe's security tonight. It gives her a way to get past the resort's guards."

"Well, Ms. Kane, is it? What does this alleged assassin look like?"

I describe Lyn, then add, "Of course, she might be disguised."

Headley chuckles. "The lady sounds attractive, though older than I prefer. I'll alert my staff to detain any woman who comes uninvited or claims to be Kylee Kane."

"Well," I fumble. "I may actually show up at your door. I'm sailing to Jade Pointe—"

The general cuts me off mid-sentence. "I'm beginning to wonder if you're who you claim to be." His voice has lost all hint of amusement.

"Relentless media hounds and commie liberals have forced me to take security seriously. I bet you're another goddamn reporter. I don't open my door for any strangers. If you're not a fraud, don't worry your pretty little head. I seriously doubt some lunatic female is hunting down Sedgewick alums, and no woman is a match for the ex-soldiers on my staff."

Headley disconnects. I'd hoped to ask about beaching the River Rat on his property. Not a chance. His bodyguards would shoot first, ask questions later.

His smug dismissal of any female adversary almost makes me want to forget trying to save his sorry ass. After all, we warned him and the authorities, and we were unanimously ordered to butt out.

I turn to Ted. "We could give it up. We're wading into a dangerous situation with little upside. If we get killed, the sheriff will blame us for interfering in law enforcement business. Even the intended victim says we're not welcome or needed."

Ted smiles. "You don't really want to quit, do you? You're offering me an out to be fair, right? I say we go for it. I feel responsible. Lyn Adair pulled the wool over my eyes and used my company to stalk her victims and plan their deaths. I won't be complicit in another murder."

I smile. "Okay then. Take the helm, while I get the marine charts."

Ted maneuvers the River Rat out of the marina slip. As we enter the Beaufort River, we fight headwinds and the in-rushing tide. The winds, predominately from the south, seem to swirl on a whim, churning the river into a frothy rollercoaster. It's starting to rain.

"No way we can hoist the sails," Ted observes.

"You're right. The winds are fickle, and it would take forever to tack back and forth in the river's narrow channel. Hate to say it, but we're better off relying on the motor—at least until we reach Port Royal Sound. When we turn east, the wind won't be trying to blow us back to Beaufort. Then maybe we can risk a jib."

"You want the helm?" Ted asks.

"No, you know this stretch of the Intracoastal. Just remember to keep the yellow triangles starboard and the yellow squares at port since we're heading south."

"That assumes I can see the buoys," Ted grumbles as he shields his eyes from the stinging raindrops blowing in at a slant.

"I'm going to get us rain slickers and my Ocean Scout. It's a nifty thermal imaging aid that uses Forward Looking Infrared Radiation—FLIR. Should help us spot floating logs and other hazards with this poor visibility. Come to think of it, the Scout will be a bonus on land after dark. Always nice to detect hazards like alligators and psycho assassins before they attack."

"Since you only have one Scout, and you're its rightful owner, I hope you'll give me a heads-up if you spot any alligators or assassins in my vicinity."

"Just stick with me, kid," I add with a grin.

I feel bad about leaving Ted on deck to get soaked. But he doesn't know where I store things. In a few minutes, I rejoin Ted and hand him a towel and a heavy-duty slicker. I take the helm while he dries off and shrugs into the raingear.

"Remember when we visited Hank, the Hemp Isle artist Mom loves?" I ask. "He made those arty fish perpetually swimming on your morning room wall. When I checked the charts, I noticed Steelhead Cove is next door to Jade Pointe. Hank has a dock on Steelhead, and I bet he won't mind if we tie-up. Mom has referred a pile of customers over the years."

Ted frowns. "We walked out on Hank's dock. I could call it rickety, but that's too kind. It's dilapidated. Hope a wind gust doesn't blow it and the River Rat away. Still, it's probably safer than attempting to beach at Headley's place. Can't believe you remembered Hank's dock is on Steelhead Cove."

I shrug. "I asked Hank how he decided to buy the property. He said the name Steelhead Cove seemed like a sign from above since he uses steel drums to make his fish. The cove's named for a pirate, who wore a metal helmet for luck. Thought it made him look like a knight."

"Don't suppose you have any metal helmets stashed below deck?" Ted asks. "Have the feeling we can use all the luck we can get."

Chapter Sixty-Six

The Twin

Friday, October 2, Late Afternoon

The ferry captain gives a weather update as we dock. Not like I can't look out a portal and see it's raining. Thunderstorms and gusty winds are forecast to continue until midnight.

Shouldn't pose a problem. Though it'll be harder to appear on Headley's doorstep as the ravishing and ready-to-be-ravished Alexia. Luckily, I packed no-nonsense raingear. It'll help keep my wig from getting soggy. If I'm to wiggle my hips inside Headley's boudoir, I need to maintain my horny, groupie image.

Meanwhile, I'm glad I stuck a flimsier rain poncho in my backpack. I pull the crinkly plastic on as I wait for the passenger rush to end. The stampede's temporarily stalled by a wheezing pile of blubber, who can't seem to navigate the four stairs leading from the enclosed passenger cabin to the open deck. On the plus side, fatso's blocking rain from blowing in.

I give Tubbo and the back-up he's caused a few minutes to clear the ferry before I climb topside. Winds twirl the steady rain, transforming it into a full-body shower head. I hope my rental golf cart is zipped up and dry.

Peering through the rain, I spot the ferry attendant holding the keys to my ride. Have to remember I'm Kylee Kane as I identify myself. He hands me the keys and points to my rental. The heavy-duty vinyl is zipped in place. Unfortunately, the rental company parked it on sand, and I'm not about to wheel my very heavy case through the muck. The island's sandy soil contains just enough dirt to become as sticky as just-poured concrete when it rains. I sigh and leave my suitcase in the rain, while I run to the cart.

Once I load the suitcase, I zip myself in the vinyl enclosure and head to the cabin I reserved. After three miles, I leave the paved road and turn into a dirt road that's become a sandy field of mud. The golf cart bounces and wallows in the ruts.

After thirty minutes of slogging through the wilds, my cabin comes into view. I rented it with a new Jan Bishop charge card. According to the owner's online come-on, the hut is "an intimate, cozy home-away-from-home for a nature lover's getaway."

Yeah, right. Location is its sole saving grace. The tiny, tin-roofed dump sits just beyond Jade Pointe's boundary, making it a handy base of operations.

I find the key under a flowerpot as instructed. *Tight security.*

After I haul my big-ass suitcase inside, I slip off the rain poncho. Though not drenched, I'm damp and chilled. I rummage in my backpack for a teabag, and head to a kitchen alcove. There's a sink, a microwave, and a two-burner cooktop. Good enough. A hot cup of tea will be a nice pick-me-up while I unpack.

My how-to-murder-Headley-and-not-get-caught plan recognizes four challenges. One, circumventing Jade Pointe security. Two, dealing with Headley's beefy bodyguards. Three, convincing Headley to invite me and my murder paraphernalia into his bedroom. And four, perhaps the toughest, leaving the island undetected.

Have I solved all four? Maybe. I mentally repeat the Helen Keller quote that's become my new mantra: "Life is either a daring adventure or nothing."

How I wish I'd lived by that motto sooner. Then Uncle Wade would be dead, too.

Chapter Sixty-Seven

Kylee

Friday, October 2, 6 p.m.

"I'm glad to see Hank's dock still stands," Ted says. "The small craft warnings were no joke. Those roller-coaster waves have me as unsteady on my feet as a blind drunk."

I half-listen to Ted as I maneuver the River Rat downwind of Hank's pier. I'm circling to pit the engine's thrust against wind and waves. Attempting to dock with the wind would guarantee a crash landing.

Once we're within a couple feet of the dock, Ted hops over to secure the bow. In the time it takes to tighten a line around one of the weather-beaten pilings, the wind shoves the boat's stern at a ninety-degree angle from the pier. I go aft and throw Ted another line. He'll need to apply some brute strength to haul the River Rat's backside close enough to tie off.

Eureka! He's got it. Below deck, I trade my deck shoes for high-topped hiking boots. While I had an extra rain slicker for Ted, he's stuck with his running shoes. No spare pair of size thirteen boots in my closet. I quickly fill my small backpack with both our guns, my Scout scope, my wallet, and a few miscellaneous supplies.

Topside, I swallow a fleeting sense of panic when I can't see Ted. While it's just a little after six, the rain's doing one heck of a job obliterating daylight. Finally, I catch movement in the murky twilight. Ted's arm, encased in the rain slicker's neon-yellow sleeve, waves as he talks to another rain-drenched soul. I hope it's Hank and not an irate stranger who shares the artist's dock.

I'm a few yards away when the men turn. Squinting, I see Hank's bushy red beard. Unmistakable, even though the dim light mutes the color.

"Hi, Hank," I half-yell over the storm's din. "Hope you don't mind us using your dock."

"Not at all," he hollers back. "Ted explained your predicament. Wish I could do more to help, but I have my little girls this weekend. Alice is seven, and Maya just turned five. They're too young to leave alone. I stepped outside to check on a tarp I threw over some just-painted art. Couldn't believe my eyes when I saw you tying up to my dock in this weather."

"Hank knows where we can enter Jade Pointe without sinking in marsh or wrestling alligators," Ted says. "The area used to be protected wetland but the general filled it in."

"It's a short hike," Hank adds. "But you best be careful going over the perimeter fence. They recently added a strand of electrified wire about five inches off the ground to discourage armadillos. It might set off an alarm if it's cut or damaged, not to mention you'd get a nasty shock. But security patrols are your real problem. They visit that area regularly because it does offer easy access."

Ted looks at me. "Can't say I'm thrilled about running into a guard the minute we set foot inside Jade Pointe."

"Well, there's another option," Hank says. "You could paddle my two-man ocean kayak around the tip of the peninsula. You'd end up at the Carlyle Estate beach, but it would be a real slog against the wind and current. You're less likely to meet up with Jade Pointe guards, but that doesn't mean bullets won't fly. The general's goons have threatened me when I paddled there in broad daylight. They seem to think they own the ocean."

It sounds like a toss-up. "You know me, Ted. I love the water, but it takes two to paddle."

Ted shrugs. "Can't get much wetter. Let's do it."

Hank eyeballs our attire. "Maybe you can't get wetter, Ted, but the pluff mud will suck those shoes off soon as you wade ashore. I'll loan you my fishing waders."

"Great."

We follow Hank to his cabin. When the door opens, his red-haired daughters run to greet their daddy, then screech to a halt when they see us. Hair plastered to our scalps and water dripping off our noses, Ted and I must look like ghouls. Hank urges us inside, but we insist on waiting by the door. We've imposed enough without forcing Hank to mop his floors.

Ted steps into Hank's one-piece waders. They stretch from his feet to well above his waist. Over-the-shoulder suspenders hold them up.

Hmm. If we tip, those waders will fill with water and drag Ted toward the ocean floor faster than a mobster's cement shoes.

As Hank begins to describe how to find his kayak, I interrupt. "Sorry to be so wishy-washy, but I realized the land route's better. We don't care if we accidentally set off an alarm or get stopped by a guard on patrol. Lyn's handed us a catch-and-release guarantee. If we're stopped, I just prove I'm Kylee Kane—my driver's license says so. We do exactly what Lyn will do if she's detained—tell the officer to radio his boss. Then, like magic, Kylee Kane, and her associate, will be free to go."

Chapter Sixty-Eight

I hear deep-throated grunts and thrashing noises.

"What's there?" Ted asks in a hoarse whisper. "You've got the Scout scope. Please tell me we don't have alligators chomping at our heels. I can't exactly do a zig-zag jog in these waders."

I use the Scout to scan the brush. Heavy-duty snorting sounds and snapping twigs are loud enough to hear over the rain. "Ye gods. Not alligators. Two armadillos, big enough to ride. Now I understand why Jade Pointe electrified their fences."

"How did armadillos get on Hemp Isle?" Ted asks. "Surely people didn't bring them as pets."

More loud snorts and rustling a few yards away. "Are those monsters headed our way?"

"No. I'd be worried if I hadn't read about them last time I visited Hemp," I say. "They've colonized several islands. Air trapped under their spiny shells makes them buoyant, and they're exceptional dog paddlers. They have teeny mouths and peg-like teeth. They tear up lawns going after grubs and such, but don't harm people. That is unless you pet them or eat them. They are carriers for leprosy."

"Well, I promise not to eat them, if they won't eat me," Ted says. "Hemp Isle is beautiful in the daytime. At night, it looks like a set for some horror flick, especially with moss draping every tree and rain churning the soil into gritty quicksand."

I trade the scope for a small flashlight to see what's ahead on the muddy track Hank recommended for our hike. "We're almost at the fence that marks the Jade Pointe boundary."

"How long do you think it'll take for a patrol to find us after we cross into Jade Pointe?"

I shrug, then realize Ted can't see me. "Depends how many security officers patrol at night. Best guess? Fifteen minutes to never. But fifteen minutes is more likely if we don't ditch these bright yellow slickers."

"The rain's let up," Ted says. "I'm game for losing them."

"Me, too. Let's stuff them in the crotch of that tree. It'll be hard for anyone to spot them there and pick up our trail."

My ears tune to every noise. Plenty of creatures, large and small, seem to be rustling through the leaf litter. I shiver thinking about the damage done by that copperhead trapped in Alex's blueberry netting.

Do snakes ever hunt at night?

We use the bolt cutters Hank loaned us to cut the non-energized portion of the fence, and I return them to my backpack. The live wire is so close to the ground it's easy to step over. We plod through the jungle-like undergrowth as quietly as we can, trying not to sound like an armadillo brigade. We have to be near the general's property, but I can't see a smidgeon of light in the deep woods. Hope we aren't walking in circles.

I hit a button on my watch to illuminate the digits. 7:19 p.m.

Ted grabs my arm and hauls me to a stop. "Hear that?"

An engine's whine. Some sort of off-road vehicle? Blinding bright lights. We duck behind a massive live oak, hoping we haven't been seen.

"You're trespassing. Come out now!" a disembodied voice booms. *So much for hope.*

"I'm a Jade Pointe security officer, and you're under arrest."

I can just make out a silhouette of the man standing beside a rugged utility vehicle.

We've been inside Jade Pointe less than ten minutes. Got to give the resort's security an A-plus.

We step out with hands held high. As the officer walks toward us, I see how young he is. If it weren't for his acne, he'd almost be a clone of Officer Adam, the youngest on Hullis Island's force. Our guard's trying his darndest to look stern and mean. The trembling gun hand suggests he's scared. Probably his first intruder encounter.

I smile. "Congratulations, officer. My name is Kylee Kane and my associate and I are here to test your security and response times. If you'll radio Chief Alan Watson, he'll verify."

The youngster asks to see ID, and I ask permission to rummage in my backpack for our wallets. Fortunately, our guns, at the bottom of the pack, aren't visible.

He radios his chief. In less than two minutes, he says, "You're good to go. The chief says I'm to go back to my routine, and give you half an hour before I try to locate you again."

Chapter Sixty-Nine

The Twin

Friday, October 2, 7:30 p.m.,

While I told Alan I'd test Jade Pointe security between six and midnight, I never intended to start before sunset. That's officially 7:05 p.m., though the rain makes the sun's leave-taking irrelevant. Still, I keep to my plan. The rain's drumbeat is growing softer. The longer I wait, the better.

I eat the sandwich I packed and sip two mugs of hot tea. Any more and I'll need a time-out to pee. No fun for a woman in the island's woodsy bramble.

By seven-thirty, the rain's a gentle patter. I load a duffle with my bimbo clothes, wig, and fire-engine lipstick in the golf cart. For the moment, I need to be Kylee Kane. I'll change clothes later. The passenger seat well also holds my "camera case" which contains many interesting items, none resembling a camera.

A five-minute drive delivers me to my pre-selected spot of dense brush and deep shadows. An ideal place to hide my golf cart outside the Jade Pointe perimeter. No security patrol will come near. It's also invisible from any of Hemp's dirt roads.

I position a few branches against the cart to perfect the camouflage before I start walking. My entry spot is miles from General Headley's property. While it's doubtful anyone can connect the dots and figure out the real reason I'm here, I won't leave any clues about my final destination.

At my crossover spot, I check the time—7:27 p.m. I use the insulated wire cutter I brought to sever the fence's single live wire. I do so knowing it will set off an alarm. When Jade Pointe added the electric wire, it paid extra for a twofer. The wire discourages armadillos and, if there's a break, it identifies which fencing section is damaged.

I want to set off the alarm now so there won't be an alert later when I drive my golf cart through the gaping hole in the security system.

I smile, imagining how security will react to the breach. Initially, they'll assume a tree limb's fallen or a squirrel chose the wrong snack. But, when a guard shows up, they'll see my neat cuts, and all hell will break loose.

Once the search for an intruder is underway, I won't play hard to get. I want to be caught so Alan will assure his peeps it's a test. That means they'll figure I'm probing security elsewhere and quit looking at this particular section of the property. But I'll be baaaack.

I'm wearing my black ninja-look outfit. Once I hear an officer coming, I'll make myself easy to find by "accidentally" stepping on a twig. Maybe I should shout "Marco…Polo." That hide-and-seek game's been around long enough for even the older guards to know it.

My night-vision goggles turn everything a weird, watery green, but they make walking through swampy areas less risky. Now is not the time to step in a sinkhole and break my ankle.

The hiking is getting old. I glance at my watch. 7:35. Where are the officers? Can't say I'd give their security system good marks.

A flare of light temporarily blinds me. One of the drawbacks of the damn night-vision googles. I rip them off. Let my eyes adjust. Look for a twig or two to snap.

"You're trespassing," a guard yells. "Stop and raise your hands."

The spotlight aimed at my eyes isn't helping the whole vision recovery thing.

I raise my hands. "No worries. This is part of a security test. Call your chief. Alan will tell you. Just take it easy. I'm going to reach two fingers in my pocket to pull out a business card. I'm Kylee Kane, security consultant."

I'm relieved when the guard holsters his gun, though it looks like he's substituted one of those telescoping batons. They're capable of becoming painful weapons with a flick of the wrist. The baton's in his right hand. He takes my business card in his left, and reads it.

He pulls a radio off his belt, and a voice crackles in response to his call. He's no spring chicken. The old guy took this job because he's bored or desperate to supplement his pension. He repeats my name a second time. I can't make out what Alan's saying, but the guard's body relaxes.

"Alan wants to speak with you." The guard hands me his radio.

I smile. Undoubtedly, Alan wants to rub it in that I've been caught so easily.

"Hi, Alan," I say. "Guess you were right—"

"Kylee, if indeed it's you. What do you think you're doing?" His brusque interruption cuts me off mid-sentence. "I didn't approve you bringing in a whole crew. Not ten minutes ago, a guard detained two trespassers near the old Carlyle Estate. The woman said *she* was Kylee Kane. I know very well you can't both be Kylee. No way could you get from the Carlyle Estate to where you are in ten minutes. What's going on?"

I'm shocked silent. What the hell? A crew? Another Kylee Kane?

While I'm usually good on my feet, I stutter. "Sorry, Alan. Yes, I really am Kylee Kane. I can prove it. When we had drinks at the club, you ordered a boilermaker and a plate of dim sum appetizers to share. I, uh, didn't tell you about the other woman because I thought it would be a better test. I'm sorry if you're upset. Told my colleague to use the Kylee name so your guard would know she's part of the exercise."

"She wasn't alone," Alan says. "There was a man with her. How many people do you have out there?"

"Uh, just the three of us," I answer.

"Better be," Alan says. "I have a mind to end this security audit right now."

Oh, God. Say something to appease the man.

"Alan, please don't blow off the rest of the test. I've spent a lot of time and effort planning it. Your guards performed with flying colors." I drop my voice an octave into a low purr. "I'll treat you come midnight, promise."

I hold my breath.

"Okay, Kylee," Alan says. "But when it's over, I expect Welch HOA Management to pay for repairing the fence and any other damage."

"Oh, they'll pay," I say. "I can promise you that."

* * *

My brain begins to catch up and cope with the new reality. Kylee and Ted are inside Jade Pointe, roaming freely near General Headley's property. My chat with Alan basically told me those two know I'm posing as Kylee and that I set up a security test to circumvent Jade Pointe guards. Smart of them, using my security test against me. I can't let that happen.

"Officer!" I yell to be heard. The old guy is cranking up the loud motor on his all-terrain vehicle. "Sorry, I forgot to tell Alan something important. Can you get him back?"

He kills his engine, walks back toward me, and radios Alan. "Chief, it's me again, Officer Cruikshank. Kylee Kane wants another word."

He hands me the radio.

"Alan, I have an idea. It'll give you a more complete assessment of your officers' capabilities. They've already proven they're good at detecting intruders. Now, let's judge their ability to subdue and detain trespassers. Why don't you radio the officer who just freed my two-man team? Tell him, you've learned those two are frauds, and it's his job to confiscate any weapons they may have and take them to the Security Office for questioning. My associates may struggle to make it look good, but they won't harm your man."

Alan doesn't respond immediately.

What is he thinking? Is he having doubts about me, about this security audit?

"Okay." He chuckles. "You're one devious lady, Kylee. Your friends may not appreciate the strategy change, but I do. You're right, we've already demonstrated how hard it is for trespassers to slip past our security. I'll make the call."

Chapter Seventy

Kylee

Friday, October 2, 8 p.m.

"I'm having a déjà vu moment," I say. "Hiding in the brush, being snacked on by no-see-ums, waiting for a killer to show. Can't believe we were doing the same thing on Hullis Island a week ago. Hope this vigil doesn't end the same way, with a dead body."

Ted shoos whining insects away from his ears. The rain's stopped earlier than predicted, and the humid air hums with ravenous winged pests. "I'm ready to flag down a Jade Pointe security guard," he says. "Tell him to contact his chief, this Alan Watson. Then we clue Watson in. That might have been our best play when the first guard stopped us."

I shake my head. "Tempting, but I'll bet the imposter Kylee has met Alan Watson in person. He has every reason to believe she *is* the real Kylee. If they're in touch, and I'm sure they are, she'd spin our story as a lie to create chaos and weaken security. Our best option is to catch Lyn when she sheds her Kylee impersonation and goes after the general."

Ted's look tells me he isn't buying. "Here's another option," he suggests. "We knock on the general's door. Yeah, I know Headley told you his bodyguards would *handle* any Kylee Kane. But being *handled* inside doesn't sound half bad. And, once the fake Kylee arrives, he'll know we're telling the truth."

I bite my lip as I consider the pros and cons. "His bodyguards would truss us up like Thanksgiving turkeys until the general sorts out what's what. We'd be helpless to stop Lyn from killing Headley, and, then murdering pesky witnesses—us—after the general's dead."

"You do know how to argue your case," Ted says. "Okay, we wait."

A few minutes later, a tightly spaced set of headlights appears. Though it might be one of the general's toughs checking out the estate's outer edges, the vehicle looks to be a twin of the one operated by the Jade Pointe officer who stopped us.

"Kylee Kane, come out where I can see you," the voice commands. "The chief wants a word."

What now? I hope none of Headley's bodyguards can hear the Jade Pointe officer. If so, we've been outed.

Ted and I slip out of the brush and walk toward the officer, who edges out from behind his ATV—all-terrain vehicle.

Uh, oh. His outstretched hand holds a gun, not a radio.

"Hands up," the young officer barks. "The chief knows you're frauds. He's not sure who you are or what you're up to, but you're not part of any legit security audit."

"What? You're kidding, right? I showed you my driver's license. I'm Kylee Kane."

"Yeah, and I can buy a driver's license that says I'm Santa Claus." The young man's sarcasm tells me he's not inclined to debate.

"Both of you, get your hands up and lean against the vehicle. Feet spread."

Frustration tempts me to mutter "Screw you" or "Make me." Ted's small shake of his head signals not to antagonize an inexperienced kid with a gun. Especially since that guy's boss just told him we're mysterious, and possibly dangerous, intruders.

We raise our hands and spread our feet. The officer searches Ted first and absconds with his beloved Swiss pocketknife. He lets Ted keep his cellphone.

Finding nothing of interest in my pockets, he throws my backpack in the back of the ATV. It holds my heat-sensing scope and both our guns. Glad he didn't look inside.

"Hands out front." He handcuffs Ted's right wrist to my left one. I'm guessing the officer's utility belt only holds one set of bracelets. Since Ted's a leftie, and I'm a rightie, we're in luck. At least, our predominant hands are free.

He points to his ride. "Get in front. You—" he jabs a finger in Ted's back—"you drive. I'll be right behind you. We'll take it nice and slow. No funny business."

"Officer, this is a huge mistake," Ted tries. "Let us explain to your chief. We're trying to protect General Headley from an attack by a serial killer posing as Kylee Kane. She's the imposter, and she's already killed at least two men."

The officer laughs. "The chief said you'd have some tall tale, but I gotta admit that's a hoot. No one's gonna mess with General Headley, even if they could get past Jade Pointe security. Two bodyguards provide round-the-clock protection. Besides, the chief just spoke with the real Kylee. Not another word out of you two. You can blab all you want when we get to the Security Office."

Ted and I both get in on the driver's side. No choice with our steel-linked wrists. My arms aren't long enough to permit entry on the passenger side. Scooting my butt over the center console isn't one of my more graceful moves.

As I'm scootching over the gears, the guard holsters his gun and substitutes a nightstick to ensure our continued submission. We're handcuffed and his pat-down assured him we weren't carrying. He must figure he has few worries.

Ted does a Dosey Doe with his eyes, signaling that he also noticed the guard's weapon change. He starts the engine and grabs the wheel with his unfettered left hand. He shifts our joined hands my way and squeezes my thigh. A definite attention-getter. I look down. Ted scrunches his fingers together to look like a foot, then mimics the foot slamming down.

I'm not sure if he intends to stomp on the brake or the gas pedal, but I appreciate the heads up.

I shift our conjoined hands to his leg and tap one, two, three before I copy his pretend foot slam. Does he understand?

Ted duplicates my taps and foot slam on my leg. Okay. I think he's promising a one-two-three heads-up before he floors the gas or stands on the brakes. We're not belted in. Hope I can brace myself to keep from becoming a hood ornament.

Thank heavens, the dude behind us put his gun away. No accidental trigger pull. Of course, having the youngster thrown on top of me wouldn't be a picnic.

Chapter Seventy-One

The Twin

Friday, October 2, 8:20 p.m.

Time to go into overdrive. The minute I end my conversation with Alan, I make a beeline for the golf cart I left outside the Jade Pointe perimeter fence. There's no one about to watch me strip off my ninja duds. No need to change my underthings. Despite the discomfort, I've worn the black lace teddy with its push-up bra all night to speed my costume change.

I towel off the nervous sweat worked up on my jog back to the cart and treat myself to a few blessed seconds of cool air whispering over my skin.

Reluctantly, I slip on the clingy red-silk dress and my Alexia wig. I apply wet-look lipstick. Since I have no mirror for a smile check, I scrub a finger over my teeth to remove any hint of a blood-red smudge.

Ready? Yes. I zip the cart's vinyl enclosure to make it harder to see inside. The weatherproofing eliminates any chance a gust of wind will mess up my styled wig. The cart bumps over rough terrain. Despite the rain, I don't worry about getting stuck. I'm driving over a hard-pack dike that predates Jade Pointe by more than a century. While it's now overgrown with weeds and brush, it offers a solid connection between the fence and Jade Pointe's network of paved roads.

Still, I'm happy when I see the posh resort's main palmetto-lined thoroughfare. Now I have a straight shot to the old Carlyle Estate and Headley. I take my eyes off the road for a minute to check on my "camera bag." All secure.

Headlights flash, a golf cart or off-road vehicle is approaching in the opposite lane. The compact silhouette says it isn't a car. No surprise. Most Jade Pointe residents and visitors tool around in various souped-up versions of golf carts. They're well aware no officer will arrest them for driving unlicensed vehicles on the private roads. The general and his ilk don't need to follow the rules set for chumps who can't afford to live here.

Tonight, though, there are rules. And I make all of them.

As the off-road vehicle glides by in the opposite lane, I'm tempted to laugh. Ted and Kylee are seated in front with a guard who barely looks old enough to drive perched behind them. What a come down!

Did they even glance my way and wonder if the lady driving in the opposite direction might be me? Doesn't matter. My cart's vinyl weather protection is cloudy. Even if my adversaries stared, I doubt they'd recognize me.

I estimate it will take the young officer twenty minutes to deliver his prisoners to the Security Office, which sits beside the enclave's private marina at the southern edge of the property. The general's estate is at the opposite, northern edge of the crescent-shaped resort. So, even if silver-tongued Ted can convince Alan I'm a dangerous assassin, I have at least thirty minutes before an alarm is raised.

Sure, Alan could try to phone the general, but he'll be much too busy to take any calls. Plus, his henchmen have met Alexia. In their minds, a boudoir heart attack is the only possible danger my Alexia persona might hold for their boss.

Before I enter the estate's private drive, I pause to unzip the cart's vinyl sides. I want anyone patrolling out front to instantly recognize me. I practice my fetching smile and bat my extended eyelashes.

Good. I see Jacob, the courteous gorilla, who chauffeured me to and from the marina on my last visit.

"Hi, Jacob, so nice to see you. I had an unexpected schedule change and decided to surprise the general. Sorry I didn't call ahead, but I couldn't seem to get a signal during the storm. I hope he's not busy, or, uh, entertaining someone else."

"No, ma'am." Jacob's bushy eyebrows bunch together in a single line. "How did you get on the island?"

I'm primed to answer. "Oh, John and Jane Clark, two of the general's Jade Pointe neighbors, are friends. I ran into them in Beaufort. Told them I hoped to call on the general, and they asked me to join them on their yacht once the worst of the storm blew through."

"I'm sure the general will be pleased to see you, ma'am," Jacob says. "I'll let him know you're here. Then I'll see you to the door."

Jacob moves out of earshot to tell the general he has company and get approval for my visit. In no time, he's back at my side. "Can I help you with anything?" he asks.

"Yes." I smile. "I brought some camera and lighting equipment in that bag on the floor. I hope the general will allow me to take some candid photos to run with the story I'm writing. He's so handsome and virile."

Jacob grabs the bag in his massive left hand and offers his right arm to escort me up the sweeping staircase. I'm steps away from success.

The general opens the front door before I finish climbing the stairs. Headley looks a little less put together than the last time we met, but his leering smile says he can't wait to get me alone.

Imagine that. Me, too!

I repeat my story about wanting to surprise him. Then, I bend my head close to his ear and whisper. "I haven't been able to stop thinking about you. I hope we can spend some time alone. I brought a camera. I told Jacob it's to photograph you for my story. But, if you want, you can take pictures of me, too. That bag also holds some interesting adult toys. I can demonstrate how to use them while you video."

Headley licks his lips. "Let's take care of those photos right away." His voice is a tad hoarse, but he speaks loud enough for Jacob to hear him and share his plans with any other bodyguards or servants who happen to be on duty. "Let's go to my bedroom so you can help me pick out what to wear.

Here, I'll carry your camera bag."

The general leans in. "We'll also decide what clothes you don't need to wear."

Gotcha!

Chapter Seventy-Two

Kylee

Friday, October 2, 8:30 p.m.

When we need a pothole, we can't find one anywhere. The pavement is silky smooth. Unlike the rest of Hemp Isle's residents, Jade Pointe owners aren't subjected to dirt roads with their muddy ruts and potholes. Any of these road hazards could add pizzazz to Ted's driving maneuver when he tries to eject our guard.

Houses are set far off the road. Now that the rain's stopped, the night's soundtrack is full of tiny, chirping tree frogs. And another sound. What is it?

A long, low building sits off the inland side of the road. White fencing hems in a sizable pasture. The sound? Muffled banging. Couldn't be construction this time of night.

Horses? I'd forgotten Jade Pointe boasts an equestrian club. Lacking sufficient land for a golf course, the developers promote horseback riding as an elite pastime, and couple it with a save-a-species appeal. They breed Marsh Tackies, the rare, sturdy descendants of equines the Spaniards brought to the Lowcountry centuries before.

There are no horses trotting down the road tonight, and only one buttoned-up golf cart has passed us. Given how deserted the road is, it seems unlikely anyone will report us if we manage to escape our guard. Of course, it also means there won't be any eyes on Lyn, the assassin, either.

I try to nudge the guard into conversation. "How long till we reach the Security Office?" I ask. No answer. "Where's this other woman who claims to be me?"

Grunts and silence are his response. Not a big talker.

A hazy gold glow appears on the horizon. It's the Security Office, where we'll be detained indefinitely. No illusions we can convince Chief Watson our story's true in time to stop Lyn.

I squeeze Ted's leg to get his attention, then dip my head toward the lights. "Can't wait much longer," I mouth.

Ted taps my thigh three times. I brace myself as he gradually speeds up, then jerks the wheel hard right, flinging us off the road like a wobbling top. The guard yells as he's thrown to the edge of his bench seat.

When we nosedive into the lumpy remains of a one-time sand dune, the front of the cart stops, and the rear leaps in the air. Our guard isn't braced for it and pitches forward, half-in, half-out of the four-wheeler. When the vehicle settles, I wriggle sideways and use my feet to shove him completely out.

He lands on his back in the sandy muck. As he struggles to regain his feet, I pray he doesn't go for his gun.

Ted's attempt to get back to pavement and flee isn't a slam dunk. After two failed rollbacks, our ride finally gains traction and bounces onto the road. Ted turns north away from the Security Office and toward the general's estate.

A gunshot sounds like a cannon in the quiet night. "Keep your head down!" Ted yells.

I scrunch down and peek around the seat at the guard. "He's not shooting at us. His gun's pointed at the sky. Imagine he's shooting to rally reinforcements. Anyway, I think we're out of range."

As Ted speeds toward the general's estate, I glance in the backseat. "Crap, our little NASCAR maneuver not only ejected the guard, it jettisoned my backpack."

Ted laughs. "Oh, good. Now we're handcuffed and have no guns and no night scope. We needed more challenges. After all, our potential adversaries only include a successful assassin and the general's goons, all U.S.-Army trained in a dozen ways to kill."

"Don't forget Jade Pointe security officers," I add. "Our young guard kept his radio. By now, every Jade Pointe officer is hunting for two dangerous intruders in a stolen security vehicle."

I look down the road, searching for any signs of lurking Jade Pointe patrols. That's when I notice the squat outline of the equestrian center.

"Turn in, turn in," I yell. "There must be tools inside. Something to break these cuffs."

Ted swerves into the drive. "Worth a try."

We pull behind the building. Nervous snorts and restless horses shifting inside stalls indicate our arrival hasn't gone unnoticed.

The back door's unlocked. No light needed to tell we're in horse territory. The aroma's a rich mix of oiled leather, hay, and manure. But we need a light for our search.

Ted's hand fumbles along the wall. He flicks a switch, and the bright light makes me blink. We're in what I think is called a tack room. The walls are hung with a wide assortment of gear from horse blankets to bridles. Stainless steel and leather. It could be a dominatrix's closet.

"I'm looking for hoof nippers or rasps," Ted says. "Either might saw through a link in these handcuff chains."

"What are hoof nippers?" I ask. "And, how the heck do you know about them?"

Ted chuckles. "I did lead a full life before we reconnected. Horse culture is big in the Middle East. Grant and I rode a lot. Hoof nippers are made of steel. They look like giant tongs and end in vice-like cutters. There." He points.

Ted moves toward them, tugging me, his handcuffed sidekick, along. He shakes his head. "The nippers might work if I had two free hands to apply enough pressure. I don't. See if you can find something else."

In seconds, I spot a hacksaw and yank Ted's arm as I point. "Will a small hacksaw do?"

"Perfect. A mini with a ten-inch blade. A demolition necessity. Use mine all the time to cut through screws and nails."

Given that our internal clocks are set to trying-to-stop-a-murder time, it seems to take forever to saw through a connecting link. In real-time, it takes less than ten minutes. Guess that explains why the Coast Guard taught us to never leave a handcuffed suspect alone. Too easy to get free.

"While we're here, let's round up some weapons," Ted suggests.

My haul includes a hammer and a knife. Ted chooses the hoof nippers, a rope, and a heavy-duty flashlight. I start toward the door we entered, but Ted grabs my arm.

"This way." He nods toward the horse stalls.

"Why?" My whisper is unnecessary. The only beings close enough to eavesdrop speak in whinnies.

"The Jade Pointe guards are looking for a stolen off-road vehicle. So, let's switch to a different off-road transport." He lifts an eyebrow as he motions toward the stalls.

"Uh, no. I've ridden exactly twice, and it's dark. Those poor horses might break a leg."

"People ride horses at night," Ted says. "Remember the midnight ride of Paul Revere? Marsh Tackies are sure-footed and hard to scare. There's no time to argue. Hide the ATV, while I ready our new ride."

Great! Why did I notice the equestrian center? I'll fall off the horse and break my neck.

I shove bales of hay around the ATV to make it harder to spot from the road. Then I hear hooves and a little nicker.

"Stand on that bale and give me your hand. I'll pull you up," Ted says.

"What? Bareback? The two of us on one horse?"

Ted chuckles. "A horse can sense a nervous novice. If you're nervous, she's nervous. Better if you come with me. Riding double we'll make less noise and be harder to see."

I grumble as Ted hauls me onto the horse's stocky back. "You sure he can handle this much weight?"

"She's a filly. I'm guessing fourteen and a half hands, the tallest of the barn's inhabitants. And yes. You do weigh under two hundred pounds, right?"

"Har, har." I know Ted's humor is intended to ease tension. Not sure it's working.

As the horse starts bouncing and swaying under us, my arms circle Ted's waist, and my fists grab healthy helpings of his shirt. If I fall, his shirt comes with me. Each step jars my bottom. As the horse comes up, my butt always seems to be coming down. And as the horse's back drops, I seem to be rising.

I'm doing my best to match the animal's rhythm when Ted says, "Hold tight. Use your knees to get a grip. We're going to take it up a notch."

The horse trots. And I thought my bottom was being jarred before. I command every thigh muscle I possess to squeeze. "Holy crap!"

"Shhh. We'll reach the general's property in no time. Guards won't be looking for us on the beach. Even off-road vehicles have trouble in the pluff mud, but not this filly. Right, girl?"

"What about the general's bodyguards?"

"Good question," Ted says.

I notice he doesn't supply a good answer.

Chapter Seventy-Three

The Twin

Friday, October 2, 9 p.m.

The general shuts the door to his massive master suite. It's bigger than most living rooms, not part of the stately mansion's original layout. Headley either knocked down walls or added on. A huge bed is front and center. Another section of the room holds fitness and weight equipment. The large mirrors hardly surprise. Headley is enamored with himself.

The back window wall includes a sliding glass door that leads to the patio. Headley picks up a remote and with a click, all the glass turns opaque. Glad he doesn't want his roaming bodyguards watching. Neither do I.

"Lock the door, will you?" I make my voice breathy, urgent. "I want to make doubly sure no one walks in and sees what's meant just for you."

"Don't worry." Headley turns the lock. "My people know not to disturb me if I'm in my bedroom, especially if I have gorgeous company."

I grab my bag of toys and coyly mince backwards toward the massive bed, beckoning Headley with the crook of my finger. "Come closer," I whisper, "I have a special present for you."

When I feel the foot of the bed behind my legs, I zip open the bag and place it on the comforter. I use my body to shield what I'm doing. The loaded syringe is on top, easy to find. I grasp it in my right hand, while my left hand twitches its come-and-get-it invitation. I giggle as the leering idiot moves ever closer.

Headley reaches out and pulls my body tight to his. My left arm slides over his shoulder. I cup my hand around his neck to bring his head lower. A move he'll assume is a prelude to a kiss. My tongue glides against his lips, as I position the ketamine syringe for its sudden plunge. I've bumped the dosage to 600 milligrams, a hundred more than police might use to subdue a 220-pound psychotic.

I figure the general will bellow when the needle punctures his neck. As I stab him and push the plunger, I commence a loud series of cries and gasps. "Oh, Ronnie. Yes. Yes. More!"

Headley's mad bull roar barely lasts a second. His fingers convulse as he tries to shove me away and pull the syringe from his throat.

"Not going to happen, Ronnie," I explain in a matter-of-fact voice as he loses muscle control and starts to crumple. I thrust my hands under his armpits to pause his fall and shift his body. I want it draped across the bed. Easier to remove his clothes than if he were sprawled on the floor.

Can he hear me? Understand? I'm not sure. Ketamine has hallucinogenic properties. I talk to him as I strip off his clothes, hoping my words imbed themselves in a horrific nightmare.

"Ronnie, remember Jake Turner? Well, I'm his twin, Blake Lynd Turner." I pull off my red wig and shake my blonde hair loose. Then I turn sideways to show off my profile. "See the resemblance?"

I stuff a pair of lacy women's panties in his mouth so he can't yell. Then I remove Headley's clothes. Once he's naked, I drag his body onto the rug and roll him on his stomach. Inside my camera bag, I rummage for the handcuffs and leg irons bought through an online S&M store. After I restrain his hands and feet behind his back, I loop a rope through the two restraints and pull until the handcuffs and leg irons almost touch. Once the rope's knotted in place, he's firmly hogtied.

"Do you remember taking Jake's clothes? I know you came up with the idea for the cover-up. You were the brain behind the choke chain, too. And, looky here, I brought one for you!"

Next, comes the piece de resistance, a shiny choke chain. I dangle it in front of his eyes so he can see the glittery steel with its no-nonsense crisp edges. I slip the choke chain around his neck and thread the attached leash under the leg iron's chain. Two pillows from Headley's bed act as supports to lift his head about eight inches off the floor. Had to determine his chin's angle and height to decide what length of leash to attach to his leg irons. I test it. No give.

I pat the top of the general's head. "You always hold your head high, right? When I remove these pillows, you'll stay alive just as long as you're able to keep your chin up. When your neck muscles give out, you'll choke to death. How long will you last? Don't worry. I'll wait till you regain some function before I snatch those pillows away.

"Fair is fair, right?"

Chapter Seventy-Four

Kylee

Friday, October 2, 9:10 p.m.

A hole in the thick cloud cover lets the pale waxing moon peek through. It paints the beach a cold white and spotlights the frothy waves breaking near shore.

"I told you to trust the filly," Ted gloats. "She had no problem finding the bridal path to the beach. Now there's no stopping her—or us."

An unexpected bounce jars my back and slams my teeth together. "Argh. You realize one of Headley's goons could stop us with a bullet."

"Hey, as I recall, paddling here in a kayak would also have risked a bodyguard encounter," he replies. "If someone's shooting, we'll be much tougher targets to hit if we're riding a galloping horse. In a kayak, we'd be sitting ducks. I see lights. We're almost there. Come on, girl, let's find a bit of cover."

"I imagine you're speaking to our filly but I agree."

The horse slows, and plods through the pluff mud, then does an equine version of a waddle through fluffy sand to reach a ghostly copse of trees. Sun, wind, and high tides have polished the skeleton trees into bleached sculptures. While there's no foliage to hide us, the grotto's twisted trunks and bloated logs should make it hard to pick us out of the geometric jumble.

Ted pulls the filly to a stop. He pries my hands from his waist and helps me perform a controlled fall to earth. Flipping one leg over the horse's neck, he gracefully slides to the ground and ties our horse to a tree. I hope I can walk, let alone run. Feels like I tried doing splits, a gymnastic feat I haven't attempted in decades, and got stuck in a wishbone position for hours.

I look toward the mansion's stately columns. Even without a scope, I pick out a muscle-bound bodyguard standing maybe fifty feet from the house. I start to thank heaven for the watery moonlight's return when I realize it also makes Ted and me more visible. Movement to the right of the guard catches my eye. A waving ember suggests a second guard is taking a smoke break and joining his pal.

Ted nudges my arm. "Looks like both on-duty guards are outside. I'd have thought one would stay in the house."

"See the golf cart by the staircase?" I whisper. "Maybe Headley has company and wants privacy."

"Let's inch closer. See if we can eavesdrop."

Large oleanders, planted long ago as a windscreen or hedge, provide excellent camouflage as we creep toward the mansion. We stop at the end of the oleander row.

"How come you're outside?" the cigarette-waver asks.

"The boss showed that broad to his bedroom and locked the door," the first guard answers. "Soon as I heard the first loud moans, and her screams of 'Yes, yes. More,' I was outta there. Porn's a drag if you can't watch—or better yet, participate."

I tug Ted's sleeve. "Could the moaner be Lyn?"

"What? You think she'd screw a guy before she kills him?" Ted sounds incredulous.

"Hey, she's an accomplished actress, and Headley's a womanizer. Lyn used a stun gun on Finley, and she paralyzed Cole with ketamine. She could use either to subdue the general in the privacy of his bedroom. Maybe she's doing an audio solo for the guards' benefit. Women can fake orgasms, you know."

"Or maybe the general's entertaining some innocent—well, maybe that's not the right word—entertaining a woman who has nothing to do with

302

this."

"Only one way to find out," I say. "We just need a diversion to occupy both guards while we sneak around back."

"Okay, for argument's sake, let's say Lyn is inside, and we divert the guards' attention," Ted says. "Then what? I doubt Headley conveniently left a back door open."

"No, but I studied the Carlyle mansion on Google. The satellite view shows a modern addition around back. Looks like a four-season room. If we break the glass and set off an alarm, the guards will come running to check on the general. We can watch what happens."

"Are we doing this watching before or after the guards shoot us?" Ted asks.

"Forgot to mention I saw some baseball-sized rocks in that drainage ditch we just crossed. We throw them, from a distance, then run and hide."

Ted shakes his head and sighs. "As the night wears on, I'm becoming less concerned about saving the general's disgusting hide and more worried about keeping our hides intact."

"Catching Lyn tonight is the only sure way to prove she's behind the HOA murders not to mention the attack on Mom and me."

"There is that," Ted agrees.

Both of us go silent. I'm trying to think up a diversion, given that we have no guns, no fireworks, not even a match. My brain is totally blank.

"I have an idea if a certain filly will cooperate," Ted says. "Look for a dead tree branch that's about five feet long with plenty of dried leaves clinging to it. Oh, and I'd like to borrow your bra."

"Excuse me?"

"The bra is just icing on the cake." Ted grins. "When Grant and I lived in Saudi Arabia, I watched a man try to get his gelding to pull a log. Soon as the horse started moving, it heard the log dragging behind and decided it was chasing him. Ran like hell. If we tie a dead branch to our filly's tail and slap her butt to head her toward the guards, I figure she'll keep running."

"And the bra?" I remind.

"I'll tie it to her bridle so it flutters like a flag. For good measure, I'll take off these waders and use the suspenders to tie them around her neck. The vision should totally befuddle the guards."

I don't dare laugh out loud. "Not a good enough reason to sacrifice my bra, but you get an A-plus for a vivid imagination. I'll hunt for a dead branch."

Ted returns to the beach to fetch our borrowed filly, while I scour a forested area for a noise-maker branch. When we meet back at the edge of the oleander hedge, I see Ted has brought the horse and all the make-do weapons we scrounged from the tack room.

As Ted starts braiding the tree limb into the horse's tail, I walk to the front of the filly, my back to Ted, and strip off my top. I figure a bra donation won't even make my list of top ten stupid deeds. The cool air on my bare boobs offers a sensory wake-up call as I pull my bra free. *Didn't know idiocy was one of the side effects of too much adrenaline.*

I pull my top back down and dangle my no-nonsense white bra in front of Ted's face. He chokes back a laugh. "Didn't think you'd fall for it. But, if you did, I hoped I'd get to watch. I also pictured black lace."

"In your dreams," I say.

"Yep, you're right." He waggles his eyebrows. "In my dreams."

"Your turn," I say. "Shuck those waders and I'll tie them around our filly's neck."

Once our Marsh Tacky is fully costumed, Ted rubs her velvety muzzle and puts his lips near her ear. "Sorry about this, girl. I'll make it up to you tomorrow with a thorough brushing and a pretty red apple. If I'm alive."

He moves to the filly's backside and enthusiastically swats her rump. She immediately whinnies and shoots ahead. Within a few feet, her ears prick up and she kicks her back legs trying to discourage whatever's chasing her and holding tight to her tail.

The running, kicking whirlwind mesmerizes me until Ted gives my backside a soft swat. "Run!"

We sprint across an open area, then crouch near a grouping of neatly trimmed bushes at the back of the house. Lights inside suggest the modern addition isn't a stand-alone four-season room. I study the roofline's shape. It looks like the curved bump-out expands an interior room that opens onto a patio. Huge windows bookend a set of oversized sliding glass doors. But, despite the interior light, I can only see shadows inside.

"Looks like Headley paid big bucks for smart glass," Ted says. "No need for curtains or drapes, just flip a switch and the glass turns opaque."

"Do the doors and windows break like regular glass?" I ask.

"They're tough, but we don't need to break the glass," Ted answers. "If Headley invested in smart glass, I'm sure he installed glass break detectors. If a big rock hits any of those glass panes, I'm ninety-nine percent sure the vibration will trigger an alarm."

Out front, the guards are still yelling and chasing the runaway horse. Distraction success.

"Are we ready to rock?"

"Yes," Ted agrees. "As I recall, you were pretty damn good with snowballs when we were kids."

Chapter Seventy-Five

The Twin

Friday, October 2, 9:20 p.m.

The general is slowly regaining motor skills. I figure his first instinct will be an attempt to wriggle out of his hogtie bonds. I'm right. I smile as he learns that moving his arms or legs increases the tension on the choke chain and makes it harder to breathe.

I'm seated on the floor beside him. I lower my head to look directly into his eyes.

"You regained muscle control faster than I expected. Guess I can quit faking loud orgasmic rapture for listeners. In a minute, I'll yank those pillows out from under your chin, then I'll time how long you're able to keep breathing.

"Are you curious what I'll do after you die? Yes, no? Doesn't matter. I want you to know. I'm going to reenact the cover-up you devised for Jake's murder. Your bodyguards will find you hanging by your neck with skin mags scattered at your feet. Of course, I'll be long gone. I'll leave the bedroom door locked and exit through the patio. Since you drained that marshy area near your property, it's an easy walk to the motorbike waiting for me just beyond the Jade Pointe perimeter."

Headley's eyes widen. He tries to spit out the panties so he can yell and curse. He can't.

"Your bodyguards will tell the authorities about Alexia," I add. "But she doesn't exist. Unfortunately, Kylee Kane and Ted Welch will tell them my real name. But I already have a new identity waiting, and I'm off to England in the morning. I'd hoped to leave authorities baffled, but things don't always work out the way one hopes. Look at you. Not the night you planned."

Thonck! What in blazes?

I turn toward the glassed-in area leading to the patio. Did a large bird fly into the glass? Since Headley switched the smart glass to opaque mode, I can't see outside.

My brain's trying to process the sound when an ear-splitting siren starts its wail.

Shit! Any second, the guards will come running and break down the bedroom door.

"Goodbye, Headley. Roast in hell." I kick the pillows out from under his chin and my toe grazes his ear in the process.

I run for the sliding patio doors, unlatch them, and give a mighty shove. My pulse leaps to jackhammer mode.

Leaving the lighted bedroom, my eyes see little more than dim shapes in the nightscape. Bushes. Yes. A place to hide. Run. Quick.

Once my eyes adjust and I'm sure no bodyguards are near, I'll run the rest of the way to my motorbike.

Chapter Seventy-Six

Kylee

Friday, October 2, 9:30 p.m.

My first lob fell short, but Ted's stone made a solid hit. The alarm's blare is immediate and so loud I wonder if it can be heard in Beaufort.

"Get down." Ted shoves my head below our bush buffer. "All hell's going to break loose. That alarm's going to wake up the guards in the guest house as well as the ones on duty."

Peeking through the foliage, I expect to see bodyguards swarming the house. Instead, a woman shoves open the patio's sliding glass doors and runs like her life depends on it.

Unbelievable. She's making a beeline for our hideaway.

The moon highlights Lyn's bottle-blonde hair as she runs straight at Ted and me. Her shadowed face is little more than a smudge. Still, I'm dead certain it's Lyn.

Clearly, she doesn't see us. As she sprints, she glances over one shoulder then the other to see if anyone's chasing her. Doesn't realize she's running pell-mell into our arms.

The homicidal bitch thinks she can escape again. My anger boils. She's made her murders into lethal games. Didn't give a damn how her HOA diversion hurt Ted. Worse, she terrorized Mom.

You're not getting away this time, sweetheart!

I do a quiet duck waddle toward a gap in the bushes. My move prompts Ted to stretch in my direction and try to grab my arm. He misses. "Stay put," he whispers, "I'll tackle her."

I hear Ted, but his words fail to process. I'm too jacked on adrenaline. My body's coiled, ready to spring. Lyn's twenty feet away...ten...five. I mentally whisper the Coast Guard motto—*Semper Paratus, Always Ready.*

I leap through the opening as Lyn's glancing over her left shoulder for any danger from behind. My lunge snaps her head around, eyes wide, mouth open. Her eyes narrow to slits. "You!" she screams.

My balled fist connects squarely with her jaw. I put all my fury into the punch. Vibration and pain shoot up my arm and into my torso. Lyn's eyes roll up, and she crashes to earth. Out cold.

"Kylee Kane, didn't you hear me?" Ted's tone is exasperated. "I said I'd tackle Lyn."

"Yeah, but would you punch a woman? I decked her to make damn sure she doesn't get away this time."

Ted motions toward the mansion, and the source of the ear-splitting alarm. "Headley's bodyguards won't have any qualms about shooting us either," he says. "They have no idea who may be in on the attack. I'll phone Jade Pointe Security. We hide till they get here."

"We'd better drag Lyn behind the bushes and tie her up. No telling what she'll try when she comes around."

Once we're all hidden, we tie Lyn's hands and feet with the rope Ted borrowed from the tack room. He pulls out his cell. Before he can punch in a number, we're practically deafened by a man on a bullhorn.

"This is Jade Pointe Security. We were in the vicinity, and we're responding to the alarm. The Sheriff's Department will arrive shortly. General Headley, we need you and your bodyguards to put down any weapons. We don't want to risk anyone getting shot by mistake. If our officers see people with guns, accidents can happen. We need to take control. Let us investigate, find out what's happening."

Ted waits a couple of beats. "Officers, we're unarmed," Ted yells.

He stands up, holding his arms high, his hands palm out, to show he has no weapons. Unfortunately, the handcuff chain dangling from his right wrist probably does little to engender trust.

"We'd appreciate it if you'd take us into protective custody," he says, "We can help you sort this out."

A man in a Jade Pointe security uniform cautiously approaches. He keeps his gun pointed directly at Ted's center mass. Good, he's not the young officer we dumped by the side of the road. He might hold a grudge.

"I'm going to stand up, too," I yell. "With my hands up. We have no weapons."

Actually, if the "we" includes Lyn, I'm not sure about the no-weapons claim. But, even if Lyn has a bazooka stuffed up her ass, she can't use it. Her hands are securely tied. Even better, she's unconscious.

*　*　*

The night goes by in a blur. Alan Watson, the Jade Pointe chief, is flummoxed to learn I'm the real Kylee Kane. After his helicopter lands, Sheriff Conroy, albeit with disgust, verifies Ted's and my identities.

The sheriff's anger is evident in the way he aggressively barks orders. What I don't know is who he blames for this fiasco—Ted and me for failing to convince him that Lyn is a stone-cold killer or Deputy Nick and himself for dismissing our warnings.

EMTs transport Headley to Beaufort Memorial Hospital via helicopter. He's alive, survival up in the air. The alarm triggered a bodyguard to break into the general's bedroom and release the choke chain. Since Headley's oxygen was cut off for a time, brain damage is likely.

I notice the Jade Pointe guard we jettisoned from the ATV. Thankfully, he looks unscathed. Ted and I abjectly apologize. A slight nonverbal nod says he accepts. I have a hunch he's mostly embarrassed that we got away.

At one point, another Jade Pointe officer walks past us. He's leading our borrowed Marsh Tacky. There's sweat on the horse's neck, and she looks plain tuckered. The officer laughs as he unhooks the bra from the bridle.

CHAPTER SEVENTY-SIX

"What's with the bra? This filly doesn't look like a 34C."

Mortified, I cross my arms over my chest. Thank heaven, my loose sweatshirt isn't see-through. *What possessed me?*

We listen in on Chief Alan's interview with a bodyguard named Jacob. "The woman was wearing a red-haired wig when she arrived at the Carlyle Estate," he says. "We found the wig in Headley's bedroom. Yeah, she's blonde now and dressed a lot differently. But that's the woman." He points at Lyn. "I'm positive she's the dame the general took into his bedroom."

Lyn only says four words. "I want a lawyer." The sheriff tells her she can make her call after she returns to Beaufort in one of the sheriff's patrol boats.

Sheriff Conroy doesn't offer Ted and me a ride. Think he'd prefer we stay marooned on Hemp Isle. Too bad for him, we have the River Rat.

Periodically, Lyn sends poisonous glares my way, and every so often she seesaws her lower jaw. I hope it's an unsuccessful attempt to lessen the pain. My knuckles hurt like the dickens. Totally worthwhile.

The authorities separate Ted and me for a spell while we each give an independent version of events, first to Jade Pointe security, and then to Sheriff Conroy. Eventually, we're reunited on a patio glider and told to stay out of the way. As soon as we're alone, Ted puts an arm around me and pulls me close.

I wake with a start. Can't believe I dozed off at a crime scene bustling with activity. "What time is it?" I ask.

"Almost six a.m.," Ted answers. "I just asked Sheriff Conroy if we can leave. If I interpret his grunt correctly, the answer's a yes. Chief Watson says a Jade Pointe officer will take us to our boat."

"Hallelujah." I yawn, then shiver. "I'm chilled. Can't wait to get out of these damp muddy clothes."

Ted raises an eyebrow at my comment and smiles. I elbow his ribs in response.

The air is still, no wind. I look at the sky. While thick gray clouds hug the horizon, a brightening suggests dawn is near. *We live to fight another day.*

A Jade Pointe officer gives us a lift to the River Rat in his ATV. This trip is a sedate one with Ted and me seated in back. No handcuffs. On the ride, I do a rewind, thinking back on everything that's happened since I agreed to consult with Welch HOA Management. Some things remain a confused jumble. But about one thing I have no doubt. I couldn't ask for a better partner than Justin Theodore Welch, Jr.—Ted.

He's smart, brave, and resourceful. He also has two other virtues I prize. A sense of humor. And he knows how to kiss.

Time to stop thinking of Ted as my younger brother's pal, forgive him for being three years younger than me.

We climb aboard the River Rat, and I head below deck. Ted follows.

"Do you want to shove off right away?" Ted asks. "Get back to Beaufort before we collapse?"

I smile and shake my head. "Told you I wanted to strip off these clothes first thing."

I look straight at Ted as I pull off my sweatshirt. No need to unhook a bra. I didn't ask the sheriff's deputy to return the one I tied to the Marsh Tacky's bridle. My pants come next.

Ted doesn't move.

"What are you waiting for?" I ask. "The River Rat shower is pretty small but I'm sure we'll find a way to fit both our bodies inside."

"Semper Paratus," I whisper to myself.

A Note from the Author

Since I love the South Carolina Lowcountry, it was a no-brainer choice as my retired Coast Guard heroine's coastal home. The dozen years we lived in the Lowcountry are chockful of fond memories. My biggest challenge was inventing names for HOAs—they're all fictional—that weren't in use. Fingers crossed that I succeeded.

My choice of Beaufort County geography does not mean I think the area has more homeowner association (HOA) feuds than other regions. What's more, my fictional sheriff and deputy are not meant to reflect on the competence of any law enforcement officers (LEOs) or the professionalism of the Beaufort County Sheriff's Office. It's just that my heroine would have had nothing to do if I'd let my fictional LEOs promptly solve the mystery.

How do I feel about HOAs? Like all organizations managed by human beings, their potential for good or harm largely depends on the ethics, personalities and agendas of those in power. I've served as an HOA secretary, vice president, and president. I've also joined a lawsuit against an HOA. I admire the vast majority of volunteers who serve on HOA boards and committees. Fortunately, for my series, less altruistic homeowners are quite adept at generating the conflict every mystery novel needs.

Acknowledgements

While it's tough deciding where to begin a thank-you list, it seems appropriate to start with Katherine Ramsland, Ph.D., non-fiction author and professor of forensic psychology. One of her fascinating Writers' Police Academy classes sparked the idea for my villain's motivation.

For help in planning my heroine's Coast Guard career, I pestered two retired Coasties—Lt. Commander Diana Wickman, Ret., and Rob Spencer, Chief Boatswain's Mate, Ret. Their help was invaluable. Any Coast Guard errors are purely mine. Thanks also to Downtown Beaufort Marina staffers for suggesting my heroine's floating home might be a 38-foot Island Packet sailing cruiser.

Artist Bess Ciupak generously allowed me to photograph her fun fish mailbox for the book cover. Of course, the original had no protruding arrows.

Since my husband and I couldn't attend the wedding of our grandniece Kylee Mann to Justin Welch, I gave my heroine Kylee's first name and my hero Justin's last name as a belated wedding toast.

Some time ago, Kay Barrett won a character-name drawing at a Seneca Woman's Club literary luncheon. I hope Kay likes her fictional namesake. It took me a while to find the best fit.

As always, I'm indebted to fellow authors who serve as critique partners and Beta readers. I can't say enough about their input and encouragement. Hats off to authors Howard Lewis, Robin Weaver, Lorraine Quinn, Ann Chaney, Cindy Sample, Donna Campbell and Danielle Dahl, Howard, proud owner of a horse and a mule, gets extra credit for his input on equine psychology.

Level Best Books, my publisher, and editors Harriette Sackler and Shawn

Simmons also deserve kudos for suggestions that definitely improved the final copy.

Finally, thanks to my husband, Tom Hooker. Our multi-mile walks often include "what if" plot and character discussions with Tom serving as an honest sounding board for my fledgling ideas. Thank heaven for spouses who share our love of reading!

About the Author

A journalism major in college, Linda Lovely has spent most of her career working in PR and advertising—an early introduction to penning fiction. With Neighbors Like These is Lovely's ninth mystery/suspense novel. Whether she's writing cozy mysteries, historical suspense or contemporary thrillers, her novels share one common element—smart, independent heroines. Humor and romance also sneak into every manuscript. Her work has earned nominations for a number of prestigious awards, ranging from RWA's Golden Heart for Romantic Suspense to Thriller Nashville's Silver Falchion for Best Cozy Mystery.

A long-time member of Sisters in Crime and former chapter president, Lovely also belongs to Mystery Writers of America, International Thriller Writers, and the South Carolina Writers Association. For many years, she helped organize the Writers' Police Academy. She lives on a lake in Upstate South Carolina with her husband, and enjoys swimming, tennis, gardening, long walks, and, of course, reading.

To learn more, visit the author's website: www.lindalovely.com .